Also by Leon Rooke

SHORT STORY COLLECTIONS:

*Last One Home
Sleeps in the Yellow Bed*

Vault

The Love Parlour

The Broad Back of the Angel

Cry Evil

Death Suite

*The Birth Control King
of the Upper Volta*

*Sing Me No Love Songs
I'll Say You No Prayers:
Selected Stories*

A Bolt of White Cloth

How I Saved the Province

The Happiness of Others

Who Do You Love

Muffins

*Narciso allo specchio
(Narcissus in the Mirror) (Italian)*

*Narcis u zrcalu
(Narcissus in the Mirror) (Croatian)*

Oh, No, I Have Not Seen Molly

*Arte. Tre fantasie in prosa
(Art. Three Fictions in Prose)*

Oh! Twenty-seven Stories

*Painting the Dog:
The Best Stories of Leon Rooke*

POETRY:

Hot Poppies

NOVELS:

Fat Woman

Shakespeare's Dog

A Good Baby

Gentil Bébé

Who Goes There

The Magician in Love

The Fall of Gravity

En chute libre (The Fall of Gravity)

The Beautiful Wife

Balduchi's Who's Who (Novella)

PLAYS:

Sword/Play

Krokodile

Ms. America

A Good Baby

Shakespeare's Dog

FOR A COMPLETE LISTING:
www.leonrooke.com

HITTING THE CHARTS

LEON ROOKE

HITTING
THE CHARTS

SELECTED STORIES

with a foreword by
JOHN METCALF

For Emily

Much love to you. Em

Leon Rooke

BIBLIOASIS

FIRST EDITION

Library and Archives Canada Cataloguing in Publication

Rooke, Leon
[Short stories. Selections]
Hitting the charts : selected stories / Leon Rooke.

1-897231-17-2 (HAND CASED)
1-897231-18-0 (PBK.)

I. Title.

PS8585.O64A6 2006   C813'.54   C2006-904557-7

We acknowledge the support of the Canada Council
for the Arts for our publishing program.

PRINTED AND BOUND IN CANADA

For Connie and Jono
and for 'lit mag' editors
wherever they are.

Contents

FOREWORD / 9

THE DEACON'S TALE / 21

MAMA TUDDI DONE OVER / 37

HANGING OUT WITH THE MAGI / 69

SIXTEEN-YEAR-OLD SUSAN MARCH CONFESSES
TO THE INNOCENT MURDER OF ALL THE DEVIOUS STRANGERS
WHO WOULD DRAG HER DOWN / 87

ADOLPHO'S DISAPPEARED
AND WE HAVEN'T A CLUE WHERE TO FIND HIM / 101

SWEETHEARTS / 125

THE PROBLEM SHOP / 129

WINTER IS LOVELY, ISN'T SUMMER HELL / 149

THE END OF THE REVOLUTION AND OTHER STORIES / 161

SOME PEOPLE WILL TELL YOU THE SITUATION
AT HENNY PENNY NURSERY IS GETTING INTOLERABLE / 181

IN THE GARDEN / 189

WY WN TY CALLD YOUR NAM YOU DID NOT ANSWR / 207

WHY AGNES LEFT / 211

SIDEBAR TO THE JUDICIARY PROCEEDINGS,
THE NUREMBERG WAR TRIALS, NOVEMBER, 1945 / 217

GYPSY ART / 229

THE BROAD BACK OF THE ANGEL / 237

FAZZINI MUST HAVE YOU EVER AT HER SIDE / 253

HITTING THE CHARTS / 257

BIOGRAPHICAL NOTES / 269

FOREWORD

H *itting the Charts* brings back into print stories of Leon Rooke's that go back to 1980. Over the years since *Cry Evil, Death Suite*, and *The Birth Control King of the Upper Volta* first appeared, Leon's stories have worked themselves into our hearts and minds and have become part of our emotional and mental furniture.

I am particularly pleased to be associated with the republishing of such performances as "The Deacon's Tale," "The Problem Shop," "Sixteen-year-old Susan March Confesses to the Innocent Murder of All the Devious Strangers Who Would Drag Her Down," "Some People Will Tell You the Situation at Henny Penny Nursery Is Getting Intolerable" and "Mama Tuddi Done Over."

I use the word "performances" to describe these stories because that is precisely what they are. If we come at them with our busy intellects asking earnest irrelevancies, we'll miss the pure fun and uproar of language and cadence being presented on each story's stage. The most fruitful way to approach Leon is to think of him as a jazz musician in full flight of improvisation. I'm often put in mind of Illinois Jacquet or Eddie "Lockjaw" Davis erupting into solo from the Basie ranks. Sit back and listen. Dancing is not forbidden.

Leon approaches stories as improvisations. He tries a few notes, a few chords to see what will happen. Sometimes the story takes off; sometimes it peters out.

In a book called *Singularities* edited by Geoff Hancock, Leon wrote: "I don't have many rules for the writing of short fiction. One of them is, if a thing is going wrong, then start over. If it is going nowhere, then give it up, or start over. If it goes awhile, and stops, then you stop too because maybe you have gone as far as the story wants you to go. Which often means, of course, starting over. The piece lays down its own laws; that's another thing I mean. That's why many very intelligent, very gifted literary people who want to write, can't. They operate under the fallacious notion that the writer is Creator-God, whereas intervention of another sort is more frequently the case. The thing, at a certain point, and usually at the start, creates itself, it is of value, or it isn't. Does it matter so much anyway, since the story that awaits the telling awaits as well the teller, and as many aren't found as are?"

He also said in a *Canadian Fiction Magazine* interview with Geoff Hancock:

"I've also written ten or fifteen stories that came out of no-where. I sat at the typewriter, typed out one sentence, and that sentence invited another sentence and that demanded a third. Several hours later I had the first draft — even sometimes the final draft — of a story. These stories happen very fast and where they come from or where they're going I don't know until I get there."

Improvisation, then.

It should not surprise us that from early in his career Leon has written plays and been closely connected to theatre. Many of his stories are simply voices talking directly to us. Who are these people? What do they mean?

Listen.

The talking voice will tell you if you listen.

* * *

A quarter of a century ago now, Leon wrote an essay for my anthology *Making It New.* The essay was about his story in this present volume called "Winter Is Lovely, Isn't Summer Hell." The essay was entitled "Voices." Here is an excerpt.

Many, many years ago — whether twenty years or ten or *last night* it is all part and parcel of that fabled once-upon-a-time — I went to the public library in New Orleans, La. in search of *The Man Who Was There* by the American writer Wright Morris, an early novel I had been searching for without success over a long period. And there it was on the shelf. I pulled it out and the pages fell open to a scrap of lined school paper on which was scrawled, 'she have to check up on her hygiene.' The handwriting was close to illiterate, but it seemed to me there was something highborn and noble about the text, something that struck to the heart of the identity of that anonymous 'she,' while at the same time conveying something quite remarkable about the speaker. There was *appeal* here, stress and urgency. Moreover, the writer, so it seemed to me, was speaking with undeniable truth. *She*, whoever *she* was, would indeed by better off — lead a happier, more stable life — if only she would, and with some haste, check up on her hygiene.

I could easily enough imagine the situation: three school girls (for I had already added a third member to this party) located at one of the long library tables, preparing homework or class report, suppressing giggles, having been several times shooshed quiet by a grim librarian (keeper of Clock and Titles) — each of these three in a dither now because what they really want to do is get across the street to the drugstore before it closes, and there wreak havoc with assembled boys. And one of them, the brightest, scribbling this note to her mate about the third: We can't go yet, this albatross with us has to first check up on her hygiene assignment; *then* we can have a Coke and eat our chips and monkey with the guys. But having neither need nor inclination to spell all this out, theirs being a closed world, reduced in firmament in which all matters of importance and significance are understood through lifted eyebrow, hand-fluttering, through shrieks and moaned syllables, through giggles and signs, coded behaviour that has no more to do with language than the grunt and throat-jerk of prehistoric man or the zoo's enfeebled baboon in his cage. Language (its study), this trio would tell us, is useless paraphernalia, a heavy burden, something *else* the addled world would heap upon their feline shoulders. Subject *this* and predicate *that*, and God protect us from a thumping modifier.

Thus this note passed with surreptitious gravity to her friend: *she have to check up on her hygiene.* And here the magic. For with its writing her wit has momentarily become unshackled from the dead world of denial, from that one which preaches *language sucks, language stinks, language is The Curse.* She has scribbled it out of mind and sky, without fear of the teacher's brutal punishment (teacher as blunt instrument); liberated in that instant from the gruesome bondage of grammatical instruction, she has got it exactly right, has said precisely what she means. *'This stump beside us has not finished yet. Bear with us, Mercy, yet a while.'* Has produced, that is, a sentence perfect in all its parts, every word working to her purpose, no frills, no beating around the bush — first and last time in all probability, in her entire life that she has ever — will ever — use language with such exactness.

And it pleased me enormously that I'd discovered the note in *The Man Who Was There* (novel, I soon learned, of a man who *is*, and *isn't*) for it added that extra dollop (donation *from* charity, flower from the cupped hands of Mistress Good Fortune), reminding me again that libraries are public in more ways than one.

Another country heard from, I thought.

The Girls Who Were Here . . . are here.

My cup runneth over.

It only remained for me to hijack the line and put a story to it, with narrative speech or voice, with style and content and form that retained some fidelity to the original. Say, in a story entitled 'Winter Is Lovely, Isn't Summer Hell,' in which the changing seasons exist as unreliable backdrop to the characters' ups and downs — their quick shifts of loyalty and passion against the weather's quick reversals; all as narrated by an anonymous figure struck up herself from that same neighbourhood, holding vested interest in those whose story she relates, but with an eye that wants at the same time to be objective; narrator who feels no necessity to condone or accuse, one who seeks through *tone* (language's

solace) to find a satisfactory dignity in the embrangled diction —
search through her world for what can be found that will usefully
suggest its essential qualities. *Her*, yes, this peculiarly female (as
the sea is female, as the wind is) voice that proclaims the story of
Ruby Tucker and Thomas Jones is in effect the story of an entire
neighbourhood (any neighbourhood is foreign country, a nation, a world) caught between impermanence and transition, between tradition and new ground, between poverty on the one
hand, pleasure and purpose on the other. Utilizing dream
(Ruby's dream) as solid rock ('I want and will have!') to alter experience, and all circling (thus the insistent employment of time
in the story, time as a pepper pot's sprinkle) forward towards
some dimly glimpsed destination, with *reckoning postponed* (there
the rub). Leading towards that future hour when the children
churned up within this neighbourhood

> 'So it is that each night now the boys can drop off to sleep
> snug and warm and no doubt wondering whose side of the
> story they going to hear tomorrow. Wondering what going
> to happen next. Feeling how the story of one is the story of
> them all and wondering why if this is so they remain so
> fearful of how their own fortune going to fall.'

will inherit what is theirs by unresolved law of blood and lair —
pointing towards that time when they will find themselves living
out their own variations on and extensions of . . . *the story*.

Maze, as in the Sunday comics, it being each new generation's
labour to trace down the undiscovered exits.

This being not so much what the story is about as what it
comes to.

So the teller's voice is the face over the back fence: voice addressing (not us the reader so much as) another woman (sea and
wind are female, is the audience, too?) standing shoeless at her
own back door, there waiting the story out, but a little irritated
(in all probability that she can't get in her two-cents, tell the story
herself, for she surely has her own version of the story and her

own preference for the way it should be told, wanting at every instant to highlight or drive home this or that difference, thinking always, 'That's not the way I heard it, no, you've got it all wrong, what really happened is this!' The narrative voice moulded, then, (First Person in Third Person Disguise) to be fabric and part of what is being revealed, one intentionally crafted out of the region's soft clay to affirm that message the distant author holds most vital: voice that says, 'This is *their* story (Ruby and Thomas), but it is *mine* as well, and that of friends I have here, and *your* story too if you live (or ever find yourself living) in this neighbourhood.' And saying furthermore that 'your neighbourhood, whatever you may *think* it is, may not be so different from ours, since this I *know to be true: We are not so different from you. Don't let my idiom mislead. We are not the odd — and stupid — people you may take us for.*

A sentimental view?

Well, no. All a matter of good clean hygiene, mental this time.

And so a scrap of lined school paper is transmuted into the music of *the story.*

"He wondered did she wash her hands before she fall in love. Whatever he wanted he got but mostly that was because he know what he want. Her, for instance. But up to that time he only have dreams of her. My Dream Girl, he say to friends, she like this: and he slice his hands through the air like what he really want is a Coca-Cola bottle. Next thing he know it have happen but *how* it have happen he slow to realize . . ."

* * *

Or here's a different kind of voice.

Dust. I am thinking that.
I am thinking street-pavers.
I am thinking big orange machines, giant rolling pins that weigh
    twenty tons and can mash you flat.

I leave my room that last time, I see these thundering buggers,
    I am thinking, Yeah, just throw yourself down.
Down on your belly, go head first. Let fate handle the rest.
I am thinking that.
I am thinking Expo.
Clean-up, I am thinking that.
Mostly I am thinking Princess Di. On the face of it, yeah,
    no kidding, I am thinking Di.
Street-pavers, they come and go.
But Di?
Her picture in all the papers.
That *wan* face.
So forget street-pavers, forget my eviction from flop-house hotel.
Forget those Spruce-up/Renovate-me times.
Forget I left the room that day, saw the paver, said to myself:
Just throw yourself down. You're gone. Let fate monkey with you.
It's allowed.
Dust, I was thinking that.
Okay, I didn't have a clear head that day, nothing to live for,
    let's say that.

Can you see him in the spotlight?
Can you hear him weaving words into a spell?
It makes me itch to get on stage and build the piece using "I am thinking" as a kind of delaying, tantalizing punctuation in a striptease of slow revelation.
Oh, cunning Rooke!
It seems so effortless.
Leon's novel *Who Goes There* opens:

> *"Bud?"*
> *"Yes."*
> *"Where was I?"*
> *"Jack Dreck."*
> *"Jack?"*
> *"Yes."*

Okay. Jack Dreck, his tight slick hair, his white bony hairless ankles, is reading the fine newsprint through splayed knees, going uh-oh, there's mayhem in Angola, uh-oh, them bikers over in Enfield are on the war path.

Ugg, I goes.

Like if he don't tell us the latest then we are never to know civilization's carrying on.

Outside the EatRite, this is, on the loading ramp: me and these gooneybirds grabbing the break.

Mental don't want any, he goes. He's off carrots. He's into unwashed spinach, so's he can tongue the grit.

Ugg, I goes, pulling a face.

"Grit's good on yous, girl," Mental goes. "Yous a kid, yous dint eat dirt?"

No, I dint, I goes.

"I dint either," goes Jack Dreck from Meats.

Dint is how them two speak. Juice them till doomsday, they don't never catch on. They's I.Q. below sea-level, see?

* * *

Leon, then, is improvisational and theatrical. He is in love with words, with style. One might say that his *subject* is words. He spoke about style to Geoff Hancock:

Rooke: . . . from the start I was gravitating towards the strong stylists. Wright Morris, for instance. Stylists, I find, are rarely disappointing. If the style is strong then the content usually is as well.

Hancock: By style, you mean the surface of words? The music of the language, the pushing of language towards its razor's edge?

Rooke: Yes. The unique imprint of the single writer. Style to me is like a woman walking in high heels. The way they know how. And one never exactly the same as another. The way the toes are pointed right, the way the legs shoot up straight, how the head is carried. That's style. Put the woman in high heels and give her a name and put her on the road: that's what the stylist does, putting words on the page.

What a lovely image. And quintessentially Leon.

All those winsome women titupping down that road.

Kent Thompson, story writer, editor, teacher, impressario, reviewed Leon's 1992 collection *Who Do you Love?* in *Essays on Canadian Writing* with great insight and generosity and I need to quote him at some length.

... Rooke's writing is also authentic of time and place — and here you have to take my word for it, and trust that I, who share something of Rooke's background, can recognize in the following the authentic American voice of the boonies:

'Your grandfather let you walk down the rows with him, he let you hold the plow, and he said, Just let the mule do the work, but you couldn't hold the plow handles and the reins at the same time and the plow blade kept riding up out of the ground. When you came to the end of a row the mule would stop and your grandfather would look at both of you, look and flap his hat against his leg, and say, Now let's see which of you has the better sense. You stood behind your grandfather's chair in the evenings and combed his balding head, but your grandmother said, I've got enough plates to get to the table, why should I get theirs? Why can't she come and take away these that are hers and leave me with those that are mine?

'No one asked her to marry that drinker.

'Didn't we tell her sixteen was too young?

'She made her own bed. There ain't one on their daddy's side ever had pot to pee in or knew what pot was for.'

It's a skill for which Rooke will not likely receive much credit in Canada — for who will recognize it and value it? But it is there, for all that, and I think it is wonderful.

Kent Thompson continues:

My favourite story in the collection, however, is the stunning and violent 'Want to Play House?' in whose title is an echo of two forms of the favourite children's game of carnal knowledge. Sometimes the game involves going into the bushes and taking off your clothes to look at one another like Adam and Eve, because you know, somehow, as a child, that this nakedness and connection is what makes a family. And sometimes the little theatrical game with the same name refers to a performance of home as we know it. Rook's story hints at the first and performs the second. The two are intertwined. It is a story of playing house in which the little girl insists upon three revisions. It is her story, set in the imaginary kitchen. The little boy — probably her younger brother — is to play the man who comes home after work. And it is a story of rural poverty and despair that ends with a butcher knife. Its language is that of the Bible Belt and the miserable little house or trailer off the dirt road; you can hear the King James Version in both the vocabulary and cadences:

'Okay, I will take you through it step by step, though that's precious little fun for me. I will tell you, it is precious little fun for me, and I don't know why I go through it. All right, you are here at this line, which is the door, and you come in and I am sitting at the table crying my eyes out because I am full of woe.

'That's right. I have changed my mind, I am not standing at the sink when you come in. Let's play this way instead. I have been full of woe all day and I have got nothing done, nothing is ever done because I am unable to rouse myself from the loathsome woe, and now I have lost all track of the time and I don't know which way to turn.'

I cannot imagine better writing, anywhere, than this sample. It is the equal of Flannery O'Connor's best work, and it is Rooke's bad luck to share with O'Connor a common background and similar concerns, because she has had the more powerful literary establishment asserting and demonstrating her virtues. She is accorded the American reputation.

But Rooke at his best is her equal, and he's still writing. Let's not forget either of these facts.

Amen to that.

John Metcalf
Ottawa, June, 2006

THE DEACON'S TALE

Here's a story.

Although it has been going on for years, the crucial facts are fresh in my mind so I will have no trouble confining myself strictly to what's essential. Nothing made up, have no worry about that. I live in this world too: when my wife, lovely woman, tells me that people are tired of hearing *stories*, they want facts, gossip, trivia, how-to about real life, I'm first to take the hint. So this is plain fact: yesterday my foot was hurting. The pain was unbearable. I was in mortal anguish and convinced I'd been maimed for life.

My wife, naturally enough, was concerned. Now and then she would look in on me: "How's the foot?" she'd ask. I'd grit my teeth and do what I could to keep from screaming. I hate sympathy, faked or otherwise. Had she come in with a sharp axe to ask whether she could chop it off, I would have felt better. But she was all politeness, you see: "Is it better? No? Shall I bring you a magazine? Fluff your pillows? Comb your moustache?" Her comments are precious and I want to leave out none of them. According to her, the people in my stories are never polite and nice the way people really are. In my stories it's always hocus-pocus, slam-bang, and someone has a knife at your throat. Turns people off, she claims. I'm influenced too much by TV and radio and by what I read in the papers; in real life people are not nearly so anxious and unhappy as I make out. Put in a little comedy, she says. After all,

21

you live in a pleasant house, you've got liquor in the cabinet, a beautiful wife, and most of our *urgent* bills are paid. Why be morbid? It gives people the wrong impression.

All right, I can see I've already gone astray. All this past history is irrelevant in a story meant to be about my foot. I'm getting too subjective, too interpretive, that's another of my flaws. You sound bitter, she'd say. Just stupidly sarcastic. Never mind that she's scowling in the doorway, grumpy and embittered herself because the bedroom is such a mess. When she's in *her* sick-bed, you understand, she likes everything immaculate: tables dusted, all knick-knacks pointing in the proper direction, flowers smiling from every ledge. Anything less is apt to depress her and I grant you her view is not unreasonable. It just happens that I don't like to be surrounded by that kind of false cheer. If I'm on my death-bed, I want two or three undertakers standing by and if a hearse is out in the garden, so much the better. So:

"Are you in pain?" she asks. "Do you think you can eat your lunch now?"

I groan. I can't help myself. Lovely and generous women like my wife think that all the ills of the world can be cured by a small wedge of cucumber sandwich or a nice salad with a little lemon dripped over the top. My mother is exactly the same and she is still going strong at ninety-five.

"Speak!" she shouts. "You're the big word-man around here."

The fact is, although I was starving, I wasn't talking to her just then. We'd had a tiff earlier in the week about my alleged promiscuous behaviour at a party but that's not why I wasn't talking to her. I simply *felt* like keeping my silence. It had nothing to do with my outrage over having been falsely accused. I'm accustomed to that. No, all my compassion, all my sympathy and love and concern, was invested in this wretched foot. I was in agony, I tell you. I was worn out. All night I had been in the grip of a fever — fever and chills — and hadn't slept a wink. None of my medicines helped. Penicillin, codeine, morphine, a bottle of eighty-year-old Scotch — nothing had offered any relief. Meanwhile, she had slept like a princess. Her story would be different, of course. She'd have you think she was up every minute putting hot or cold compresses on my brow. She'd tell you that when she finally did doze off she couldn't get any peace because my hands were all over her. That's not true. It is true that about four in the morning she jumped out of bed shouting. "Why don't you go and feel *her* up!" — and went running off to another bed. "What *her?*" I shout. "That bitch Gladys!" she screams back. Then the door slams and I don't see any more of her until breakfast.

Okay. I see I've fallen into my old trap. My stories don't *move*, she says. That is, they move but they don't go forward. I'm always botching them up with too much extraneous material. *"Who cares?"* she'd say. *"You throw in your mealy-mouthed references to Gladys and expect us to interpret them any way we wish. We're supposed to predict all sorts of dire consequences for these people, for their marriage, because you've invoked some slut's name. Well, it won't wash! Get on with it or shut up."* That, of course, is what she'd say after first denying that she'd said anything remotely similar to *Why don't you go and feel her up!* I put that part in, she'd claim, only to get the aroma of sex in my story.

"You get into this trouble only because you have nothing to say."

All right, I've made it clear I had a restless, terrible night. Now she comes in with my lunch on a tray. I'm supposed to comment on how heavenly it looks. She's even brought a little daisy in a vase and has dug out one of the bright yellow napkins she picked up in Mexico. I'm supposed to be touched. She's had to pick this flower from the garden and she's had to wash this napkin by hand and slave over it with a hot iron. I'm not supposed to remember that she's got a trunkful of these faded things or how she came by them. In Mexico, I mean to say, while on a decadent trip with her beloved Arnold, in the days before she met me. I'm supposed to think she's still a lady when in actual fact she's toured three continents with that jerk! Arnold, I should add, is a first-rate story-teller. If you ask her to, she will put one of his platters on the stereo to prove it: "The Ballad of Johnny Cool," which hit the Top 40 and became a great movie by the same name. But do me a favour and don't take your children to see it.

He's successful, she sometimes tells me, because he knows when to employ dialogue. *"So you've decided to tell us a story about a man with a bum foot. You're smart enough to give him a beautiful, sophisticated and intelligent wife. But right away you impose an impossible burden on yourself. You have him so mad and stupid he can't talk to her. Result, no dialogue. All we get are his lame-brain buckshot musings. It's Dullsville. And I for one couldn't care less about him or his foot. Chop it off indeed. How did he hurt it in the first place? You always deliberately avoid revealing what most people would regard as a most essential part."*

He got it caught in a crankshaft.

"There you go being cute. You ruin every story you tell with these touches that you think are so cute. Nobody believes for a minute that this character's foot got caught in a crankshaft. Most of us don't even know what a crankshaft is. You will go to any extreme to avoid rooting your story in a basic, common, SHARED *experience."*

It got caught in an elevator door.

"Not believable."

A rhino stepped on it?

"Oh yes, any old lie will do. Anyway, by this time it's too late. Who cares? We're not dunces. If I didn't know any better, if I hadn't had to put up with it, I'd never believe your foot hurt at all."

Forced to, I will tell you what happened to my foot. It was nothing very dramatic. A week ago I was pouring concrete for this absurd gazebo she wanted built on the rocky cliff beside the house. *"Up there, honey,"* she says, *"so we can see for miles!"* Somehow my feet got tangled between bucket, hoe, and wheelbarrow. I lost my balance and fell forty feet on this foot which I'd already sprained when I tried kicking a fire hydrant. Then I had to hobble two miles to the hospital because naturally she had the car, out to one of those treasured lunches with friends whom I never see. After treatment I collared a kind Ladies' Auxiliary person and for ten dollars she agreed to help me get home. I'm in bed, half passed-out, when my wife finally comes in. *"So this is how you build my gazebo!"* she exclaims, and tears out in a huff to see whether I've even started it yet. I can hear her up there stomping about, cursing, kicking rocks down the hill, telling neighbours, *"I knew it! I knew it! He's a lazy sod, he's done nothing and I rue the day I ever met him."* Meantime, I have revived somewhat and am trying with my bleary sight to find the front door. I'm going out there to strangle her, to push *her* off the cliff. My crutches slip, I topple over, and damned if the same foot isn't banged again. They sweep up my blood and guts and somehow return me to my bed of pain. Naturally she is all remorseful now, and solicitous, and for the next thirty-six hours baby-talk bubbles out of her: "Does my poor diddums forgive me? Won't my pretty diddums give me his pretty poo-doo smile?" She is so warm and contrite she could cook me in this syrup. Finally, one frostbitten night, I relent and go to put my arms around her in matrimonial harmony: I get her knee in my stomach, a slam of insults, and the next second she's scrambling for another bed. Even if I have chased Gladys, which I deny, it seems to me that our crimes ought to balance out.

Right, so onward, she's now brought the lunch tray in. Ham on rye, a big pickle, a glass of milk, and fresh strawberries under a blanket of homespun cream.

"Eat it," she says. "You know what will happen if you lie about drinking whisky all day."

"What will happen? Let my dark secret out."

"You'll get blotto."

"Ho-ho as my Daddy would say. Big deal."

"Is your foot still throbbing?"

"I don't know. Hit it with a hammer, then I can tell."

That's enough dialogue for a while. She's got her eyes on my strawberries and has already eaten half the bowl. I'm not supposed to notice that and certainly should not remark on it: she's on a diet. It occurs to me that the reason my foot's in such pain is because the bandage is too tight. No circulation. My foot is puffy and red outside the wrapping, my five toes like shrivelled apple peels. It's one of those surgical bandages, the kind that stretches. I try to reach it, but can't. Every time I move, a thunderbolt rips through my leg and a spike bangs into my skull. My wife takes an interest in my contortions. She's quite bedazzled. Her eyes enlarge. My agony sends the blood rushing to her face. I have her sympathy but I certainly can't expect any help with the bandage from her. She won't touch it. It hasn't been washed in seven days. Nor has my foot. That's just what I don't need: to get trapped in a tub with a hundred-pound foot.

"What can I do?" she asks.

"Nothing," I say. "Go away." Howling pain makes a person rude. I lie still, exhausted; the pain diminishes somewhat. My wife's feelings are hurt, but she insists on feeding me. Each time I turn my head there's another spoonful sliding between my lips. "Eat, eat!" she says. "Your mother tells me she had to feed you this way until you were nineteen years old." Oh, she knows how to get at a man. She knows how to humiliate him. "I'm sorry," she next says, "about last night." She knows how to make old hatreds live — to make repulsion for one's swollen foot embrace other swollen members too. I must pay for the sins of every man who has ever clawed at her when she wasn't in the mood. "It's just that I wasn't in the mood." I raise my head to look at her. What I see are her wet eyes. Luscious, trembling lips. Hair trained by Mister Divine to shroud her face like a tent. *Déjà vu.* I have been here before. And the thought I have now is the same I had then. Better, old sport, that you had married a hag. Staked out the most vile neighbourhood witch and mated with her. One glance at this woman's proud, suffering face and I am hit with instant self-doubt and loathing, I am awash in sentimentality. Old True Love is hooking its claws into me. She's the one who's miserable and misunderstood. *I'm* the brute. We don't need God to remind us of our evil deeds; all we need is another person.

I find myself reviewing this most recent encounter with Gladys. A snaky wink through my bifocals. A tawdry giggle under the tree. And yes, three years ago, a single scuffy kiss in the pantry where a fuse had blown. Crimes microscopic in size but all the same I ask myself: am I not better than this? Would I tarnish reputations, cheapen myself in the eyes of the community, betray this fine woman for the sake of such a pale and fleeting lust as poor Gladys can engender? I tell you the experience gives me pause. I grip the neck of my Scotch bottle tighter and that's a fact.

I got gloomy and distressed. Oh, I plunged into a deep foul mood, no doubt of that. Down there where only mole eyes perceive. Me with stubby legs and no visible neck, chomping on earth worms, aware that my path must take me through solid rock. The same thing happens to her. She sulks, she moans, she sweats: you'd think my flaming foot had been transferred to one of her long limbs. As usual, she combats her depression by lashing out.

"Stop complaining about your foot," she cries. "If you mention that goddamned foot to me again I'll scream!"

"But it hurts."

"Shut up! You didn't appear to have any trouble tracking that bitch Gladys! Or Hilda! What a barge pole *she* was! No, your foot didn't hurt then, you were a four-minute miler so long as you had their buttocks shimmying in front of you!"

Hilda? Hilda *Who? Barge poles!* What on earth can this hysterical woman mean?

"Yes, *you*, you twit! You stump-toed turd!"

Hold on a minute. I can't go on without inserting one tiny aside. My spouse is constantly criticizing me for what she calls my dirty mouth. I can't say a word to friends but that she doesn't first have to chase about the room with her pine-scent spray and cotton for the children's ears. *Reduce the filth*, that's what she's always saying. I get it from bartenders too. *Muzzle it, Deacon, or it's out you go.* I go to a movie, for instance, with naked bodies wallowing all over the screen and language that would drive killer bees to suicide, and if I mutter *Pee on this*, right away I've got six ushers driving me to the door. Fellini can have a hundred bodies copulating in a Roman bath but if I have a couple holding hands in a snowstorm I'm accused of being degenerate. *Yes*, she will say, *but your material has no redeeming quality.* Her friends will nod and grandmothers may come back into the room. So hold on. I'm not to be blamed for *her* filthy mouth. The accusation isn't true in the first place. I learned long ago to clean up my act. They used to say about my Daddy, that rascal, that he had a mouth like a cat's rear end. You can bet your money I wasn't going to model myself after him.

My wife has no ear for this or any other criticism. Not for nothing has she attended the best schools, known the best people, committed her entire being to this marriage. Her efforts are to be recorded in the Guinness *Book of Records* (under section-heading TOOK MOST CRAP); even now, angels are at work on scrolls to be hung at the Gates of Heaven. I, too, in my dreams, when they are not of dinosaurs and other amiable and extinct creatures, compose encyclopaedic encomiums to this woman:

Mama Fournose — WIFE. *Married to erstwhile stonemason and oral traditionalist known as* Foot. *At great personal sacrifice she fed & preserved this oaf's soul, nurtured his body, saw to it that his house was not overrun with tramps, drunkards, rogues, deadbeats, Hedonists, etc. All this sweet woman wanted out of life was a marriage that would go down in history* (dinner by candle light each evening of the year — Famous Quote: "Isn't this romantic!"), *and loyalty. Got neither of above.*

Betroth me, O serpent, to my fate
Let my bones lie still.
A ludicrous sadness overwhelms us both at times. It charges at us with a banshee zeal, routing us from the careful defences we have laid. We pick up the pieces and limp for higher, more neutral ground. Reach for Rule No. 1 of the *Survivor's Guide to Home Warfare*: after any skirmish, win or lose, effect a quick retreat. Tend to your wounds. Keep a fresh whisky close to your left elbow. I must forget what I know of this woman. A college fraternity, in her tender eighteenth year, voted her Most Impressionable Girl; a year later the same group named her Most Desired; competition faltered and within the season a new crown had been bestowed: A Woman Too Good To Be True. What had happened to my beautiful princess to warrant this impossible title? How many dreary days she must have sat, swilling sherry, staring out of windows in makeshift rooms, paced cities like a loaned-out cat, knocked limbs with phantom shapes, yearning every moment for the day when her heart would truly crack and love's childhood dream of her perfect knight could at last draw to its deadly close. *Look, Father, I am a stranger to you now! Look, Mother, at the woman I have become! Oh, lover, I have survived the best and worst you could do to me! Oh, world, send me a man out of your darkness! I have toyed with prince and rabble and am prepared now to wed whatever stranger next steps into my light.*
"This can't go on," laments my wife.
Most Fashionable now. Her clothes, no less than her black moods, put her at the vanguard of her age. Tomorrow *Chatelaine, Vogue, The Womans' Own Daily* no doubt will call: *We're in a real quandary, honey: this season is it to be mauve or green?*

My rancid foot is killing me.

"Think of something pleasant," she advises. "Try remembering your first wife."

I remember a story that a fellow down at the Motherlode used to tell me. It seems there was this woman down on her luck who one day sat down by a pool thinking she'd throw herself in when this frog suddenly hopped into her lap saying *Kiss me* and she got out her hatchet and chopped off its legs and immediately fried them up on her hibachi and ate them and decided on reflection that she hadn't had such a fine day in years.

All right, forget that story. I can see it's not relevant, what a guy in a beer-hall told ten years ago.

My first wife *was* demented; ever in study of her L. Ron Hubbard; I hardly see how I'm to be blamed for that.

"Or how you wet your bed until you were twenty-one."

Feeble. Such weak humour will not provoke my ire. Anyway, I have more serious matters to ponder. I've had a suspicion now for several days: my foot is only a symptom of the deeper trouble I'm in. I have some dreaded disease of the blood. That's why my doctor has been so guarded in his report. It's why a simple X-ray was not sufficient. Numerous tests were required: my blood was drained, my urine analysed, my body strapped to numerous unidentifiable machines while four hefty nurses held me down. I am either sick in a most complex way or another patient has been confused with me. I suffer weird discolorations of skin: black here, blue there, a purplish tinge all over. The doctor tells me, *Well. Sir, you drink too much. And you had a wicked fall.* He means to keep the news from me. To let the poor soul have a few happy days.

I'm a normal man, I worry about problems such as this. Yesterday I called a friend of mine, Fromm, a practising psychiatrist. Can you help me, Doc? I asked. Am I in trouble or is this delusion? He refused my case. You're terminated, he said. Deacon, I have bigger fish to fry. *I am at work on a case that could change the entire face of Europe.*

A good man but a dope, what does he know?

My wife is, of course, in on the secret. That explains why twice in the past week she has raised the subject of our financial affairs. *It's absurd, darling, but do you by chance have a secret bank account? I ask because I simply can't figure out where all the money goes.* She wanted me to believe her inquiry could be routinely explained: she had seen a hot item in a dress shop and wanted my enthusiasm before spending what amounted to a small fortune. I might have been deceived. But the next day she brought up the question of wills: *everyone writes a will these days. Don't you think we should?*

It explains too why, on the whole, she's been so nice to me lately.

Nothing she can say, however, will induce me to reveal the presence of my secret account. It's there as a buffer against hard times, and because when my first wife left she cleaned me out. The furniture, my dog, my neckties, my thousand-franc Swiss note, and a Maytag appliance repairman all went away with her. *You deserve it*, she told me. *Say any more and I'll take away that silly toupée you wear.*

Ignore the above. I've read the Book of Job and know when I'm well off.

Her successor is now fluffing my pillows and straightening bedclothes, polishing the bureau — ploughing like a moose through the trash of seven days. Into her "White Tornado" housewifery act.

"In case anyone calls," she says.

Because that is how she is. Although I can go six months in this house without seeing another living soul, and often do, in her mind the front steps are forever packed with visitors queueing to get in. I sink my teeth into my arm, and watch. Women are mad. *All* women are demented. That's what makes them women in the first place. But how else are we to be saved? Who else would go to the trouble?

"Lift your foot," she instructs. "You can't rest with the sheets in this untidy state."

"You expect me to be concerned about sheets when I have only a few hours left to live?"

She laughs. Oh, she has a fine old howl at this. Then she becomes reflective, her cheeks puff, her mouth goes tight, eyebrows leap into her scalp: "Ah," she says, "I've got it. You've been trying to think up a story to tell those deadbeats down at the Motherlode! Haven't you? Is it about your foot? But now you've realized that not even those idiots would be interested in a yarn about a foot, so you've thought to deepen your tale by inserting some nonsense about your approaching death. Or about your first wife running off with your neckties. That's it, isn't it?"

"What is wrong with a story about a foot?"

"The average person cannot relate to it."

I remind her that everyone has feet. I even laugh because I know the remark is funny. But she does not crack a smile. I can scent the malice of more criticism in the very way she breathes. My wife the acid-thrower.

"Yes, but their feet don't ache. How many of your average listeners have recently been so drunk at ten o'clock in the morning that they've fallen off a cliff? Your stories are merely extended jokes. No meat. No heart. No humour. They are of no consequence."

I know what she has in mind. She has this theory, for instance, about sex. My stories ought to have more sex. "But don't make it goofy," she will say, "and for God's sake avoid your nasty specifics.

"Or about money. They should be about money. Everyone wants or needs a certain amount of money. You'd have people around you all the time if you ever talked about money. But for God's sake don't make it too intelligent. You always want to appear so smart. It puts people off. You can't stand people knowing you were born a hick and didn't wear shoes until you were twenty years old."

Well, that's what she says. Actually, I was born in a porter's closet in the Louvre, Paris, France, and didn't go country until I was four, after my parents were killed in a tornado in the Aleutians.

"And don't tell it in that twisty language. Or with that hound-dog face. As for that, you'd be a lot better at it if you stayed sober."

She pauses there. She doesn't want to go too far, she knows I have feelings. She knows I can be hurt. She sits on the bed now massaging my poor, hot, throbbing foot. Her hands are deliciously cool. Or perhaps it is the other way around. Perhaps her hands are hot and my foot is cold. I can't be sure. That illustrates another of my faults. I have too many *perhapses* and far too many *can't be sures*. "*I like,*" she has told me a thousand times, "*the simple declarative statement.*" Not a busload of adjectives. Although she does not call them adjectives. She calls them "*extra words.*" That's understandable, after all I'm the one around here who considers himself the professional. "I'm the amateur," she will say. "Just a darned good Eaton's buyer, just cook, maid and sex object. But that doesn't mean I'm ignorant. If I say your stories stink, they stink."

She's saying nothing at the moment. In a half-trance she strokes my foot. Her face catches the sunlight and I can't deny she's lovely. She's lovely, she's nice, she's employed. The truth is, my foot may be either hot *or* cold but, more important, the ache is absent. It may be there but I can't feel it. She stares out the window. Placidly strokes my foot. Probably she is thinking about dinner. Or about the new suit she didn't buy after all. I lie there luxuriating, so to speak, in the touch of her hands. They tickle. I like it, I mean to say. Now and then she runs a hand up my leg. Fingers fold lightly over my knee. There is a soft glide along my thigh. Now back to my foot again. Again. Again. Then once more the somnolent climb up my leg. I dare not move. I'd like to, though. I am definitely getting interested. Her hand strokes and my body of its own accord sinks down, trying to urge the hand ever higher. I dare not speak. One wrong word and this moment is lost forever. I'd like to hire a violinist, Isaac Stern perhaps, and give him permanent residence in the attic. For times such as this. I wonder what will happen when she stops looking out the window. What will happen if *she* gets interested? I close my eyes and think: stroke! . . . stroke! . . . now higher! Higher! *Ahhhhh!* That's the ticket! Nice! Nice. . . .

That's where the sex comes into this story. I thought I'd try it. I wouldn't want it said of me that I'm not open to criticism. My idea, moreover, is that by including it I can kill two birds with one stone. I see it as a nice, positive moment in the lives of these two people. That's another criticism she makes of me. "You're too negative. People are tired of all the negative crap. Who wants to hear a story about another loser? What's the point?" As proof, she usually drags in that story someone told about two guys buried up to their necks in sand. Or the one I like to tell about four shoe-salesmen who fall into a cave and argue for hours about which of them wears a true size ten. "Big deal!" she says. Not that I exactly disagree with her on this score. "People are not a bunch of sows," she will say, "wanting to wallow or root in another's misery. Or in their own, for that matter. Leave us a little hope, will you? A little dignity!"

She ought to know what she's talking about. She gets out much more than I do, she has her lunches three or four times a week, she's in and out of people's houses and gets to know what they are thinking. When she tells me people want realistic, happy stories, I believe it. I know her remarks are meant to be helpful; I realize some of mine are getting a bit ripe. "I've heard that," she will sometimes say. "You told me that one last week." And I can imagine her final assessment of this hurt foot piece: *just another sleazy monologue! It's the same old story, sugar, we practically know it by heart.* She will admit too, if pressed, that she didn't appreciate that part about her stroking my leg. It was insulting, it questioned her natural sensuality, and what about her privacy? "Keep it up, sonnyboy, and roses will grow out of your ears before I stroke you again!"

Don't I honour anything? Is nothing sacred?

That is what she will be saying next. "But do go on. Don't let me hold up your precious story. Your audience is breathless!" How would you react to such ridicule? Do you think you might momentarily flounder? I'm a professional but that's how it affects me. I get red in the face and can't sit still — the thread is lost, you see. I laugh and try to put a light face on it but everyone can see she's stopped me in my tracks. "Where was I," I will lamely persist, "before I was so rudely interrupted?" She will smile knowingly: "You were talking about how I know more about what people are thinking than you do."

I plough stubbornly ahead. Sometimes people *will* drop over. They do. They ring up and ask whether they can shoot over — because they've heard I've been ill or depressed or they haven't seen us lately down at the Motherlode — that sort of thing, all perfectly natural. So we will be sitting down to a drink, eating roasted almonds or cheese or a pizza, say, with these people, and it happens that it is not altogether unheard of for one of them to ask outright for a story. "Tell us a story," they will say. "Let's hear what's been going on with you two." *Long time no see, Deacon, lay one on me, we're all ears!* That sort of thing. I am, naturally enough, happy to oblige, since I have come to think of myself in those terms. As a storyteller. It's what my mother tells her friends: "Deacon doesn't do anything, he just tells stories. That's all he does. He could have had a good trade as a stonemason but it seems he's content to let his wife support him." So I, as I say, am happy to respond to these requests. I get right down to it. *There was once,* I might tell them, *in darkest wintertime, in this most foul time of the year, a man who went about our country with his feet bound in rags, with horrible leaking eyes, and with a great hump on his back in which you would think he carried all the troubles of the world. Now one day, on that very day in which this poor rogue was to breathe his last, on that day a young girl innocent as the dew came dancing along his path.*

As a rule I am interrupted at about this point in the narrative. *She* wants to tell the story. Or *they* do. For her part she doesn't trust me with it. I have, she will claim, already got it wrong. "You are flogging a dead horse and no one in this company wants to hear it." What is wrong with it? "It is pseudo-literary trash," she informs me. "A hump, indeed. If we want Dumas we can go to the library. And your young innocent tra-la-la, what garbage!" She will go on to tell me how my plot is to develop: the stupid old bugger bleeding to death in an alley somewhere, our young innocent then walking up and kicking the corpse — because it's symbolic, you see. Both of them rotten and dirty and disagreeable creatures and somehow all of society having to accept the blame. "Either that," she informs our group, "or he will have no plot, he will simply have the old fart walking down the street thinking his own vile accusatory thoughts while the girl hovers innocently, symbolically, in the background waiting to be redeemed through true love. Nothing ever happening, not even any description except the odd streetcorner lamp now and then and maybe dog feces in the gutter. So don't tell it. It won't make any of us feel any better. It won't make anyone want to rejoice that they are alive. So what if people like your ugly hero do exist, you think that's any excuse? What percentage of people in the world do you think your old bastard represents, him with his filthy psychology and his dog crud in the streets? He's probably out hunting Nazis, right? Why don't you tell a story about an average person for a change, one with average wants and needs? I know too that before you're another minute into this oral beauty you'll start trying to make it sound deep, you'll drop vague hints, the situation will get so tangled up and messy we won't know where we are. It's just another of your hateful disgusting creations and we will want to go and take a bath and regret we ever asked you to open your mouth. Gloom, gloom, gloom, that's all you preach."

The truth is she is better at storymaking than I am. At least if our friends are any judge. They smile and laugh and feed her good lines. In my story, which she appropriates, my sour old man's hump is barely noticeable. She refers to this growth as a *pretty ridge* and speaks of his scarred but ennobled face, his good manners, and benevolent attitude. He meets a nice mature woman at a bus stop who turns out to be the daughter separated from him in a train wreck years before. "Why, I thought you were dead!" she remarks. Pathos carries the day: for a decade now the daughter has been placing flowers on the grave thought to be her father's. It is this journey, in fact, which has today been interrupted. "Come home with me," entreats the girl. "Mother could not accept your death. All these years she has faithfully waited." He stops off for a shave; she goes in and buys a new coat she's been eyeing in Eaton's.

I admit her stories make me feel good. I concede that her tales are populated with characters one might willingly invite into one's own home. I am bothered a little by the coincidence of this bus stop meeting, though she waves aside this minor reservation. "A story has got to be true to life," she opines. "Every day I meet someone on the street whom I have not seen in years." Others agree. They give examples.

"All right," I argue. "Even so, you must admit that her version does not sound modern." This observation is met with instant derision. Hands flap in the air, everyone wants to talk at once. Would I be done, then, with Goethe? Are Sophocles, Dante, Shakespeare to be thrown into the incinerator? A hundred names collide in the air. "What about Woody Allen? Sam Shepard? Cecil B. De Mille? Would you throw them out because they do not sound modern?"

I try to edge in my one thin line of defence: that I am speaking only of and for the oral traditionalist.

"Spit!" my wife declares. "You think your kind of oral history is an end in itself; I say look where your lies have got us. Abnormality creates more abnormality. You will have people expecting it of themselves and disappointed when it is not achieved. You will not be content until you have us walking about on all fours. You must encourage us to nobility. You must inspire us. *Inspire* us, you fool!"

I don't know. I can't refute the arguments of these people. I despair. How can I go on in the face of such accusations, such hostility, with a story, for instance, about my miserable foot? Why not give up? Retire into a world of pleasant chat. The only pleasure I have left is to look back with a wet nostalgic eye to the good old days. In the old days I was to be found every night down at the Motherlode. Folks would spin off their stools and clap me on the shoulder, saying, "Tell us another one, Deacon!" And they'd spin the other way and punch a neighbour, crying, "This guy is great, his stories will put hair on your chest!" So I'd rock on my heels and launch into the first thing that entered my head. It came easy as breathing, I had only to open my mouth and the magic would fly. "Listen," I would say, "have you heard the one about . . ." and before you'd know it they'd be doubled up, laughing, wheezing, pounding on the floor and falling against walls, or they'd be sobbing, the tears plopping down their cheeks, their poor hearts bursting. "By God, that was a good one!" they'd say. "By God, Deacon, that was a pip! What a beaut!"

So I don't know now. The heart has gone out of it. Maybe I need the enthusiasm of those good old days, expectant faces lining the bar, urging me on, quiet as snakes while they waited for what was to happen next and always knowing there'd be a good solid snort of another man's liquor at the end. I don't know. Can't tell. Maybe I have begun to lace my tales with too many non-essentials like that rubbish about Gladys or even that my foot was hurting in the first place. Maybe my whole approach is wrong. I've become fancy, gone twisty in the lingo and the mind. I'll have to think about it. Have to lay off the newspaper and TV for a while. Go easy on the booze. Try to recapture what I had at the start. Go back to scratch. Anyway, that's the advice my wife will give, late at night when I roll hurt and trembling into her arms. "*Stick to a single incident,*" she will say. "*Make use of chronological time. Keep it simple. You will get your confidence back in time. I'll help you. If you get into trouble, you know you've always got me here to fix it up.*"

Mama Tuddi Done Over

You have heard about Mama Tuddi. If you got eyes and ears or a brain in your head then you know that Mama Tuddi is a big celebrity, that she have her own show The Mama Tuddi Show on TV and radio where she sell soft drinks by the bottle and the crate, especially on TV where everyone know what she look like and how much she enjoy her work. On this day I am talking about, Mama Tuddi arrives at the doorstep of the house where Reno Brown have lived his life and said goodbye to it and there she pause and take a deep breath and think a final time about what it is she have to do. It is not right, that is what she think, but it is too late now to talk anybody out of it. Her sponsor have told her it is the right thing to do, she owe it to the public, that is maybe in bad taste, a little on the obscene side, but it is good public relations all the same.

So she knocks on the door and waits. Somebody will come soon for sure because everybody must know it is Mama Tuddi at the door and she don't have all day, she got more important business elsewhere and she only have a little time to devote to the public service the Brown family and relatives and friends have ask for and apparently expect.

She is thirsty, Mama Tuddi is, waiting in the sun, and she wish she have swallowed down a soda pop or two before she start out on this job. Also it happen this afternoon that her teeth ache. She have time for this nonsense, but no, she have no time for her health, no one care if she ever find a minute to go to Dr. Pome and get her bad tooth knocked out. That is what Mama Tuddi think as she fidget at the door, how selfish everybody is. So this put her in a worse mood and she stand there beating on the door, grumbling to herself that it ain't right, all the time impatient for someone to come roll out the red carpet, give her the official greeting she expect.

But they don't come, it is like everybody inside — not just Reno — is dead.

Finally she say to herself *I be damned if I'm going to wait out here all day in the boiling sunshine*, and kick open the door and stride right in.

"Yoo-hoo!" she call, "Mama Tuddi have come!" But the room is empty, not a sound anywhere.

But she know she have the right address. Looking around, the first thing Mama Tuddi notice is that all the mirrors are turn to the walls, all the pictures on the walls and tables have a black cloth draped over them, all except the face of Jesus who is looking at her. She don't mind the look, it seem to her natural that Jesus is going to look over anyone who walk into the room and that he especially will want to take a long hard look at someone famous as Mama Tuddi. She even give him a little nod and a smile. It occur to her for her next show that maybe she can have a big picture of Jesus at The Last Supper and the sponsor can hire a man to paint in a picture of Double Ola in front of all the apostles at the table. That way, it seem to her, her work is done before she speak a single word. So the look of Jesus give pleasure to Mama Tuddi, it seem to her he have the same idea.

However, the black cloth hanging everywhere and the mirrors turn to the wall, that is another story. They send a shiver up Mama Tuddi's spine. It seem to her a tacky thing to do, what you'd expect from ignorant folks but not from anyone in the Mama Tuddi Fan Club. Not from anyone who like the Mama Tuddi Show. She hate it, that is what Mama Tuddi think to herself. She have a good mind to sail on out the door and never come back.

Still no one come and Mama Tuddi don't know what to do with herself.

It remind her of her early days in the Green Room when she was waiting to go on after the weatherman, a long time ago before she make a name for herself.

"Tooth, be quiet,"she say to her tooth, but it go right on aching.

Mama Tuddi opens up her purse and takes out the aspirin bottle and she pick out a pill and put the top back on and goes to one of the mirrors on the wall which she take off the hook and turn around so she can see herself. Then she puts the mirror back up on the hook again. She hold her face real close so she can see inside her mouth. It is hard to tell which tooth hurt, so she does the best she can. She push the tablet down beside the most guilty-looking tooth, then she close her mouth to see what kind of bump the tablet make in her jaw.

"It look all right," she say to herself, "nobody notice a thing."

"I be good as new," she say, "soon as that pill dissolve."

Already she can feel the medicine flowing round her gum. It is on the sour side, but Mama Tuddi don't mind pills, she think it taste pretty good. She puts the aspirin bottle back in her purse and gets out her lipstick tube. Again she hold her face up close to the mirror, she scrunch up her nose and shape her mouth and paint on the red paint and licks her lips and backs up to look at herself. By now she is feeling pretty good, Reno Brown is the last thing on her mind. Her only regret is that in the rush to get here, the Double Ola man pushing and pulling her every which way she turn, she have not had time to black out her two front teeth which is how she always look on the Mama Tuddi Show and which is what her public have come to expect. She always feel much better when she know she have done all she can to please her public, when she spare not one iota of herself. It is proof to her mind of the kind of world we are living in and how bad things have got that the station people and the Double Ola man have not give her time to black out her front teeth, a Mama Tuddi trademark known far and wide. Be just as bad, she thinks, if she show up at the studio without her special Double Ola shoes or if she forget to put on her hat or get out her chequebook when she talk about the money a family save when they buy Double Ola by the case.

A smell was bothering Mama Tuddi, something in the air. She had got a whiff of it first coming in, but now it was heavier and if Mama Tuddi had a spray she would use it right here, she thought, her house or not. She liked a house where folks were not stingy on the spray, and she was beginning to have some second thoughts about these Brown folks and whether they were the right kind of people, the kind to appreciate a personal appearance from Mama Tuddi and know how much she was putting herself out for them, never mind their ignorance of how to run a clean, happy home.

Things was dusted, she could say that much for them.

And arranged nice, if you was to shove this studio couch back against the wall.

Mama Tuddi pulled the black cloth off a pair of bronze baby shoes resting atop a pile of maple leaves also in bronze. She poked her finger inside one and brought out a shriveled up spider which she flung with a gasp to the floor. Beside the shoes, under another cloth, was a picture of a boy with a flat nose and curls of tight black hair growing low over his forehead. He was spruced up smart in a Ben Blue short pants suit and to Mama Tuddi's mind he would have been a real heartbreaker but for his smart-alecky expression, which his mama ought to have smacked off his face before she let him step up to the camera. He had broomstick legs too and his socks was bunched up at his heels, what part hadn't been eat up by his shoes.

She wondered if this was the Reno Brown who had loved her so much.

She heard a giggle behind her and turned in time to see the same face jumped out of the picture frame to poke itself out at her from the doorway across the room. Mama Tuddi waved the picture at him, about to say "Well, your nose have improve!" but before she could get it out the boy's teeth flashed white and he have vaporized.

A minute later the whole back part of the house seem to blow up and people, men mostly, men in blue seersucker suits and men in nice sports jackets all yellows and blues, in stripes and in pin wheels like targets to be shooting at, were springing at Mama Tuddi from every side, their faces plastered with the biggest grins, running around her like a pack of dogs let loose suddenly from whatever was fencing them in, shouting out their welcomes to her, reaching for and shaking and then letting another of these creatures take her hand. Before Mama Tuddi know it she have been shove back against the wall, her breath all sucked out of her from so many faces to say "How you do?" to the way a lady would, with the dignity an entertainer of her standing have to maintain

— but still they are coming, more men folks thrusting out their hands, beaming down on her, saying what an honour it is, while the few women who crowd in, as dowdy uninteresting females as Mama Tuddi have ever seen together under one roof, mill around the edge casting glances back and forth and smiling quick polite smiles when Mama Tuddi let her eyes light on them.

"Now listen here," Mama Tuddi find herself saying once the gentleman have done pawing at her, "what is that smell I smell?" — which someone say is cabbage, just pot luck, nothing special, only something the women folk have been cooking up for after the service. Mama Tuddi is about to inform them how a can of good spray can cut through a smell like sand stifling a fire when it strikes her that a man is standing over by the mirror she have turn around, just standing there with his mouth dropped open and a look of horror on his face. So Mama Tuddi forgets about the spray, the man with the open mouth have reminded her and she say, "Listen here, how come all these mirrors are turn and all the wall pictures except Jesus covered with this black cheesecloth double-folded over them like that, I never see the like of it to this day?" Everyone's look is blank followed by surprise, then they begin at once to jabber their response, saying "Sho-nuff, Mama Tuddi, you pulling a laig, don't you know what they is thataway faw!" or some such variation, while all through this time the struck-dumb man is staring from the mirror to Mama Tuddi as if he think his very life or hers is in peril.

"No, I do not," Mama Tuddi say, keeping her eyes off him for she is beginning to think may be she have done something wrong judging by the few gasps she see, wishing these boisterous people would take her on in to see the dead boy so that she can get on back to the station for her evening broadcast and her TV Mama Tuddi Show which have an audience growing by leaps and bounds and which she have her duty to keep inform and entertained.

"Mama Tuddi," they say, "why Mama Tuddi how you do be a cutup, what a rascal, here pretending you don't know why they is thataway faw!" — poking each other in the ribs and swarming around her like they have lost the little mind they have. The man with the open mouth have put the mirror face-away back on the wall, and now he is bearing

41

down on her, his face set like he is face to face with death. "Why, don't you know, Mama Tuddi, whoever see hisself in the glass a time like this don't you know the devil take his soul, Mama Tuddi, we surprised at you!"

"Hogwash," Mama Tuddi say once she find her voice. Someone is pushing behind Mama Tuddi and a little child is down between her legs trying to crawl through after another one on the floor. She want to kick both of them and tell the man behind her to get his hands off her, but before she can someone else have take her arm while another person shove in front and swing open the door so it seem to her finally that they are ready to get on with what they have ask her here for; in some way-off part of the house she can hear a tin can piana making feeble notes of reverence. Mama Tuddi have a rush of mixed thought, not wanting to go in to see the laid-out body of Reno Brown she presume, not wanting to look on anybody dead, not even if he have love her like a mother, which is what the program manager and the Double Ola man have told her when they say she have to come here for the public service of the thing. Mama Tuddi's hands and feet in fact have gone cold, her legs are stiff and in fact she would not be moving at all but for the elbow pushing her in the back. Her throat have gone dry too for want of a soda pop or even a drink of water now that she think of it. She lick her tongue over the two front teeth which ought to been blacked out because that is the Mama Tuddi trademark, though she glad these people recognize her all the same. She glad at least she have remembered to wrap the fox tail around her neck, never that she have yet gone a place without it. She crane her head round to catch sight of Reno Brown or to see where the music is coming from and what kind of creature must be propped up on the stool playing it so bad with his bony fingers that have no weight on the keys. She can see nothing but the sway of shoulders and backs and ugly-women faces turning to study her as she enter through the held-open door and move slowly down the aisle that is being cleared for her. Now some wretch can't control himself and he catch at her arm. Without looking Mama Tuddi smack out at his hand, she struggle to go on, but he have arms like an octopus, he catch her again. Turn out it is the struck-dumb man, now climbing over someone to root his worried face up close to Mama Tuddi, his eyes lit up like orange peel, tugging at her to get a firm hold and spitting his saliva into her ear drum. He is screaming something at Mama Tuddi, she can't tell what because other folks are hugging the aisle wanting Mama Tuddi to touch them, but Mama Tuddi know it is not good news he bring. People in her walk of life, people above the crowd, they have to put up with so much from the unruly mob, from crazy people in the mob, that sometime Mama Tuddi rue the day she ever start The Mama Tuddi Show, she wish she back at home in her rocking chair maybe dipping a little snuff, talking quiet with neighbours, seeing the best in people. *It wear her out all this public-service stuff*, that is what she think as she try her best to sweep on down the aisle, it plumb tire her out and ain't worth the effort no how.

"*Pray!*" the man is screeching, "*Pray*, Mama Tuddi, for you have look in the mirror and Satan himself will run amuck inside your soul!"

"Shoo!" Mama Tuddi say, "Shoo!" — fanning her arms like she have walk into a nest of bees. One of the men beside her says, "Shut your mouth, Rufus, what you want to be upsetting Mama Tuddi faw?" and another one push the man called Rufus back while a third person whispers into Mama Tuddi's ear, "That's Rufus, he got the devil on his brain, don't you mind Rufus, he just a stupid superstitious type." Mama Tuddi does not know what to say to this, she hardly know what to think. Clearly the man have religion, he wearing a nice tie and is no lazy driftabout, all the same Mama Tuddi think they be doing everyone a favour they lock this Rufus creature up. Still, she don't mind, a person in her position have to learn to take the icing with the cake or they sink back under the mud. The pain in Mama Tuddi's bad tooth have vanish thanks to the aspirin tablet, her hands and feet are no longer cold and her limbs can function normal now, she have conquered her vexation and is as a matter of fact beginning to be glad she stoop to come, she glad to do these folks a favour, their good friendly feelings and the love they have for Mama Tuddi remind her of the time she first set foot on a naked stage, with hot lights around her and the little red light on the camera she have to look at for the zoom. It remind her of the joy she feel the first time she sit down with a Double Ola on the table and her front teeth blacked in good, and the wonderful way she have scored a big hit with the public who have tune in not even knowing in them days who she was. She got no time now, she tell herself, to be bothering about no trashy Rufus; she in no mood for ignorant superstition, folks will stay ignorant no matter how many times you tell them what's what.

It never cross Mama Tuddi's mind that a crowd this large will be on hand for the service of Reno Brown, she guess it is news of her presence which have bring them out, maybe a hundred or so with not enough chairs to go around, the windowsills full too and everyone squirming for a place to put their knees. She give these onlookers her best smile, her Double Ola smile, which keep the station phone ringing every time she do her show. These folks are all smiling too, whispering, "Dare she is, Dare Mama Tuddi, lookadare, son, Dare she is. Our own Mama Tuddi!"

Mama Tuddi keep her poise, she have a rule never to let cheers go to her head: she walk with the same regal bearing she have learn by heart at the Poise Clinic she have attended for one day, her head kind of thrown back, her chin stiff and erect, not walking like her legs made of rubber like some tarty women do. Mama Tuddi know she have sex appeal, if you got it flaunt it, that is what Mama Tuddi say. Over in a side room Mama Tuddi spots where the music coming from, a piano with a dark oak frame, and playing it is the most skinny woman Mama Tuddi have ever seen this side of a pickling jar, though to give the music lady credit she have on a stunning hat in black layers like a wedding cake, which Mama Tuddi very much admire. But she got her fox collar and her jewels, Mama Tuddi ain't worried none. Down near the front row Mama Tuddi see a man standing, pointing out his arm at her, shouting "Lookadare! What I tell you? Mama Tuddi is got tooths, I tole you she have tooths!" and the man next to him dig in his pocket and it look to Mama Tuddi like he pass the first man a dollar bill.

It is at this point that Mama Tuddi observe at the front a tiny coffin stretched over two sawhorses there. "Is that Reno?" she ask, and a figure near her nod in a sombre voice, "Days old Reno, bless the poor Chile's heart," and Mama Tuddi can't take her eyes off the coffin which thank the Lord have a lid on it.

Suddenly her escorts touch her elbows, they do a little dip, and a second later to Mama Tuddi's astonishment they have fade away.

Suddenly the room fill up with total quiet.

Mama Tuddi licks her lips, she have a mild case of nerves, wondering if now is the time to do her speech in praise of the dead boy. That is all she have been told she have to do, maybe cry a little as she read off the credits for Reno Brown and tell how he is bound for heaven on the glory train.

Mama Tuddi feel a tug on her skirt but she have her poise and won't look down.

The music lady play three quiet notes on a new song.

Suddenly a low groan begin in the room:

Ummmmmmmmmmmmmmmm. . . .

It stretch out on the same key and commence to grow:

UmmmmmmmmmmmmmmmMMMMMMMMMMMMMM. . . .

It hold on for the longest time, then it advance up a note and swell, it keep on swelling, sending a shiver up Mama Tuddi's spine.

MMMMMMMMMMMMMMMMMMMMMMMMMMMMM. . . .

The floor under Mama Tuddi shake, she got goose bumps on her arm: it the most beautiful singing Mama Tuddi have ever heard, she think for a second God himself is lifting her out of her shoes. *MMMMMMMMMMMMMMMMM.* . . . Then the sound just explode out of these folk's popping jaws, it wham into Mama Tuddi most to knock her down, in the split instant before it sweep on past her like a mighty wave:

Bringing in the sheep
Bringing in the sheep
We be here rejoicing
Bringing in the sheep

Mama Tuddi unhook her fox, she close her mouth, and sit down.

Amen, murmur a soft voice next to Mama Tuddi. *Amen. De Lawd is bringing in de sheep, de Lawd is taking Reno home.* Then the woman whose voice it is begin to wail, she begin to wail and shriek, and Mama Tuddi hold her mouth tight, she look straight ahead over the coffin lid, correctly figuring in her head that the broken-hearted woman beside her must be the bereft mother of the child. They have give Mama

Tuddi the seat of honour but although she think the world of mother-hood Mama Tuddi wish they give her another chair.

A few other women join Reno's mother in the tribute to her son, their moans kind of snake around the room, but the grief does not get very far. It seem the outburst have been premature, for one thing Mama Tuddi overhear a remark that the preacher have not yet come, he held up in traffic on the freeway. This cause Mama Tuddi some concern since it have always seem to her that preaching ain't now what it was in her day, that their heads are too big, they ought to take their lesson from her and be on time, that is what she think.

A heavy hand fall on Mama Tuddi's knee, and although she give a little jump of surprise it does not go away. She look down at the man's big hand and slowly turn her head meaning to give the hand's owner a cut of her tongue, it rile her the familiar ways certain men have who are so full of themselves they think they can get away with anything. But she see the man in question have a friendly smile, he have a certain charm to him. "I'se LeRoy," he say teasing-like, fixing on her a half-wink. "You was Reno's favourite to the end." He have nice black hair all straighten-out and smooth on his head, he a handsome man, Mama Tuddi can see, with winning ways, and she hear a small voice inside her head saying *Mama Tuddi you watch out for him.*

For some reason Mama Tuddi gets it in her mind he is Reno Brown's daddy. "Pardon me," she say, "I assume you are the departed boy's father?"

LeRoy just grin. "No'm," he say, "I's the boy-friend."

"The boy-friend," Mama Tuddi repeat, not knowing what else she can say.

"Of Mrs Brown," LeRoy explain, leaning forward to poke his head in the direction of Reno's mother on her other side. And Reno's mother come out of her crying spell long enough to look Mama Tuddi in the eye and present her hand, saying, "So please you could come. Me and LeRoy was worried on Reno's account, this mean all the world to him."

"He was a dear little boy, I'm sure," Mama Tuddi say.

"Old Reno," observe LeRoy, "they break the mold when they make him. They throw away the key."

Scrunched up in the seat on the other side of Mrs Brown, with his hands covering his face and looking out at Mama Tuddi between split fingers, is a small boy. Mrs Brown smack at his hands, saying, "This here be Reno's twin brother Lasvegas, he the man in the family now." The boy give Mama Tuddi a grin and once more hide his face. Then he wrench around and whisper something in Mrs Brown's ear.

"He say to tell you he's older," Mrs Brown informs Mama Tuddi. "He older by three minutes, to tell the truth. You knock me over with a feather when the doctor tells me another one knocking at the gate."

Although Mama Tuddi nod and think to say she never have a child herself and proud of it, her mind is elsewhere. LeRoy's hand have crept up her thigh, it continue to rest there, and Mama Tuddi have her hands full trying to decide what to do with it. He certainly a forward type, she think, and it strange to her that Mrs Brown don't appear to mind. He a flashy dresser, this LeRoy, he is too young too, and plainly Mrs Brown have snatched the cradle to get him. Mama Tuddi puzzle to herself how Mrs Brown have manage to bring this off. She is not an overly smart-looking woman, sorry to say, with not much meat on her bones and none of the *savoir-faire* a man appreciate. She is over the hill, Mama Tuddi would say. And in the wardrobe category she is running a pretty bad race. The black mourning dress is all right, but it have a three-inch hem of fancy lace, which have no place at a funeral. Not to mention black net stockings. At the moment Mrs Brown have one leg crossed over her knee and she is swinging it pretty good. Also she have something flashing there. Mama Tuddi reach down to scratch her own ankle, wondering what it is. Turn out it is a gold anklet Mrs Brown have on, with a big moon disc which have inscribed on it the word MINE.

Pretty tacky stuff, Mama Tuddi theorize.

"LeRoy give it to me," the woman now say, leaning close. "He a cutup from the word Go." Then she hook up her dress and show Mama Tuddi her other ankle, which have the word HIS.

Although Mama Tuddi is interested and she nod, she have her mind elsewhere. LeRoy have lifted his hand from her leg and now either a fly landed on her neck or that Romeo have put his hand there. She hope it is his hand. Mama Tuddi have a fear of little fly feet walking all over her neck, getting his dirt and disease everywhere. Now the little feet are walking around, it tickle and tingle until it drive Mama Tuddi almost

47

to distraction. She clamp her knees together and hold her body straight, wondering where it going to walk next. She hears the little boy whine, "Mama, I wants a drink," and "Mama, I wants to go the bafroom" and "Mama, I'se hongry," and Mama Tuddi wish Mrs Brown would tell him to hush up. The piano lady starts up another tune, and another woman pass in front of Mama Tuddi, saying back to someone that she think she best go stir up the runnin beans. Mama Tuddi wish all these people would hush up so she could give her attention to the thing on her neck. She no longer think it is LeRoy's hand on her neck because he have both his hands down in front of him looking for "The Old Rugged Cross," which is the song the piano lady is playing. Although the fly have now stopped walking it have not gone away, and Mama Tuddi think standing still is worse than moving because she can not bear the thought of what the fly might do next. She think to herself that if they kept this place clean they wouldn't have so many flies around here, and it seem to her that was the least they could do since they knew she was coming. Reno Brown may have love her like everybody say, he may have believe the sun and moon rose and set on Mama Tuddi, but there is a limit to what she will put up with, whether from him or somebody else.

The fact is Mama Tuddi have sunk so deep in thought she have failed to observe that the audience is now getting up and filing by the box which hold the remains of Reno Brown, the lid lifted and held up by a red broomstick, the folks who have already had their last look at the boy now crowding around Mrs Brown to tell her what their last look at Reno have meant to them, telling her that he look so peaceful you would swear he was only sleeping, telling her they never seen him looking so good, he the prettiest child they ever sat eyes on, he is safe at rest in the arms of the Lord — hugging her and patting her hands and sort of being swept along until they come to Mama Tuddi where they bend their knees and take a close look at her fox tail with the head of the fox still on it and at her two front teeth, which they know now is real, and at her dyed-orange hair and even at her shiny black purse which have the words Double Ola in big letters on the flap — then to slouch on by and return to their seats or their standing place and join in on another verse of "The Old Rugged Cross," which is the cross Jesus and Reno and everyone in this room have to wear until they exchange it for a crown.

The song goes on and everybody files by to pay Reno their last respects. Then the music lady half-lifts from her stool, she fix a look on Mama Tuddi who is slapping at her neck, she lets her eyes go bong-bong and roll around in her head, then she shrug to show her confusion and sit down again to play "The Old Rugged Cross" all over again in the hope that Mama Tuddi will stand up and do what's right, that being the same hope others have, which is why they are beginning to whisper and shuffle about and wonder aloud why Mama Tuddi will not pay her last respects to Reno, wondering if maybe she have something up her sleeve.

Mrs Brown in the meantime know nothing of this, she is up by the coffin sobbing and moaning, crying for her dead child, now and then letting fly a big shriek which go through the room like a fast curveball which send others down on their knees weaving and moaning and shrieking back. Mrs Brown is telling Reno that Mama Tuddi have come, that old LeRoy have come, that Lasvegas is standing by, that Reno be happy to learn all his close friends and loved ones are here paying their last respects, that the preacher will be here to say a few kind words soon as his car gets off the freeway jam, that they are all praying for his soul and never forget him till their dying day. She is looking up through the ceiling and flailing her arms to get her message through to heaven, reminding the Lord to look after His humble servant Reno, her poor beloved son Reno, to place a chair for Reno close-by to God's own chair, to watch over his growth the way a mama would because she know in her heart Reno would have make something of hisself if he had the chance, a nice bright boy like Reno who didn't have a hurtful bone in his body, a believer who commit his heart to Jesus on the very day he was born, who turn a helping hand to his mama anytime she ask and who love his daddy and treat him with respect even if his daddy was a sorry worthless no-count snake who never walk God's road a day in his life, that worm who also gone to his reward praise be to God, taken away by the Grim Reaper and none too soon if God want to know the sorry truth of the case. His daddy burning in hell where he ought to be, Mrs Brown cry out, but her precious lamb Reno he will walk right out

49

of the valley of death into the stretched-out arms of Jesus, GLORY GLORY, to ride around heaven in the golden chariot God have carved out of ebony bone for all the innocent children of the world. "GLORY GLORY!" She Say, "LIVE AGAIN!"

"Thine the glory!" come the chorus behind Mrs Brown; *"Hallelujah Amen!"* the chorus shout, now drumming their feet on the floor in a quick rhythm that makes the whole building shake, that cause the saw-horses on which Reno's coffin repose to quiver and bounce as if old Reno himself want to climb out and show these folks how grateful he is, to show them the power of God's love, that His power have no end, that God Himself have climbed down on Jacob's ladder from heaven to show He approve, to show the poor people's welfare is ever close to His heart. Mrs Brown now have a grip on the coffin, her head momentarily disappear as she stoop down to give her boy one final kiss on his sorrowful closed eyes, now emerging with tears streaming down her ravaged face, her body twisting about, her mouth opening and closing though silence have the day, her feet lifting and lifting as if she have set them down in a bed of burning coal, while her friends in the audience look on with half-envy, with their hearts caught up in their throats, for it is plain to them that Mrs Brown is now in the rapture of God's strong embrace, that God Himself have taken hold of her tongue, that He have come to claim this hour for His own. And they is proud in fact that this have happen, for in no other way can it be explain why this innocent boy have been plucked away in his tender years, poor Reno who have never done no harm to no one, as nice a boy as you ever hope to see, with always a kind word for the old and the lame and the sick, who give his last dime to any stranger ask it of him. This is why they have come in the first place, it is why they are thumping their feet so hard against this floor, and clapping their hands, and twisting about themselves, and aiding Mrs Brown with their shouts as best they can — all to urge God on, to argue Him into showing His face or showing His presence with a sign like He have give to Moses with the burning bush, or to them with their tents pitched by the Red Sea. If you love God He will not let you down, that is what they think and know and believe, and they have not doubted He will show up today because God have plucked out of a mother's arms an innocent child and even God would

not do this without some good excuse, He have a reason for it just as He have a reason for the sun and moon and for resting on the seventh day. God's power is awesome, it is both a terrible and beautiful thing, it take the breath away, all the same He will not take an innocent child less He have to, and it is clear this time He have been force to for how else can He remind them they are a sorry bunch and evil live in their hearts, the eyes they see with are blind as whale bone, the mouth they talk with is bitter as a snake's tooth, their soul is slick as marble, they come to Truth slow as a wheelbarrow. They are sinners all. Only by plucking away poor Reno have God been able to make them face up to the error of their ways, only by this pilgrimage through a mother's grief can He guide their footsteps after His into the everlasting Hereafter. *"Gone!"* Mrs Brown cry out, *"My baby gone, done gone, first he here and then he gone, out of my arms he stolen like a thief in the night, my poor baby gone on High, gone on ahead to Gloryland!"*

Throughout this Mama Tuddi sits high in her seat, her backbone straight as a barber pole, even so her breath quickening as if hurried along by the drumming of feet. Except for sheer willpower and re-minding herself who she is her own feet would be beating against the floor. But she have her dignity to uphold so she hold herself steady and oppose the tide that sweep the rabble along. She blink her eyes and hold on tight to her fox, fearing for her personal mortal safety as this untidy crowd invoke the Lord and exalt this doomed child Reno above any station she expect he might have truly achieve. It do no harm she guess, but still to her mind it is a tacky show, it hardly the sort of perfor-mance to go down well on TV. All the same it have a point, she kind of like it to tell the truth, it have the hocus-pocus that keep her on the edge of her seat, some of it have hit like something from a slingshot, she too have felt a stirring in her breast. Now she see Mrs Brown pulling at the red stick which hold up the coffin lid, yanking it away with fire in her eyes, slamming the lid down with a loud crack while she shout over Mama Tuddi's head and everyone else's loud enough to cause anyone walking by in the street to stop and think: *"Gone! Gone! My sweet baby gone!"* — and she sink down in a puddle, which LeRoy leap up and bring back to its seat.

"Mama Tuddi," someone calls, "Mama Tuddi, for shame!"

And Mama Tuddi cannot believe her ears, it have been ages since she hear anyone speak her name in vain. She rise in her seat and glare around, she search these faces looking at her with accusation and re-proof, these looks that say *Mama Tuddi you have let us down.* Mama Tuddi is in a dither close to outrage as she look perplexed at a man standing in the rear who jab out his finger and keep on jabbing it her way, yelling "She in league with the Devil, pray sinners pray!" and it is the man Mama Tuddi recognize as the man who have said Mama Tuddi in her vanity and pride have looked at herself in the mirror, thereby prompting Satan to enter her skin, the man who have first ac-cused her with his stinging eyes. LeRoy have Mrs Brown back in her seat now and Mama Tuddi swing on her, she wanting Mrs Brown to tell this man he is a fool, that Reno have wanted Mama Tuddi to come here because he love her so, which Mama Tuddi have done as a public service on her own time with no question of money in the bank, she wants Mrs Brown to tell this buffoon that very thing.

But Mrs Brown shrink away, it looks like she is angry too, that she too believe Mama Tuddi have not done right by her departed child. Mama Tuddi switch to LeRoy, she gets his ear and whispers to him "What went wrong?" but LeRoy only give her a quick sad smile, he duck his head toward the close coffin and that is all he do before he go back to tending Mrs Brown, now a weeping ghost of her former self. Suddenly it come to Mama Tuddi what she have done wrong, it hit her like a flash; she have been too high and mighty in the eyes of these peo-ple to give a last look at the remains of Reno Brown. She have remain in her seat fussing about flies and thinking of the pleasures of the flesh while others have paid tributes to his name.

Something scrunch up in the brain of Mama Tuddi, it form a tight ball and pulse there to gather strength, it seem to get down on its hind legs awaiting the perfect moment to fly forth — that is what everyone feel watching Mama Tuddi, and a sigh of relief goes up, you can see it and feel it rising dense as a cloud, the tension leave these folks for they can see now that Mama Tuddi mean to make matters right, she have only been jiving them, she have something up her sleeve sure as night be night and day be day and dream be something in between. They see Mama Tuddi square her shoulders back, they see the way her tongue is licking over her front teeth like she intend to black them out, they see the blood swelling in her face. They hold their breath as she stride around Reno's coffin, as she position herself behind it on her spread-out legs, her both hands gripping the fox tail and pulling at each end like she mean to tear it in two. They fall silent, waiting in a hush for what it is Mama Tuddi will say to them.

Indeed Mama Tuddi have at last got into the spirit of the thing. She glaring out at these folks, she is letting them see she have poise and dignity and above all she have nerve. She letting them know she don't like it that they have even for a minute give up on her. She stroke the coffin slowly as she stare them down, she sweeps her body over the lid and both her hands now move over it like she is washing this body of Reno Brown, bathing Reno with her own hands for this holy trip. LeRoy comes out of his spell, he the first one to sense what Mama Tuddi require, and he leap up to retrieve the stick which have propped up the lid, he is all business as he pass it to Mama Tuddi who reward him with a stern nod of her head.

Mama Tuddi props up the lid though she don't yet look down. She is looking out into this sea of faces, compelling them to admit the personal wrong they have done to a celebrity of her importance. Now she lick her lips, she take a breath way down so folks know that when she speak she is someone to be listen to. The cords thicken in her neck, she let out a big groan sweeping up both her arms. *"Now let me see,"* thunders Mama Tuddi's TV voice — *"Let me see this heah Reno Brown!"* Her eyes rake on past everyone, they roll over the ceiling, then they drop and settle peacefully on Reno Brown.

"Praise the Lawd," someone murmur nearby. "Praise the Lawd." And the spirit pass around, it multiplies as Mama Tuddi study the face of Reno Brown, her own face softening as she study his tender remains. Mama Tuddi is in fact quite a bit surprised that Reno is as he seem: so young, so composed, yet so small, so tiny, so shrunken almost to nothing in the Ben Blue suit which lie flat on his bones. For a second she let her eyes dart over the space in that box, space which to her seem horrible, more than a person can understand or cope with and which she hates to believe — a terrible thing, that is what Mama Tuddi sees. It is like doom stretching all around, defeating not just this shrivelled child;

not something simply lying in wait for Mama Tuddi and everyone else sharing this globe, but just bigger, bigger, so big one almost want to hang the head, condemn God, cuss Him out, say "It ain't right, God, this little space You let us have, how can we live it well when death loom so large?" But Mama Tuddi falter only for a second, no one in fact realize she falters at all; quite the other story for in fact everyone is amazed. Mama Tuddi bends right down, her orange hair descend inside the coffin with Reno Brown. Then she straighten up and suddenly both are there, Mama Tuddi with her arms around Reno, Reno with his head stiff against her breast.

In that position she look down on him, she stroke his hair. Her voice when she speak is quiet as a lamppost at first dark, it have the soft lick of a single flame under glass. "*This heah be Reno Brown,*" she intone. "*This heah be Reno Brown who adore his mama and his poppa and who love LeRoy and all you folks. He dead now but Mama Tuddi say he not dead, he live forever in the Book and in The Mama Tuddi Show. I now rename this child, I rename him Calvary, for Mama Tuddi can do what she please and it please me to name him that. Now I say adios to Reno Brown renamed Calvary from this moment on. I say to you that this boy Calvary alias Reno have withstood the birth, he have withstood the pain, he have stood off the infidels and let his light shine wherever he go. Now he gone like his mama say. She right insofar as she know but she don't know yet Mama Tuddi going to speed him safe and sound on his way.*"

That is all Mama Tuddi say. She grip the boy's shoulders firm in each hand. It seem a marvel to everyone that Reno's head don't fall back but indeed it stay there flat and indeed it seem to some that Reno lifts his head to meet Mama Tuddi as she come down to put a kiss on his mouth.

"*Glory!*" some folks cry, "*now he riding fast!*"

"*Lickety-split! Look out Lawd, here he come!*"

Mama Tuddi complete that kiss pretty soon, she give a smart look all around and stand a minute patting her foot. It seem she still have more to do. She suck in her breath through her nose, she unwrap her fox fur and stretch it out full-length over Reno. Then she give it one last look goodbye and close the lid.

The man in the back row who have accuse Mama Tuddi can only

shake his head and try to drop down out of sight. Everybody else too stunned with happiness to do anything but sit and look. It a long minute before they collect themselves and give Mama Tuddi her earned applause. Then you can see them exchanging smiled-at remarks, saying as how Mama Tuddi have sure speed him up to heaven with her kiss — laughing at the thought of old Reno — old Calvary — streaking from star to star like a fox. "From now on," one of them suggest, "I reckon it will be the swish of his tail making them blink and swing." "If he don't make it to heaven," LeRoy tell Mrs Brown, "at least we know he have made it to the Milky Way."

* * *

After that it seem the people have enough and they breaks up, though milling around, still waiting for the preacher to come. For good as Mama Tuddi have done — and she have done more than they bargain for — it take the preacher to make Reno's passage complete. Folks pass on to the kitchen to get their food, they pass on through and eat in the yard, after first seeing to it that Mama Tuddi have started in on hers. She is the guest of honour and they don't eat nothing Mama Tuddi haven't tasted of first. She eats the ham biscuits and she eats the corn, she eats the mashed potatoes and pokes at the succotash. She eats the cornbread and the yams and she have a bite or two of the greens, she eats the chicken livers. She pass up for some reason, maybe not seeing them or because her plate is limber and won't hold no more, the runnin beans. Everybody else have no choice but to pass them up too, which riles somewhat the woman who have cooked them up. But she is a forgiving sort and is the first to let Mama Tuddi know she don't hold no grudge.

It is out in the yard by the honeysuckle vines that Mama Tuddi learn the story of Reno Brown and what have happen to him; there too that she learn what LeRoy have done when the boy's daddy out of spite and meanness thought to put the killing stick to him. It is hard telling some of this to Mama Tuddi because, much as they regret it and hope the misfortune here will end, the plain truth of it is Reno's death have a bearing on her. So they mostly leave that part out, that part about Reno looking in the mirror at the burying for his daddy that took place. His daddy had been whupped fair in a knife fight with LeRoy, which nobody could blame LeRoy for doing since it was a case of doing it or having it done to him. Reno's daddy was no good, the wonder of it was it hadn't been done to him long before. He like his drink that man did and whenever he had it he lit up real good and nobody could do a thing with him, he as soon light into a person as look at him. Usually who he lit into was Reno or Lasvegas or their mama because she wouldn't give in, she'd stand between him and them daring that drunk fool to raise his hand to her own flesh and blood. She had any sense she would of run, but she never did. So he'd pour it on, or try to, even if he couldn't stand up. You never saw a man so keen on beating the daylights out of what was closest to him. Everybody have seen the licks that poor woman receive fighting him off her boys. Nor did they blame her for taking up with LeRoy. LeRoy was young and high of blood, but he was dependable where it count. He wasn't about to let nobody walk over him. Or over those what were dear to him. Mrs Brown was older but she know her own mind and LeRoy make it plain that he like a woman who is mature in her views. And she have a warm way with him, she know how to please a man who return her love. That is all she was looking for, that and a man who is soft with her boys. She don't mind taking a stick to them herself when they do something low-down and deserve it, but she don't like it when her husband just takes up a stick to them for no good reason.

So yes she is with LeRoy one night trying to have a good time and forget for a minute her bad homelife when her husband catch up with her. He calls that woman names no one here will repeat, for no need to offend Mama Tuddi with name-calling she no doubt have heard herself, being a woman who have got around and not one who hide her head under a stone. He calls her names and starts beating up on her and on Reno who it happens is tagging along. He pulls out a knife he have obviously brought with him intending to do bodily harm and he start swinging it around.

LeRoy is not going to stand for that. He lays into him and somebody throws him a tool just to even it up. Her husband don't even have the excuse of drinking this time, he's just mean. He just want to carve on someone, it don't matter who. LeRoy he don't mean for it to happen most likely, he just want the man to come to his senses and stop but he don't so after LeRoy take a nick or two on the wrist and have that blade switching over his throat when he is down, after that he gets down to business, throwing Brown off. They tumble in the grass, they roll in the bushes, folks looking on hold their breath — in a minute it's LeRoy who crawl out. He's looking for Mrs Brown, who is standing over under a shed hiding Reno under her dress so he can't see, and LeRoy get them and take them on home. I guess he stayed on after that.

Some folks claim the law ought to be called, but anyone with eyes could see it happened too fast. LeRoy was scratched up bad, he must of lost a gallon of blood. Brown he was dead, nothing anybody could do to change that. He got what was coming to him, what he been asking for. The truth is everybody breathes a little easier around here with him gone. Nobody like him. Everybody know he worse than dirt. We glad to be rid of him.

Anyway, it ain't right that a man, bad as he is, be left to rot so we have a notion to give him a decent turn in the ground. We hold the service right here, after all she is his wife. We try to think of something good to say about him. We hedge a little on his virtues is what I mean. Some of the women say he was a right good looking man, for he was that. And sometimes he would work, though naturally he throw it all away. No need grieving, that's just how some folks are. He was one of them: plain no good.

He stupid, that what the trouble was.

* * *

So that part they tell Mama Tuddi and glad to get it off their chest. The part that more directly concern Reno is the part they attempt to skate around. How he raise the black cloth which he knew better than to touch and which he been told a dozen times to keep away from. Reno was a good boy, but nobody ever deny he have a hard head. Stubborn as the day is long. A service for the dead no time to be primping, he told that time and time again. Still he look. He in one of his know-everything jackass moods and he do it anyway. He took sick pretty soon after. Nothing anybody can do, he have done it to himself. He hung on for five days, wasting away, wasting down to skin and bones. No use to call in a doctor, but they call in one for lack of any better idea and the doctor all he can do is throw up his hands. He bring LeRoy and Lasvegas and Mrs Brown into the kitchen and he says, "I throw up my hands." He say this boy have been looking into mirrors, and the family have to agree. "All I can do," the doctor say, "is give him something to stop his foaming at the mouth. If the devil have walked in you will be seeing a lot of that." Mrs Brown cry, what other relief she have? Lasvegas cry, LeRoy cry too I guess. Mrs Brown blame herself, thinking she have not parade the danger enough across Reno's brain. That don't do no good. LeRoy blame the husband, he gets to feeling low just when he was bouncing back from what he have to do to him. LeRoy ain't killed nobody before. Mrs Brown she comforts him. LeRoy he comforts her. Lasvegas he a little short when the brains passed out, he don't much seem to know what is going on. He just a nice fella, he do the best he can. LeRoy and Mrs Brown they get their heads together, they agree they doing nobody no good, so they figure out what they can do to help Reno pass the time in his final days. They pools their money and come up with enough to buy Reno a little twelve-inch TV set. That is how Mama Tuddi come into the picture. Reno never have no TV of his own to watch before. Still nothing cheer him up, he don't care a hoot about no wagon train or shootumup cops nor none of that soapy doctor stuff.

Then one night Lasvegas have turn in and LeRoy and Mrs Brown are drinking tea in the kitchen when they hear a shriek from Reno. They run in fearing he is dying on the spot, but what they see is Reno rolling on the floor, giggling and wheezing himself blue in the face, getting up to point at Mama Tuddi on the screen then rolling on the floor again. Old solemn-faced Reno who is on his sick bed, at death's door, yet they have never seen him having so much fun before.

"I going to marry her," Reno say. "She going to be my bride. What her name?"

"Why shore," Mrs Brown answer him. "You know her! That's Mama Tuddi. Everybody know Mama Tuddi."

Reno drag himself up to the tiny screen, he get close enough to look Mama Tuddi in the eyes and trace out her face with his finger on the glass. "She don't have no tooths," he say, "that woman have no tooths," and he laughs hard and kicks his thin legs into the air with a loud whoop that wake Lasvegas in a yonder room.

"You never seen Mama Tuddi before?" his mother ask. "Land sakes alive, Mama Tuddi is a household name."

"No tooths," Reno repeat, and he clutch his sides laughing all the more.

"Yes, she is," LeRoy say, "she got tooths all right, they just blacked out because that her trademark."

"No she ain't. If she had um I could see um, you trickin me."

"You watch," his mother say, "we prove it to you."

Mama Tuddi is talking about her sponsor Double Ola, a bottle in her hand with the other hand pointing to it while she tell them how good it is. The camera come in full-face on her, she opens her mouth wide and recline her head and put the bottle between her lips. The liquid go chug-chug in the narrow bottle neck, Mama Tuddi hold it there a long time, her eyes growing bigger with every swallow she take. They count fifteen swallows and Mama Tuddi bring the bottle down, she say "AHHHHHHHHHHHH!" and with the backside of her hand wipe the spittle from her mouth. Then she tilt the bottle back between her lips, she swallow fifteen times more and then she say "AHHHHHHHHHHH!" and hold the bottle straight out in her hand and study it awhile, her head shaking as if she cannot believe her luck. Then she hold her head way back and hold the bottle upside down, the liquid go chug-chug down the neck, and when she have finish the last of it Mama Tuddi again cries "AHHHHHHHHHHHHH!", smacking her lips and rubbing her belly and standing with her shaking head and winking eyes so that everybody watching The Mama Tuddi Show will know that Mama Tuddi love Double Ola and they will too the first chance they have to go out and get some.

"Now look here," Reno's mother say.

For right there the camera come in on Mama Tuddi's mouth alone — wide open, smiling, inviting anyone who want to have a look — and Reno lets out a shout, "SEE! SEE! I TOLE YOU, SHE GOT NO TOOTHS," Mrs Brown and LeRoy at the same time screaming, "SEE!

see! she have!", Lasvegas also yelling from his part of the house for them to hush their mouths, he sleepin — while in the meantime it seem the camera have gone right on through Mama Tuddi's mouth to come out on the other side where it turn so that Mama Tuddi's hind-side can be seen as she throw her fox fur over her shoulder and maybe pin a small hat on her head and pick up her Double Ola shopping bag, on her way out now to get some more.

The screen fade to black and that is all of Mama Tuddi for this hour.

"I loves Mama Tuddi," Reno say. "I going to marry her."

There is no other way around it either, that boy have fallen head over heels. He keep the TV set running 128 hours straight, he will let no one turn off the thing for fear he miss a minute of her show. Even when later in the week he can't hardly walk or crawl or see his own hand in front of him he have somehow drag himself in front the box and laugh for joy as he trace out her picture on the screen.

"I saving up my money," Reno say. "Her hand gone be mine one sweet day."

Then he die.

Mama Tuddi, hearing this tale told, is sure it is the saddest tale she have heard since her own daddy's mule have run away with him and broken three legs. "Hush up now," she say to Mrs Brown, "you have my heart clanging and twisting like someone have taken a meat cleaver to it. You have me wanting to go back in there and lift the lid and give that sweet boy these very shoes I have on, my best walking pair. I wants to take off these jewels from my neck and string them around his."

"They nice jewels," Reno's mother agree. A sorrowful look reclaim her face, and she add: "He was a sweet thing. No one ever take his place."

They with some others are now sitting out in the yard, enjoying a leisurely chat while the debris — white paper plates and Dixie Cups — is being cleaned away. Plates and cups blow about the yard and dogs chase after them, pouncing with their front legs to lick at them.

Everybody getting a little drowsy after this fine feed. From time to time a family will step up to shake Mama Tuddi's hand and give Mrs Brown a good hug, to say what they have to say while they have the chance.

LeRoy is over by the rose bushes kicking a tin can with Lasvegas who now seem a kind of dreamy child.

"I hopes you don't mind him," Mrs Brown confide, meaning LeRoy. "His hand on your leg, he don't mean a thing, it just his way of showing he like you."

"I hardly notice," Mama Tuddi reply. Her heart have been moved today, but now the juice have gone out of her and she is beginning to wonder how she is ever going to get out of here.

"Well, maybe not, but I see lots of women slap his face. First month I know LeRoy he walk around with my hand print on his face six or seven times a day. I say to him, Listen LeRoy if you see something you like if you like it enough it is worth waiting for. Finally he ask me if I see anything I like, and it was his saying that that baked the cake. It don't pay to argue with LeRoy."

Mama Tuddi have a watch on a dog's wagging rear-end. She feel somehow she is slowing down, getting tired — "Losing my zip," that is what go through her mind. She feel a mite woozy in the sun and come close to asking if there is a place she can use for lying down. But her pride save her in time. One person is already here lying down and that to her way of thinking is enough. It occur to her that some prankster have put a spike in her tea. The top layer of her head seem to be floating away from the rest of her.

She is aware of the peculiar way Mrs Brown is looking at her. Of how she keep leaning forward to ask, "Is something wrong, is something troubling you." To be sure, something is. Mama Tuddi have a notion that the air have thicken between them. She can hear a bluejay prattling in a tree, she can even see the limb the bird is sitting on, but it seem to her the bird's song come from another place.

"I was just thinking," Mrs Brown confess, "I like you better off the air than on. It seem to me you have more poise." More "paws," she say.

Mama Tuddi nod. She try to focus on one part of the woman's face the way she have to learn to look at the red button on the camera box.

"Your dignity come through."

"That my trademark in life," Mama Tuddi agree. She turn her head to look out over the yard and down to a leaning shed which LeRoy with Lasvegas is standing beside. It appear the two are trying to plant a tree.

The tree to her eyes is nothing, maybe three feet tall, a couple of scraggly limbs which the foliage have drop away from or it never have.

"That a fruit tree," Mrs Brown explain. "Apple, could be. Reno was partial to apples. He had it in his head that one day he like to plant a orchard full."

"I like trees," Mama Tuddi say to keep her end of the conversation going. Her voice sound strange to her, like it have entered her ear from some distance far away. She switch her head back to notice Mrs Brown have her leg crossed over one knee, swinging that free leg hard. The gold anklet catch a glitter from the sun and Mama Tuddi see she have on her face a wayward smile.

Mrs Brown catch Mama Tuddi looking and laughs out loud. "My motor running," she say. "It a disgraceful thing to be feeling in this time and place with my Reno not yet in the ground, but it have a way of coming over me when I looks at that man." She hitch her head off LeRoy's way, wanting herself plainly understood.

Mama Tuddi give a little push and her head wag slowly up and down. "He have any other women?" she ask.

"Could be he do but they don't have him."

"You lucky, I guess."

"I guess. I have my cross to bear but cross ain't all."

Mama Tuddi at a loss to understand what have come over her. It been ages — since way before she embark on a career — since she have sat rocking in a chair out in the yard talking to another person like she have all day. She observe Mrs Brown and think to herself she could like this woman, she could be friends with her. She is part trash, maybe more trash than she let on, but Mama Tuddi find herself admiring her. It sadden her, now that she think of it, to realize she never have any woman friends, never have the time, always from the minute her alarm clock ring it is a case of GET UP AND GO. Get up and go because if you don't whatever you are after won't be there.

Yet now she surprise herself by wondering what it all come to. She wonder if maybe she ought not to gone into politics, since she get along so well with people. She wonder what the Double Ola people say if she march in and tell them, "You can get yourself another Mama Tuddi, this one's retiring."

The roof, she is sure, would cave right in, they would have a fit. She wonder if she can chalk the fox fur up to her expense account.

A chill suddenly steal through Mama Tuddi. The sun is shining bright on Mrs Brown, the sun shine all over the yard, but it seem to her as if dark shade have suddenly envelop her chair. Her bad tooth begin to ache again, the throb spreading all through her mouth. She feel weak clear through to her bones.

Now there be fresh excitement in the yard. Folks are scurrying this way and that, relating that the preacher have come, he have escaped with his life from the freeway jam. Mama Tuddi looks off at the gate where five men are turning through single file like they are playing a CHOO-CHOO game. The one in front she take to be the preacher since he have a Bible in his hand. She spots right away he have back trouble because of his stiff legs with the feet pointing off opposite each other and the way his shoulders are slung back like they can't quite catch up with the rest of him. He have a pointy head, Mama Tuddi can tell even though he have a hat on.

The train come right on up to her chair. The man behind the preacher step out from the line, coughing a few times while Mama Tuddi scramble to get her shoes on. Then he grin and say, "Mama Tuddi, this heah be Preacher Teebone who express a pleasure to meet you."

"T-Bone?" Mama Tuddi inquire.

The preacher's eyebrows, trimmed to a boomerang shape and pomaded down, now shoot up, which make his pointy head more extreme.

"T-E-E-Bone," the preacher say, spelling it out. He have an expression of doom which never change and he stares deep into Mama Tuddi's eyes, which is why she can't stand preachers in the first place. "I heah," Preacher Teebone say, "you have kiss the boy and give him a fur coat. My feelings is you be best off kissing the Holy Book, but I ain't against kissing in the circumstance irregardless of which wherever he go thet coat ain't liable to hep him none."

Mama Tuddi stay quiet. Her experience at the station have taught her that the preachers of the world are engaged in an international conspiracy to take over every second, minute, and hour of TV time.

63

And if they doing it, she tells herself, you can bet this T-Bone is in on it.

The minister abruptly turn on his heels and him and his train wheel along inside the house.

Wouldn't you know it, everybody out in the yard having a perfectly nice time up to this point, toot along after him.

Folks would follow a toad frog, Mama Tuddi thinks, *if first you slick down its hair and put the Good Book into its mouth.*

After a minute or two of sober thought during which time Mama Tuddi expect someone to come superintend her needs, she gets up and follows them. The preacher is already down at the front wiping a white handkerchief over his face. One of his sidekicks takes away his hat while another one is setting up a speaker's stand which have draped from it a red cloth with a gold fringe which have stamped on it the words ONE GOD and something like a lightning bolt shooting down the middle. The music woman is taking her seat at the piano and Lasvegas have been set up with a candle on a plate and told where to stand up by the coffin. Curtains are being pulled and it is almost dark by the time Mama Tuddi is able to claim her front seat. LeRoy's seat is empty and for all Mama Tuddi know he have gone for good. It gives her a funny feeling that empty chair beside her, and a second chill come over her when she is surrounded on both sides by empty chairs because Mrs Brown is now being led up to the coffin also, she and her boy now standing with lit candles at both ends like a pair of watchdogs. That is Mama Tuddi's view of the matter and it is all *tacky tacky tacky*, that is the only word she have for it. Preacher Teebone himself lights up a row of candles on the coffin lid.

The whole room then plunge into darkness except for the light up there. Preacher Teebone, standing behind the coffin, stretches out his arms and his hands fall square on top the heads of Mrs Brown and her living son. His face have a yellow glow, his ears stand out from his head like he would flap right on up to heaven unless he have this duty to hold him down. He have not yet spoken a word but the sweat is already pouring off him, and Mama Tuddi is beside herself thinking *tacky tacky tacky, I could do better with my hands tied behind me and my feet in a bucket of concrete.*

"LAWD GOD IN HEAVEN rings out the preacher's voice, "PROP
THESE HEAH TWO PEOPLE UP ON THEIR WEAK AND LEANEST SIDES
IN THEIR HOUR OF SACRIFICE FOR THEY ARE BUT THE CHILDREN
OF YOUR HANDIWORK." Mama Tuddi almost falls out of her chair
since it comes to her such a big surprise that this pointy-headed man
with his bad back have got so much thunder up his sleeve.

"Prop um up!" replies a few in the back. "Preach on, Reverend."

The preacher withdraws into the darkness and the music lady does a
roll on her piano. When next he appears, behind the rostrum, his suit is
washed in shiny magenta and he have his head thrown back so that all
Mama Tuddi can see of his face is mouth. "*Friends,*" he begins. . . .

Something crawls over Mama Tuddi's skin, first up her legs and over
her knees then wrapping her thighs and hips and finally settling like a
feathery waked-up thing that thinks to play possum in her lap.

And suddenly the preacher's voice have leaped out at her, forcing
Mama Tuddi's spine straight back against her chair: FRIENDS WHEN
YOU GO TO SHECAGO YOU KNOW WHAT TIME YO BUS DEPART AND
WHEN YOU GOT YO TICKET TO BATON ROUGE OR FOWT WAYNE OR
IF YOU GOING TO NU YAWK OR MONTRAWL OR WHETHER YOU GO -
ING TO DEETROIT OR THE YUKON TERRITORY YOU KNOW WHAT
TIME THE BUS LEAVE AND WHAT TIME SHE GET THERE AND SO YOU
GOT YO BAGS PACKED AND YOU GOT YO SKIVVIES IN ORDER AND
YOU WOMEN'S GOT YO FACE MADE AND YO HAIR CURLED AND YOU
ALL SET CAUSE YOU KNOW —

— CAUSE YOU KNOW THE HOUR AND THE MINUTE AND THE
DAY YO BUS GON GO CAUSE YOU DONE SEEN THE TIMETABLE OR
YOU DONE ASK OVER THE TELEPHONE AND THE VOICE DONE TOLE
YOU THAT BUS LEAVE AT NINE FAWTY FIVE OR TWELVE P.M. OR ON
THE BUTTON AT SIX O'CLOCK AND YOU IS HAD TIME FRIENDS —

Tacky tacky, Mama Tuddi think. Yet even as she say this to herself the
thing in her lap darts up its head, listening to her, and Mama Tuddi's
scalp tightens as once more it begin to crawl.

— YOU IS HAD TIME FRIENDS TO MAKE YO PREPARATION
COMPLETE!

"*Amen!*" someone cried.

"*My baby gone,*" moan Mrs Brown, "*he gone.*"

"*Gone!*" everybody sing.

BUT BROTHERS AND SISTERS WHEN YOU TAKE THE TRIP THAT
RENO BROWN TAKE WHICH IS ONE THE QUICKEST RIDES YOU GON
EVER HAVE — WHEN YOU TAKE THE GLORY RIDE YOU AIN'T GOT
NO TIME TO PUT THE CURL IN YO HAIR —

"No, you ain't!"

OR TO SLICK IT DOWN —

"No, you ain't!"

OR TO POLISH UP YO SHOES OR PAINT UP YO LIPS —

"No, you ain't!"

CAUSE THERE AIN'T NO TIMETABLE OF THE LAWD'S PLAN AND
THERE AIN'T TELEPHONE POLE OR FREEWAY TO THAT FAR
KINGDOM —

"No, you ain't!"

AND SO MY FRIENDS UNLESS YOU CAREFUL AND GOT YO FIN-
GERS CROSSED YOU GONNA HAVE TO MAKE THAT TRIP WITHOUT
YO PREPARATION COMPLETE CAUSE THAT ONE TRIP WHAT RUN BY
NO SKADULE YOU LIKELY TO UNDERSTAND —

"Praise the Lawd!"

YOU GONE BE CAUGHT WITH THE WINE IN YO MOUTH AND YO
FOOT IN THE TRAP! YO BED OF PLEASURE GONE BE YO BED OF PAIN,
YO PATH OF SIN GONE BE YO PATH OF WOE, THE DEVIL HIMSELF
GON COME AND SWEEP YOU UP LIKE A MONKEY WITH A BROOM,
YES MY FRIENDS THE HIGH AND THE LOW!

"The high and the low!"

The room is aquiver with this preacher's work, in the din Mama
Tuddi cannot hear herself think. Teebone's eyes are boring in on her
from his face gone shiny-slick, she can see the flash of his gold teeth and
the sweep of his arms as he grab the red banner and flaps it hard and
fast, like he mean to shake out the words ONE GOD and hurl them
around her neck. Mrs Brown and her boy are down on their knees,
bent over like two melted piles. Candle flames jump off their wicks and
spin through the black air, clearing a path for Reno's spirit to follow.
His spirit is climbing out of the box. Mama Tuddi sees it clear as day
passing on up through the lifted lid, walking barefoot through the
throbbing air. Mama Tuddi sucks in her breath, she grind her teeth

together and sucks again. She press her hands tight between her legs, whining all the time, whining despite all her desire to maintain her dignity and poise, for the crawly thing have twisted down over her stomach and is hissing out its tongue and she can feel its rough nose pushing cold and wet under her hands, aiming to slide up through her woman's trough to lodge inside of her. *"How many?"* Teebone asks. . . . The snake thing slides in.

HOW MANY OF YOU FOLKS BEEN TO THE RIVER?

"We been there, preacher!"

HOW MANY OF YOU POOR SINNERS HAVE BEEN TO THE RIVER?

"The river, amen!"

I SEE SOME OF YOU FOLKS HAVE BEEN TO THE RIVER AND I KNOW YOU HAVE BEEN THERE AND JUMPED RIGHT IN —

"Right in!"

— WHILE OTHERS OF YOU HAVE STOOD ON THE SHORE AND WAITED FOR THE WATER TO DIVIDE SO YOU COULD WALK A DRY BOTTOM RIGHT INTO GLORY LAND NOW AIN'T THAT THE TRUTH?

"It's the truth!"

YOU HAVE STOOD ON THE SHORE BIDING YO TIME AND WHILE YOU HAVE BEEN BIDING YO TIME THE DEVIL HAVE CUT THROUGH THE WATER LIKE A SILVER FISH AND HE HAVE COME RIGHT ON UP INSIDE. YOU HAVE STOOD ON THE SHORE WATCHING YO FACE IN THE WATER AND LIKING WHAT YOU SEE AND THINKING YOU ARE ABOVE GOD'S PLAN AND THE DEVIL'S HUNGRY FISH HAVE JUMPED OUT OF THE WATER AND DROVE HIMSELF SMACK-DAB INSIDE YO EVIL HEART.

"Save us, preacher!"

I SAY TO YOU THE SAME AS I HAVE SAID TO THAT BOY IN THE BOX I SAY BROTHERS AND SISTERS IF YOU WENT TO THE RIVER WHY WERE YOU NOT BAPTIZED? I SAY TO YOU IF YOU WENT TO THE RIVER WHY DID YOU NOT JUMP RIGHT IN AND SWIM CLEAN ON HOME?

"Show us how, preacher!"

"You bring us home!"

MAYBE YOU THINK YO FUR COAT OR YO TV GON GET YOU THERE—

"No, we don't!"

MAYBE YOU THINK YO DEEP FREEZE OR YO POCKETBOOK OR YO LOOSE WAYS GON GET YOU THERE —

"No, we don't!"

MAYBE YOU THINK YO SODA POP GON SWING IT WITH JESUS MAYBE YOU THINK YOU CAN GIT OUT ON THE FREEWAY AND THAT GON TAKE YOU THERE OR MAYBE YOU THINK THIS BOY GON GO ON AHEAD AND PUT IN A GOOD WORD AND THAT GON GET YOU THERE BUT I SAY TO YOU THE SAME AS I WOULD SAY TO A MAN BLIND IN ONE EYE AND UNABLE TO SEE OUT OF THE OTHER FRIENDS I SAY THERE IS BUT ONE GOD ONE HEAVEN AND ONE WAY OF GETTING THERE WHILE THE WAY OF THE DEVIL IS LEGION AND HE CAN CLIMB INTO YO HEART AND TAKE CHARGE WITH NO MORE SECOND THOUGHT THAN A VAIN WOMAN HAVE WHEN SHE APPROACH THE LOOKING GLASS!

"Amen!"

"Thine the glory!"

Preacher Teebone speaks on. The music woman's fingers roll over the keys like someone stripping bark from a living tree; the voices in the room shake the roof with their song and one by one the long line form to head down to Teebone, who have a bucket of water to sprinkle from, saying "Sister, I baptize thee."

Going home, we going home, the song goes.

But Mama Tuddi can see through her heart and she like what she see. She like what she feel. The thing inside her is warm and quiet, he have come inside and curled up and it seem to her he have brought her peace. He have taken her a long way from these people, she hardly aware of them. She have her hands full just thinking how good she feel.

The thing inside her is sleeping now. He satisfied now. But she have a notion he is going to wake up the minute she tell him to. She going to have new strength for her show; this thing going to lead her out of this backwoods town into the bright lights of bigger places and more important work: pretty soon all the world going to know Mama Tuddi's name and bow down to her esteem.

Hanging Out
with the Magi

The minute Velma saw the delivery truck creeping slowly up Jacksnipe Lane in front of her house, motor whining, driver's head poked out the window like weeds on a stick and no way you could ever bring yourself to think of that ugliness as human hair or even a human head, she stopped scrambling Willy's breakfast eggs to say over her shoulder to him, "Oh Lord, there goes another one." Another one *lost,* she meant. Meaning more than that too, as she knew and her husband ought to have, because since Velma had got married and stuck out here in these scratchgravel hills all her good times, her dreams and easy temperament, her way of seeing life as a thing to be enjoyed and led to the fullest and not a thing to be denied or held in contempt the way Willy did his — all these had got lost too. Sidetracked, anyhow. This being God's truth and one she was likely to harp on and throw up to Willy's face day in and day out or at any rate every waking minute she had him underfoot to remind her of what an aboutface her life had taken. *"My misery beginning,"* she'd tell him, *"from the first second my lucky star got hooked up with yours, William Shotte."*

But she didn't say that to Willy this morning. She had already said all to him that she ever wanted to say on this earth, and what words she spoke were meant for her own ears and for those of whatever kindred spirits — kindred to her — hovered in the room.

"Now what is that fool out yonder up to?" is what she said.

Scowling, wondering how he could go on and what was the use, Willy spoke his thoughts to the table in front of him. He had slept like a dog. He had tossed and turned and slept on rocks. But that didn't satisfy anyone around here. He'd have to go through hell and show her his burning feet, before Velma would be satisfied.

He raised up to his own window to see what the fuss was about.

Outside on Jacksnipe Lane the driver had got out and was walking around the truck, kicking the tires and looking — so Willy thought — like what the TV shows called real strung out. Lanky scarecrow type spitting and rubbing up the toe of one shoe on the back of his trouserleg, now shading his eyes and peering off into the wild blue yonder.

Looking for a house number, Willy figured. But it was just forest out there — forest and mean hedge and ivy so thick it could strangle a man. The driver could hunt till doomsday turned over and still be none the wiser, because nobody in this part of earth which God had forgot had ever had sense enough to put up numbers, or even to hammer in a post saying Jacksnipe Lane is what that poor excuse for a road was called.

"You're scorching them eggs," grumbled Willy, returning to his seat and drooping there with his elbows on the yellow dinette and thinking how his life was hard, so hard, one difficult moment after another, and what in God's name had he ever done to deserve it? "Go ahead," he said, his voice rising, "go ahead and burn them good and proper. My mama cooked me eggs for thirty years without singeing them once!" But with that his eyes lit up and he decided to keep the rest of his thought to himself. *Yes, she did. While all you can do is stand over there gawking out the window, too lazy to stir the pan and not yet with sense enough to run a comb through your hair. You ought to have stayed put away in the loony bin where you would be this very minute if I hadn't come along and rescued you.*

Silently he regarded her. He truly believed she belonged in a madhouse but he knew too that this was now a forlorn hope inasmuch as no self-respecting madhouse would have her.

Velma spooned more lard fat into the skillet and stood for a few seconds with her feet planted in utter concentration, her lips puckered, stirring with a frenzy. Then she ladled the egg lumps onto a flimsy paper plate and brought them over.

"Here are your eggs," she gaily reported, blowing hair up out of her face and into his eggs too if that was where hair had a mind to fall. "Here they are, hard and greasy and not fit for a buzzard and just like your mama used to cook them when she was up and able."

Willy pushed the plate back.

"My mama would have sprinkled sprigs of parsley on the top," he complained. "And she'd had laid on a spot of buttery toast, I reckon."

"I reckon so," Velma smoothly replied, "because you and your mama have the appetite of split-neck hogs and you never worried once about the children going starving in the world."

Willy thought: *This woman is nothing but a bucket of meanness and spite. She ought to be broken up into concrete and dropped into the first river.* Aloud, he said: "My mama and me may have a slight weight problem, but no one can say we have not always done our duty by our fellow man."

Velma scorned any reply to such nonsense. She went back to her window and stared moodily out at the delivery van — whose driver was now unabashedly urinating against a front wheel.

"It seems to me," cooed Willy, his mouth full, "that if a man is going to put in a full day hard at work in the salt mines, if he's going to have the difficult moments I've had, then he ought to have a full breakfast under his belt. My mama would always make me a nice little pancake on the side. And we had us a fine little room to eat in, a glassed-in porch it was, cheerful and pretty as could be, and we could sit out there and take the sun and watch birds pecking around in the yard if we wanted to. We had us a little red rose on the table." He reared up his chair, glaring at Velma, daring her to refute this. "That's the kind of woman my mama was!"

"*Is!*" jumped in Velma. "Still *is*, unless she's passed on and I haven't yet heard the good news." She broke off, suddenly stomping both feet down, letting out a wail of disappointment: "Hell's bells, I was hoping there was something for me!"

The delivery driver, it seemed, had made up his mind. He'd revved his engine, thrown the big truck into gear, and was now rumbling on out of sight down Jacksnipe's twisty vine-besieged lane.

"That's you to a T," observed Willy. "Always expecting something for nothing. In that regard you are one with your age." He smiled, patting his stomach, taking pleasure from that last remark — and now holding up his empty plate for Velma to come and take it.

Velma did not say *You're one to talk*, although she thought it. She didn't say any of what was on her mind because for one thing you could not get blood out of a turnip and for another her Willy was all turnip. Velma felt like hanging her head in shame, wondering anew why she had not listened to the spirits when they warned her that marriage to a man like William Shotte would be the same as having a yoke around the neck for the rest of her natural life.

Willy was worse than yoke — over there waving his empty dish like he didn't have two legs of his own — he was log and chain. One of the spirits, the flaxen-haired one who could have been Little Boy Blue's brother he was that sweet and pretty, materialized in the far doorway, pointing a silken finger at Willy and shaking his head ruefully.

"Oh, Velma, my heart aches, aches, aches for you."

Willy of course pretended not to notice.

His eyes were fixed on nothing, absent-mindedly chewing a thumbnail, as the beautiful spirit moved sadly over and took the plate from the table and brought it politely over to Velma.

"Thank you, darling," she said.

They had such good manners, her spirits. They were all charmers. *If only*, she now grieved, *I could have married one of them.* But people would have talked. They would have worried about her. They would have said, *Well, you've done it this time, haven't you? You've finally stepped off the deep end. You can't expect us to come to your home and have a normal visit with you, when it's a spirit-husband we've got to sit down with and talk to and us never knowing where to look or what kind of conversation a spirit would want to have.*

Willy, too, had his thoughts. *There goes another one*, he heard the voice in his head saying. *That goddam blue Fancypants, with his silk stockings and lacy sleeves, and that nasty smirk I'd like to slap off his silly face. Little snot-nose toe-walker. There's my dish, you little fruit, go ahead and take it, but if ever I find you alone I'll wring your head off.*

"Thank you, darling," he heard Velma say.

Velma Thicktitty. As nice to these spirits as can be, but can I ever get a kind word out of her? Not one. Just eggs on a paper plate and noodles for dinner and my own bed in the corner when finally I lay my head down at night.

No, the spirits get all the favours, around this house.

What's left over, the hard times, they are all for me.

"Here, darling. Here's a kiss for my beautiful Boy Blue."

The spirit went up on his toes to receive Velma's kiss. Then he pranced by Willy, sneering.

There he goes, the little turd. Off to see what's cooking elsewhere with those other half-wit spirit freaks.

Meanwhile, there Velma Longnose stands. A pain in the behind. Always thinking how life has let her down, how I have, and how she'd be better off sent up to some glue factory to be melted down, so she can come back as candles to light up a rich man's table.

Sassy cow.

Not that a rich man would have her. I knew in the beginning she was stuck on herself. That she had airs. But I thought her airs kind of pretty. She was different, you know. She was vixen and siren and she hung on to me like a baby on sugar. 'My Precious Willy,' she called me.

Now look at her. She ain't yet made me a cup of coffee. She ain't yet asked me how my night's rest was, what I dreamed, what my mood this morning is. All Thelma Twotitty can do is stand there in her dingy gown looking out the window, hoping to get something for nothing. Born with one silver spoon, now looking for another. All she can do — all she is fit for — is ragging my nerves and spending money. Spending it, and holding out her hand for the next dollar. That, and coddling spirits. Letting them take over house and home.

There is no doubt about it. I fell knee-deep into Hell's Hole the day I looked twice at Velma Fattitty. The day I gave my hand to Miss Velma Tittytitty.

The voice in Willy's head fell silent, and the space where voice had been abruptly clouded over and went black, as the Little Boy Blue spirit came running into the kitchen in high excitement.

"*Me, Me, Me!*" he was shouting.

He veered around the counter and began tugging at Velma's house-coat, still shouting "*Me, Me, Me!*", but more insistently now, his golden

73

curls dancing and his beautiful eyes flashing — thrusting up before Velma's face the framed dimestore print he'd taken off her bedroom wall.

"Me?" he shouted. *"Me?"*

"Yes, it's you, darling," Velma sweetly told him. "Now you go on outside and play."

The spirit scooted happily off, a blaze of blue and gold.

"I declare," said Velma, "he does take such a delight in that old Gainsborough. But he's right, you know. For him, it's just like looking into a mirror."

Willy groaned. *If I was a spirit, he thought, I wouldn't need no painting to tell me who I was. I wouldn't need no mirror, either.*

Willy had it on the tip of his tongue to tell Velma exactly what he thought of her and her spirits; instead, he blushed, his eyes enlarged; he gave a long sigh, and his body went limp all over.

Virginia, not a day over thirteen, had come in. Had drifted in. Looking more bereaved and struck-down even than usual. She was wearing the thin cotton dress, pinkish and see-throughish, that swept down in a puddle around her ankles, and today she had on her nice pink hat with the feather as well. Her travelling hat, although as far as Willy knew, she never went anywhere. Went, so far as he could determine, in her slow liquid-like fashion, only from room to room to room. Pining away. He could see her little breasts pert against the fabric, and a darker smudge where her neat little legs came together. A narrow black ribbon, velvety in its smoothness, circled her slender white throat; her tiny feet were whitish and bare. Head and shoulders were bent. What he could see of her hair was straggly, in knots, one could almost say. As usual, both hands were up over her face, as if lured there out of some sense of quiet and perpetual shame, or as if she feared someone might at any moment step out from behind a door and begin beating her.

Poor, wan spirit-child.

Willy wanted to reach out and hug her. He wanted to press her to him to kiss away all her troubles and to tell her a thousand times that she must not worry, that she had him to count on, that his shoulder was always available. But he knew how such touching could unnerve her. He knew how his lightest touch might drop her spiralling into deep fits; might send her spinning and weeping and down on her knees to pass the next days and weeks sobbing in a corner.

Poor wraith. Poor ravaged, always-hurting child. Poor orphaned freak to the spirit world.

He wondered what on earth had happened to make her like this. What vile and vicious act had been done against her while in her natural life. He wondered what depraved man had got his paws on her.

She was so high-strung, so frail and penitent — so burdened down — was his Virginia. Yet, for all of her despair, she brought into this house the essence of femininity. Divinely elegiac, brainless in her torpor and woe, this phantom girl represented, to Willy's mind, pure Womanhood. Her pale shape, as he considered her now, was awesome. She was the one thing that reminded him of what lust was. Of what wonders lust could accomplish. A spirit, yes, but he could do it with her. Longed to. Was in a fever to crush her to him, to have his member go hard and swollen into her — sweetened! — and to hear her cry out *Yes Yes Yes, pound me with it, blind me with it, Oh give me more, more more!*

Even dim Velma would sit up and take note. Even his sainted mother would:

"Oh, Willy!" they'd say admiringly. "Oh, Willy, you're a rogue, a rake. Oh, Willy, what a fearsome man you are!"

Virginia brushed by him, stumbling, sending up a weak cry. There were times, it seemed, when the poor spirit hardly knew where she was.

"Is it . . ." she asked now, her voice tender and wispery, *"still morning? . . . Is the sun . . . shining today?"*

She did not expect any reply. She continued her slow, aimless drift through the room.

"Has anyone seen . . . Granny . . . this morning?"

Velma, poking and prodding the Mister Coffee machine, which was at last beginning to drip, raised her eyes to the ceiling. She loved her spirits, but felt it was just her luck to have one of them crazy. I've got my troubles too, she thought, but I don't go around parading them. I don't walk around half-naked, either, with men underfoot to see everything I have.

Yes, she thought, I've got to have a hot talk with that little lady.

Virginia criss-crossed in front of her, hands wringing. The dress practically flapped right through her, she was that thin and skimpy.

"Is poor Granny . . . out in the woods? Has anyone seen . . . my dog Barney?"

The way Virginia sometimes talked a thousand spirits had nothing better to do than to swing on vines and hide behind trees, hunt mushrooms and kick up stones, out on the lane and in the thick woods.

Slump-shouldered and bemused, moaning softly, Virginia wandered on off. Probably into the living room. A dozen times Velma had come across her there, speaking to the empty rocking chair. Saying, *"Are you . . . lonesome, Granny?"* Saying, *"No one . . . touched me, Granny."* Saying, *"Will I . . . bleed much? Will it . . . hurt me, Granny?"* Saying, *"Would you like me . . . to tickle your feet, old Granny?"*

But Granny was never in the rocker. Sometimes a grown manspirit would be. Scary creature with blue chin, dressed in dark serge suit, twisting a toothpick in his mouth. Crooking his finger at Virginia, saying, *"Come sit on my lap, little girl. Little nice girl. Come play with me."*

And Virginia, sobbing, in the end would climb up on his knees. Saying: *"Will it . . . hurt me, Daddy? Will it hurt me? Oh, don't hurt me, Daddy."*

It amazed Velma that so much — and so much of it disgusting — went on, even in the spirit world.

* * *

Willy was putting on his shoes. Now bent over, grunting and straining to get his laces tied. *How many times in my life have I done this?* asked the voice in his head. *How many more? I want to stay home like Velma does: wash a pan, scrub the floor. Mend Virginia's addled spirit, get some sanity back into this house. Take a walk in the woods, blaze a trail. But, no, I'm stuck at my nine to five. Velma gets the gravy. All I get to do is go out the door. Fight for my place out there among the Spit & Shines. It isn't fair. No, it isn't fair. Break my back, and all for what? I'm going to quit one of these days. I am. I'm going to say, "Velma, YOU go out the door. See for yourself what it is like out there."*

She'd say, "No, you're not. Pull yourself together. Go on out there. It's a man's world, and you've got to believe you're one."
"Not any more," I'd say. "Now it doesn't belong to anyone. Home, even with these spirits, is a paradise compared to what you will find out there." That's what I would say. But why bother? Why try talking to a wall? Willy looked up. Velma was cooly drinking her coffee, not even thinking to offer him one. He looked down at his shoes, reminded for some reason of his mama. His mama would have buffed up these old Thom McAnn's. She'd be stooped this very minute at his feet, tightening his laces, saying *You don't want them coming off in the rain. Willy, when you go out your mama's door, you go out proud. Because that's what a Shotte is. You can leave this house smiling, because you know you go with your mama's love.* And she'd swish a little talcum over his neck, fold his collar down, and send him on his way. *Go like a Shotte,* she'd say, and give a little wiggle of her hips at her joke.

But his mama, his sweet mama, she could not help him now. She was half-way to the other side of the world, and no help to anyone.

He stood up, heaved back his shoulders, and said: "How do I look?"

Velma flopped a tired hand his way. "You'd best go on," she said. "You're going to be late if you don't, and you know what happened last time. I declare, you dawdle about worse than a sick child. Anyone would think you were halfway to losing your mind. I put your coffee right there in front of you, and you have not touched it once."

* * *

A few minutes after Willy's departure, a knock sounded at the door. Velma wheeled around with a look of embarrassed surprise, much as if she had been caught in an indecent act. In fact, she was in deep conversation with a Dr. Schuler — tall, pin-striped spiritman who had taken over Willy's chair and who was explaining that he had sold insurance to the poor and disabled while in his previous life.

"Previous or future," he interrupted himself. *"Lord only knows."*

The door sounded again.

"Now who can that be?" she said to her visitor.

Dr. Schuler did not seem to hear the door. He was saying, rather excitedly, that he hadn't enjoyed selling policies to such people. *"Although they make the best customers,"* he now went on. *"You get a poor person, trying to raise a family, he wants nothing more than a sense of security. False or otherwise, he doesn't care; if it is called security he will sell his soul to have it. Yes, the poor more than anyone are really willing to shell out the bucks. I raked it in."*

Velma remembered her own childhood, when they had been as poor as chickens, with her mama gone all day and finally gone for good, and her daddy mired down in drink and self-pity.

In his spirit life, however, the doctor continued, he had set out to improve himself. He'd gone to a good university and got himself a Ph.D. in rural psychology. Unfortunately, there was not much demand for his services, as the bottom had dropped out of that profession just as he was entering it. *"That's why I called by this morning,"* he said, his manner turning serious. *"It was mentioned to me that you had a young girl here who might be needing council."*

"That's between you and Virginia," replied Velma, feeling her face redden for no good reason. "I don't interfere with anything my spirits want to do. They are free to lead their own lives."

The front door again rattled, louder this time, but when Velma moved to answer it her visitor stopped her. *"I heard, too,"* he murmured, *"that you could use some help yourself. I'm told you have had some difficult moments along the way, up to and including a plague of bad dreams lately."*

Although the tall spirit had a kindly manner, Velma did not feel disposed to speak with him of her problems. She was not the confessional type, having trained herself to believe that what was personal and private should remain that way. Talk was futile: she'd learned that much at an early age. It would pain her too much to dredge up those old issues now. They were dead and buried, so far as she was concerned. The doctor was nice, he was easy to talk to and appeared to have all the time in the world, but she had never mentioned a word of her difficult moments to anyone — not to blue boy or Virginia and certainly not to Willy. She liked to remind herself that she had had her satisfying moments too, enough to balance those others out. She was not one ever to be swamped by her own misery, as Willy was inclined to be —

although what accounted for Willy's misery was totally obscure to her, and was largely, she believed, self-induced. He had a fixation on gloom — to use the doctor-spirit's term — or so anyway it seemed to her. The door had been silent for a time. Now a hand shot up and rattled its knuckles against the window over her sink. "I know you're in there!" she heard someone shout.

Strangely, Velma was not startled by this, not even sufficiently moved to see whose hand it might be. The Schuler spirit was nodding his head sympathetically, saying he understood. Saying it over and over, smiling sadly at her. She could not imagine what he thought he understood, since she had not said a word to him. All the same, she would like to have told him of her recent dreams. Last night's, for instance, had her still puzzled. She had waked sprawled on hard ground near her own house. She could see the lit windows. From a tree close-by, an owl hooted. She tried to move, only to find herself completely enclosed in vines. Two people stood not far away, both totally oblivious to her screams. One she recognized as Willy. The other was bathed in darkness from the shoulders up, and although his figure seemed some-how familiar, she could not fathom who he might be or what his pres-ence signified. He dashed silently over and began whipping her with a stick. The vines abruptly slackened, yet she did not rush to escape. The dark figure lifted her nightgown with his stick. He spoke, but she couldn't hear his words. Then he lunged forward and seemed to come down, but instead his black shape went on past her and she waked sweating in her bed, clenching her fists, thinking how his shadow must eventually fall somewhere.

"Well, it was a difficult moment," the spirit said, patting her hand. *"But I'd say you waked up in time."*

The door was now being kicked repeatedly by whoever was there. Blinding sunlight flooded the hallway as Velma opened the door, and she saw the spirits — blue boy and his friends and even the doctor — fall away from it in a swirl of tumbles, with small cries of agony.

This so disconcerted Velma that all she could think to say to the boy blinking at her with a stolidly contemptuous expression was: "No one is home."

It was the same whisky-faced, strung-out, straggly-haired boy she had seen earlier urinating against the truck wheel. The truck itself she now saw parked in the lane behind their hedge.

The boy wiped a filthy rag across his face. He said nothing. The sun blazed behind his shoulder, directly into Velma's eyes, hiding away entirely the boy's features and in fact his very head. She thought of spook stories read as a child, and shuddered, stepping back a pace. Her hands flew up to her face. A sensation passed through her, radical and ungovernable, and perfectly shocking. She thought she had caught sight of a scrunched-up Willy peering back at her from a dark pocket inside the hedge. But that could not be. Willy had gone. Willy was on his way to work.

"None of these houses out here have any numbers," the delivery boy stated. His words were clearly meant as a rebuke, for his mouth was twisty and his eyes had come close together. His foot was loose in the right shoe and he kept sliding his foot into and out of it. His voice rose. "It's against the law not to have your house numbered, don't you know that?"

"They fell down," Velma quickly lied. "You could see them up big as day for a long time, but they fell down in the last snow." She pointed with a vague finger where the numbers had been.

"When was that?" the boy demanded.

But Velma, now recovered, refused to put up with any further insolence. "State your business," she told him.

The boy ran first one hand and then the other through his tangly hair. Then a black comb appeared in one hand and he brushed the comb unhurriedly across each ear. All the time he stared intently, almost ravenously, into Velma's eyes.

"I never saw no snow," he said cunningly. "I like snow, but I never get any snow where I live. If you get any snow away out here I would say you're lucky." He licked his lips, awaiting her reply. He slid his foot again into his shoe, but this time he gave it a great stomp against the porch floor.

"There was some," Velma said, surprising herself. "But that was years ago. It snowed more in the old days."

The boy pensively regarded her. "That's what I thought," he agreed. "I thought it snowed more in the old days." He withdrew a wrinkled slip of paper from his hind pocket and waved it under Velma's nose.

"You got to sign this," he said. "You got to sign this before we can re-lease your goods." He was practically shouting. "Where's your pen? It's got to be in ink, you know."

Velma did not hear this. She was pivoting about, swinging her head high and low, trying to get a good view of the yard. She thought she had seen movement in the hedge, but now nothing was there and she was convinced that there was no way anything could have been.

Maybe a rabbit, she thought. *Maybe a big cat*. Cats were numerous in the neighbourhood. Most of them half-wild and a considerable nuisance to the spirits. For some reason the cats frightened them. It did no good to ask why. The faces of the spirits would simply go scarlet and they'd stand about whispering and nudging each other in the ribs.

Apparently signing of the form did not matter to the boy any longer. He had stuffed it back into his pocket and was now down on the lower step signalling to some unknown other person out at the truck. "You can bring in the goods!" he shouted. "This is the place!"

The man he called to stepped through the hedge-opening, mumbling indistinctly as he brushed vines and holly aside with one arm. He wore floppy trousers coloured like a barber pole, and a barber pole shirt. He looked about eighty. His cheeks were sunken; tufts of white hair sprouted under his nose and out of his ears. An ugly, festering spot on his chin was swollen the size of a half-dollar. Emblazoned across the front of his shirt were the words THE NEW DAY CARTAGE and, in small script, *We Deliver The Goods*.

"Watch out for the skates," the boy said.

The old man carried the package cradled in both arms. He was sweating. His eyes had that faceless and untroubled look of someone sightless.

"What say?" he asked.

He tripped as he reached the top step; the package thumped down, bursting in one corner. The boy up-ended it quickly, and slid it over to Velma.

"It's C.O.D.," he said. "You'll have to pay up."

* * *

81

Velma settled the package up on her kitchen counter. "It's not very large," she told the spirits. "It's not very heavy either." She shook it. "It doesn't shake," she said.

The spirits huddled back against the wall, as if afraid of it. Virginia was shivering. Her face was whiter even than usual and her knuckles were in her mouth; she was breathing heavily. A trickle of what looked to Velma like blood ran down one leg, and spread out from her toes. An instant later, she was retching. Doubled over, turning and turning, she gave a prolonged cry, then fled the room.

"Go see to her," Velma told the blue boy. "Make her stretch out in bed, and put a hot towel over her face."

"She makes such a fuss," the blue boy complained. But he seemed happy enough to go attend her.

That left only the Schuler spectre with Velma in the room.

"Look!" the doctor said. *"It's moving!"*

Velma put her ear to the package. She could hear something inside kicking. She heard a faint cry, too, as one might hear from a small animal that had lost its leg in a human trap.

I know that sound, she thought. I'd know that sound anywhere.

With a wild cry herself, half delight and half panic, she ripped the box open.

Outside, high in a tree that overlooked the house and the thick maze of vines, that had a view of lane and hedge and nearly all of Jacksnipe Hill, Willy rested. His cheeks were scraped raw; his stomach burned; his feet were scratched and sore; he had blisters on his hands, and pinpricks of blood decorated much of his naked body. He panted, not yet daring to look down. Heights confused and frightened him. There was that, but also many years had elapsed since he had climbed a tree. It had been hard. He had climbed it the way he climbed trees as a child: with his arms wrapped around the trunk, clinging with shoulders, stomach, and thighs. Pushing up with his bare feet. Pulling with his arms. Inching steadily up. Feeling the rough bark go wet and hot against his stomach. Straining. Keeping his eyes ever skyward. Pausing when the limbs above him swayed like a golden web and the earth below him seemed to shake. Dizzy. Waiting for the dizziness to pass. Then opening his eyes and pressing on. Inching steadily up. Holding tight. *The old snake-crawl*, his mama would say. *It was how your daddy said he did it as a boy. You can do it, Willy. Go like a Shotte. And don't give up until you have reached the top!*

And he had done it. He still could. The effort left him shivering; it left him cold with fear. But he had made it. He had made it to the top. His only question now was *Why?*

* * *

Velma paced to and fro with the baby, laughing down into the lovely and perfect face, letting her eyes and her free hand rove with fine pleasure over the perfect body. When the baby smiled, Velma smiled, and when it giggled she did the same. If its mouth puckered, hers puckered, and when the baby went *Goo* her own voice involuntarily produced the identical sound.

Oh, bliss, Velma thought. *This is bliss. I now know what true bliss is.* And she meant it, too. Sentiments which only a few minutes ago would have quite astonished her she now took for granted as having been hers all along. She would have called anyone a liar who now said to her that Velma Shotte had never until this moment been heir to, custodian of, these warm, strange, inarticulate motherly urgings.

It quite passed Velma's reckoning that she had not herself given birth to this beautiful child. It seemed to her that already ages must have passed since the delivery people dropped their package at her door; nor did it occur to her to question how this miraculous thing had come about. When the baby *gooed*, she gooed, and when it wiggled, when it arched its back, she arched hers as well — and smiled down on the baby — and smiling down on the baby was enough for her. Just having the miracle gift in her own arms was enough to think about.

She's mine! she thought. *She's mine! Velma has a baby!*

"*Let it nurse,*" the spirits advised Velma. "*The baby is hungry.*"

And without any shame or even the smallest acknowledgement that she might be incapable, Velma peeled her housecoat back, and let the beautiful rooting mouth snatch at her breast, and suck-suck-suck away.

And white milk poured forth and it did not occur to her to think this strange. It was extraordinary, but it was not strange.

She walked the floor with the child and the child nursed; the child slid into peaceful sleep, and Velma went on with her walking, because she could not bear to put the sweet child down.

"Let Virginia hold her," the blue boy said.

Virginia wept and called out from her bed, rent the air with her violent, choking sobs, although Velma heard this not at all, so enraptured was she by the tranquil beauty of the sleeping child's face, and by the little hands that, even in sleep, curled and uncurled over Velma's finger or nose or lock of hair.

"Let Virginia hold her," the blue boy said again.

Velma was offended. It amazed her that the blue boy would betray her with such a thought.

"Be quiet," she said. "You'll wake the baby."

"It's what Virginia is crying for," the blue boy said. *"It will help her to rest. It will give her great happiness, for it is no ordinary satisfaction, this holding of a baby in your arms."*

"Only for a little while," the Schuler spirit agreed. *"Extend yourself."*

Velma walked the floor, blowing kisses at the child in her arms, rocking it, singing over it lullabies that rushed out of nowhere into her memory. But she had never known the blue boy and all the other spirits to be so insistent about a thing.

"No," she said. "No, I cannot bear to part with this child even for an instant."

Thus she was astonished when, a few seconds after making this declaration, her heart softened and tears spilled out of her eyes at the sound of Virginia's cries. Her heart seemed to part itself in half, and then those halves parted too, and the pieces kept on parting, providing room for everyone. There was room for Virginia, who had not her backbone and fortitude and strength to combat the difficult moments. There was even room for Willy. She wished he could be here to see this glorious baby.

She went into the room where Virginia lay, and sat down on the bedside. She rocked the baby and swooned over it, delaying that instant when she must surrender the baby. Only a moment more, she thought. Let me hold it one instant longer. Velma's face lit up and a big whoop erupted from her: "We must name this child!" she cried. "We must give it a fine, noble name that it can carry proudly through life." But Virginia was reaching. "Hush, Virginia," she said. "Hush, darling. Don't cry. We can both be mothers to this adorable child."

She placed the baby beside Virginia. It seemed incredible to her that she felt no jealousy, nor had any wish to grab the child back, as the spirit girl rolled to one side and with a deep sigh brought the child snugly into her arms.

Velma felt joyful beyond all her ability to comprehend. It was as if the whole of her once innocent nature had been bestowed on her again. "The baby looks like Willy," she heard herself saying.

Nor did this observation blacken her heart, as she feared it perhaps would. She was gladdened, for she was next saying: "The baby looks like me. The baby looks like all of us."

At this the baby's eyes opened. It seemed to Velma that they did. They opened into a grand and bewitching smile, then closed again, and whether the smile was conspiratorial, whether it was witless or blessed, she could not say.

* * *

Willy, up in the tree, was thinking how much like a monkey he must seem, for being there. But this did not worry him. He could see his house, and through the windows of his house Velma passing back and forth, and he had no further curiosity about what parcel had been delivered. Nor in what manner it had been received. Velma was a good woman. He loved Velma.

It came as no surprise to him that he was thinking this. Always, once away from her, once out of the house, he found himself thinking so. And he knew these feelings were truer to his nature than those others. He loved her and he loved the spirits. He would not like to live with any other woman, in any other place.

"*We love each other*," he said aloud.

His voice carried full and strong above the trees, and although he could almost see those last words spreading apart and dropping down and finally fading into the thick underbrush, he was unconcerned that they did not come back to him.

He only thought it strange, up here in the trees, that he didn't have more to say on the subject. Mostly he thought of himself as a boy. His mama had dressed him in blue shoes and a blue suit; she had spun his curls and called them golden then. Mostly what he thought of was that.

Sixteen-year-old Susan March Confesses to the Innocent Murder of All the Devious Strangers Who Would Drag Her Down

O LOVE, DADDY,

the first day the first hour the first lovely moment I met him O that first afternoon in my mother's lonely home I said to myself O God Susan March you're going to lose your wits and your heart over this man for look at him he is beautiful isn't he the most beautiful gentle charming exciting man you ever saw and why of course Daddy he was and even as he sat in my mother's chair primly inspecting the room and judging its contents for value and taste and ourselves my mother and me for the way we fitted or did not fit in with it and wondering probably where you were Daddy or even if I had a father or what he would think if he were our father/husband/lover even then I was murmuring in my heart THIS is the man I would lay down for THIS is the man I would have for no Daddy I did not think I could bear to let him perish as those others had and I knew he was aware of my thoughts and was listening to my secret words as I said them over and over

O! O! O! O! O! Oh I said

Mr Reeves I know it's crazy and absurd and out of the question even but I declare myself I yearn I ache I love you Mr Reeves for god's sake don't let me keep sitting here too fragile in this instance even to remove my eyes from your face O tell me what I should do how I might give myself help me Mr Reeves because this has never happened to me with those others I shall show you in our lake for I am my father's virgin and have waited here for you but of course it probably happens to you all the time because you're so perfect women can't help themselves O say something Mr Reeves I said and

Lovely tea he said Daddy

though how did I hear for I was dancing all around the room even as I sat brittle and moist with sweat and apprehension in my mother's Queen Elizabeth chair without a hair out of place or a smudge any place and nothing to do with him Daddy until we could circumvent mother's stern presence across the room and advance towards each other over the Persian floor and take each other in our arms

O crumple me Mr Reeves I said almost a scream I wanted this so much O melt me within your

but wait Daddy what were they saying my mother and Mr Reeves that day that hour in our quiet house O what a wasting of time and cruel that time was

I would love to he said I would adore sailing on your daughter's boat out on this beautiful lake but no I've never sailed haven't the knack but yes I can see your daughter is/would be the ideal yachtslady you're all so tanned and beautiful here I can see you love to get out and get your share of

Oh we get our share of pleasures Mr Reeves my poor mother said and already I saw myself out on the lake with him Daddy with you Daddy and hungry for the breeze to quit the lake to lie calm that we might drift under the sun and our eyes closed his arms around me Daddy his lips on my lips his fingers in my hair his

and we would not come back oh would not come back at all until the sun dropped down and mother stood on the shore in the darkness screaming her fear of waves   wind   the night that hid all danger in that greedy spread of water and knowing all the while that the nice Mr Reeves would love me and leave me and break my heart so that I might never again look into the eyes of any man and every man thereafter would look on me with soulful pathetic eyes

O sad Daddy sad sad

and pity that I had given up my heart to someone not worthy of my heart and now no heart left Daddy for anyone

Mr Reeves my mother said would you like tea? cream with your tea

and sugar here's the sugar if sugar is to your taste she said and he said
No thank you don't use the stuff bad for the complexion or so I hear
and nervously laughed and I did too I touched my burning cheeks and
watched him spin the silver spoon inside mother's fine china cup and
balance the cup on his knees and oh I spun I spun myself watching him
sip and sip and pat his lips and nod his thanks and all the while curling
his lashes at me his looks secretive his gaze furtive oh furtively on mine
because that day Daddy that first hour the first moment I set eyes on
him I/we/he declared our love oh I was not missing even his heartbeat I
was attuned to his every breath and on him like a leech and waiting oh
waiting pining to be alone with him holding him yielding and giving
Daddy although there was not even the need for that because we were
together and joined from that first lovely second our eyes met our
paths linking and forging a thing massive and insoluble and bound for
all eternity and all created out of that first instant when I opened the
door   said   you must be Mr Reeves   here to see about the
Queen Charlotte house here to   oh please do come in mother
is   why yes we have both been expecting you
    and I seated him in the drawing room and scurried away to catch my
breath
    O! O! O! to catch my breath!
    My daughter is worried Mr Reeves my mother said to him the child
can't decide whether to return to school or to stay here with me by the
lake this year what do you think she should do Mr Reeves can you advise this troubled girl advise me I am afraid I am of such little use to her
in these affairs I've always held that people should make up their own
minds don't you think so too but of course life now is so unpredictable
and plans hard to keep the roof is always falling in and advice is the last
thing I care to give especially where my own flesh and blood are concerned and perhaps you think so as well my own life you see is so un-
tenable and masked I should say so deceptive and riddled with mistake
and misdirection and misuse and broken vows at every turn oh I admit
it Mr Reeves I am at the mercy of whatever forces at any moment stir
yes I think I could say that but as for Susan well my pretty Susan does
have her own secret life you know her own curious way of seeing things
come to that I suppose we all do wouldn't you say? So what do you

think Mr Reeves should my daughter return to school plot her path up through the indifferent world or has she got all the good out of that of course I realize that all these difficulties will end once she leaves me once she meets and marries the man she loves and has children you see a life of her own and all that that involves all my other daughters are quite well-placed in marriage and in the home they are away and settled you see and I know it's difficult for poor Susan who is the youngest child and our prize and was always my favourite and yes her father's too he pampered her gave in to her every whim oh they were very close inseparable which is why it was so cruel what he did Mr Reeves cruel and there was no excuse for it whatever he might say or you might think

and OH OH Daddy I could have gone through the floor could have hung my head in shame for my eyes were suddenly wet and you were beside me Daddy leading me down to shore explaining this explaining that and *going* Daddy *going* while I cried *You can't You can't* and held on to you Daddy held you tightly my arms around your legs crying *You can't You can't* and my mother running berserk at us and away from us through the trees tearing up the earth and finally flinging herself down and calling helplessly to me *Don't let him Susan Stop him Susan* while you walked steadily away

oh vicious Daddy vicious you were

So how do you see it Mr Reeves my mother said don't you think our Susan will have a nice and normal life whatever advice we may or may not choose to give her now can't she expect the same as any other girl with her advantages might expect a home a family a man to look after who will look after her

Oh Mr Reeves I saw it saw his heart leap his eyes shroud over saw gloom walk over him at mention of any man other than himself in my life his tea cup clattering down his shoulders drooping at the thought of my body bearing children not his own at the vision of the cold hands of these men bewitching me

I wanted to stroke his face to bring his face up close to mine and calm him saying Oh don't listen to her Mr Reeves ignore her Mr Reeves only listen to me

I have no one

have had no one

want no one

want only you Mr Reeves and will offer you my proof the minute we are alone I will be yours Mr Reeves and you will never again be made to feel these hot splashes of jealousy this false treachery this pitiful acrimony my mother would inflict on us she is only worried Mr Reeves vengeful and remembering because the truth is she knows how we feel can remember what it was like to know desire and love like ours she's nervous and frightened Mr Reeves and certain that you will murder my soul and mangle my heart and take my pride and whatever beauty I might have whatever innocence and hope and trample me humiliate me leave me at last alone and miserable and waiting out my life as she is waiting hers

but oh Mr Reeves Daddy may I describe him now?

His eyes lovely his shoulders lovely his face smooth oh smooth Daddy as a tailor's dummy his nose straight as a postman's and his hands I loved the way he kept lifting his hands and letting them fall with nothing said the palms turning and settling soundlessly down his long fingers fluttering through air and then descending like something that had forgotten why and all the time fidgeting uncomfortably in his chair so anxious that the moment of this meeting would pass and moment would be all there was and this all so unnecessary I thought for how could a thing so grand as how we felt ever perish so soon but

ah, ah Daddy

his tweedy suit his fine shirt his hand-loomed narrow tie worn how many years now past its rightful hour like the wing-collars of my ancestors in their oval frames his trousers with their wide cuffs and pleats his baggy knees and shiny shoes I wanted to get him out of those clothes knew he had only dressed up for us wanting to be proper and distinguished when he called around for the keys to our summer Queen Charlotte place and I wondered if he knew I had had to do the same my mother instructing me to change out of my levis and the sleeveless yellow blouse

because we don't want Mr Reeves to think we don't care   must make ourselves presentable mustn't we   can't have Mr Reeves thinking the worst of us can we   we should all be ladies shouldn't we   so change my darling make yourself beautiful for Mr Reeves my mother had said and she had proved right again I was glad I had made myself beautiful for him I couldn't wait for him to put down his tea for mother to go away the two of us to rush upstairs into my room and throw off our clothes and close the door oh

close the door Daddy and

O! O! O! the clock would spin and at last we would bound back down the stairs leap into my boat glide and sail

sail on past darkness

darkness towards dawn and it would be too late for him to leave on his long drive home and my mother would say Oh stay the night Mr Reeves

more than enough room

glad to have you and he would come to my room once silence settled over the house and enter my bed slide warm beside me on the sheets and enter me and joined oh like that joined Daddy we would meet the dawn and of course at breakfast mother would give him withering looks accuse him of taking advantage of her hospitality of my innocence and youth and Mr Reeves would leave steal away and I would never see him again poor Susan would pine away become embittered and HURT Daddy HURT with nothing now ever to take the place of that stolen love

of your betrayal Mr Reeves

and nothing ever again to keep my breathing firm my cheeks flushed my eyes without the look of painted death

and yet even with this knowledge I ached to give myself and this although I knew nothing of him except his name and what he wore how he looked at me how he wanted me and this despite the wife he had the poor woman waiting somewhere for him to return with our keys to the Queen Charlotte place so that she might go there with him

which hurt Daddy it did

for I should be there with him I love that place it's a thousand miles from here and in a place so beautiful I ever have it inside of me and all just the way I had him inside me that first day that first hour as we sat in our swoop-backed chairs in my mother's spotless sitting room my mother politely describing the tea

It's jasmine Mr Reeves

Lovely lovely he said it's lovely tea

So sorry your wife couldn't come Mr Reeves my daughter and I were so looking forward to meeting both of you

Ah yes well

he said and oh how my eyes bored into him I would wrench her from his skin and slice her with razor blades slice her for all those parts of him I couldn't have and slice her my mother too so much I wanted to be alone with him

So hot in here my mother said so mercilessly hot whyever are we sitting in here when outside there's the lake the breeze oh but you'll find the island weather perfect this time of the year

You don't like jasmine Mr Reeves

and closed her bodice demurely desperate hands quietly raking the air above the pot of tea which we were all too nervous for perhaps she said you'd like to go for a swim while you're here   in the lake   or in   I'm sure my daughter could   we could find   a suit for you the lake you see well the lake well yes better perhaps the pool and O Daddy I thought it had all been given away that he was lost to me would turn and run but no she was saying the pool you see because the lake water is so   cold   so deep and cold Mr Reeves and O Oh Daddy he was satisfied he suspected nothing at all he was even amused for mother was saying it seemed to her it seems to me she said that death is afloat out there accident and suicide and well I never go in myself although of course Susan goes in all the time lake or pool it makes no difference to her she says she likes the lake all lurking snares and slimy silken skin over submerged logs booby traps and

O Daddy she was laughing she was teasing me

but

in the next second her mood changed she fell silent she sat with closed eyes her body rigid her lap napkin twisted taut between her hands while Mr Reeves contemplated the air above his cup and cleared his throat a dozen times and squirming until at last my mother stood   said

if you will excuse me Mr Reeves

and he and I were instantly on our feet

headache she sighed so tired oh always something

and then going oh going she was actually going and Oh God I was suddenly alone with Mr Reeves alone and trembling with Mr Reeves

So you're Susan he said and Daddy I laughed I truly did for of course I was Susan and I took his hand I said this way please and led him through the dining room set for twelve and out through the archway into the sunroom so dazzling green with its potted monstrous plants hulking against the glass walls like evil persons placed there to breed and out we came onto the green tiles of the enclosed pool and looked the two of us at the placid queer chlorine-scented water and at the translucent green-fluted walls and he murmured O Love Daddy yes he did

pretty pretty Susan

he said my Susan Oh Susan he said and I thought how perfectly he stands how tall and iron-trapped and what a hush there was too with mother gone he took my breath away into his eyes into his very hands as he stripped off my clothes and stepped out of his own and ran naked diving head-first into the pool and I followed fast and swam abreast of him midway the pool and in the water beneath the diving board our arms closed around each other closed Daddy and I knew I could not would never get enough oh god of him

And afterwards he scooped the water up in his hands and said this is your water the water in which you swim I love this water because it held you before I came and because it will hold you after I have gone and thus I drink this water Lady Susan and he did

but you'll be sick I said and he said

oh no I'll drink some more he said and I said why then I will drink you and did and afterwards we made love on the sobbing diving board mindless of whether my mother might return for I was determined to love him until there was no love left in me once he walked away

Thus we entered the afternoon had lunch and walked downhill with my mother between tall evergreens to shore and stood by the water's slushing edge looking out across the glistening surface to where perhaps a dozen boats sailed in vivid solitude and the sky that day was absolutely clear and

I heard him say to her

Such a pity that you and your daughter must ever leave this lake this house these trees how can your Queen Charlotte house compare and

My mother sighed and sighed for what answer could she give could she say Mr Reeves I have buried my husband here and it is sordid with all the reminders his death bequeathed to me oh Mr Reeves how stupid and cruel men are and how stupid I was myself ever to put my trust in him never once imagining that the vows of a lifetime could be broken easily as I break this twig or that she was herself now flotsam or floating half-submerged coated by the green algae his memory gave

that stupid man

I thought oh stupid Daddy stupid all of you and stood myself in that instance forlorn and perishable and hating everyone my head bent low and now on my knees that the grass might fold up and cover me and I might lie forever only with myself in the cold cold ground all the fragments of the past stitching and binding me to that bed and that final grave whose surface was even and unmarked and less disrupted even than the waters of the lake under the hidden wind but

Deep he asked deep is it deep is the water deep this lake how deep is it in its deepest parts

and oh my Christ my mother and I stood like dull burdens cast to shore by some long-forgotten storm and unable in that moment to comprehend even the most simple question put to us and

My mother there holding herself oh holding herself within her own arms and trembling while I stood transplanted within her skin single bereaved and haunted image of what is left after flesh has emptied itself of soul has yielded to time and pain and abandoned love oh the stark winter trees that cloak the Queen Charlotte place how like them we are but

Deep Deep he asked is it deep and

at last I cleared her skin heard her reply

we have had drownings here the latest no more than one week ago a young woman my daughter's age it's said she swam out too far committed suicide committed but oh men Mr Reeves you know how extraordinary and despicable how ruthless and faithless men are Mr Reeves the lengths they will drive us to and

I shuddered thinking yes wanting to tell him of my father that my father was there now and abandoned too but we started to walk the beach instead the three of us my mother saying the real she was saying is only what we see through these lampshade torches we call eyes the tree falls Mr Reeves in the empty forest and makes no sound and those people out there on the lake in their boats when I turn my back to them they also are no longer there the real is only what stands here in front of me this these trees this landscaped earth the two of you here beside me and this hand I place in front of me all the rest is as nothing and no concern of ours if indeed we accept the notion that the falling tree makes no sound

and oh I wanted to take him in my arms and love him insisting that our lives could not be so arbitrary so much accident without design that the tree the sound the tree makes in its silent forest is what compels it to stand in the first place Daddy like you once stood and that when the tree falls the earth goes on shuddering for a million years that what we are seeing now in front of us is not nearly so real as what we saw yesterday or the day before or will see again past this ambush of years this trap of fateful circumstance that finds us here now Daddy looking to find you O look look I wanted to say O Love Daddy let us celebrate this life by pointing our eyes directly at the sun for in its flash and fire do we become transmogrified and replenished and ever in the end purified for no ghosts live outside that fiery centre we swim Mr Reeves in fields of unremitting heat and our lives extend only into its pull but

Ah Mr Reeves my mother was saying so you're interested in suicide and her voice was raised and pinned him Daddy to where he stood so much as if she had enclosed him within a vault or tomb

why yes he said in the vague conventional way I suppose I am

and of course I thought *liar liar* why does he lie and saw my mother smile place a light placating hand over his arm and guide him back along the beach and into the shadowed coil of trees

while for my part she said I am more interested in murder

in murder he said

and my mother told him yes Mr Reeves murder is so much more interesting than suicide for the simple reason that what others would do to us is ever so much more desperate than what we could do to ourselves although I see what you mean for instance only a month ago a woman I know went out alone in her boat a small runabout I forget was it a

Brampian a Rawson I can't be sure though she called it her Sundance
boat was that the name Susan
and I trembled whispering yes
nice name he said and
I slid my hand in his and walked a little behind that my mother would-
n't see and closed my eyes to hear her say
at night it was so dark oh very dark the boat rammed at high speed
into a floating deck that some of the young people here had con-
structed out of abandoned logs and twigs and
Look
she said
Look
and I turned with him to follow her floating hand for sight of that
speck far out over the lake's surface near the shore on the other side
where the boat
Can you see it
she asked him and said my daughter Mr Reeves goes there sometimes
to dive she takes off her bathing suit and the people whose houses share
this beach put binoculars to their eyes and watch her dive nor can I
blame them she's so beautiful wouldn't you say so Mr Reeves and
I hung my head thinking oh all the trees are falling tonight oh every
one of them but
he said why I think I see it is that it he said way over there but my
mother and I walked on because we knew he could not see it at all and
very likely it was no longer there not a scrap of it because the boat had
exploded into it and even the splinters now had washed ashore
even so he went on studying whatever speck his mind had fixed
there and seeing in his mind's eye as I saw it in mine the boat surging
powerfully over the black skin of water with a blind berserk woman at
its wheel and smashing into the platform and then in the darkness the
sudden meliorative burst of flames and noise and shattered fragments
rising in the smooth darkness looping into sky and falling in thinnest
silence with no more mark on the water's roof than the summer rain
and then the darkness expanding to hold it there Daddy the way my
mother and I held it when you said *I'm going going* and walked steadily
away from us

vicious Daddy vicious

just as my mother that moment was as she lunged past Mr Reeves crying Oh take her Mr Reeves take this foolish girl why not have your fun with her and struck off then to disappear into her own private ambush of trees and

Oh Mr Reeves I whispered hold me Mr Reeves I need you now and he did

our twin bodies struggled against ground and the earth yielded explosions shook my flesh my parts burst into the air shot high outside of me and cascaded weightlessly back down again inside of me without a sound my parts looping up and looping back and cascading weightlessly down as the red sun spun and hovered above us near enough to be lust itself my mother shrieking from her ambush of trees

Leeches Leeches

she shrieked you have only to look around this lake Mr Reeves it's awful awful and weeping I leaned my head past his and stared out over the water its face a shelter of warm eiderdown and far away up there the thin mist rising where the lake's mouth opened out to sea

where warm water met the cold

and all to obscure defeat and deny this pirate's cove with my body pressed against his body and my mother shrieking

Leeches Leeches

why can't we build houses to live with the lake the way our trees live with the sky the way I was meant to live with him and I knew what she meant I felt it myself the fierce clutch we have on love like the clutch these houses have the hooked claws these houses have upon the lake

and you Daddy gone

and so I rolled from beneath him I stood and let my dress fall and shook down my hair and stood erect as Eve hearing him say I don't want to go to the island now no never I would stay here with you always with you and I smiled and took his hand and we took the path down through the trees coming upon my mother there kneeling in an ancient garden plot holding in her hands a wanton delicate green new shoot and rolling its tender nub between her fingers quietly moaning

Diseased diseased

and now crawling on her knees to search the rampaging grass while

behind us he stalked out of impatience and need to have me forever
with him and whispering

Let's go out in your boat now

and so I took his hand and said I would and mother stood with her
dirty knees and dirty hands and smudged cheeks and rolling tufts of
grass between her palms and flinging the rubbed grass aside so that
now her hands smelled of grass and her sleeves which she wiped them
on and finally now reaching into her pocket and producing our key to
the Queen Charlotte place saying Mr Reeves we know you and your
wife will be happy there but

And then we got the boat my mother and I and him and rigged it up
for sail and went slow out onto the lake guiding for the centre which
yet was free and pointing out to him as we drifted by all the imprisoned
bodies chained to our submerged rotting logs our lake floor thick with
the rocking corpses of those who had entered our lives and now swaying beneath the surface and our green and slimy mould growing everywhere but over their eyes staring up from the deep and the water that
day perfectly clear Daddy and littered to its furthermost depths with all
the naked strangers we had known and you there in my ear to steer us
Daddy whispering

O Mr Reeves

O Mr Reeves

Ohhhhhhhhhhhhhhhhh. . . .

Adolpho's Disappeared and We Haven't a Clue Where to Find Him

We had not seen Adolpho for the whole of one month and were beginning to wonder if evil had not befallen him. It must have been about two weeks ago that Skoals, in response to a casual inquiry, remarked that Adolpho was just the sort of innocent, airy person to whom evil was ever liable to occur — "the plucky, dim-witted sort," he said, "who will step into a thug's net with his eyes wide open and not know he's been done wrong by until he wakes up at the bottom of a well."

Nettles objected to this unkind assessment of our friend's character and wanted to know whether Skoals had any cause for suspecting violence had been done him. "No more than you," Skoals told him, laughing in that mirthless way he has. "No more than any one of us." There seemed sinister intent in this odd comment and for a moment our group fell silent. Then Nettles could stand it no more and in a loud voice emphasized that, speaking only for himself, *he* knew nothing. "Our friend has simply dropped off the face of the earth," he lamented, appealing to me, "but he's a resourceful fellow, I don't suspect he's come to any harm, do you, Philby?"

I felt unaccountably exhausted and could not bring myself to contribute anything useful to the discussion. That is the way I have been of late: as if an incomprehensible maze has opened in front of me and I have stepped involuntarily into it.

"Oh, I expect the bloke will show up in time," amended Skoals. "I mean only to point out that criminal acts against those of our station are becoming more and more prevalent. You will recognize, I might add, that Adolpho's habit of going about with a full purse was quite well known." I suppose each of us gathered around the Statacona fire at that moment patted his breast pocket, for if Adolpho had the habit so did we.

Our servingman Mole at last arrived with fresh drinks, and Skoals felt obliged to ask him whether he could account for Adolpho's mysterious disappearance. In a splash of rude monosyllables, that oaf professed to a total ignorance of our affairs.

"Gawd," said Nettles after the man had gone, "from the way he acts you'd think he never heard of old Adolpho." A few more remarks were passed on that sullen, impenetrable creature as we tossed back our brandy. It was a slow night at the club, the place being deserted save for ourselves and a clique of newer members, all rogues, and so vulgar and disreputable that no proper gentleman will have fellowship with them. They had been gathering all evening round the fireplace some thirty feet from us, taking quite the best chairs and generally conducting themselves as if they had a direct line to the Queen's bedside.

Then Gerhardt, whom we knew only in a nodding way, decided to make himself familiar. He padded up and stood the longest time by our table, breathing hard and smoothing down his moustache like a diamond merchant. We were finally moved to inquire what the deuce was the matter with him. "I have news," he said gravely. Before we could tell him to peddle it elsewhere he rose on his heels and declared that Adolpho had been abducted. "Yep," he said, "ransom note came this afternoon. Thrown through the wife's window, I hear, tied to a stone."

Skoals's eyes sought mine but I looked away, feeling a surge of nausea. I scarcely saw Gerhardt. I could hear the lick of flames in the fireplace, the clink of glasses, a murmur of voices, but what I was most aware of was the moose head on the panelled oak wall above us. Old Adolpho had donated it to the club.

"How much?" demanded Skoals. "What figure have these reptiles asked for?"

Gerhardt shook his head in what we took to be abject misery, leaving us to our anxiety while he meditated on the ceiling. "Have to dig deep," he finally grumbled. "All of us. The culprits want a ridiculous sum. Poor Orpha will never be able to raise it."

Gufstaffson kicked out his stubby legs, stood and strode to the fire, there throwing himself in a slouch against the stone facing. Skoals was scrutinizing Gerhardt with an expression of dreamy consternation. Like him, I couldn't make head or tail of Gerhardt's story. I felt a deep fatigue at that moment — rancid and bitter vision of all the evil set loose upon the world.

"Yep," said Gerhardt, "that's the upshot of it. A dangerous business we have here."

Eventually I became aware of Nettles's hand resting on my knee. He peered at me over his wire spectacles, his flesh coloured like a skinned rabbit, his eyes actually moist. "What can we do?" he whispered. We were all in partial shock. I guess it rang in our ears, the coincidence of having just speculated on the possibility of harm coming to our friend.

Gerhardt lifted his arms in a gesture meant to emphasize his magnificence, his voice now booming: "I'm good for a thousand! What about you gents? I know your group was as tight as quails nesting. I know you won't let Adolpho down." He thrust his open palm at me. "How much can we count on from you, Philby?"

I noticed my shoe-laces were untied and reached down painfully to set the loop in them.

My heart was pounding. I've not been in the best of health lately. These days I take my physician's advice seriously: *You've got many good years ahead of you, Philby, if you'll just learn to relax and enjoy yourself. No necessity for you to lead a dog's life any more.*

"You know we can't do enough for old Adolpho," I heard Skoals remarking. One of the rotters across the room laughed, but when I looked up they were all hidden behind their papers. Nettles and Gufstaffson were whining that their funds were all tied up, any other time they'd happily add to the war chest. Nettles puffed on his cigar. I wanted to lift a foot and kick him.

"Times are unpredictable," he muttered. "Our group is not exactly sitting on the treasury, whatever the rumours." Gerhardt ignored these declarations, though his scorn was apparent. He was still tumbling his fingers under my nose, entreating a donation. I started to speak but my throat went dry and I shrugged my shoulders helplessly. Skoals jumped back in.

"Like to hear more about this ransom note," he stated gruffly. "Don't pay to give in too easily to such ruffians. How do we know they haven't already done in old Adolpho?"

Gerhardt's lips curled away from his teeth, his features became truly malevolent. I realize in that instant the he was something other than the noisy upstart we'd taken him to be. He was treacherous and unpredictable, a man to watch out for. Even as I was formulating these thoughts the transformation was continuing. His frog eyes sluiced shut, his lips compressed, his cheeks ballooned, his face turned cherry red. He went high on his toes, trying to keep whatever it was inside. Then his lips shot open and a monstrous laugh suddenly erupted. *"Haw-haw!"* he cried, spurting saliva . . . and *"Haw-haw!"* . . . and the laughter kept spewing. Tears streamed down his cheeks, he clutched his sides and bent over wheezing, yet those mad Haw-haws continued to rain down on us.

We thought the man had gone stark raving Jupiter.

He took to pointing at us and each time his nasty frog eyes opened anew, his guffaws burst forth in greater volume. *Haw-haw-haw* now and *Haw-haw-haw* and more of it, the contemptible dog. After a time we came to realize that the entire club was laughing with him. They were thumping their knees and collapsing in fits against the walls, a bunch of randy hyenas. "Can't do enough *haw-haw*," wheezed Gerhardt, "for old Adolpho *haw-haw* . . . times unpredictable *haw-haw* . . . not sitting on the treasury *haw-haw-haw!*" It was an embarrassing few minutes, I don't deny it. Gerhardt finally howled his last and dispatched himself over to where his cronies were collecting. Their laughter gradually subsided, though the atmosphere worsened. The club became a black, reeking miasma; suspicion and hostility seemed to engulf us all. We were aware of the spread of sinister whispers and could hear the isolated, anonymous catcall.

We ignored such boorishness as best we could. We realized that Gerhardt, by this action, had proclaimed himself leader of the opposing

Statacona faction, that his was precisely the kind of low-born, debased element against which we would have to contend as long as we persisted in our efforts to uphold and perpetuate the club's time-honoured standards. "We have given the Statacona our best years," fumed Skoals, "and this is how they repay us. It would have been a shambles long ago but for Philby and our crowd."

Shortly after Gerhardt's exhibition our group dispersed. Gufstaffson provoked a mild astonishment by declaring his intention to go that evening and solidify relations with his often estranged wife. Skoals and I thought it best to withhold comment on this reunion. Nettles was more than a little angry and hurt by the suddenness of this announcement. He fell into a gloom and went off soon afterward.

Left alone, Skoals and I brought our heads together in a brief conference. "What do you make of it?" he asked.

"Of those two?"

He shook his head irritably. "No, no," he whispered, jabbing a finger toward Gerhardt's crowd. "Adolpho. That gang of cutthroats over there."

My mind refused to move. For a moment I couldn't think what he was talking about.

"Have we reason to worry?" he asked. *He* was worried, I could see that.

"I don't know," I managed. "This is deep water we've got into."

He nodded, lapsing into momentary silence. I watched Mole clearing cigar stands at a nearby corner. The man's baggy breeches were soiled at the knees, his cuffs damp and rolled, as if he had been out digging in a field. "I don't see why Gerhardt pulled that trick," muttered Skoals. "He hardly knows Adolpho, surely his whereabouts are of no concern to that wretch."

"He thinks we've done it," I said, looking squarely at Skoals. "He thinks we've done old Adolpho in."

Skoals's face dropped. He looked haggard and appalled, an old, old man. It was a face, I thought, that might have been staring at me from a grave. Then his eyes lit up, he found a bright refuge in wit. "I didn't," he murmured. "Did you?"

My own smile felt pasted on my face. I was too tired for Skoals' lame humour. Nor did I receive his remarks so innocently as perhaps he in-tended them.

A minute or two later we shook hands and he took off.

I pulled my chair nearer to the fire and put my feet up and con-tented myself watching the flames. The three neighbouring chairs forming our cove remained vacant, even those members of long-established amity avoiding me, aware no doubt of my disdain for the pious oaths they would feel called upon to utter. I couldn't have toler-ated any decrepit wag coming along to tell me that I and my friends had been wronged, that rogues like Gerhardt should have their hands fitted with thumbscrews, that this nasty business would soon blow over. Blast them all, I thought, blast the whole kit and caboodle to hell, I thought, and sought to relax, sliding deep into the cushions, closing my eyes which recently seemed to be running to water more and more. . . . I found myself humming a soft, jagged little tune I hadn't thought of since my childhood. The tune had to do with two young, foolish lovers who become separated while on a long journey. Evil times befall them, the years pass. The heartsick maiden is deceived into marrying a dreaded woodsman, ancient and embittered. Marry him, a witch tells her, and you will be reunited with your lover. It doesn't hap-pen that way and our maiden grows old, weeping. Then one day the woodsman goes hunting and his arrow brings down a deer. The dis-traught woman sobs at the sight of the animal slung so irreverently over the old man's shoulder. Dress it, he tells her, that we may have food for the winter. Unknown to him, she buries the beast in soft earth. That night her lover comes to her bed, reborn, he tells her, because his love is the warm heart of the deer. They murder the dreaded woodsman and in the morning it is his body which is laid in soft earth. Yet the next night, in the arms of her lover, the woman is ravaged by shame and guilt. She sees herself flying through the sky on a stick. She sees a heart-sick maiden weeping by a pool and tells her of a dreaded woodsman liv-ing nearby and that if she will but marry this embittered old man she will one day be reunited with her lover.

This ballad tormented me, the words kept tumbling over in my head. However had I come to remember such ridiculous tripe? Its childish melody served as a further insult, mocking me for my vain susceptibility, taunting me for my barren life. The tune was insistent: it bounced merrily through my mind, at the same time hovering outside my skull as if God Himself were its punitive composer. Innocence seemed to have no place in the story, it was not germane to God's little hoax. The maiden, the lover, the woodsman: they were all guilty. Murder is done with the same ease and aplomb as one gathers flowers and the right or wrong of it is not an issue. It was very well, I thought, to have said to Skoals that this was deep water we had got into but, I reasoned, it would get deeper yet. We stood to the side, executed this or that careful motion; in the meanwhile God steered us willy-nilly into His maze of traps. Gerhardt, for instance . . . had he actually possessed a motive for his depraved joke, or was he merely giving impromptu expression to the current divisiveness in a club which for a full century had pledged itself to the all for one, one for all concept of charity and brotherhood? Was the rogue in league with the devil, I wondered, or did he know something? The fireplace flames licked gently, shadow-patterns on the lids of my closed eyes, ghost figures dancing without threat. I relaxed under that suffusive warmth, lulled almost into slumber, submitting almost with pleasure to my drowsy contemplation of the nature of evil. It seemed to me that Adolpho's fate was of no consequence, that whatever mercy or violence had come his way evil would continue to stalk us and always with the same abandon and whimsy and steadfast loyalty to absurdity that it had stalked him. Evil wanted only to make us look and feel ludicrous, then it could rest. And we were privileged to have it that way, I reflected. For only in tripe of my song's kind could man be transformed into a beast and back again. We were stuck with the life that had been ordained for us. We perceived our agony and were allowed our brief sojourn, however futile. It was given to us to divine God's scheme and add our laughter to His. This itself was evil, but evil of a sort that alleviated much pain. God no doubt approved of our laughing at Him. It let Him know what we knew: that while He amused himself with our lives, and duck-walked us through our maze, other, stronger forces were toying with and ridiculing Him. Stars, rigid after their long waltz, mocked His small power.

I suddenly sensed I wasn't alone. I opened my eyes and found Leland, the club rake, standing in front of my chair, cheerfully smiling, his eyes riveted on me. "Why the black mood?" he inquired. "A fellow would think you had lost your best friend." His polite demeanour, his gay humour, the emptiness with which these remarks were uttered, caused me to sink even more into despondency. I felt my ire unaccountably rising and although I would have liked his company I told him to go away. "Happy to oblige," he laughed. "Mustn't cross swords with our oldest member. When you kick off I'm going to see that we name a footstool after you." He saluted Adolpho's wall moose, turned his grin on me, then wheeled about and strolled away. I watched his retreating backside, feeling envy for this man who took nothing, not even death, seriously. Adolpho too, it seemed to me, had been like that. Flimsy, arrogant creature floating above life, having his fun with us.

I yearned for the rascal all the same. I drank my brandy down and looked off toward the door, half-expecting to see him there waving his chubby hand in greeting. What I saw was a trio of members in fancy duds whispering importantly and I grasped that they were speaking of Adolpho, of the void his departure left in our ranks. From the hang of their long faces I perceived more: they too were pointing the finger of suspicion . . . *Adolpho is missing, old man. You must tell us where he is!* Evil, I thought, how evil these men are! What prompted them to go about with their scurrilous whispers, their accusations, their foul murmurings behind every chair? They advanced toward me. I closed my eyes, waiting for the hand to descend on my shoulder, for their vile words to fall. Yet no hand touched me and a moment later it seemed to me I had dreamed them there. The logs hissed in the fire, the flames scratched at my lids. I was alone.

It is not in my nature to want to understand what isn't meant to be understood. It was too much idleness doing this to me. It was not having old Adolpho any longer to regale me with his cockamamie fancies, his airy boasts, his buoyant jibes, his concoctions, his endless tales about the enchanted and enchanting Orpha. I missed his capacity for enthusiasm, his facility for finding beauty in the most fetid, puerile pond, pasture or field one ever came across when walking with him.

His moose head held me to my chair. Adolpho, on the occasion of its being hung, had told us how this stuffed head, with its bland and ignorant eyes, had all but brought his house crashing down. Orpha, it seems, had seen such a beast pictured in a book and had mooned over it until Adolpho determined that her happiness was dependent on her acquiring one. He had gone to a far country where the animal roams unfenced, like sad prehistoric cows that are too insipid to fear any person or thing, and he walked directly up to one of these animals, settled to his knees, and shot it in that portion of the chest which rises between its tall front legs. He had the head properly stuffed and mounted and brought it back in a crate to give to his Orpha. She had taken one look at it and fallen into a dead faint. "Her eyes rolled," he said, "her face went white, it was as if she had been made to stand toe to toe with all the wickedness man had ever invented." For days she was joyless, bereaved. He could see, he said, that Orpha took no pleasure from his gift and eventually concluded that perhaps what the dear woman had wanted was a live beast which could go about unhaltered in the deep woods surrounding their house, and thus provide company when his wife was lonely or made low by her womanly sorrows. So he was presenting the head to the Statacona, he said, making the best of a misguided affair. "It isn't a moose anyway," he confessed to me somewhat later, after its moose identity had lodged in my mind, "but a kissing cousin, the North American caribou." Despite its imbecility, he claimed, the animal had an aristocratic air, dignity of a plodding sort, and would be quite at home in our club chambers.

It is the moose then and remembering Orpha's part in the story that has served to draw me each evening to the same club chair. Under spell of the soothing fire I have only to lift my head and gaze into the gleaming orbs which are the beast's eyes and I am instantly transported, my spirits lift, the thought of evil deeds, the sundry imperfections to which we are heir, all dissolve, practical considerations of everyday life ebb away, and I find myself sharing the innocent, dignified, enchanted world of Orpha and her stolid, benign, antediluvian beast.

As is usual, I ruminated at some length over Adolpho's Orpha, endeavouring to construct in my mind a picture of this elusive, now no doubt besieged and frightened woman. I tried to imagine what she would be doing at this hour: her husband gone the whole of one month and herself abandoned in isolated countryside, probably without so much as a stick of firewood to keep her warm. I resolved soon to go see her, to let her know that she had a kindred shoulder to lean on. We owed it to Adolpho to do this much for her. I would kindle the fire, sit her down at the warm hearth, pour her the best soporific . . . hold the child's hand . . . discuss her future in sympathetic, practical terms. Because, despite my fancy which saw Adolpho materializing in the club doorway, my bones knew the man was not going to be returning, that Orpha had seen the last of him.

"Must go now, old man," he used to say.
"Must go tend my little nightingale!"

I dozed. I must have, and for some little while, before waking with sticky, wet eyes. A hot sweat lay on my brow. The moose appeared to be holding me in mournful judgement from its place on the wall. The space around me seemed stuffy and sour, the air so tainted with an unknown stench that my first baffled thoughts were of a decapitated, rotting thing that some wretch had placed next to me. Yet I beheld nothing in my vicinity to justify this extravagant sensation. More likely, I reasoned, a rogue of the first order had deposited his rubbers in my fire. Yet when I poked among the ashes I could discern no such pollutant and was in fact much distressed to discover that my fire had gone out. I trembled with cold. The empty brandy snifter had been removed from my hands. My cigar had tumbled from its stand. I found it smouldering on the Persian carpet under my chair. I made an effort to rise. My seat and backside adhered to the leather so that the chair lifted with my person in the second before it clattered down. My head drummed like a racetrack. My timepiece had run down, though I gauged midnight could not be far ahead. The club had emptied, not a solitary member could I see. A sheet of parchment had been left near my chair. Large Gothic script spelled out a single word. ADOLPHO, it said. My initial reaction was one of consternation. I thought: Adolpho has been here, he has left this himself. He has found me asleep and has wanted me to be informed of his safe return. . . .

An immense weariness, wind from a pharaoh's tomb, swept over me; I could not compel myself to think about the matter. A multitude of questions hung like curtains behind which I dared not peer. Why was the Statacona deserted? Had traps been set for me, to spring the moment I stepped beyond the Statacona door? Was Gerhardt lying in wait? Had he conceived stratagems whereby I alone was to be held responsible and punished for the evil that stalks our world?

Even Mole, that cur, was gone.

I could find no one.

This insolvency of character proved a temporary one. I retrieved my hat and stick from the cloakroom, made my way down the corridor and out the door. I set out for a walk in Great Statacona Green, from which our building a century or so earlier had drawn its name. I had need, I reasoned, of a long walk. Far from being too much alone, as had earlier seemed to be the case, I now realized I had of late been too little accustomed to being by myself. My friends had been making too many demands on my time. In recent months, there had always been Nettles and Gufstaffson, Skoals or Adolpho grabbing at my sleeves, waylaying me, inducing me to accompany them on this or that escapade. *A long walk, Philby, a bit of solitude,* I heard myself saying, *and you will be restored to full form. Nothing is so grave as it purports to be. Our fates are not carved in granite after all.*

The night was damp and milky, my feet churned along through cool fog — indeed, it was a fit night for a mariner. Statacona Green, that unkempt lay of land preserved by the Borough Council much in its natural state, stretches from perimeter to centremost point for a distance of close to one city mile. It was to this wilderness heart that I now directed myself. It was here on just such a walk, at just such an hour, in fog bathing us, that Adolpho and I had last been together. Here that he continued his account of Orpha's moose. "Apparently," he told me, "in that country the animal is viewed as legal prey only during certain periods of the calendar. In the space between hunting seasons the animal forgets, his docile, friendly nature emerges anew, and the creature will venture from his home in thick brush and come almost to a solitary farmer's door. You will even see them drawn to outlying city hovels, standing forlorn in this or that open field, lured by the hope of easy food, I should suppose. I saw mine not thirty yards from my hotel. He gave me no difficulty. I had only to load my weapon, advance a few paces, and shoot him."

I came now to Black Pond in the Green's centre, a pool, it was said, whose depths had never been calculated, and seated myself on the very path of ground where he and I that night had sat. "Naturally," he told me, "for Orpha's benefit I had to embroider the tale. She would have you believe I trekked a thousand miles over snow and mountain trail and that the beast was menacing me." His voice as he confided this had a melancholy tone quite out of keeping with my knowledge of him.

"How much," I asked him, "has this expedition set you back?"

"My life," he groaned. "My life. My beautiful Orpha remains unhappy, you see."

The moon that night was as yellow as a round of cheese. It lit up the black water to the extent that I found myself thinking of it as a giant evil eye watching us in cold detachment, although I saw too that this same moon transformed the pool's slime into a pretty field of glass. We sat side by side on the damp, reeking earth there at the water's edge, our images reflected in the glassy surface where our sticks jabbed. It is so dormant, this pond. Ageless. One is tempted into believing there is something almost sacred about a place that can preserve itself unaltered past all the years of one's mortal life.

"She's unhappy, did I say? More to the point, she's in another world. My poor nightingale." He spoke in a hush, recognizing, I suppose, as much some interior truth about himself as about his lovely Orpha. "Given all this," he next asked me, "in your opinion what should I do? How may I recapture the child's love?"

I had no advice for him.

Once, one cold day when I was a child, my father had brought me to this black water. I dragged a dead limb from the brush — fully forty feet in length it seems to me now — and plunged the long pole in. I pushed it down and down, the pond consumed my stick as if it had been no longer than a witch's broom, and I never touched bottom. It was my moment of truth, a revelation I would carry with me. Horrible, yet fascinating — these depths that are measureless, incalculable. The thrill and the horror I felt at that moment I shall never forget.

It is such a deep pond then. Nor is it a pretty pond. For very good reason casual strollers prefer to avoid the place. Wilderness grows up to Black Pond's shore for three-quarters of its turn, rendering it largely inaccessible. There is that. Moreover, it is a brackish water, half-covered with green slime, and its odour is putrid. Gnats in warm weather hover perpetually over its surface while in the black water itself nothing lives. Now and then a lazy turtle may decide the place is satisfactory. Later you will find his empty casing at anchor under the slime. I often come here. I dislike the place. It offends me enormously. I come here because my father brought me here when I was a child. It was stagnant and repulsive even then.

Adolpho that evening found cause to make one observation about me which I emphatically denied: "Rot and beauty," he told me, "in your mind walk hand in hand. The older you get the truer this is for you. Yet you have a romantic disposition, Philby: it gives you pleasure to regard them as a loving pair." I do deny it. Decay does not interest me. I find no fascination in it. I loathe it, my spirit recoils. I abominate what is happening to my body.

A man should not utter such accusations to one he counts as his friend. I would never have spoken in this fashion to him.

No one has seen the poor devil since.

* * *

A few days later I ran into Nettles on the street. He reported that he'd been in the grip of an unholy influenza and had been keeping indoors. His pallor seemed normal, though I refrained from comment. I cannot say he was as kind to me. He said that I looked distinctly unfit and wondered aloud whether my doctor hadn't diagnosed some new ailment or whether I had been treating myself to a proper night's sleep. Naturally I made light of these remarks.

"Have you any news?" he asked in a low voice, dragging me away from the lamp-post into shadow.

"None," I said.

"Then all is serene?"

I replied that our affairs had that appearance.

The next day Gufstaffson's houseboy came around with a message informing me that he and his spouse had repaired their nuptial differences and would in the near future be receiving once more. But the letter's contents and his sending of it in the first place I found curiously offensive, and hoped he had spared Nettles this ignominy. Like Nettles, the boy was moved to comment on my visage. Was there anything I required? he asked. Could he run and fetch a doctor to my house?

I sent the imp packing fast.

I took my medicines and nibbled at the light supper my help had left me. I wasn't up to dining at the club.

Skoals, someone told me, was deep into his maps and avoiding everyone.

I had my own affairs to attend to.

The time passed. Finally reassembled, our group exchanged surprised remarks on the oddity of an entire fortnight having elapsed in which not a single member of our circle had visited the club.

Adolpho, it turned out, was still missing.

"Nothing," said Gufstaffson. "Not a word. No one has seen or heard from the fellow."

"Ditto here," confirmed Nettles. "It's as if the old boy has dropped off the pier."

Mole was compelled to come stoke up our fire. He was unwashed, his pig-eyes lit as if by the rigours of an imbecilic brain — an oilish rodent of a man. It was impossible to regard this repulsive specimen without feeling a pang of contempt for the human race.

Nettles dropped his hand on my knee, laughing. "Calm down," he said, "you're in such a state these days." He yanked his handkerchief from his breast pocket and dabbed it at my wet brow. I kicked at him and the others laughed.

Mole poked clumsily at the fire. He spat at and cursed and jostled the logs glaring at me when I told him he'd never learn to lay a proper fire. Then Nettles had to chase after the brute to order more drink. The fire was too hot and I had to push back my chair.

I dozed. It was Skoal's voice which awoke me. "Heaven help me, you're a grim bunch," he was saying, "but you'll be more cast down yet when you hear the news I've got."

Gufstaffson asked what was meant by these words. Had evidence been found as to Adolpho's whereabouts after all?

"Not a bit of it," Skoals said, dropping into a confidential whisper.

"I've been going through the account book in which Mole records our expenditures. It appears a bolt of pages has been torn from the ledger." He lowered his voice still further, his expression wary. "Adolpho's entire account has been removed. We'd be hard put to prove that the man had ever been a member."

Nettles gave a cry of astonishment. He and Gufstaffson were most keen: what barbarian, they asked, would commit such mischief? What could be the explanation? Skoals motioned their heads near. "It's my notion," he declared, "that Adolpho himself, prior to his disappearance, removed the pages. I suspect the poor devil couldn't pay up!"

They thought this a scandalous suggestion. "The theory is incompatible with what we know of the man," offered Gufstaffson. "Adolpho had his faults, perhaps more than most, but he was hardly the criminal you portray."

Then one of them was shaking my shoulder. "Wake up, Philby. Tell us what you think."

I quietly dropped the news that Adolpho had been into me for a large sum, if this fact was of any significance.

Skoals smacked his hands together, jubilant.

"But Adolpho was well fixed!" cried Gufstaffson. "He could have bought us all many times over!"

"That's true," agreed Nettles. "The rogue spent money like a sultan."

Skoals murmured something to the effect that a great many rats lived in walls where one could never see them. "I should remind you," he added, "of what you must at times yourselves have sensed: that despite his fellowship with us, his way of life — not to mention that of his precious Orpha — remained an enigma."

They denied this with vigour — as did I, though no one listened — accusing Skoals of singing a different tune now that Adolpho was no longer among us. But on the question of money they were vehement. Only a few months back, they pointed out, Adolpho had been speaking of returning home, of erecting a great mansion for Orpha which would stand for centuries as a monument to her memory. This did not sound to them, they said, like the talk of a man courting ruin.

Skoals scoffed at this, muttering that we had more gold in our teeth than Adolpho could have raised in a year. "No," he went on testily, "our knowledge of Adolpho was confined strictly to what he himself elected to tell us, and I for one took what he said with a grain of salt. The man was a dreamer, a fool, as devious as a one-armed wheelbarrow. I could never make head or tail of his stories. And as for returning home, well, except for Philby who has always claimed this place *is* home, we have spent most of forty years talking of little else."

Our group went temporarily silent, directing black looks at one another.

Mole tried sneaking by but Nettles threw burning sticks at him until the rodent agreed to bring us another round of drinks before dinner.

Gufstaffson quickly splashed his down and turned surly, feeling that everyone was against him. "Next thing I know," he whined to Skoals, "you'll be saying that I'm a fool and a cad also, or that Nettles is. So what if we do occasionally express the wish that we could go home, or if I for instance wish that my mate for life had been a little more wisely chosen? Just because you and Philby have been bachelors all your lives doesn't excuse you for heaping derision on us and on poor Adolpho just because he was so fortunate in his choice. It seems to me that we ought to be able to expect a bit of loyalty from each other after forty years and that includes loyalty to our missing member. I don't hear Philby saying much about all this. I remember though that he was crying in his cups and running off to see his doctors when Adolpho was talking about pulling up stakes and taking Orpha back to her roots."

He fell silent but his amazing speech had got Nettles shaking. "I say amen to all that," put in Nettles. "Much has been going on here that I don't understand. There have been nothing but whispers and insults and innuendo since poor Adolpho disappeared." He paused, a glint came into his eye, and he turned his rudeness on me: "What happened that night?" he snapped. "The last we saw of Adolpho the two of you were going for a walk on the Green."

This brought Skoals angrily to his feet. "You're whipping a dead horse," he told this pair. "Unless you want to straight out accuse old Philby of a dastardly crime I'd suggest you hold your tongues."

Nettles instantly deflated. He took off his glasses and wiped them, mumbling that he hadn't meant to suggest anything.

"Well, you'd best clam up," Skoals warned him. "You know what these Statacona villains would make of talk of that kind." Gufstaffson hurried away and came running back a moment later with a glass of water which he seemed to think I needed. Skoals patted my arm. "Ignore the fool's prattle," he said. "You know how rabid he can be. Drink it down, old friend, that'll get your juices flowing." Nettles offered me his hand but I wouldn't take it.

He and Gufstaffson drifted off to engage in a private conference. Skoals and I forged the pretence of a smile as a member passed. "Eavesdropping," whispered Skoals. "Reminds me of the war." This remark touched me deeply. My eyes flooded. We had been through a lot together, old Skoals and I. He drew closer, our knees all but touching. It struck me that he had aged considerably in the last few days. "How are you?" he asked. "Feeling better?"

I nodded. My tongue felt as if it had swollen.

"I've still got that numbness in the limbs," he confessed. "My trouble got so bad I had to have a feather mattress made." His manner was just short of bereavement, as if he feared we both might shove off then and there. "No need to be touchy about it," he told me. "You get to our age you've got to expect a bit of suffering, a few aches and pains."

I gave an evasive nod, not being really very interested. A curious lethargy had come over me. I had not the strength to lift my hand. Concern for my health from Skoals and these others puzzled me no end. I felt queerly distracted, and I wondered vaguely whether there was not among my acquaintances a conspiracy to undermine my self-confidence.

"Why'd you never marry?" Skoals abruptly asked.

I shook my head dispassionately.

"Ever come close?"

I had no stomach for the topic but hinted at the casual nibble in the past. Skoals accepted this, his own memory nudged. "Must have been in about my fortieth year," he reflected, "that I fell in with a near-perfect little woman. Such a delight! Such a pretty laugh, like a string of sleigh bells. Part apparition she seemed." He laughed. "I never could believe the little filly was mine if I wanted her."

I reminded Skoals that I had known him for half a century and asked him why, if this story were true, I had never heard of this grand passion before.

"Afraid you would steal her!" he hooted. "That's why I never told you. Glad I didn't too, after seeing the way you got steamed up over Adolpho's Orpha!"

I remained silent.

"That's one thing I hated about that fella. The way he had of putting that woman on a pedestal. I got sick of hearing about her, you want to know the truth." He patted my knee. "Not you, though. Hung on to his every word. Even crossed my mind you'd gone and lost your heart to the woman."

I had no interest in Skoals's fishing. My attention was on the moose head. Some peculiarity in the light was causing the entire club-room to be reflected in the beast's smouldering eyes. The heavy curtains, the paintings on the dark walls, the fine leather chairs, the beautiful carpets, the golden span of ceiling — all found distorted replication. Members could be seen slowly moving, small and bent, like black twig-people enacting in silent pantomime a play of sinister description.

Nettles and Gufstaffson soon returned, gesticulating wildly, their rage spilling over. "The foul dogs!" exploded Gufstaffson. "The villains!" shouted Nettles. "There is no end to the deceit in this rathole!" Both were talking at once, a shriek of mad accusations.

"What is it?" demanded Skoals. "What puts you into this fever?"

Gufstaffson spun on him: "That vulture Gerhardt!" he roared. "He's been putting his liquor on our tabs."

"Not only Gerhardt," broke in Nettles. "Others are beginning to do the same!"

"That cur Mole says we shall have to pay, he will give us no satisfaction. I'd like to throttle the swine but there it is in the ledger, page after page: *Two whiskies Gerhardt, charge to Nettles. Four whiskies Gerhardt, charge to Skoals.*"

"Even his dinners!" chimed Nettles. "We owe a fortune!"

One exclamation fed another until the two were in a proper fit. Their solicitors, they said, would hear of this. They would, for their part, refuse to pay! They would resign from the club, see Gerhardt in chains!

There was no soothing them, our cautious replies only fuelling their rage. They would not listen to us and took themselves off again, intending to round up Gerhardt, to give him a good dressing down. "Evil," Skoals muttered when they were gone. "The man is evil. I fear he will not rest until he has the slime covering us all."

I lacked the stamina to pursue these issues. I was weary of Gerhardt's skulduggery, I found his very name tiresome. Skoals fell silent, hands folded over his large stomach. I could see he agreed with me. We did not have much longer allotted to us, we asked only to be left alone to enjoy the remainder of our days in peace and quiet. I know that is what I was thinking. All of this business was over nothing: so a man had disappeared, suppose he had been murdered or had done himself in, was that a reason for the ground under us to shake, for our friends to go yelping about like lunatics?

I fell into a sombre, half-mellow mood, remembering my father. An eccentric man, I suppose, though I prefer to think of this as an advantage. In Statacona Green one day he had pointed out to me the tree from which the highwaymen were hanged. The many ropes had stripped the bark and in half a dozen places these ropes had cut deep grooves into a favourite limb. The earth underfoot was trampled firm and the grass refused to grow. My father crouched on his heels, scratching at the earth as he told me this. Flesh rots, he told me. This is what a lad comes to in the end, be he evil or be he good.

I tremble to recall that hour.

When the renegade is cut down, my father told me, the soul comes shrieking from the body and flings itself downhill into Black Pond, because neither God nor the devil will have it. It is the tears of all these doomed souls that had made such a putrid hole of Black Pond. *Horrible! Horrible!*

* * *

We soon went in to dinner. I recall a plate of food set in front of me and that I could not eat it. I recall Gerhardt's entry. He was all fine-scented, done up in a velvet suit like a man who gives speeches at a circus. He raised a frequent glass, calling out this or that toast: *To*

Adolpho! I'd hear him sing. I recall the laughter that swept the room
when he said: "Old Adolpho is still missing, gentlemen, and we have
not a single clue to his whereabouts. Are we soon to see nets dragging our ponds? Shall we unloose our dogs and have them nose the
bushes in Great Statacona Green? What fortune awaits the fair and
fragile Lady Orpha, woman of mystery?" I recall the fascination with
which I studied the faces of my incensed friends: Nettles with his
bald head and pink skin, his overlong nose and the wrinkles which
made a birdcage of his mouth; Gufstaffson with his eyes like two
cave apertures, with his jowls and beard and his great mane of hair
hanging about his face like a red lampshade. Obscene! I thought.
Have these men been friends of mine? I recall Gerhardt's uplifted
glass and his merry voice intoning, *To wickedness, here's to wickedness,
my mates!* and it seemed to me my own laughter joined that of others
in the room. Skoals gripped my arm and I stared, bemused, at his expression of appalled wonder. Nettles and Gufstaffson were out of
their seats, their eyes boring into mine, outraged. I marvelled at this
venom, yet could not see how it related to me. Leland entered. He
floated by our table, a woman's arm hooked over his. I could hear
the rustle of her petticoats and smell her heavy perfume. Her presence struck me as most incredible, for women had never been known
to grace our halls. Yet it seemed to me entirely appropriate that
Leland had brought her, that she should be here hanging on his arm,
her face lit in a smile for everyone. "What, still no Adolpho?" I heard
him call to our table. "Well, I'll wager he's hanging out down by the
public bath, his eyes peeled for a wench! Where else would rakes like
us go when we're wanting sport!" He was his usual high spirits, no
one could take offence at Leland. He was our favourite, there was
not a man in the Statacona who had not wished to be more like
Leland. "Ta!" now he said to the room, smacking his lips in a kiss
above our heads. "Carry on, old beauties! Keep your willy flying!"

The woman laughed; then they were gone.

I could not eat my dinner. It was mutton and had gone cold. I could
not imagine how this dish had come to me. I hate mutton. Yet I raised
no complaint, I took no offence. I would eat it in good time or I would
not eat it and either way it would not signify. I dreamed. Wide awake,

staring at my plate, I dreamed. At any rate, I heard Skoals saying I did. I felt a pressure at my elbows and submitted to it. Tables clattered back, people stood. "Get a physician," someone cried, "Philby's finally gone and done it." My friends were at my side, supporting me, and I let them direct me where they wished. The commotion was considerable and I could not get them to understand that there was no cause for alarm. Everyone seemed in a big rush, flitting this way and that; I could not make them understand that they should remain very still. This seemed essential. I tried to warn them that if they continued in this manner they were inviting danger, their positions were in jeopardy. Their movements and voices I found irritating, distasteful, on the point of being obscene. Faces familiar to me through numerous years I saw suddenly as treacherous, decadent, vile masks designed solely to torment me in this hour.

"He's coming around," I heard Skoals say, "move back, give the man air."

A lap robe fell across my knees.

Figures stood by, murmuring. I stared into my old fire. I detected Leland's woman-friend seated opposite me. She smiled, radiant. Her dress was of scarlet and brighter than the flames.

"This Orpha," I heard her ask. "Is she young? Is she beautiful?"

Someone chuckled: "So old Adolpho would have us believe."

The Statacona lights did a jig. It seemed to me my feet left the floor.

Members were forming a close circle around the woman's chair, fussing over her. Again I felt an urgency to warn them. I thought it uncanny that they lacked the sense to know that they should remain absolutely still. "Don't worry about old Philby," someone said. "He's a horse, he'll make it." Another said, "He's been pushing himself too hard, worried about Adolpho, I would guess."

That they should speak at all I found to be the height of conceit. Whatever terrible thing was to happen to them they would deserve it. "Ah, well," someone said, "it's been a dog's life and I don't suppose he'll be sad to leave it."

They went on talking. Above their voices I could hear the woman's waltzing laughter. In a while I could see only patches of her fiery dress.

"Old Adolpho, what a wizard! One never knew when he was telling the truth or when he was making up a tale. To this day I'm not convinced his Orpha exists."

I felt faint, as if my heart was slowly enlarging.

"It will be different around here," someone remarked, "without old Philby to cheer us up."

Everyone laughed.

I could feel my head folding onto my chest and my every limb collapsing.

* * *

I peered in at Adolpho's black window. It was Adolpho's fault I had not got to know her. He never appeared in public with her, never brought her to any of our functions. "How unfortunate," I would say to him, "that Orpha couldn't come. Is her health unstable?"

"Oh, she isn't sickly," he'd reply. "Far from it. She's fragile to look at, I grant you, but don't be fooled. Five minutes with her and any man would be eating from her hands. I've seen it happen a thousand times."

I was quite at sea with talk like that.

* * *

The most we would ever see was the pale back of the woman seated beside him as the two retreated in the distance.

"Was that Orpha I glimpsed yesterday?" I'd ask.

"Yes, so sorry you missed her."

* * *

"Thin-skinned as a water reed, gentlemen, a smile to tear out your hearts. Graceful, my word. She could fill your teacup and you would never know she had come near. Oh, I'm happy to tell you about Orpha, I can never sing enough praises to my Orpha! Flesh soft as bird's feathers or bride's bottom, a complexion with a blush to sadden radish or rose, oh she's a marvel, is Orpha . . .

". . . About fourteen hands high, eight stone light, a warm breath

*of a girl! Hair yellow as lemon peel! Wonderful lovely dewdrop eyes
that have all the innocence of pearls, oh she's a dream, is Orpha!"*

* * *

Blackness hung like a mirror, extending the black window.

I did not want to pop in unannounced and risk alarming Orpha.

Creatures the size of turkeys flapped like black umbrellas from one
nearby tree to another.

The house groaned like a coffin.

Thick, smoking sky widened and darkened.

The door opened.

"Orpha?"

The stench was sudden and overwhelming, an ageless fetid rot spilling out from the unbreathing room. *Horrible, horrible!*

Yet it passed, or was lifted into abrupt inconsequence.

Her small frail hand eased into mine. Her shoulder swayed against
me. Musically, her voice rose out of the darkness:

"Is it Skoals?" she whispered, "or is it Philby?"

"Philby," I murmured.

"Ah," she sighed, "Adolpho told me it would be you."

Her grasp tightened. I lifted a hand to touch her but where her face
should have been I felt nothing.

"He has been waiting," she said. "Let us go in now and see him."

My dream cracked like a window, I cried NO! in horror and sought
to pull away but her strength was unyielding, she led me hurriedly
along, down and down, through levels stagnant and repellent beyond
belief, myself weeping now, sinking with her, shrieking that I was *innocent, innocent!* while all the evil of a thousand days licked at my
heels.

SWEETHEARTS

Hey Sweetheart, come on over. She calls me on the phone, that's what she says. Hey, Sweetheart, come on over. I say, It's late, baby, you come over here. So we argue about it. She says, But I was over there last week. I was over there last night. Wasn't I over there last night? We argue about that. I say, Was it last night? Are you sure it was last night? She says, Wait now, I could be wrong. I could be. What's your name anyhow? That's what she says: What's your name anyhow? And we argue about my name. We argue about her name. We argue about everything under the sun. She says, If you are going to argue I don't want to talk to you. I say, Talk to me. I've got to talk to someone. She says, Sweetheart, now you're talking. I'll be right over. I'll hop into a cab. Okay, I think, that settles it. She's coming. Don't get in a sweat. She'll be here pronto. Then I say, Will you spend all night? Will you? Can I count on that? And she says, Are you kidding? All night? Have you lost your senses? What about my kids? What about my tooth-brush? What about all the nights I did spend all night and nothing ever happened? What about that? I say, Hold on. Hold on, I say, I think you've got the wrong party. Let's check that number again. Do we know each other? She says, If that's how you feel I'm not coming. She says, If that's how you feel you can call somebody else. I say, what I say is, Who called who? What I say is, I don't recall ringing your num-ber. What I say is, Sweetheart, this isn't working out. She says, Whose

125

fault is that, if I may ask you? Who started this? You always want to argue. Why do you always want to argue? You'd better get straight with yourself before you want to start making time with a woman like me. Am I making time? I say, Is that what I'm doing? I say, How much time am I making if you come over and nothing happens? She says, Did I say that? Did I? So we argue about what happens and what does not happen. We argue at considerable length about that. We are shouting into the phone and she says, Why are you shouting? Stop shouting, get a grip on yourself. But things have gone too far, I can't get a grip on myself. I can't get straight with myself. She says, I know. I know, that has always been your trouble. I say, What trouble? I wasn't in any trouble until I met you. She says, You're right. I don't doubt that for a minute. She says, I'm always trouble, I've been trouble for every man I've ever known. What I say is, No, you haven't. I say, You're a life saver, that's what you are. Thank you, she says. Thank you. It is very nice of you to say that. Even if you don't mean it, it is nice of you to say so. I mean it, I say. You've saved my life a thousand times. She says, If only I could believe that. If only we could start over. I say, Every time I see you is a new start, every time, even if nothing happens. She says, Oh God, what can I do? What can I say? When I say nothing happens I don't mean it the way you think I mean it. My head's in a whirl, that's what she says. I say, Tell me about it. She says, I can't talk now. She says, I've got to see you, what I want to say can't be said on the phone. We're in deep water, she says. How did we get in such deep water? I say, Let's talk about it. Okay, she says, okay. I'll be right over and we can talk about it, although that's all we do, is talk about it. Do you really think we should? What I say is, Yes, yes, we owe it to each other. Fine, she says, I'm on my way. Shall I pack my toothbrush? Shall I stay the night? Can we have a nice friendly dinner somewhere? The truth is I haven't eaten, I haven't eaten in days and days. I say, Same here. I say, God, I'm starving, let's do that, let's eat somewhere. She says, Good, good, I can't wait to see you. I think to myself, God, what a shot, what a woman! I can't wait to see her, that's what I think. Wear a jacket, she says, it's cold, it's very cold out there. You too, I say. Dress warmly, don't let the cold get next to your bones. She says, You know what I want next to my bones, don't you, don't you, you've always known. I say, Hurry, let's not waste any time, why have we been wasting all this time? I'm on my way, she says, I'm flying out of the door. Me, too, I say, goodbye for now. Goodbye, she says, kiss-kiss, she says, into the phone. What a woman, I think, why are you always fighting with her? No fighting, I say, anymore. Get straight with yourself, Jack, go to a nice restaurant, hold her hands, look into her eyes, get lost inside her eyes. Get inside her coat with her, run your hands over her body, warm each other, let the flesh commingle, be bone against bone, the bones in harvest, go at it breath to breath, breath with breath, forget this ashes to ashes business, just forget it. Hold her, lock eyes, get inside that coat with her. And don't stop there. Why stop there? Call the children in. Say, Children, do we have news for you! Say, Children, gather around, assemble your bedrolls, for we have important announcements to make. The world does not belong to those whom you thought it belonged to. No, it doesn't. You see this coat? Come, get inside this coat with us, let's hug each other, warm each other. Look into our eyes. Did we say "lost"? We don't mean "lost," we mean "found," as in "Eureka! " as in "Boy oh boy! " as in "new continents," "larger horizons," "greater expectations," "warmer seasons," "fabled heights," etc., you get the idea. The world doesn't belong to those you thought it belonged to, and never did. Say that, I tell myself. Tell them that. Get your act in gear. So I go down and I wait for her cab, I wait for it. She's my sweetheart, I am hers. We are sweethearts to each other, we are lovers through thick and thin. She'll be here soon, any minute now, any second now. You believe me, don't you? Accept it, every word is true. There's her cab now, turning the corner, a nice yellow one. I can see the driver, I can see her in the back seat, black coat up around her ears. Come on now, hurry, hurry it up. I want to get inside that coat with you, I want to look into your eyes, to lock hearts, to say, Cabbie, turn this cab around. Cabbie, haven't you heard the news? We've got everything, we've got all we need. What you have here, in this neighbourhood, on this freezing night, are two people, two sweethearts, who utterly desire, comprehend, and complete each other. Snow? You call this snow? This isn't snow, this isn't a freeze. We're trim and fit and ready for anything.

THE PROBLEM SHOP

"AR-SALAR-SALOAM, of no fixed address and a blight on the soul of this town since you first came to birth, as witnesses against you have put in a No Show and as the Crown's Attorney has thrown up his hands in disgust and had not a shred of evidence in the first place, I have no choice but to declare you a free bird. I want it known, however, by you and by all present that if you ever again appear in my court I shall throw the book at you, guilty or otherwise. You are a reprehensible creature without, so far as I can tell, a single redeeming human trait. You are the bottom of the barrel and in my estimation would frankly be better off hung by the neck. Now get out of here!"

Ar-Salar-Saloam, the case against him so miraculously concluded, left the judge's chambers where these harsh words had been uttered, and walked out into a muggy Victoria day, to head back to his old stomping grounds in the up-and-coming but still derelict area forming the heart of the old city, the part the bloody English hadn't yet ruined with their tea shoppes and cutesy knack-knack tourist joints.

His child-bride Auriole met him on the steps.

"You old dog!" she exclaimed, smiling, cuffing him hard on the shoulder — "I thought you'd be dead by now!"

To her surprise Ar-Salar-Saloam did not cuff her back. Nor did he speak. He trudged on miserably up the street, looking at his shoes — in what she would call *one of his moods*.

"The reason I didn't visit you," Auriole said brightly, catching up, "is I been busy, real busy, it's been real hard on me out here, not knowing which way to turn."

Ar-Salar-Saloam stumbled on. The way his head hung, the way he slouched, his long arms dangling and his shoes flopping stiffly against the sidewalk, he looked like a man with deep problems — a fact which even occurred to Auriole.

She hung back, biting her nails, wishing he'd git with it. "Git with it, Dipstick!" she called.

But Ar-Salar-Saloam was already turning the corner.

She found him a few seconds later down on Douglas Street, leaning with his head against a store-front glass, his shoulders scrunched up around his ears and his hands shoved so straight and deep into his pockets that his pants were practically off his hips. She sidled up beside him, silent now, in a mood herself — and for a minute or two both stared at a window poster which had on it the picture of an airplane looking like some kind of bloated python snake, with its front part tied up in a fat knot. THANK GOD IT'S ONLY A MOTION PICTURE, the banner under it read.

Occasional Nudity, the B.C. Censor warned. *Too much swearing. Overall, a negative moral vision curiously copesetic. . . .*

"I seen not one movie," Auriole declared in a lively voice. "I seen not one movie the whole time you were in jail. That's how busy I been!"

Whether responding to this claim or to something revolting in his own nature, Ar-Salar-Saloam's reaction was most curious. With a groan loud enough to startle several passers-by, his body went rigid, he balled up his fists and screwed up his eyes and swayed high up on his toes; Auriole thought he was going to smash his head right through the plate-glass window. She bent her knees, getting set to take off: *"Do it!"* she urged in a fierce whisper. *"Do it! We be to hell and gone before anyone even know what happened!"*

But Ar-Salar-Saloam did nothing of the sort. He straightened up, sighing, shaking off whatever rigours had possessed him, fixing his sad eyes first on Auriole then on the grey street behind her.

They moved on.

To cheer him up Auriole began telling him of all the groovy people she'd met while he'd been locked up. "Great guys!" she said. "Real neat!" A lot of them, she said, would be down at The King's Tattoo this very minute — "probably happy to buy you a suds or two if you've got a real thirst on like I have."

But Ar-Salar-Saloam was off in dreamland or black hole, not even listening to her.

They arrived at Government Street where the Empress Hotel and the Parliament Building hove suddenly into view, like an old and noble but enfeebled couple come together for one last look at the world before going off to gas themselves for what it and they had come to.

They passed on, Auriole chattering, Ar-Salar-Saloam in gloom, looking at her and at the city with a mood of puzzled yet serenely elegiac scorn, moving in a stiff-legged gait, his shoulders bent — much as if he had spent the past six months sitting on his knees in a dark corner.

"Is it that old lady bugging you?" asked Auriole. "Is it you thinking it was your fault that old lady croaked?"

Ar-Salar-Saloam's head slid lower. "I never laid a hand on her," he grumbled, his eyes hooded.

Auriole was rapidly losing her own good edge. She wished he would shape up. She had her own troubles, heaps worse than his, and if this is what marriage was — walking around town to no purpose and with your tongue hanging out — she'd best call it quits right now. Without her hit earlier in the day to boost her along she'd have given him a good dressing-down the minute she saw him. She hadn't shed family and school — hadn't come to the ripe age of sixteen — to put up now with anyone messing round with her good times.

But she was afraid he'd hit her if she said any of this, so she decided to keep her trap shut.

At Johnson Street Ar-Salar-Saloam turned, and they went on down to the water: past the string of junk and pawn shops, past the flophouse rooms, past the littered alleys and dusty doorways where on more agreeable days winos would have been clutching at their sleeves

— went on past even The King's Tattoo. Past Man Tung Yi's Foot Parlour, past the City Parkade and the Upper Room and Lum's Foam Factory. Went on past Sally Ann whose great blue three-storey building stood guard over this seedy part of Flower Town like a great blue angel not about to forget which side of the bread her butter came from. Went on down to the water.

"How's it feel to be back in civilization?" chirped Auriole.

Ar-Salar-Saloam gave no answer. Mouth open, his legs wide and bent, he was gawking at something way up in the sky.

The Johnson Street bridge was up, and under its black open tongues, just then passing through towards its anchorage in the Inner Harbour, slid a magnificent long white schooner — banners flying, slicing speedily through the black water, its three huge masts looming higher even than the grey city rim and cold mountain range beyond.

"It's *BEAUTIFUL!*" cried Ar-Salar-Saloam, suddenly beaming, dancing a little jig — "What I wouldn't give to have me one of them!"

"Be a good place to dope up," agreed Auriole, her manner solemn. With a short plump finger the colour of dry seaweed she was busy raking over a number of coins in her palm.

"Dollar forty," she announced — "Plenty enough for two drafts at the Tattoo. Let's go."

But Ar-Salar-Saloam stood with closed eyes, his head thrust back and rhythmically swaying, his expression momentarily blissful — as if from some place far removed from his present location music of divine and tranquil nature was somehow flowing through to him.

"My throat needs wetting," whined Auriole, tugging at an arm — "Are you coming or staying?"

Only after the bridge had cranked down and the line of waiting cars had bolted off to wherever it was their drivers were going — only after the beautiful ship had sailed on — did Auriole get him moving.

They had taken no more than a few dozen paces, however, when Ar-Salar-Saloam halted in his tracks. "What's that?" he demanded. "That up there. What is it?"

Auriole followed the line of his outstretched arm.

"That's the new disco," Auriole told him. She didn't tell him that she had been there the last seventeen nights and that it was the swinginist place inside of a thousand miles. What she told him was: "I hear it's real good."

"I don't care about no disco," replied Ar-Salar-Saloam sullenly. "What I mean is that sign in the window next to it."

"You mean the one with the red hand on a stick pointing around the corner?"

Ar-Salar-Saloam said yeah, that's the one he meant.

Stenciled along the length of the red hand were the words NO PROB-LEMS TOO BIG. SEE US FOR SATISFACTION.

"That's Fisheye's new place," Auriole informed him. "He's gone into business. Doing real good, I hear."

"Fisheye!" muttered Ar-Salar-Saloam. "Imagine that!"

Further on up the street, painted on another dusty upper window, was another sign, this one reading IN A RUT? SEE THE PROBLEM SHOP — and in smaller letters, B. Fisheye, prop.

"'Prop' means he owns it," Auriole explained.

"Oh God in heaven, you think I don't know that?"

"Your face was all screwed up, how could I tell? Stop picking on me."

Auriole pouted. She stared at Ar-Salar-Saloam, hating him, figuring she'd never in her whole life had such a hum-drum, no-account day as this one was turning out to be. He was proving just one big headache and she wished he'd never got out of jail. Then she could be down at The King's Tattoo, having herself a good time.

She wished she had herself a cigarette, or at least some chewing gum.

"I got me a real nicotine fit on," she now told Ar-Salar-Saloam. "You don't want to buy me a pack of Players, do you?"

"I done quit," Ar-Salar-Saloam said.

Auriole backed slowly away from him, filled with rage: her lips puckered, her eyes narrowed. She made up her mind: "I'm cutting out!" she cried. "You can do what you want from here on out! I'm fed up with you! I'm going where I'm appreciated, going to have me some fun!"

Thinking surely he would knock her teeth out, she spat and kicked at him, then sucked in her breath and broke away in a fast run.

A few seconds later she disappeared behind the nearby battered door of The King's Tattoo.

Oh little Auriole, thought Ar-Salar-Saloam, only an inch away from sinking down to weep in his solitude: *All you can think of is having your fun. Life don't mean no more to you than having your glass of beer and your weeds and a place to throw down your head. You are one of the world's lucky ones, and what I wouldn't give to be that way again. . . .*

Poor me, thought Ar-Salar-Saloam. Even so, he wiped his eyes and took a deep breath and locked his shoulders — and trudged on. Onward into gloom. Pedestrians walking two and three abreast parted for him, alert for sudden moves, sensing something menacing and alien in his hooded stare, his scowls, his periodic groans.

Oh, Auriole, he thought, *why me?*

Onward, ever onward into misery, into the odious future. Into remorse and the black pit, into melancholy and hopeless sorrow — hopeless because the further along he ventured the more convinced he became that his was a route allowing no turnarounds. *Problems,* he thought, *so many problems, which way do I turn?* He had no idea what his problem was, only that it was a thing so indeterminate and insuppressible, so vast and impenetrable, that when he was able to glimpse it at all what he was put in mind of was a giant and spidery creature that crawled up out of his ears to drop its black hairy legs over his eyes and spin out its sticky black glue over his body head to foot.

Worse yet, all this, he knew, was exactly what he deserved. It was what Ar-Salar-Saloam had been coming to all these years.

* * *

Four people were in the waiting room at Fisheye's Problem Shop, five if you counted the dingy-attired man dozing under the iron hat tree in the far corner, six if you counted the proprietor himself. Not nearly as many as Ar-Salar-Saloam had expected. Not for a Fisheye operation. Not with all the troubles loose in this world.

Ar-Salar-Saloam took his place in line.

The real business, he figured, must be going on in a back room. A man with Fisheye's reputation for the fast buck wouldn't be wasting his time on no two-cents operation.

But there was Fisheye at his desk, with a yellow pencil stuck through his mouth and another lodged over his ear, looking as cheerful as you please.

I am the Antichrist, Ar-Salar-Saloam heard someone saying.

The establishment had been fitted out to look something like a church holding-station, with pew-like seats off to the left for the anxious to sit on. Near where the man was sleeping, bolted to the floor, was a stained plywood money-drop box with the words GIVE TO THE NEEDY stamped on its sides. Someone had spray-painted LOVE IS POWER on the side wall. A printed sign off to the right said HOPE I$ BETTER THAN MONEY IN THE BANK. The straw mat by the entrance door said TAKE A LOAD OFF YOUR FEET.

Fly-by-night but not *too* fly-by-night, Ar-Salar-Saloam reasoned.

I am the Antichrist, he heard again. He peered forward and saw that the person speaking was a dumpy, truck-looking woman at the head of the line. Fisheye seemed to be having some trouble with her.

Behind Fisheye, tacked to the wall with masking tape, was a large poster of Mt. St. Helens emitting steam. Next to it was a cardboard print of some yellow flowers in a jug, all sweepy-swirly like the painter had taken his broom to it. It was hanging wrong, and Ar-Salar-Saloam resisted an urge to go and make it right.

A half-dozen carpet remnants of various sizes and colours and weaves had been tossed about the floor.

A fine white mist drifted down from the ceiling.

This gave Ar-Salar-Saloam an eerie feeling, and for the first time he wondered if he had come to the wrong place.

The woman up front continued to rage. "I am the Antichrist!" she shouted.

"You are a pile of you-know-what," Ar-Salar-Saloam heard Fisheye tell her. "Stand aside!"

"That is no way to talk to the Antichrist!" stormed the woman, beating her purse on Fisheye's shaky desk. Papers fluttered to the floor; as Fisheye bent to retrieve them the woman moved over and stood on them. "I am the Antichrist!" she said again. "Do something!" Her face was bloated, the skin purple, as if she had just stepped into a vat of crushed grapes.

Fisheye, too, was losing his temper. "This is a problem shop," he yelled, "what's your problem?" With a rolled newspaper he swatted at the woman's legs until he got his papers back. "Stand aside!" he commanded. "Move on!"

Others in front of Ar-Salar-Saloam were raising their voices as well, saying "Yeah!" and "Git the lead out!" and "We got problems too!" The woman fumed. She banged her purse against the desk and said she was the Antichrist and had her rights the same as anybody else. The dust sifting down from the ceiling seemed to thicken: Ar-Salar-Saloam could see it on the shoulders of the person in front of him, and on the floor in the Antichrist woman's shoeprints as she strode up and down.

Ar-Salar-Saloam trembled; suddenly he felt fearful of his own sanity, wondering whether this strange snowfall was not altogether imagined. It seemed to him that, far from decreasing his troubles, The Problem Shop was only adding to them. A noise behind him made him turn: a small ragged boy, no more than eight or nine, stood poised in the doorway, sobbing wildly. *"Mama Mama Mama,"* wept the boy, *"When will you come home?"*

Ar-Salar-Saloam's own eyes dampened; sobs caught in his throat; the fine white mist went momentarily static, glistening; his knees weakened. He felt himself lifted out of The Problem Shop, transported back to his own stinging childhood: he was the boy in the doorway weeping for his lost mother.

Yes, and his mama — worse luck — never *had* come home. She had sent a wire from Reno, saying *Las Vegas next, I'm fed up with working finger to bone, try your Daddy or the church.*

This ragged boy was lucky, he had a mother to look after him. One who could teach him — if not love — then obedience and respect. The Antichrist woman had given up arguing with Fisheye to storm at the miserable boy, to cuff him and shake him, to beat her lessons into his head. *"Get out of here!"* she shrieked. *"I told you never to leave your room! I told you never to bother me while I was doing my work! Am I not the Antichrist?"*

"Yes, Mama," sobbed the throttled boy, "you are the Antichrist."

She ripped at his ear, smacked him hard on the fanny, and slung him back hard against the door. The boy crumpled down, groaning.

"You are, Mama," he whimpered, "I know you are."

"There!" she shouted, turning on Ar-Salar-Saloam and everyone else in the room — "There, you heard my boy! Now you know I am as I say I am!" Her mottled face glistened with perspiration, her glare was furious and would admit no denials. "Tell them again!"she shrieked, spreading her thick legs wide, sweeping both arms high above her head in a victory pose. Cords rippled in her throat; her full bosom heaved.

The boy dragged himself up, to clutch at her: *"Oh, Mama,"* he moaned. *"Oh Mama, come home! Oh Mama, let us take care of you!"* His hands wrapped about her ankles; he slobbered at her feet. *"You are, Mama. You are the Antichrist."*

The woman relented. Her fierce gaze swept over all in the room, she gave the boy another slap or two, but she relented all the same. She was content at last to let the shivering boy hug her knees.

"So long as you understand," she told the silent group. "So long as you know whose problems come first around here!"

The fine white mist leaking from the ceiling appeared to lift and thin; Fisheye's desk chair let out a nasty squeak; over in the far corner the sleeping man was waking up, rubbing knuckles into his swollen eyes and wiping an open hand across the black stubble of his chin.

The Antichrist woman allowed the boy to lead her reluctantly out. Everyone breathed again.

* * *

Half-an-hour later Ar-Salar-Saloam was no nearer to having his problems solved. He did not know what to think, and was ready — as he admitted to the now near-empty room — to throw in the towel.

"I'm on my last lap," he told Fisheye, as it came his turn to stand before the proprietor's desk.

Fisheye was scraping a knife blade under his nails, and did not even consent to look up at him.

A few seconds before, with all clients gone except for Ar-Salar-Saloam, the once-sleeping man had got up and bolted the entrance door.

"My goose is cooked," Ar-Salar-Saloam tried again.

Fisheye gave no indication that he heard. He closed his knife and rolled back in his chair and opened a desk drawer. From inside he pulled out a small sign and when he had placed it on the desk Ar-Salar-Saloam saw that it read GONE FOR COFFEE.

To Ar-Salar-Saloam this seemed too much. He wanted to break down and cry, but instead he squared his shoulders and tried again.

"What's that mean?" he asked.

Finally Fisheye looked at him. His expression registered no opinion one way or another — either of his own actions or of Ar-Salar-Saloam's timid insistance on service. He seemed, with his blue empty eyes, to be looking at something totally to the other side of Ar-Salar-Saloam. He seemed totally disinterested.

"Gone for coffee," he now said — pausing, standing up, reaching for his hat — "It's plain English, can't you read?"

The black pit opened up in Ar-Salar-Saloam's stomach and from there quickly spread. His eyes swirled. One minute he was staring at Fisheye's bland countenance and the next second a full wall of black was where Fisheye had been.

Ar-Salar-Saloam's knees buckled; he sagged down.

The black wall came with him and in another second or two it enlarged to cover everything.

* * *

"You got problems, son," someone was saying.

It seemed to Ar-Salar-Saloam, grimacing as pain shot up through his head, that it was his own Daddy's voice speaking to him from the grave.

Oh no, Daddy, not me, not Ar-Salar-Saloam. Your little boy can take care of himself, he has not a care in the world.

This time it was his own voice saying this, yet he knew he had not spoken.

It occurred to him that at last his troubles were over, that he had passed over to the other side.

"Wake up, son," another voice said — "No deadbeats allowed, where you're going."

Ar-Salar-Saloam opened his eyes. The darkness swirled away and in its place there came a rippling tide, a white rippling mist . . . which then cleared and in the clearing, standing with his back to him as he squared-off the scrub-broom print of yellow flowers in a jug, was the once-sleeping man who had earlier bolted the door. Fisheye was gone. His papers had been put away, his desk top clear and shiny now except for one small notepad and two gnawed pencils neatly aligned side by side.

"A hired hand, son," the man explained. "Got to have their coffee breaks, their little privileges — union, you know."

Speechless, Ar-Salar-Saloam studied him. The man was older than he had previously appeared, and had a kindly look, although one faintly cavalier. An unlit fag drooped from his lips, and he stood with his hands in his coat pockets, in half-smile, but shaking his legs as if he had just wet himself.

"My own little problem," he sheepishly admitted. "All of us got to have something."

Ar-Salar-Saloam shook the cobwebs out of his head. The man was clearly a lunatic — maybe worse. Yet he swept aggressively forth, throwing out a hand which Ar-Salar-Saloam accepted in his own limp paw.

"That's right," the man smiled, "you're looking at the brains behind this outfit! You got problems, you come to the right place. Take a load off your feet. I can make no guarantees, but I think I can say that if your heart's in the right place you're as good as cured." He thumped his chest, chuckling, dropping down into the empty chair. "Old Fisheye," he said, "always got his sights on the clock. But I value him, don't get me wrong. He's good at weeding out the snowflakes. Knows his job."

Ar-Salar-Saloam cowered; his inclination was to hit and run.

"Speak up!" continued the man. "I find it pays to get right down to peanuts, no beating around the bush. I can't read minds, you know. What brings a bright-looking fellow like yourself to The Problem Shop?"

Ar-Salar-Saloam could not figure where to begin. It was as if all his problems had flown right out of his head.

"That Antichrist woman," said the man, "is she what's got your tongue? You thinking we can't deliver?" He cast his head down in a state of momentary melancholy, as if sensing that Ar-Salar-Saloam was accusing him of falling down on the job. "With some it takes time," he said, his voice low, caressing fur: "Not everybody can expect relief overnight, ours is not a Magic Shop, you know." He came up smiling, however, casting a mischievous glance over Ar-Salar-Saloam's intent head: "No, for that you have to look elsewhere."

Ar-Salar-Saloam mumbled "Oh yeah, I know what you mean," — although totally at a loss to understand either what the man was saying or what he himself felt.

A deep pool, he thought, *that's what I've fell into. I've got to get myself out of here.*

"All the same," the man now said, rising, shaking his head at the mystery of it all — "All the same, she's a case, that Antichrist woman. After a hard day like this one I'm half-willing to slit her throat." He fell silent, moping, mulling the issue over.

Too worried about the business, considered Ar-Salar-Saloam, *to give any little thought to me. Rue the day I come in here.*

"Still," the man said, reflecting, striding to a closet door behind the desk — "Still, she's got the boy. We've done that much at least for her."

Ar-Salar-Saloam wisely kept his silence. *Too much going on around here,* he thought. *Too much I don't understand. I'm out of my element in this zoo.*

"What's your name?" he managed. "Who are you?"

"Some folks call me Captain. The Captain, Cap, Old Salt — take your pick."

Ar-Salar-Saloam was watching the ceiling. The white powdery stuff was beginning to sift down again.

"My costume," the Captain said. "Clothes make the man." He had taken from the closet some kind of blue yachtsman's coat, and was pulling it on. It had a gold fringe on the sleeves and a big blue and gold crest on the pocket which said in rounded letters THE PROBLEM SHOP, and a logo that resembled a parking meter.

"How do I look?"

He looked pretty sharp. He looked what Auriole would call a *lulu,* with maybe a touch too many limp shoes thrown in.

But Ar-Salar-Saloam didn't tell him that. "You'll do," he said.

"You're like a lot of people, son," the Captain off-handedly observed:

"Too stingy with the praise." He coughed, yanking out a soiled hand-kerchief, blowing his nose. "Let's get out of here. This damned white stuff is killing me. Sinus, you know."

The stairway leading down from The Problem Shop was drab and dingy, unlit except for one naked light bulb flecked with paint. The walls were peeling. The boards creaked. At the bottom a garbage can had been overturned and soup cans and gnawed bones and small balls of cooked rice littered the floor. The moment they hit daylight the Captain came to an abrupt halt.

"Well, my boy," he said, "which way will it be? Right or left?"

Ar-Salar-Saloam was buffaloed. He had hoped that if anyone knew the way this peculiar creature would.

"Or are you the kind that goes whichever way you're pointed? Is that your problem, son?"

Ar-Salar-Saloam dropped his shoulders and shuffled his feet, giving the Captain the full force of his hooded stare. The Captain's mind moved too fast; it took too many devious turns. Ar-Salar-Saloam was beginning to think he was some kind of Show Off, a Dink.

"Spell it out, son. Let me hear in your own words what's troubling you."

Ar-Salar-Saloam had one of his rare brainstorms. He suddenly knew what his problem was, and decided to blurt it out:

"I don't have no future," he said.

The Captain's mouth fell open in surprise, then mild amusement set in, and the next second he was throwing back his head and guffawing. "Why, no one does!" he exclaimed. "Where did you get the idea that anyone did? My my," he said, now strolling along, chuckling to himself, "— this day and age, imagine that!"

Ar-Salar-Saloam scrambled to catch up with him. It seemed to him beyond reason that anyone professing to run a problem shop would fail to understand. He felt angry and betrayed.

"*Nothing!*" insisted Ar-Salar-Saloam with raised voice: "*I don't have nothing! I might as well be dead!*"

The Captain gave a sympathetic shrug: "In quicksand up to your shoulder blades, is that the way it is, my boy?"

Ar-Salar-Saloam was adamant; he wanted to throttle this grinning man. *"I am without hope! Don't you understand? I don't have nothing and I am plain without hope!"* His fists knotted up as he glared at this man. *"Are you too stupid to understand that? Can't you see I'm in pain?"*

The Captain nodded, unimpressed: "It's a tough life then, you'd say? You find the space a bit tight in your jam jar?" He seemed actually to be enjoying Ar-Salar-Saloam's wretchedness, a gap showing between his teeth as he smiled and once again strolled on.

Ar-Salar-Saloam wanted to put another gap in that man's face. He was outraged by this shoddy treatment, yet at the same time accustomed to it. He groaned. His heart was squeezing up like a small hurt thing, like a tiny bird being slowly crushed, and for a moment black spots floated in front of him as his head swam. He stomped his feet down, summoning up strength for one final appeal: *"I mean it!"* he screeched. *"I'm desperate! I'd rather change places with that Antichrist woman, that's how bad off I am!"*

The Captain did not so much as slow down: "Beyond redemption, would you say?"

Ar-Salar-Saloam felt rooted to the spot. He could feel all his juices deserting him. He was all flagged out; could think of nothing, feel nothing, except for a black recognition of the abiding unfairness of this world. Through dim eyes he watched the Captain stroll jauntily on ahead in his bright blue jacket and his yachtsman's hat, not even glancing back. He thought: *Go on, it's good riddance I say. Prance off all high and mighty, thinking only of yourself. Rue the day I ever met you, go to hell you and your problem shop, I could care less what you do. Yeah, go on, just another big cheese: what do you care, forget Ar-Salar-Saloam, his life is over, when did anyone ever care one whit about me. . . .*

Morbid, dropping down to sit on the curb, slouching over, head down between his legs, groaning to himself *That's it, that's it, I'm down in the gutter now, down here where I belong, where they've always wanted me, where I've been coming to all these years. My trouble was ever thinking I could drag myself up, ever thinking I had a chance. Well it's over now, it's over, I've shot my last wad. I can say it now, I can admit the worst: Ar-Salar-Saloam, you do not have a single redeeming human trait. You'd be better wiped off the face of this earth.*

It penetrated through to him after a time that someone was calling his name. Slowly his head came up, he wiped the wetness from his cheeks; slowly he came back to the life of the street, to the sight of cars whooshing by, of dusty junk windows and tatty curtains behind the glass of upstairs rooms, of smoke spilling up from chimneys and the odd pedestrian coming or going in a slow drift, coming or going as if to or from some far-off dream. Over at Sally Ann's blue building a stringy-haired girl and a fat boy no older than him had their suitcases out and their guitars and were playing some kind of low-down twangy song. Across the street directly in front of him an old man in a droopy coat that wiped the pavement was leaning on two rag-wrapped crutches silently watching him. Further along, outside Man Tung Yi's Foot Parlour, the Antichrist woman was up on a box rattling a tambourine and intoning *I am the Antichrist I am the Antichrist I am the Antichrist* while her boy stood by with pained face, tugging at her dress, saying *Mama come home, Mama come home, Oh Mama come home now.* The sky had turned an unwrinkled blue, shafts of sunlight slanting through drifting clouds like tall perfect skyscrapers belonging to some future day.

The Captain was down near the Johnson Street bridge, waving an arm.

"Come on, boy! Don't lolligag! Hurry up now!"

Ar-Salar-Saloam's black mood vanished; he spun off to catch up with him.

The Captain steered them down to the water. He wore a bemused, lazy expression, now lifting an arm to point out this, now to point out that, approving of one thing, disapproving of another, saying how the breakfast at Smitty's Pancake House was made of chopped-up rubber with a little ratmeat thrown in to sweeten the taste; how the new pedestrian walkway along the Inner Harbour was a step in the right direction, though the city had skimped on it a bit; how the Undersea Gardens was not a bad idea, far as it went, while the Wax Museum was a rip-off and, to his mind, frankly an aberration; how the double-decker busses were a joy to his eyes, while he didn't care a smidgen for the Tally Ho mule-wagon tour; how the black water here surely with a little foresight or old-fashioned ingenuity could have been cleaned up a bit; how, overall, looking at it without bias and with consideration for all the mean problems of this world, the old city hadn't done too badly with its growth; complaining, however, that the government was an abomination naturally — "What else can you expect?" — and how everything cost too much. Reminding Ar-Salar-Saloam how even in a relatively decent city such as this one a body still had to bitch and complain to get a thing done; how you had to watch out for yourself and not let the little stops in life up and knock you flat.

"Your troubles now," he said, "what do they amount to, you still got your youth, you got your health. Now hope, that's another matter, I admit it helps to have that. Certainly it is the A-Number-One problem I've come up against in my shop, it seems half the people I see have either got too much or not enough." He sighed, shaking his head, guiding Ar-Salar-Saloam on to wherever it was he had in mind going. "Making no bones about it, though, I'd say hopelessness is our speciality, I'd say we've built up a good record on that very issue." He smiled, throwing an arm over Ar-Salar-Saloam's bony shoulder, pushing the visored cap high on his head. "Live and learn," he murmured, "learn and live. So all right, you've got a self-image problem, nothing unique there. But tell me, if you've a mind to, what else has been troubling you. Spit it out, my boy, let the cat fur fly!"

Ar-Salar-Saloam, as if in a trance, gazed out over the Inner Harbour's black water. The big schooner which he had seen earlier in the day passing under the Johnson Street bridge, rocked not more than twenty paces from where he now stood, its three masts shooting up like endless telephone poles above the shining deck.

"There's Auriole," he softly said. "I worry about Auriole, I worried about her the whole time I was in jail. I worried about whether she was being faithful to me, but mostly I worried about her on general accounts."

"Oh, she'll get along," laughed the Captain. "No, a hot ticket like little Auriole, you don't have to be bothered about her. Make a good wife, a good worker, once she gets over loving her dope, over wanting her fun and good times." He paused, then added: "If not for you, then for someone else."

Ar-Salar-Saloam nodded, solemn. "There's that woman who dropped dead," he went on. "That weighs on my mind, what I did to her."

The Captain lightly patted his back. "I should hope so," he said. "A business like that could ruin any poor boy's life. Yet, look at it this way: the lady was old and sick, you couldn't have known. Even her doctor said she was at the edge, could go anytime. Her heart failed, as I recall. No, she was a nice old lady and we can grieve for her, but her illness I think mitigates your guilt." He hesitated, fixing a stern eye on Ar-Salar-Saloam. "Don't get me wrong. Her heart wouldn't have quit if you hadn't come along to snatch her purse. I'm not saying you got any cause to feel scot-free."

Ar-Salar-Saloam turned to the Captain with a sad smile. He wanted to say to this odd man that his life had been hell, that he and little Auriole and a thousand people like them — all that strungout gang down at The King's Tattoo, for instance — had never had a chance, that everything they had ever done and every which way they had ever turned had been wrong and not their choice at the start. But he remained silent, not certain that wasn't fudging the cake. He felt better now, did not have that sunk-down feeling any more. He felt — as maybe Auriole would put it — real strange. Real weird, like his head had zoomed off to some high place. Just walking with the Captain, having this little talk man-to-man, had done it, he guessed. It was like a father and son walk, like the old times he had dreamed about as a kid but never had known. It was wonderful, that's what it was — the Captain's warm hand on his shoulder, the day turned so scrubbed-down and fresh. So beautiful. He didn't even have that cramped feeling in the knees any longer; that iron feeling in the head.

It dawned on Ar-Salar-Saloam that in fact he felt pretty good. That he felt some hope stirring around inside.

There was activity now on the schooner. Someone in a white suit had come out and thrown a gangplank down. Others were scooting over the deck, unlashing the riggings, tying goods down, giving a last buff to gleaming brass rails.

"What's that?" Ar-Salar-Saloam asked, pointing at a small bucket way up high on the centre mast.

"That's the crow's-nest," replied the Captain — and as this did not appear to enlighten Ar-Salar-Saloam, he explained further:

"In the old days, say on your arctic or whaling vessel, the lookout man would sit up there and watch for fish. Or pirates. Or land. Whatever needed watching for."

Ar-Salar-Saloam's face brightened. He looked up at the small bucket in amazement. "Now that's a job I could have gone for," he said. "I could have whet my teeth on a job like that."

"Maybe it isn't too late," the Captain answered.

"What you mean?"

The Captain pulled back a sleeve and tapped on a wrist watch: "In about two minutes," he said, "I'm setting sail. You can sign on if you've a mind to."

"All ready, Captain!" someone shouted from the ship.

Ar-Salar-Saloam's heart gave a sudden lurch. Striding down the boarding plank, his long black gown whipping up about his ankles, his face frozen into an expression of permanent intolerance and hatred, was none other than the judge who that morning had lectured to Ar-Salar-Saloam so severely.

"Is he a part of this crew!" asked Ar-Salar-Saloam, fearfully.

"Don't bet on it," said the Captain. "No, he's a passenger, I'm afraid. That old toad has got a lot of shaping up to do before I'd trust him with my sails. He has had a thousand chances and ruined every one, while you . . . well you, my boy, you've had nothing, but at least you've wound up no worse than you were at the start. Shall we go aboard?"

* * *

Some minutes later the Johnson Street bridge went up for the second time that day, and the ancient schooner with its three tall masts passed through, rocking ever so slightly in the gentle water. From his crow's-nest on the highest mast, Ar-Salar-Saloam looked out over his old haunts, over the full width and length of the city, and already he knew he was going to like this job. Until now it had never crossed his mind that the geography of this or any other place could be remarkable, that this city possessed any noteworthy beauty. Now the water shimmered, all but blinding him, but with his eyes slit so narrowly and his hands up to shade them, he acknowledged that in this respect, as in so many others, he had made a profound mistake. Life was indeed beautiful. Land

and water were magic, a dancing pair. It was breathtaking, to tell the truth, and he sensed that from this day he would forever go on thinking so. The sea shimmered, snowcapped mountains all round touched the sky in blissful dignity, clouds hovered within easy reach; the very rooftops of the city seemed to throb and swell and extend to him a personal *bon voyage*. He could see up there on the street beyond The King's Tattoo the Antichrist woman marching at the head of a motley band of fifteen or twenty and the cars waiting for the bridge to come back down strung back for a block or two and honking their horns — and down there on the corner by the lamp post the rapt face of the Antichrist woman's son waving wildly up at him, now leaving that off to jump up and down and flap out his arms even more wildly and to shout out some excited secret message at him. . . .

The schooner sluiced at good speed through the water, sending out waves to lick at the shore, and even up so high Ar-Salar-Saloam could feel the good spray, the fine slap of untainted air. It was cool and wonderful, better than any possible dream. It was the future, that's what it was — the fearless future splashing him beautifully in the face. It was hope and love and sweet mercy; it was all of these things.

Then at once the schooner turned out of the black ribbon of water that had been its path, and the city fell away and vanished as neatly as if it had never existed, so that only the great sea awaited. Ar-Salar-Saloam at that moment cried out with joy, with an excitement so feverish he would have fallen from his nest had he not been strapped in: *"Fish!"* he screeched in rapture — *"FISH! FISH! FISH!"*

And he went on so screeching, piloted by his own ecstasy as he spotted fish or land or other boats — as he watched for whatever needing watching for — through the entire length of his voyage, which, for that matter, has not yet ended.

"Fish! . . .

Land! . . .

Heaven, my Captain! It is all here! . . ."

147

WINTER IS LOVELY,
ISN'T SUMMER HELL

He wondered did she wash her hands before she fall in love. Whatever he wanted he got but mostly that was because he know what he want. Her, for instance. But up to that time he only have dreams of her. My Dream Girl, he say to friends, she like this: and he slice his hands through the air like what he really want is a Coca-Cola bottle. Next thing he know it have happen but *how* it have happen he slow to realize: he married, or mostly near to it. He have her pregnant and everybody choose to hope she is. Married, that is.

You my ideal, more than once he tell her this. What is a poor girl her age to think?

You my ideal! You Something Else!

That kind of talk turn her head.

You not bad yourself, she say.

But still he hesitate. *What's the matter, honey?* — she find herself asking him that question over and over.

Things on my mind.

That is how he try to weasel out of it. *Got me some Man-stuff to think about.* A thousand times he tell her this, and drift right away from her. Leave her standing right where she stand, trying to figure out what she have done to put him in this mood.

Take care yourself, I see you soon.

The truth is, he confused. He up to his eyebrows in trouble and don't know which way to turn. He rue the day. That is what you hear him mumbling to himself sometime as he haunch up his shoulders and slouch along. *Rue the Day! God in Heaven, I rue the day!* His friends see him coming down the street they shout out *How's the Daddy!* and double-over laughing till their sides ache.

Otherwise, he the same as them. That is his trouble, that *otherwise*. Otherwise, he be out shooting pool, having a good time, not a care in the world the same as them. Now instead she a drain on the system, she Trouble with a capital T, and he rue the day.

Back up a minute. Don't forget the fun they have at the start. After their first meeting all memory of it is filled with love. Even if he tell her she have to check up on her hygiene. *Joy*, that was it! They have a new world all their own. People on the street they see them coming they break out into big grins, they say "You two are snug as bugs in the rug, you are stuck together with Elmer's glue." You see one coming you see the other, everybody happy.

He happy too. Up to the time she can take it no more, she grab him by the sleeve to say "I can take it no more, I got a baby on the way, when we getting married, you hear?" Up to that time she have moved him to do all manner of things he have never thought of before. She have touch him where he live. He even write her a poem.

"Let's hear it," she say.

But it turn out to be a poem about Winter not about Love like she expect. "Let's hear it anyway," she say, and fold her arms over her stomach and wait. "Show me your stuff," she say.

"Winter!" he shout out good and loud, making sure she have the title right. *"Winter*, by Thomas M. Jones!

The season come but once a year,
the reason we will never know."

He sit back down. That is all.

"Is that all?" she ask.

"That is all," he say. He squirm in the seat and wait for the praise. It is then that because she like him so much she look at him a long time before she get a hold of herself to say: "I can take it no more, I got a baby on the way, when we getting married, you hear?"

What he do is he stare at her hands like that is where the harm have been done.

"You have to check up on your hygiene!" he suddenly shout, and his face it is a blanket of woe from that minute on.

She have her feelings hurt. "I can do better than you right on the spot!" she yell back at him. And she twist up from her seat, drop her hands by the side, and scream out across the yard, "*Winter*, by Miss Ruby Lee Tucker, 16 years old:

The season is not very gay
because the birds all fly away
the lawn lose it summer colour
and take on a winter cover. . . .

Snakeshit, ha!" she say, and sit back down knowing she have captured the heart of the subject.

For a long time they do not speak about anything, the cat have their tongues, you can feel their cold hearts a mile away.

Then he tie a loop in his shoelace, he gets up, and to make sure his goal is clear to Miss Ruby Lee Tucker he say: "I am going."

She don't say nothing, her eyes just burn a hole in the floor.

"I'll be taking off now," he say.

She kick out at him a small kick, but he skip away.

She look up at him and she ask in a mad voice, "What have I done?"

"Nothing that I know of," he say.

She ask is that all he have to say.

He sit back down, he take her hand a minute then he throw it down and once more stand. "No," he say, "I can't get married."

"Why not?" she say, "you already married?"

"No," he say, "but my brother is."

For the evening that settle the matter. What's done is done, what's said is said, no longer does hope and joy rule in the human breast. He goes off the porch, she goes inside, he goes his separate ways and means home.

Everybody is sad, everybody is glum. Her mama will say "There — there, honey, the worse ain't yet come to worse, you still have your health," and her daddy will say "I always said that boy was no good, none of them Jones ever was," and the friends and neighbours on the street they are sad with regret thinking how hard young love is and maybe a little relieved thinking it is all out of their hands.

Pretty soon word is come that he is seen hanging around. One time he is seen riding by in a car and he toots three times on the horn and everyone wonders whose car he have and how much rubber he lose squealing the tires. Another time he is seen in the alley across the street watching the front door and one time her mama say she heard a noise at the girl's window but she can't for certain say it was him.

All the time a few people are saying maybe he have another girl and shake their heads worried-like or maybe even say they knew what he wanted in the first place from poor Ruby Lee and boys these days they are just no good.

First thing anybody know the romance is on again.

They is back on the street hand in hand, smiling hello to everyone, denying any trouble ever come between them.

The days pass, they are always together, they are tight folks say as skin on skin, couldn't pry them apart with a crowbar.

Before anybody is the wiser he have rented a room in the next block and she have moved in with him.

In time she come to think she married already and you would guess he thought the same, though that is not always the case. To speak in a nutshell sometime she remember how he have hurt her and what is more the baby is about to come due.

"How come you won't make it legal?" she wants to know.

"Marriage," he say, "is a serious step, besides, I am scared of it."

"And what you think that step you done already took was, Mr Shakespeare?" she say, and she will put her hands under her stomach and lift the hidden baby up at him. What he thinks is that she like to throw his poetic feeling up to his face in crucial times like this, she never let him forget a thing or have a minute's peace.

"Keep talking to me that way," he will tell her, "and I'm going to be busting you one."

"You hit me," she say, "and I'll have Johnny-law on your tail before you can spit."

He tell her she know he wouldn't hit no woman, he don't believe in that sort of thing.

She say that if so his name must not be Jones because she never heard of a Jones yet who didn't knock women around.

"That's a lie," he claim.

And sometimes if she is tired she will let the subject drop. She will put the dinner on the table and if he likes it he will eat it and tell her she sure can cook. Later on about bedtime it will cross her mind to tell him this: "If my first-born Leroy ever find out we ain't wed then you better watch out because one of us or both is bound to kill you sure."

It is at such times that he set his jaw and blink his eye and try to think real hard. The whole situation it seem to him is a new ballgame, he have not yet figured out quite how he come to be here sharing this room with Ruby Lee and her first-born child Leroy by another man. He have to spend a minute checking up on his own history just as he have told Ruby Lee she ought to take time off sometime to check up on her hygiene. It is not that he not know about the child it is just that it never cross his mind to think the child will come live with them, mostly because through all their courting days when they want to go out they go out alone with no unruly child tagging at the heels. Say they are going to a movie or to meet up with some friends or only if they are taking only a short stroll up or down the road her parents would always say, "No, you young folks don't want no youngan' tagging along, Leroy's natural place is here with us, we don't mind, you two young folks just scoot along and enjoy yourselves."

So he have never had to contend with no spoiled brat before. He never before have his freedom robbed by no four-year-old who don't even have the manners to say thanks.

"You are not being daddy enough to him," she will say, and sometimes if he is already in a bad mood he will pick up a chair and smash it against a wall the same way his own daddy would, and even if later on he is sorry for his yelling and screaming and upsetting everyone he is mostly sorry for himself because he know he can't help himself, the problem is bigger than him.

"I will make it up to you," he will say to her once they are wrapped up in the bed. "You know I am good as my word, I will be a good daddy to him yet."

"You are mean," she will say, "just mean, you don't have no sense now and you never had none." And she will keep on talking through the night in that soft fierce voice, she will not let him forget what a fine ignoble rat he is.

She will let the brat sleep, yes sir, but not him. She roll over to the wall, poking her hind-part out at him, complaining of the hot and cold spells she suffer from, complaining of the cramps she have, biting on the pillow because she have no lawful name, telling him she does not care for herself it is the unborn child she is thinking of. "He's a boy and he grows up he won't be able to get no job, folks will poke fun at him. Say she's a girl, everyone will say she's a tramp, they will look down on her and boys will take what they can get and she'll be no better than what they say because she'll know she never had no lawful name. I hope that makes you proud, I'll be happy when you dead, me, you are lower than the low."

He gets mad and sorry too, he sorry for both of them as his mind drift back through all the time that have got him in this present mess, but what he find himself saying is he wonder if she ever going to wash her hands before she die, he wonder if the day will ever come when she check up on her hygiene — "Just once," he say, "without me reminding you."

She let out a gasp the same way she have done every other time he make this cruel remark and when he move to put his arms around her out of pity or love whatever the case she most goes through the wall into the next room where there is nothing but stairs going down, all to get away from him.

"Go to hell!" he say, his feelings hurt.

"It's where I am," she cry. "It's where I been!"

Gone are the days of the poetry-making. Gone are the days of the big smiles, of these two together tight as skin on skin.

She going to drive him away, some say, with her nagging; others say the fault is him. Them Jones, you know, they think they too good for any girl.

It's her mama's fault, some say, raising her like that, while some others say it's nobody's fault, folks will be folks, you can't blame young people just following a natural human urge.

"Give them time, they work it out, they still young."

"If they don't they ain't the first and I reckon they won't be the last."

Jones he walk around with his head down, nobody can get a kind word out of him except maybe Ruby Lee's first-born tagging along after him though nobody heard the boy calling him daddy yet.

Gone are the days. In them days he know what he want and he rove about the dark street to find it, wondering where in name of heaven she keep herself. Not Ruby Lee just the mystery girl who he can love who will love him. He come upon her finally and certainly for sure, he tell himself, that Ruby Lee she's the one I been looking for, she will fit the bill. Having her is better than having the dream, that much for sure. Better than searching out the lonely nights, looking for something to do, hunting for someone to do it with. Better certainly than waiting for your life to start and all the time doubting it will. So there she was that first night standing against the wall at the Shoo Fly Inn, standing there grinning at him, and he skip over feeling pretty good, giving her a smile, saying "Are you looking for me?" and she speak right up, she say "I'm looking *at* you" and give a little dip to her head and goes right on looking. And that is how it begin, they have a good time, they can see they are made for each other. He do not know then what is going to happen next, all the same he is in his own mind ready for it, everyone can see he is flying high, he have found out what love is.

Hard to think now when he stop to think about it what is on his mind when he make up a poem called *Winter*, which he never forget and which even now he remember somehow — *the season come but once a year, the reason we will never know.* When he think of it he think his life is behind him, he wonder if he have thrown it all away and ruined Ruby Lee's life in the bargain, never mind for a minute her first-born who it turn out is not so spoiled after all, not a bad little boy come to think of it if anyone ever give him the chance. "You a nice-looking boy," he will sometime say to him, "you got a good heart."

And the boy will run fast to tell his mama what the man who is not his daddy say. And the days for a time they will be good, the old loving days will return, for a time they will think they forget. But the bad news it broods in the heart, it hang between them like the calendar on the door which tell them which day is which. He will not be putting it into words, but what he want most is a love like he feel when he only have a dream of what love is. To make a long story short that is one reason he have for not marrying her at the start. That she want to marry him because she is pregnant, not because she is in love with him. That got nothing to do with it, so he think. Love, that is what he is saving himself for and nothing else. No sir! He like to tell her that. He like to and any day now he think he will.

"We be married a long time ago, you not be holding a knife at my throat. We be hitched up and have a world all our own you not always be trying to tell me what's what, always trying to get the best of me."

"I never," she say, "I never did."

"Snakespit, ha-ha, tell me another one."

"Well you can forget about it now," she say, "I not marry you now you be the last man on earth."

"Yes," he say, "well, with your bad hygiene I be surprised you ever catch anyone."

Funny thing though, she have just come from the bath and his words not hurt at all this time. It finally begin to dawn on her mind that Mr Thomas M Jones is crazy on the subject. Frankly up to this moment his preoccupation with soap and water have always been a riddle to her.

"Well, may be," she tell him, "you Joneses wash three times a day, but that don't keep you from being the dirty one around here."

The truth is who is right and wrong is hard to tell. Even the little child can see that it seem to change from day to day. Still that don't keep people from putting their two cents in. Her mama and daddy for instance coax her to come on home, stop living with the fool, being an unwed mother with an orphan child or two is no disgrace these days and may in fact be the best thing. What his folks say is Tom it is clear you two don't get along, we don't say you shouldn't marry her, we don't say you should, all we say is she got herself in this fix and as the evidence shows not for the first time, although we agree with you that her little man is a lovely boy and you'll never hear us say a word against him.

Parents can't help being parents, they say whatever parents say.

"We work it out," he tell her, "one day you know we will."

But she is not speaking to him these days, she cook his dinner when he come home from work and put the plate in front of him and he eats, but she will not eat with him. In bed at night she sleep with one eye open, a knife in her hand and her face to the wall. He feel his manhood is at stake and he drop a warm hand on her hip, he let it stay there though he hardly dare to breathe. Ah, he think finally to himself, she is close to sleep or playing possum, may be now I have her in a friendly mood. He think to let his hand sneak up, wanting her big warmth to hold, but the very second he lift his finger to test out this idea she fling off the cover with a bloodcurdling shriek and leap from the bed like someone have stuck a burning stick to her. And the next hour she will spend sitting in the cold drafty hall where other roomers in the house have to walk around her to get home and if they think to stop and pass the time she will bite off their heads.

"Ruby Lee," they will say, "you are waiting for a bus? You a mother-to-be, you do nothing but harm to yourself sitting out here in the drafty hall."

"Drop dead," she will say, "I ain't studying you."

At last he will come out, he will drag out the one blanket they own and drape it over her, he will sit down beside her but not too close saying something like "How you doing?" or "Ain't you froze?" and in a little while when her temper is cooled she will head back inside with him or she won't. Most likely she won't.

She will walk the dark street, folks coming up to her they will say, "Child, how come you out alone on a night like this, this a rough neighbourhood, you going to git your throat slit."

"What I care?" she say, "go on about your business, stop bothering me."

But folks stop her anyway, even the worse kind; they can see she down on her luck, that her chin is scraping concrete and she don't have a way to turn.

"Prop yourself up, girl," they say, "every cloud have a lining of some kind, your luck bound to turn."

"Zipper your mouth," she tell these good-intentioned people, "I am going to end it all and jump from the first bridge I come to."

But she is just talking to keep her spirit up, she don't mean herself no harm. She sooner run naked through the street or burn her feet on hot

157

sand than hurt one hair of that unborn baby's head. Already she got the periodic pain, the dizzy spell; already she can squeeze watery milk from her breasts, she can make the baby move inside her almost on command. What she dream of these dark nights is that the baby will come and be nestled all snug in her arms and she will wake up in a sun-lit room to find her folks and his standing in their best clothes at the foot of the white bed, every one of them whispering *Ain't he the prettiest thing! He look just like his Mama, just like his Daddy!* and everyone will argue about that a while. Good dreamy music will be playing on her bedside radio her special request, something like *Deep River* or *If You Want Me Baby Don't Throw The Chicken On The Floor*, and a tall man in a blue suit will step forward to yank her toe saying *Ruby Lee, do you take this man?* And she will say *I reckon so*, and the man will next turn to Thomas M. Jones with his back to the wall and he will say *Boy, take your hands out of your pockets and come up here, can't you see I'm talking to you?* Thomas M. Jones will poke his way forward, he will dither and dab and look to escape, but when the man in the suit get down to business and next say *Do you take this bride?* the hard-headed S.O.B. Jones will find it in his heart to say *I do I do I think I do.* He will say this until he git the hang of it and then he will shout it out, *Oh indeed I do!* and he will go on shouting it over and over until everyone have to tell him to shut up his mouth. And like that she will snuggle up to her sweet baby child and turn back at last to sleep with all her heartache gone. The good part and the bad part of her life will be split in half, churning on each side but with a road the bride and groom can walk that is big and high and wide and stretching all the way to the other side exactly like the Red Sea which in fact was nothing in the history of the world before it divide.

That was the dream she have. Now that dream have come and gone and since it went she have had a thousand more — and yet still her story and his go on.

"You are just like your Daddy," these days she can tell both her boys. "You are plain hard-headed and always up to something and not worth the clothes you wear, but me and him will keep you I guess until something better comes along."

So it is that each night now the boys can drop off to sleep snug and warm and no doubt wondering whose side of the story they going to hear tomorrow. Wondering what going to happen next. Feeling how the story of one is the story of them all and wondering why if this is so they remain so fearful of how their own fortune going to fall.

The End of the Revolution and Other Stories

20 NOVEMBER: Her windows are always the same. Whether she's out or in I never know. Frustrating, the curtains always drawn. Now and then a pencil of light, no more. I *ought* to know, that's what I mean, just as she ought to know when I'm on the street watching. Her glass is dirty, too. We should clean it some time. Say I am seen walking by and she beckons with a finger — "I'm so tired, I'm not in the mood, will you help me?" — and I rush up the stairs, we get out the Windex and paper towels and scrub away until the glass screeches in gratitude. That's when I draw the curtains back. Once they are open she'll not notice, they will stay that way. I'll not open them too much, of course — anyone could walk by and look in. They could stand on the barrel in the alley by the grocery and have a pretty straight shot. Probably when at home, on slow evenings, she's often in the nude. Well, not this time of the year, in the summer, I mean. People are less cautious in summer I've noticed, a good warm day they don't want to believe anyone wishes them harm.

I should mail her a postcard: CLEAN YOUR WINDOWS. THEY ARE A DISGRACE. She'd take it as joke, I've seen how she likes to laugh. I like that, it warms me to see her enjoying herself. Surprises me though, somehow I expected her to be more stand-offish, more practical, more mature. Well, at her age. No, she acts like she thinks she's the toast of the town.

161

Note, wash hair.
Pick up feathers.

21 NOVEMBER: That idea about writing to her appeals to me. I could drop it in her box, walking by, no one would notice. Save the postage, I can't be too careful in that respect. CAME BY AGAIN TODAY, SORRY YOU WERE OUT. Signed, *Anonymous*. No, that might put her on guard. Why invite trouble? Maybe, simply, *A Friend*, that would be better. If she had a phone — she might have one of course, must look into that — I could ring her up, make a suggestion or two. "Windows washed, free of charge, our Get Acquainted Special this week." Probably she'd laugh, tell me I was ridiculous, no one does anything for free. "I know you only want to get inside. Don't try it, sister, I'm alerted now." Or she might tell me she doesn't have the time, busy-busy, never a minute to call her own. She might even act nasty, say something rude: "I can tell *you've* got troubles, but stay away from me, I don't want to get involved."

Strange, this habit she has of disappearing. Around a corner, *poof!* — and she's gone. It was like that today. Frustrating, what does she do with herself, where does she go? I think I picked up a cold waiting in the alley for her to show up. *Note*, dress more warmly tomorrow.

Shh, *he's* coming.

22 NOVEMBER: The grocer had his eye on me today. What lousy luck that his place is just opposite hers. A nasty sort. Plain to see he means no one any good. I felt guilty — I *feel* guilty — knowing he was giving me those suspicious looks. To deceive him I strolled up the block, then down the other side. A casual walk, smiling, looking at numbers, the sky, anything. "Me? Oh, I'm only waiting for friends. Supposed to meet them here. This is Richardson Street, isn't it?" I've got hundreds of tricks like that, I know how to avoid trouble. But I'm careful too, I know what it is to talk myself into hot water. The grocer didn't let up, however. Vile man. I couldn't let him get away with it, went inside his shop. Thinking to buy fruit, take the wind out of his sails. Be aggressive, that's one thing I've learned. Don't let them smell fear.

Beautiful pyramids, at least he knows how to stack fruit, his shop is neat. I've seen him when a customer comes along and takes an apple or orange from the wrong place: he fumes. Often he'll rearrange the entire bunch.

"Don't pinch," he told me. I wasn't sure that's what he said. He's surly, unshaven, vulgar, a big stomach — hardly the sort she would care for. She ought to move, in fact. I could slide a note under her door: GET OUT OF THIS STINKING NEIGHBOURHOOD, IT ISN'T SAFE. I don't feel comfortable around there, I never have, it's much nicer on my side of town. Good clean streets, and although it may only be my imagination, I think people are nicer. She could afford to move, I've seen her spend huge amounts in a single day without blinking. Crazy, you'd think she'd save a little for the future. She doesn't spend it on clothes, unfortunately. Her coat is not nearly as nice as mine. Frequently she's shabby, almost drab. Of course it's the style now, I suppose the other view is that she's right up there with the latest.

"I said don't pinch," the grocer told me. Rude. I heard him that time, but had the presence of mind to put him in his place.

"Grapes, please. The white."

He weighed out a pound. "More? More?" The price, when he told me, was quite a shocker. I went blue in the face. I had to ask him to put some back, which he did. "More? More?" I showed him all I was willing to pay: one quarter. I thought he was going to spit in my hand. It's disgraceful what food costs now, I don't see how even a small family can manage. Thank my lucky stars *I* never got into that.

Lost *her* again.

The grocer hates me. It didn't matter to him that I bought his wretched fruit.

"I saw you pinching the apples." *Scum*, that's what he wanted to say, I could see it in his eyes. He was suspicious. *Up to no good, scum like you, wouldn't be surprised if you murdered your mother*, that's what was on his mind. I was afraid he might call the . . . police. The *cops*, I almost said. I hate that word, the police should be respected. Anyway, the grocer will remember me now. He might even tell her that I've been loitering around her place. Well, she should be flattered, someone her age.

"You live around here?" he asked me.

"Sure," I said, "just around the corner," although I stuttered, not at my best.

"Fine. But don't pinch. I welcome your business, but don't pinch."

I promised I wouldn't any more. I hate myself when I allow anyone to ride roughshod over me like that. But why make a scene? Dignity, that's what was required. A dreary man.

All in all, I think I came out on top.

23 NOVEMBER: Forgot to mention this yesterday. When I got home the telephone was ringing. More trouble, I thought, what next? My key wouldn't fit inside the lock, by the time I was inside my caller had hung up. *If* it was my phone. Could have been in the room adjacent to mine. It's true: I *am* always expecting something to happen to me. I'm always expecting someone important will ring me up. Not to *say* anything important, I don't care about that. If they will only say how are you, how was your day, that will be enough.

I put my ear against the wall. If it was the old man's phone he had missed his caller too. That amused me. First that anyone would want to call him, then that when finally it came he had been out. The old fool. One's entire life can turn on a small thing like that — being out when you should be in, being in the right place at the right time. It takes a certain knack. That's what Colonel Dodson is forever telling me. He has, he says, the knack. "You ought to cultivate it. How do you think I got to be *Colonel* Dodson?" Chest puffed out, one eye drooping like a sleeping dog's. That's Dodson. Yet, it's true, he *is* a colonel, he gets along.

I kept listening for the old man to come in. If he did I'd knock on his door, look him in the eye, say, "Well, old man, one of us got a call." Study him. Determine whether he had been expecting to be rung up. I think actually the call must have been mine. He doesn't need a phone; it's been weeks since anyone called him. Maybe. Of course I don't know what happens when I'm out, that's elementary. *To my own certain knowledge, however, his phone has not rung in three weeks.*

Nothing. He was definitely out.

I went to my front window without turning on the lights. I peeked through the curtains. No one there. No one watching my place, that's a relief. Mine are good curtains, I love these curtains, heavy velvet, blue.

Lined too. No one passing on the street would ever know what I do in here, they wouldn't know whether I am in or out. But the window was filthy, that surprised me. Not like a window at all, rather like a charcoal sketch of what a window is supposed to be. *Item,* clean your window tomorrow. Get up early, get up by first light, do a good job.

I shouldn't let such grubbiness disturb me. Why get upset about it? I wiped a finger over the glass. Screech! The filth was outside. That made me feel better, not much, but a little.

I had to laugh at myself. I hadn't yet taken off my coat. Three hours home by that time and I was still in my winter gear. I'm usually careful of my appearance, if I say so myself. Clothes reflect the person. You've got to sit up straight, stand up straight, walk with your shoulders back if you want people to think well of you. Throw the world a smart salute. That's what the Colonel would say.

But then he weeps and destroys the whole effect.

I don't know. It comes over me sometimes, settles over me sometimes as unexpectedly and as beautifully as the first snow, as snow on a sunny day — my change. I do change. I feel myself suddenly go beautiful under this heavy coat. I go up another inch on my heels, everyone desires me. They sell my pin-ups at the five and dime. SPECIAL THIS WEEK AT K-MART, FOUR SHOTS FOR $1.

I had to get out of bed to answer the door. I smoothed my hair back, threw open the door, and a man was standing there wearing a white apron, thrusting a box at me.

"He sent this," the man said. "Told me you needed it, put dimples in your cheeks. He's across the street, what do I tell him?"

"That's *your* problem," I said, and slammed the door.

I reacted pretty well, I thought. I certainly handled that problem.

24 NOVEMBER: A lost day.

Got hair done though, looks nice.

25 NOVEMBER: This morning, going out: A bulbous man in his underwear at a second-storey window holding a doll in his arms. That's what I thought at first, so I went by again. Not a doll, but a small ugly dog dressed in a sort of blue vest. The dog squirmed and

165

barked and the man shrugged at me and had to put it down. "Haven't seen you in the Scream Room lately," he shouted. "You get yourself sorted out?"

People can be so stupid.

She looked especially dingy today. I'm beginning to lose interest in her. That saddens me. Of course she's old. Probably a mistake in the first place.

Today I was extremely bold. I took a table directly beside hers at Ivanhoe's. Big surprise, she usually goes to La Petite Colombe on Broughton Street (well, their stove was out). A man met her there, though it soon became clear that they didn't know each other well. A trial meeting perhaps. They whispered over the table now and then, they had to push the candle aside. Each time he lit her cigarette her smile — wispy, vaguely teasing — went past him and settled more firmly on me. Oh, she knew what she was doing. I gave the smile back, I gave it to her with both barrels. She doesn't frighten me. Nor does the waiter, I have a right to take lunch where I wish. A table to myself if that's what I choose. He was mad, I only had soup, others were waiting to be seated. Their bad luck, that's what I told the waiter. I hate waiters, they're like doctors, they think they can run your life.

I observed the man with her. He seems nice enough. Mildly good-looking. More than enough self-confidence. Not quite tall enough for her. Once he placed a hand on her knee under the table. She let it stay there for five minutes or so, then she crossed her legs and his hand rose calmly back to the table. It was lovely, his motion. Like a butterfly. They were sharing a decanter of white wine. They began enjoying each other. I could see this surprised both of them.

They left together. He walked with her for two blocks, at Fort and Government they stood chatting for several minutes. They shook hands, both laughing. Then he disappeared inside Montreal Trust.

I don't begrudge the expense. I can make it up by leaving off cigarettes for a while.

I took a seat in the rear of the bus, she sat up front in one of those triple seats facing the aisle, those reserved for the elderly or handicapped. That amused me. She had bought a new pair of shoes and occasionally I caught her twisting her ankles about, admiring them. A lovely tan leather, very expensive, but they're too young for her. Hardly her style. Still, she's got nice legs. Legs just don't age so fast, you can't tell a thing by looking at a person's legs.

She looked less tacky, all in all. She had done her hair. She was excited too.

He came by her place at four.

I hate those curtains. I imagine they are like mine, they hide everything, absorb everything, nothing goes beyond them. Even with both of them there anyone would have thought the place vacant.

The grocer, glad to say, was nice to me.

"You again? Be glad when this cold spell breaks. What can I do for you today?"

I think he likes me. I've got to be careful, he might get the wrong idea. He may think I find him interesting. The way he looks at me. I couldn't tell him it was cold, that was why I was hanging around his shop.

"You married?" he asked.

I rolled my eyes and let loose a loud Ha-Ha. It baffled him, he's not overly smart.

"I shouldn't have asked. Person like you would be snapped up quick." I saw that he wanted to get familiar with me. But he didn't dare, didn't have the courage, he was afraid of what I might do or say, even create a scene perhaps.

"More grapes today? You do like grapes, don't you, that's good, a lot of vitamin C in grapes — though you are too late I'm afraid, that looks like a bad one you have."

What a fool. They get nervous, they can't help talking a blue streak, they'll pass any stupid remark to make you think they're an average Joe.

My cold *is* worse. My nose is red, it hurts. My head feels like they've been stuffing eggplant inside. I feel awful.

26 NOVEMBER: Stayed in today. No improvement.

Just after two this afternoon someone knocked on my door. Softly, hardly more than brush strokes. I had heard him coming up the stairs but had decided it was the old man next door. I listened for the key in *his* lock. Soft as the sound was, I jumped when it came to my door. I held my breath, the blankets pulled up to my neck. I waited. Finally I heard him going down the stairs again. I peeked through the curtains but he must have kept close to the building when he came out.

I don't know why I say *he*. My first thought was that it was *her*. Creepy, but I do have a cold. I don't want to go through that again.

This morning I noticed a sheet of paper had been slid under the door. I CAME BY, it said, SORRY YOU WERE OUT.

27 NOVEMBER: Surprise, surprise! Actually I was deeply shocked. *He* knocked on my door this afternoon, the old man. Said my coughing was a nightmare to him, he couldn't sleep, he couldn't think. "Don't you have any medicine? A little cough syrup? You're driving me crazy." I hadn't even known he was *in*. I thought he had been out of town for the whole weekend. Ridiculous.

Another thing: he isn't old. Not nearly as old as I thought. Forty, forty-five.

"God," he said, "you look terrible. I think you've only got an hour to live."

Up to this moment I had simply stared at him. It seemed to me someone was playing a joke, that the landlady had moved another man into the next room.

"Can't you talk? I know you can cough."

He was almost yelling at me but he didn't seem angry. Just loud.

"Oh, hell!" he shouted. "Go back to bed!"

And he pushed me back — he actually put his hands on me and shoved me back — pulled the door shut and went away. Amazing behaviour. It worried me. It crossed my mind that he was a lunatic, that I was in danger. I put a chair against the door. I stood there, ready to scream, staring at the door, certain he meant to come back. He was large, he looked strong, he didn't look to me like the sort who would be able to control himself.

Half an hour later he was back. He stood out in the hall shouting at me: "I've got medicines! Cough syrup. Juice. Capsules. Tonics. Aspirin. Open the goddamn door!"

I told him to go away.

"You *can* talk," he said. "But shut up, you're sick, you're dying. I'm saving your life. Open the door."

"No!" I said. "Leave me alone." He frightened me, he was obviously the violent type.

"Dry up," he said. That was to himself, I barely heard it although my ear was against the door. I heard him walking away. I breathed freely again.

A minute or two later he strode right inside. He held up a key, kissed it and put it in his pocket. "Authority," he said. "Works wonders. Sit up, you've got a lot of junk to take. Open your mouth."

He meant it. He had a white sack jammed full of medicines. He even had a tin of Campbell's soup. "Beef broth," he said. "Thin as eel's breath but better than nothing I guess. Don't you have a hot plate?"

28 NOVEMBER: I feel better, thank God. What a bore he's been. He kept my head aching with his shouts. "What a pigsty! God, open the drapes. Why are there feathers on the floor? Have you been plucking pigeons, eating pigeons? It's against the law, you know. You can't just walk along, bash a pigeon on the head, bring it home and pluck it and eat it. I've wondered about you. You're nuts, is that the case? How old are you? Don't you know better than to live like this?"

Yak-yak, I thought my head would split.

29 NOVEMBER: I'm not going to keep going on this way. He's quite sure he can walk all over me. He dashed in early this morning and moved my bed, with me still in it, over to another wall. I breathe too deeply, he claims. Everything keeps him awake. Sirens at night, planes overhead, everything. Even the fish in the ocean a mile from here. *"I want silence at night, do you understand?"*

I've asked the landlady to get back her key, I've told her and told her that man is bothering me. She pats my arm. "Don't worry about it. He's like a moose up there, he throws his weight around. But you're not Cinderella, as I see it this business is between you and him. I learned early in life, don't interfere."

Impossible woman. Once each month she dresses up, splashes toilet water on her neck, goes in a taxi across town to sit at her husband's grave. No, I don't expect assistance or understanding from her.

169

30 NOVEMBER: Sunshine at last. I know now I can make it on my own, I've proved that much to myself.

I've been lucky, it seems I haven't missed anything. While I've been cooped up over here she's been ill over there. I got that much from the grocer. "Oh, yes," he said, "she's gone through five boxes of tissues, hasn't stuck her head out the door in four days, I didn't know you were a friend of hers."

He was glad to see me, he kissed my cheek and forced a bag of over-ripe fruit into my hands.

Funny man.

I worry about the Colonel. In a postcard that came yesterday he says he's got his orders, he's shipping out. Big activity in the South Pacific, watch the newspapers for his name. He has a feeling he won't return. Pray for me, he says.

1 JANUARY: I have figured out why I thought he was so old, that idiot next door. He hasn't shaved and his beard must be half an inch long, growing all whirly-whirly and grey on his face. He walks stooped, especially when he's in a hurry, which is the case most of the time. I can't say I respect him but I have got used to the abrupt way he behaves. He thinks he's my daddy, that's a guess. Last night he wanted to know what I do with myself all day. "First you're here, then *poof!* you're gone, I can't count on you, where do you go all day?"

We were drinking champagne, turning the old year out.

"Got a lover, have you? The old bench-warmer who has finally made it into the game? Cheers, let's meet like this again next year."

Turning it out, this year that has rolled by day by day and which to me seems fair enough and good enough only when seen that way.

"Ah, you're moping," he said, "don't mope!" — and he thumped his chest, saying, "The only strings we have are those in here."

Then *he* turned sour, he wanted to know when I was going to pay him back for all the money he's spent on me. "I'm broke now, lost it all in a Tuesday night poker game. So pay up, you don't get a free ride on my trolley."

I told him I had no money, he'd have to wait, and he picked up the champagne and went away disgusted with me.

I didn't know what to do with myself, it was too late, too late to go anywhere. I picked up the phone and dialled her but the line was busy, probably she was having a party over there.

Later on he came back. He thinks he's Lord Nelson, he strides right in. I was taking a bath. He sat down on the edge of the tub, sat there with his legs crossed, staring at me. "I didn't think you washed," he said. "That crust looks like it hasn't been disturbed in years. You could sell that mould to a geology lab. Unfold your arms, I want to have a good look at you."

I let him. It hurt me but I closed my eyes and let him. I don't know what I expected him to do. After a while I opened my eyes and he was gone. The water was cold, I was sneezing again.

It's true about the feathers. If you sit on a bench and the birds strut all around you they ought to expect it. I hate it, that cocky, you-mean-nothing-to-me air that they have, while all the time they are strutting around your feet, pecking up whatever you give them. I despise their throaty sound, that maddening little hop they take when you or another bird does something to vex them, that wooden-legged strut that they have. You're supposed to sit there and grit your teeth and let yourself be humoured by them. I tried to kill one with a rock but they have necks like a rubber hose, they can scoot faster than guinea hens. I stunned one and brought it home folded up inside my coat. It revived and I had to chase it all over my room. It put me in a fury that I couldn't catch it, the chase left me breathless on the floor. I crawled to the door, opened it, but the bird didn't have sense enough to leave. Well, by that time it had squirmed into a corner and lay there on its side kicking out its scaly matchstick legs.

Contemptible creature. It wouldn't have crossed my mind to try to eat it. I'm aware there's nothing to them except gristle and bone. Their bones shred, they're like hat-pins. Anyway I'm nauseous as a rule, there isn't much I can get down.

If the feathers disturb him I hope he knows what he can do, he can get off his high horse and sweep them up in a dustpan, he's God Almighty and can do that and anything else he wants to.

2 JANUARY: God, I've been in a state all day. I must have taken a hundred pills.

I've been staring at this page for two hours.

A dozen times I've gone down to talk to the landlady, I bang on her door and ask her why there's no heat in my room, I'm wearing three sweaters under this coat and still I shiver, my hand is blue on the page.

"Sorry," he says, "about last night."

I'm supposed to leap up and throw my arms around him.

"I wish I could get through to you."

I want my privacy, I want it and expect it and that's all I've ever asked for.

"It's this holiday season," he says, "everything is up in the air, people are not themselves, routines are disrupted, you'll be shipshape once everything returns to normal again.

"I know you hear me," he says, "your eyes blink when I speak, I know I'm not talking to a dead wall."

I've been remiss, I haven't thought of her once all day.

I'll survive; I will, that's what I do when nothing else works.

3 JANUARY: People think it's easy. They say, "Stand on your own two feet, be yourself." Then they crawl on to say the same to someone else while the rest of us who can't move remain in our circle screeching at each other.

That's what it was like today.

Yet he's been going out of his way to be nice to me, he promises he won't shout any more. He said that, holding my hand, looking deep into my eyes, and I had to laugh, being incapable of believing he could even *seem* to be so sincere.

"Good. Are we friends once more?"

I remember the first time I learned how easily and innocently one can wound another person, how with the smallest remark one may damage them. I remember my father had only four fingers on his left hand. I remember the winter when I was five years old and how with my play scissors I snipped the extra finger off his left glove and how this wounded him, how my mother took me to a corner and shook me, saying I was a frightful child. How he was the one who felt ashamed.

"I told you once things got back to normal you'd be your old self again."

He can sit on my tub and look at my breasts, perhaps he can even put his hands on them and he can accept that the scale of this deed is heavy, no apology can erase that, it's a betrayal of vast proportions and this insight is new to him, it's a revelation, he thinks by this recognition he's improving himself, he's on his way to becoming a decent human being, but in fact he's become worse because he will only be looking for his larger meanness now and this will blind him to the fact that it's the legion of trivialities we can't forgive. I don't care if he wants to look at me in the bath, I can even see pleasure in the episode, but I don't want to be studied like a piece of clay unless I have early warning, unless I can believe there's warmth of feeling, coexistence of spirit between the viewer and the viewed.

Dubious developments elsewhere today: I've been invited to join a theatre group, it's official: the Fine Line Players will take the city by storm when they present six weeks from now Odessa del Rey's memory play, *The Suicide Club*.

"No doubt you wonder," the director told us, "what will happen when you take your problems into the streets. Cheer up, good people, six weeks from now the house applause will tell you that your harboured secrets hold previous anchor within the breasts of all solid citizens of the town, that's art, friends."

"Ah Judith, Judith," *he* tells me, "put away your scissors, you'll find old Holofernes isn't such a bad guy. Close your eyes, I'll rub your back."

4 JANUARY: I find it so interesting. The banker had a fight with her today, right outside her front door. She called him dirty names, half a dozen people came outside or stopped in the street to stare, including the grocer whose job, it seemed, was that of timekeeper; each minute or so he'd pull a watch from his apron pocket and whisper to those near him that they had been going at it for eight minutes or nine or ten minutes now.

"Oh, it happens," he said, "all the time, though usually they keep it indoors."

The man was meek, he didn't try to defend himself. She saw this as indifference, it was this, I think, that fed her rage. "An emotional cripple," she shouted, "that's what you are!"

I couldn't help laughing, it's a line I have in my play.

She told him she hoped never to see him again, he was lower than low, she ought to have her head examined for putting up with the likes of him. Then she shook her fists overhead and fled inside.

With her gone he tried treating it like a joke. "Women," he smiled, "what else can one expect?" Everyone still scowled at him. No one doubted the fault was his. "Women," he muttered, "there's a difference all right, women are different." Someone in the crowd hooted, he whirled around on her. "Don't get me wrong. They are not different from us, just from each other, from themselves. Name me one woman who's the same from one hour to the next?" Women among us began throwing out names: Sonja Henie, Bathsheba, Mary Magdalene, Cassandra, Mamie Eisenhower, the Queen, Lotus Blossom, Little Mary Sunshine, Henny Penny, the names went on.

"That's enough," he snarled, "my case is proved!" He strode across the street; at the grocer's door he turned. "Laugh," he yelled, "that proves it too. Name me one man so able to forget himself that he'd cause a disturbance in the street." Idi Amin, someone shouted. Charles Manson. The Wright Brothers. Jesus, Hitler, the Bee Gees, anyone from Australia, the list went on. "I can see you're not serious," he shouted. "That's another thing, you women don't know how to seriously discuss an issue." Lizzie Borden, one of the women called. Lucrezia Borgia. Madame Tussaud.

He gave up, sweeping on inside the store. Behind him the grocer paused to consult his watch. "Fourteen minutes," he piped, "a new record for a Friday." The street crowd cheered; apparently this was old stuff to them. They dispersed. I felt lonely, unsure of where I should go. Finally I went into the grocery.

The man was telling the grocer he wanted a case of sardines.

"Sure," the grocer replied, "anything you want, nothing you two do surprises me."

"I want them delivered to her," the man said. "We're having this trouble because of the diet's she's on, she eats like a bird. No protein, how can she expect to enjoy proper mental health? If you have a few frozen steaks throw those in."

"Anything you say," the grocer replied.

"Of course I haven't known her very long," the man continued. "She's difficult, a difficult case. I drew her a bath this morning, washed her back, even her hair. I was convinced she didn't recognize me. Don't misunderstand me, she has no strings on me, our relationship is innocent, whatever anyone might suppose."

The grocer took his money, he said he'd deliver the order right away. He winked as he went by me with the goods.

The man decided he'd wait. One of his socks was on inside out, a tie hung from his side-pocket. His eyes were bleary, as if he'd been losing a lot of sleep. "What do *you* want?" he asked me. "Who do you think you're staring at?" I drifted back, turning away from him, turning to the bin of grapes. They were beautiful grapes, perfectly formed on their slender stems, their skins so translucent one could see the seeds inside.

A woman came through the door. She strutted to the counter and from there disdainfully surveyed us, looking from one to the other. "Well?" she said. "I'm in a hurry, which of you is running this place? I want eggs and milk and your best roach powder, don't make me wait all day." The man shrugged, stepping forward. "Why not?" he said, "I got my life's start in a store much like this." He got her milk and eggs but couldn't find the roach powder. "I see it," she said, "down there, lower shelf, the pink box. No, not the big box, the small box, don't you know anything?"

He bagged her groceries; it was then that she announced she wanted to put it all on charge. The man told her he didn't know about credit, she'd have to wait. I thought the woman was going to slap his face. She put the groceries under her arm as if she had already paid for them. The man paced the aisle, he kept running a hand through his hair, now and then pulling out a handkerchief to blow his nose.

The grocer returned. He had brought the sardines back. He put these down and hitched a thumb over his shoulder. "She wants to see you," he informed the man. "She says for you to get over there quick."

I looked through the store's plate glass. A slither of light showed at her window, I saw her knuckles gripping the drapes, her face staring down on us.

"Is she crying?" the man asked.

"What do I know about crying, no, she's not crying, she was on the phone when I got there. Talking to someone named Judy. You know a Judy?"

The man shook his head, he knew no friend of hers named Judy.

I said I knew Judy but they weren't listening to me. The man didn't appear to be in a hurry to go to her. He smiled stupidly at the woman with the roach powder while the grocer said to her, "Lady, you want credit, who are you, do I know you, what is it you have in mind putting up for collateral?" He stepped between them, asking the grocer for cigarettes. "Anything mentholated, brand doesn't matter, whatever's best." He asked where he might be able to buy flowers, was there a stall nearby? The grocer replied that he didn't know anything about flowers, what was he running, an information bureau? "You got troubles, take them to the Eric Martin Institute of Psychiatry, that's nearby."

We all had a big laugh at that.

The man left the grocery, I stepped out behind him. The streak of light disappeared at her window.

"Where are you going?" the man asked, turning on me. "Are you following me?"

"Of course not," I said, "I'm going home, why should I follow you?"

He laughed. "Excuse me," he said, "I'm a bit distracted, I need to be alone and think this difficulty out but can't manage the time just now. Do you mind if I walk along with you? I've got to buy flowers, perhaps a box of candy although flowers would certainly be better, surely there must be a place around here where one can find them."

"I wouldn't know," I said. "I'm a stranger to this neighbourhood."

"Didn't I meet you last year, Open House at the Institute? You were wearing a red dress."

"Not me," I said, "I look like death in red."

How peculiar I felt walking with him, nice, I could hear my heels clicking on the sidewalk while his made no sound. The sky had whitened to near chalk and it had turned colder; our breaths formed small bags in front of us and in the time it took to step through one, another was there.

"Are you warm enough?" he asked. "I like that coat, black suits you. But it looks too thin, you'll catch a cold. You wear a lot of make-up, don't you?"

I wasn't offended, it was clear that he was saying whatever came into his mind while reserving his deeper thoughts for his own problems. I do that sometimes too.

At the first corner I turned; he went on ahead.

"I hope you find them," I called. "The flowers."

"Oh, I'll find them," he answered. "I'm not such a kluck as I appear."

I laughed, I liked him, I hoped his life would be happy.

I felt hungry. For the first time in weeks I had a true appetite, I was ravenous and walked all the way downtown to a vegetarian restaurant I know about called *Deer Crossing* and there I had split-pea soup in a cup and an open-faced cheese sandwich with bean sprouts sprinkled on it.

I felt listless and sleepy, I couldn't wait to get home.

5 JANUARY: I couldn't write this last night, it was too ludicrous and funny.

When I got back to my place I found a man propped up in my bed.

Someone had left twelve red roses in a vase on my table.

"Who left those?" I asked.

"Be reasonable," he said, "I only just got here."

He was reading my diary.

"You need help," he said, getting up, "and you came to the right man." He thumped the diary. "What happened to December? Why did you tear out all the pages?"

I didn't rush out screaming. The truth is he looked harmless.

"Who are you?" I asked.

"Sigmund Freud," he said. "I've just finished the last page of *Drei Abhandlungen zur Sexualtheorie* and I'm tired, so don't make this any more difficult for me than it has to be."

"What do you have in mind?" I asked.

He tapped his skull. "I'm going to cure you."

"How do you propose to do that?"

"In your case all that's required is an active imagination. Lie down and get busy."

6 JANUARY: I've moved. I didn't want to but Sigmund said I should.

"New interests, new horizons, *involve* yourself, Judith."

Here it's nicer, cheaper too, I have the only room on the top floor. From my window I can see anyone coming, or leaving, for a distance of seven miles.

Note, windows wrong size, snip off bottom of drapes.

I've been lucky, right away I've found someone interesting. She's older than me, on the thin side, she's nervous and dresses badly though I don't find her unattractive. I think she's the kind of person one can depend on. I was on the street not two doors down from here, when I heard her telling off a young boy who had bumped into her. An accident, he claimed — "Lady, I didn't mean to!" — but she wasn't having any of it. "You don't own the street," she told him. "You think you can knock us all down, your kind, and go your merry way, but I won't have it! You're nothing special, it's time you realized that!" She really was in a rage. Although I was on her side I found her behaviour shocking. The boy was helpless, she had him in tears. Finally he broke loose and ran, just a small boy, barely more than five or six.

Well, his mother should keep him home.

She doesn't know what to do with her hair, it's silly the way she wears it, someone ought to tell her. I might slide a note through her mail slot, MAKE AN APPOINTMENT AT HOUSE OF BEAUTY, MR SAXONY IS A WIZARD WITH PEOPLE LIKE US.

We might be good company for each other, I think we could become friends.

Sigmund is staying with me for a few days while looking for work. He says he won't be much trouble and will do his share of the chores. I like him though he's too chummy in my opinion.

That *she* needs my friendship is obvious. She's discontented with herself, she hasn't learned as I have how to cope with life's small realities.

Sigmund says she wants to be useful to society, she wants to be liked and respected.

I say, "Sigmund, you don't even know her!" and he shrugs, he says, "I know women."

She *is* the kind who drifts from mistake to mistake, she *looks* for trouble. For instance, today before her encounter with the boy she was in the dry-cleaning place on the corner arguing with the counterman. "Your sign says one hour," she told him, "one hour Martinizing, it's in all your advertisements, what do you mean I can't have this coat back in one hour?" But all the time I could see the way he was looking at her, he was interested, that much was clear. And *she* was, too, I saw how sweet she got at the end.

Something as a matter of fact may already be going on in that department.

Sigmund says no, he says she's a long way from being ready to make a commitment to anyone.

7 JANUARY: I couldn't leave her like that, I had to go back. The grocer saw her through his window, I must have been pacing back and forth trying to make up my mind. He came outside, he touched my elbow and put a bag of grapes in my hands: "Take them," he said, "don't worry, she'll be happy to see you, I know she will. Take these grapes up to her, she likes grapes, the two of you will get along fine."

"She's taken down the drapes," I said.

"Ah well, drapes get dirty, she's having them cleaned, I guess."

I had in mind a quiet chat. I'd introduce myself and shake her hand, we'd sit down and over tea I'd tell her I knew what she had been going through, that I had been in that boat myself and while I agreed with her that we had to stand up for our rights and be on guard every minute of the day there was no point in going overboard with it, if a man was halfway decent and good to us we should make sacrifices, be forgiving, give them the benefit of the doubt. Yes, she'd say, I see what you mean, I've been thinking along those same lines myself, it's impossible but what else can we do? The discussion would become intense, we'd sit on for hours comparing notes, quite unaware of the passage of time, probably amazed at how much we had in common.

179

"That's right, go ahead," the grocer said, "nothing to be nervous about."

He was so convincing, I had never imagined he could be such a warm and sympathetic man, he even walked me across the street and opened the door for me. "Go on," he said, "you won't regret it, you'll find you're doing the right thing."

"Is *he* here?"

"I wouldn't know."

Climbing the stairs, I had the most extravagant fantasy: her door would open, she would turn with a soft smile, she would hold out her arms. I would glide across the floor and enter her skin. He would embrace *me!*

The door was open.

He was there.

"At last!" he said. "Where have you been?"

I walked in.

"You look beautiful," he said, embracing me. "That Mr Saxony is a genius."

His hands moved gently over my body. He closed his eyes, moaned and kissed my neck. I closed my eyes too.

"You've done a nice job, arranging those flowers."

I loved it, I loved what he was doing to me.

"Sure," he whispered, "sure you do. You treasure your schizothymia, you rise above the hoi polloi. There is so much *more* to you than there is to other people. But what about me? What about next week or tomorrow or even one hour from now?"

I pressed against him. I thought: *you* say nothing, *she's* the shrewd one, let *her* handle this.

"In the meantime, where does that leave me? What kind of life do I have, what am *I* to do?"

He held me tighter. I could barely breathe, nor could he. He wanted what I wanted: to become one body that contained all bodies, to look out at the world from the settled, comfortable, perfect silence of a single eye, to have no need even to think *satisfied, satisfied, we are all here!*

Some People Will Tell You the Situation at Henny Penny Nursery Is Getting Intolerable

We got fifty-two (52) kids in the nursery, the Henny Penny Nursery, only one teacher, and she's retarded. They come to me, the parents of these kids do, and they say, "Sir, Mr Beacon, excuse us, sir, for butting in like this, but some of us parents, mostly those of us you see right here, what we've noticed is that Mrs Shorts, running your place, well, sir, to make no bones about it, she's retarded." And they look at me and blink their eyes all bashful-like — "Sorry we raised it, forgive us for noticing it," sort of like that, I mean — and, well, I blink right back because frankly I don't know what they expect me to do.

"She's *slow*," I tell them, "Mrs Shorts is slow, she's *dim*, but what makes you think she's retarded?"

Because I was looking for evidence, you see. You can't just go around sacking somebody because you hear stories passed along by every Dick and Harry.

"Begging your pardon, sir," they say, "but here's one thing, what we think, us concerned parents here — that's what we call ourselves, the Concerned Parents of Henny Penny Nursery — it's like this, you see. Mrs Shorts, she's been on the job six months now and we think we've given her every fair chance. Fact is, at the start we *liked* her, we were really bowled over, because she's so sweet and all. But, sir, Mr Beacon, what concerns us is that now after six months on the job she don't yet know where the kids hang up their coats or where their galoshes are kept, and worse yet, she won't let them out on the playground some of us hobby-type parents put in at our own expense, because she says they could get run over by streetcars. *Streetcars*, Mr Beacon, and we've looked it up: there hasn't been streetcars in this town for sixty-two years. Which is another thing, Mr Beacon, her *age!*"

"I take your point," I tell them. "I have noticed myself Mrs Shorts is on the feeble side, and elderly, though saying she's retarded is maybe going too far."

"She *dithers*, Mr Beacon, she *dithers* all the time, and the place under her is a madhouse, it's pandemonium in there."

"I see. So you're telling me you're dissatisfied."

"We wouldn't go that far, sir, no sir. We the Concerned Parents of Henny Penny, CPHPN, we're called, we just think the matter ought to be looked into. We're paying good money to have our little Johnnies and Susies and whatnot get the best education available, have all the best opportunities like most of us never had, and, well, we just think this matter ought to be gone over some, maybe looked into with a fine-tooth comb."

"I see," I say, picking up my pen. "You're registering a formal complaint."

"Oh no, sir! This is all off the record. We just sort of hoped if we brought it to your attention that —"

"That something would be done about it. Good idea. The Concerned Parents of Henny Penny, CPHPN, may certainly consider that indeed I shall, first chance."

"Yes, sir. We know you will. It isn't that, sir, so much as . . . well, there is the question of the petition that other group — our parent group, so to speak, the Tiny Totlers Protective Parents Association, TTPPA, of which we are a spinoff — there's that list of grievances they brought in last year, you'll remember, about nails in the floorboards and the Doze Room without any cots, and all that rat business, and such. We were wondering couldn't we get some action soon on that, as four or five of the totters had to go to the hospital on account of the ptomaine."

"Ptomaine?" I say.

"Yes sir. And the pneumonia. There don't ever seem to be any heat in the place, except in Mrs Shorts' room."

"Imagine that!" I say.

They kept blinking their eyes at me, waiting, leaning this way and that and nodding encouragement at each other and at their speaker, so I began to get a whiff of a suspicion that this bunch meant to play tough. That they had come prepared with facts and this time meant business. A much tougher bunch, overall, than the TTPPA.

So I pulled out my upkeep file. I spread out all my figures on my desk, face-up, so that if they wanted to they could lean over and see them.

I pointed at my *heat* figures.

"You can see here," I said, "that Henny Penny paid out over seven hundred dollars in heat bills this last quarter alone. Now that's pretty hefty *heating*, I think you'll agree, I'm shocked to hear you saying you think Henny Penny would ever let a little tot go cold."

That silenced them right up. One or two of those up front sort of leaned over to glance at the heat file, but mostly they seemed quite willing to take my word for it. "You can rest assured," I told them, "that Henny Penny doesn't shirk on expenses. If seven hundred dollars is what it takes, then seven hundred dollars is what Henny Penny will pay."

There was some whispering in the back of the room. They went into a huddle back there and after a while I heard someone say, "Ask him about the toys. Why there ain't no toys."

"Yes sir," said the leader, "there's that too. We think it'd be nice, a real joy for the kiddies, if Henny Penny provided toys and equipment to keep the little folks busy. Seems every toy our boys and girls *bring*, well, they sort of disappear or they wind up in Mrs Shorts' lap. Mrs Shorts, she gets them and has *herself* a good time, but *our* kids, well, they are just left to cry out their eyes. Now that's painful for us, Mr Beacon, it's more than most of us can bear to see these little fellas and gals weeping their hearts out because Mrs Shorts is playing with the trucks or the dolls, what-have-you, and she won't *share!* That's what we mean by retarded. She's not all there, is what we mean."

I told them I could see their point. That I could see it and — if true — I was horrified. *Naturally* these little kids, here in their formative years, their important years, when their entire mental attitude and approach to life was being formed — here when they were at this sensitive age, their character being molded and all that, *naturally* they ought to have nice toys and equipment, *good* equipment, *safe* equipment, and all they wanted. "But look here," I said. And I tapped a finger on *that* file. "Look here. Henny Penny paid out — and I know it because I wrote the cheque myself — Henny Penny last month alone paid out thirteen hundred dollars for new toys and that Space-Age Ghost Rider machine! For stuffed animals, big bouncy balls, fire engines, Hootenanny Dolls, picture puzzles, colour books, and games — the whole shebang! So when you tell me we don't have any toys over at that school, why I'm alarmed!"

"Mrs Shorts broke that Ghost Rider thing," someone put in. "She hit it with a hammer, then put her foot through it!"

"I'm *alarmed*, I say, I certainly am, and I have to wonder where thirteen hundred dollars have got to. Now I know once in a while one of these sweet children in all innocence will stuff a nice new toy in its pocket and take it home, meaning of course to bring it back, but what you folks seem to be telling me is that something more organized than this is going on. Something more systematic, of the rip-off variety — something that looms as out-and-out *theft!* So you can be assured I and Mrs Shorts will give this matter our undivided attention!"

"That hammer," someone said, "she threw it at one of the children!"

"Yes, our undivided attention! That we can guarantee. We *will* get to the bottom of it, since I think you'll agree thirteen hundred dollars ain't hayseed, and, why, we'll just have to let the chips fall where they may, and if criminal charges are to be brought we will just have to bring them, without regard for race, sex, or family background. How's that? I hope you can see you've put me in a corner on this, and *action will have to be taken!*"

A few of those in the back started pushing and shoving and raising their voices, and pretty soon they all were, and it looked to me as if the whole business was about to get out of hand.

"What about the hammer!"

"The dirt!"

"Fist fights!"

"No treats!"

"Plopped down in front of the TV!"

"Ah!" I said, "the TV! Now hold it! Hold on! You can see right here that TV cost Henny Penny nine hundred dollars. Nine hundred. Nine hundred dollars don't grow on trees. It's an example of Henny Penny always providing the best. Nothing's too good for those tykes, that's Henny Penny motto. Quality first!"

"Only one channel works," said one loudmouth. "And no sound on it!"

"Hold it!" I shouted. "Now hold on! You're all adults, all parents, so I'd like to see some resemblance of order around here. Not everybody shouting at once. We can't expect our little folks to grow up with a proper perspective if the parents don't lay down a good example. So hold on!"

"I was opposed to that TV," one loudmouth said. "TV's stoopid."

But I got a few tentative apologies. Their leader was telling everyone to hush up. "First things first," he said. "Is Mrs Shorts retarded or isn't she?"

I rode in over them. "You know," I said, "if you don't like Henny Penny's outlook on child care and child-rearing, you can always withdraw your fine children and enroll them elsewhere. There is, for instance, that Howdy Powdy Nursery next door."

"But that's all boarded up," someone let out. "We thought that place had shut down *eons* ago."

"No," I said, "begging to correct you. Howdy Powdy is operating every day, every week of the year, seven o'clock till midnight, the same as we are. And doing quite well, by my understanding. I don't mind saying a nice word for the competition. Of course, they may be full up, I doubt you'd find a vacancy there just now, but fine by me if you want to grab your kid out of Henny Penny and throw them in Howdy Powdy."

"I've heard stories of that place," someone said. "Whippings and such."

"There used to be this nice place out on Willows Road," one said. "Any time of day you could ride by, see the kids laughing and playing, singing and such. Maybe we could put our kids there."

I could see the group getting all hepped up over that idea. I let it ferment a while. Then I jumped in: "Hold on!" I said. "Hold your horses. I remember that Willows Road place the same as you. A real lively, jumping place, full of the greatest kids in the world. But I hear tell it's been bought out. By a syndicate bunch. I hear tell it's got this tall barbed-wire fence around it now, with armed guards at the gate. Nope," I said. "Nope, it looks like for the moment there's just Howdy Powdy and us."

The leader spoke up again. She was a short, thick lady touching forty, I guessed, wearing thick eyeglasses and a gray business suit with a ceramic moose on the lapel, painted green and swirly. I'd had my eyes on that moose practically the whole time her group had been inside my office. My wife, before she ran off, had one exactly like it.

"We could start our own," she was saying. "With the fees we pay for Henny Penny we could in no time have the greatest little nursey ever hit this town. We could rent us a nice roomy house on a cheerful street, hire us three or four bright graduates from the childcare school, paint it up pretty, put in a nice playground! Why, it would be the greatest thing in the world for our little kids. They'd love it! We could make it their own little home, you know, just beautiful and clean!"

The discussion got heavy. I could see they were getting truly excited. They milled about my office, exchanging ideas, toting up figures, flashing smiles — making plans.

I raised my hand.

"Hold on," I said. "Just one dang minute. I'm not opposing your ideas in the least. It's a fine idea and I want to tell you that Henny Penny is behind you one hundred percent. We will give you all the advice and encouragement you need."

That quieted them down.

"Funny thing is," I said, "you are reminding me of my very own self, some fifty-three years ago, when I marched in here, head of a concerned parents' group just like yours. I demanded the situation improve at Henny Penny School. You won't believe it but in them times the plight of the little lads and lassies was truly sickening. A real sweatshop. Little three-year-olds making wallets. They knew nothing but misery. Whippings day in and day out. Typhoid, whooping cough, measles. A true dirt hole. But I and my then wife and some of the others, we decided to march. Get organized. We marched in here and laid down the law — to a Mr Magruder it was then, sitting behind this desk. Kill the rats, we said. Pull down the rotted trees. Cut the grass, burn out the snakes. Haul away the litter to the junk yard. Slap on a dab of paint. Put in a stove. Buy toys. Hire a nice worker. On and on we went, a list long as my arm.

"And Mr Magruder, he laughed. He laughed in our faces. 'Try it,' he said. 'Go ahead and try it. *You*,' he said, talking to me. '*You* take this chair. This desk. Here, take it,' he said, 'it's all yours. I give you one year. Maybe two. I give you as long as it takes you to get your kid out of short pants. Once your own kid has moved on, you're going to start forgetting about the rats. About the refuse. About the beatings. You're going to forget about it all. You're going to wish you could go somewhere where you could never see another little child through all of your born years. You're going to *hate* the darlin' little rascals. You're going to learn that these little brats, up to and including your own, are the ugliest, rottenest, stupidest, noisiest, most venal, selfish, hurtful, *dangerous* sonsofbitches ever put on this planet since God was himself an ape. And you're going to want to *hurt* them, to *menace* them, to *wreck* the little bastards while they're in knee pants, because you'll know that is the only chance you'll ever get. You're going to want to drive home the message once and for all that adults have lives too, that not *all* the world belong to these sniveling, bug-eyed, innocent, knock-kneed, big-eared fools.'

"That's what he told me and my wife. And we spat in his face. We said, 'Not me! We love kids. Kids are the hope of the universe and we never saw a bad kid yet.' My wife and I, we stood right on this spot, pointing the finger of accusation at him. 'So yes,' I said, 'I'll take that chair. Move your fat butt over.' And I took it. And I have been sitting here ever since. Fifty-three years I been sitting here. My wife too, at first. Then she took our little Johnny and ran off. Where to, God knows. Who cares. Now I am not going to tell you what Mr Magruder told me. I've got more respect for you than that. I want you to know I am on your side. Start your new nursery. Paint it blue. Put up your white picket fence. Call it Andy Pandy, Starky Larky, Monkey Funky.

Give it your best. No, I am not going to repeat Mr Magruder's words. All I am going to tell you is this. Mr Magruder told the truth. Yes, he was quoting the gospel. God help the miserable cur. For every day that knowledge has been killing me. Chiseling away my heart and soul. Paring me down. I was a Henny Penny kid myself, you see. Back in the old days when the sky was truly falling. I'm a Henny Penny graduate, member of the very first class. The last surviving member of that class, I'd suppose. I owe all I am today to Henny Penny. Good old Henny Penny. Three cheers for Henny Penny. God knows where I'd gone, what I'd be today, without it."

In the Garden

The woman — the one who stands here at her apartment windows in her blue stockings and blue shoes and a blue raincoat that hangs to her heels — the woman up here behind her windows high over the city's wayward slopes (Oh snow, oh hoary winter's drool!) and over the murky green waters (Needs stirring, I'll say) of Fisherman's Bay . . . is thinking: *What next? What to do with myself today that can be half the fun yesterday was?*

"Life *calls!*" she suddenly trumpets, surprised herself by the sound of her voice and by all the joy that, like a grinning lunatic, has leapt inside her. (I'm happy as a tick, one might conclude I've been drinkin'.)

She carefully puts down her glass.

"Eleven A.M.," she gloats, "all's well."

She steps out on her narrow balcony, shivering (Merciless winter, oh sweetjesus will spring never come?), bending low and dangerously over the railing to peer inside the recessed sliding doors of the apartment below.

Feet, feet, she thinks, that's all I've ever seen. Shine your shoes, Mister-Man-Down-There.

No feet today, however. The glass needs cleaning and he ought to throw out those two dying ferns.

"I'll call Estelle," she says. "My good friend Estelle."

Do *do* call Estelle, give the little lady a fine thrill.

But Estelle, it turns out (Dear me, I've split my britches), is not home. (Not in? At this hour? What is that elfin horror trying to prove?)

So Rebecca — woman by the window — goes back to the window and again looks out over the close-rippling water (Ten years in this place and I've yet to see a fisherman there, only boats and more boats, teensy putt-putts, you'd think civilized people would have better things to do) — looks out over the city slopes to the high, snowy mountains beyond (Oh fold upon fold upon fold, tedious and exhausting, but rather exquisite; yes, I *do* like it, this is such a friendly part of the world).

Oh, she thinks, what *can* I have been thinking of!

Of course.

She goes into her bedroom and takes her time selecting a nice scarf from her dresser drawer, something in a fetching complimentary blue —

"Yes, this one I think," and ties the silk loosely about her throat.

"Now I'm so pretty," she remarks aloud, "I am pretty enough to *sing sing sing!* And why not, while I'm at it, telephone Estelle?"

Estelle's phone — can you believe it? — rings and rings.

But Rebecca — following a crow's black flight across the bay (Oh look at him swerve and dive, if only I could fly like that!) — is not fooled. Oh, she's *home*, she thinks. Certainly she's home. Where else could she be but at home!

In one of her moods, possibly.

Mustn't discount her elfish moods.

One of her I-don't-want-to-see-anyone days. Doubtlessly nursing old grudges by the tonne. Got the brush-off from Harold, could be. Oh, the poor little downtrodden bird.

"None of your business," Rebecca tells herself. "Honey, you stay out of this."

She laughs. Estelle is so funny when she's in her moods. No, one can't help laughing.

A fruitcake, that's what Estelle is on her rainy-day days.

"No way out of it," Rebecca says. "I'd better shoot right over."

* * *

A swarm of gnats — fruit flies, she supposes (Genus *Drosophila*, diptera, transparent of mind and wing, oh go away, gnats!) — hangs in the air just short of Estelle's door, which swarm Rebecca steers straight through, thinking surely they will scatter. But they come right along with her, a net of floating black dots. They swirl about, an inch up, an inch down, untouched, as she swats. "Shoo, shoo!" she says, "oh, scat!" Finally she wades through, knocks on Estelle's bright red door.

All the curtains drawn, house sealed up tight. Estelle, honey, is it as bad as all that?

"Yoo-hoo! It's me!"

She can hear music playing over the stereo — or radio — something classical. Harpsichordish, may be. Old Worldish anyway.

Estelle being *grand*.

Grim *church* music to aid and abet the foul downspin.

"Let me in *at once*, darling!"

The door opens an inch and no more. The chain remains in place.

"Why have you kept me waiting here for so long?" Rebecca says. "You should do something about this plague of wild gnats."

All she can see of her friend Estelle is one eye in the crack. She appears to have a bandage of some sort half-covering it.

"Go *away*," whispers Estelle.

"But I've walked miles," replies Rebecca, not worried in the least by such rudeness. Ooo-la-la, that's Estelle. "My feet hurt. It isn't easy in these high heels. I've probably got a blister, if you want to know. Anyway, I've got to talk to you. It's imperative. You *are* my best friend."

The door quietly closes.

Uncanny. Oh Estelle, why are you treating me this way?

She can hear Estelle's footsteps across the floor, something clattering down (Temper, temper, oh what a temper she has!) — then the music coming on again, bit louder this time, some kind of silly piano piece, like four birds chirping from a high fence.

* * *

Rebecca swatted at the gnats. "Shoo!" she said. "Shoo! Oh, rats! . . ." She walked slowly out to the street, her head down. At the curb she turned and regarded Estelle's house most pensively. (Drab, Estelle, very drab. Most shoddy.) The house was indeed drab, small and low-slung, like a Crackerjacks box down on its side, and ridiculous with its red door.

Rebecca patted one foot against the pavement. She knotted the scarf tighter against her throat.

Poor Estelle, she thought, how *can* I cheer her up?

She wondered if any of the other people in their houses along the street were watching her. I certainly should be, she thought. I would *continue the investigation* until I knew precisely what was going on. Who *is* that woman? I'd ask myself. What can she *possibly* want? Or, if I were another woman watching me, I'd think: where could she have *found* that beautiful blue coat!

I'd smoke, that's what I'd do. I'd light up a lovely blue cigarette, oh I'd have a killing-good taste of the weed.

I will anyway.

No, no, children might be watching.

An old man, four houses down, was out in his driveway washing his car. Rebecca studied him. Wouldn't it be pleasant, and a nice thing to do, to go and talk to him?

". . . I was dropping in on my friend up the street," she said, speaking from a distance of several dozen yards, "but she does not appear to be receiving."

The man, less old than she had presumed, was down on his knees sudsing a hubcap; he did not look up.

"Her name is E. Beverly Sims," Rebecca went on, drawing closer. "She lives in that flat house with the scrawny box hedge by the front porch. I'm sure you must know her well. Estelle is the very outgoing type, and she has a splendid figure. In a nice friendly neighbourhood such as this one is everyone must know everyone."

The man, she now observed, stepping up beside him, had a pokey face and practically no hair. He was chewing on the nub of a cigar while squinting up at her. She admired his way of sitting on his heels.

"Where I live it is not the least like that. I live in a small but very efficient apartment down by the Bay. A condominium. You wouldn't believe what it cost. I'm way up on the twelfth floor, and can see for miles.

Do you know that huge ships pass my window at night? Far out, of course. But I have a large telescope mounted on a nice tripod. I am continuing my investigation of these ships. It's easily the most interesting hobby I ever had."

"I'm washing this car," the man grumbled.

Rebecca realized that the remark was somehow meant to put her in her place. She laughed.

"I can *see* that. It must have been extremely dirty."

This comment clearly interested him. He rose up off his haunches, backed up a few paces, lit his cigar, and stared appreciatively at the automobile.

"It *was* filthy," he said. "My son had let this car go to the dogs." He spat, very close to his feet, and backed up a bit more. "They tell me young boys like nothing better than sharp cars to show off with the girls, but I give this car to my son and he has not yet got behind the wheel once."

"Oh my," said Rebecca. "That is curious behavior indeed."

Soap suds all along the car side were drying in the sun. But the man seemed more interested in the hubcap. He stooped beside it, buffing up the chrome with his sleeve. "Of course, he doesn't have his license yet. I give this car to him for his sixteenth birthday, but he has some months to go." He peered up at Rebecca. "Do you know Harold?"

"Your son? No, I —"

"You wouldn't like him. He is the most stuck-up boy I ever saw. Something of a sissy, too, you want to know the truth. Bet you can't guess why."

"Hormones, I bet," said Rebecca. "I bet his hormones got sent straight up a tree."

"Not hormones," he said. "His mother. His mother has pampered the little rat since the day he was born." He paused, flipping his cigar in the dirt. Then he walked over and ground at it with his heel. "He is out now at Symphony School. Harold. He plays the oboe." He picked up the cigar, examining its mangled leaves between his fingers. "This cigar," he said, "it's real Havana. I got a pal sends them to me from Canada. Real cold up there. I got maybe twenty, twenty-five these rascals left." He spread the tobacco out in his palm and poked at it with a finger. "Real beauties, these cigars. I bet they cost my buddy a mint. But he owes me. He owes me a fortune, tell you the truth. You know why?"

Rebecca batted her eyes. "Why?" she asked. It had struck her that this man was somewhat *odd*.

"Because I stole his wife. I stole her right out from under his nose. One day there he was, married to the prettiest woman you ever saw, and the next day she wasn't there anymore. She liked me best, you see. I had the real goods but Ralph — old Ralph — well, old Ralph didn't have *nothing* and the next thing he knew he was out in the cold. Yep, between the two of us we really put it to him."

Rebecca considered this. She wasn't sure she liked it.

"Happy?" the man said. "You never saw two people so happy as the wife and me. Regular lovebirds." He shot a hasty look at Rebecca. "Then we had Harold. Beginning of the end."

Rebecca laughed. That phrase had always been one of her favourites.

"You probably know what I mean," he said. "Kids! Look at Job. He had a house full of kids, but what good did they ever do him? Only more misery."

Rebecca felt that she had been silent far too long. She thought it only right that she should point out *there was another side*.

"You would not think that," she told him lightly, "if you were in India, or in Greece, or even in Japan. Suppose you were in China and believed as you do? At the minimum, you'd be ostracized, and probably you'd be shot."

"Fine by me," he replied. "If I had to live in those places I'd *want* to be shot."

Rebecca walked over to the concrete steps leading up to the front door and sat down, crossing her legs prettily. She lit up a cigarette with her gold lighter and closed her eyes, holding her head back, blowing out the first draw of smoke in a long, measured stream.

"Nobody told you to sit there," the man reproached her. "This is private property." He seemed suddenly very angry.

". . . But sit there if you want to. What the hell, who ever listens to me?"

"I'm sure you've a very strong character," said Rebecca. "I'm sure you must dominate any circle you enter."

He puzzled over this a moment, then, shrugging, dropped down on his ankles again and began scrubbing the rear hubcap, his back to Rebecca. She noticed for the first time the baseball cap stuffed into his pocket. She found this intriguing, a strongly personal touch. She wondered what kind of hat he would have stuffed there had he been born in India. She found it charming, where men put their hats. He looked so round and full, stooped like that, a complete little world, total to the point even of where he put his hat. She smiled. She liked the way he bobbed up and down on his ankles, how his heels lifted up out of his shoes; his little grunts, too, were very charming. She could see an expanse of pink skin and now his underpants — swatch of black polka dots — rode up over his hips. She wondered if he would be interested in hearing what she had read about Babe Ruth — not so long ago that she had forgotten — in *The New Columbia Encyclopedia*. Sixty homers, imagine that. And born of people so rag-tail poor he had to be sent away to a training school, made to sweep floors for his daily bread. A pitcher, too. Eighty-seven wins in five years, now that was true pitching, that was real horseshoes.

She became aware after a while that the man was watching her out of the corners of his eyes.

She took off one shoe and held it above her head, shaking it as if to dislodge pebbles. But secretly she watched him.

He dropped his sponge into the sudsy bucket, spinning on his heels. His jacket was wet up to the elbows. "Harold's brother now," he announced sullenly, "he's another case. Been begging me for a car for years, but I wouldn't give him the time of day, not even if he got down on bended knee."

Rebecca nodded. "He must have done something extremely reprehensible," she said.

The man gave her a blank look, then shook his head. "Not *my* son," he explained darkly. "No, Norman's the *wife's* son. I keep telling him he ought to go off live with his real father, but he just whines 'Aw, Dad.' Can't even wipe his nose." He picked up his bucket and went around to suds up the grille.

"Estelle is like that, too," Rebecca said.

The man hiked up his pants. He looked off at the closed windows of his house and over at a stunted, leafless tree at the edge of his yard. "That friend of yours," he said gruffly, ". . . that Estelle, she's moved out, you know. That place is *empty* now. No, you'll waste your time knocking on *that* door."

Rebecca decided to let this pass, and the man dropped back down to his bucket. "I wouldn't give ten cents," he grumbled, "to know anybody on this block. Including your long-gone friend."

Rebecca ignored all this. "Beverly was her maiden name," she told him. "She married a man named Sims when she was twenty-eight, and although that union lasted only a short time she and Mr Sims remain good friends to this day." She smiled mischievously. "Nowadays Estelle has other interests, I understand. She's in love."

"Spit," he said.

"Actually, she's feverish about this particular gentleman, but I have reason to believe the relationship is undergoing its difficult moments."

"Pa-tooey," the man said.

"I'm sure you must have seen him. He drives an orange Toyota."

At this the man perked up. He wheeled about, pointing to a spot on the street vaguely in front of Estelle's house. "Orange?" he said. Rebecca took this to mean that he had seen the car in question parked out in front of Estelle's house through nights too numerous to mention.

"They may be good cars," he said gruffly, "but only a traitor would buy one." He smacked a flat, wet hand against the top of his own automobile. "I've seen him," he said. "He wears a hat."

This news tantalized Rebecca. She had never seen Estelle's lover wearing a chapeau of any sort. She stood up now. She had smoked her cigarette and had her visit and was now ready to leave.

"Where you going?" the man asked her.

She smiled, surprised. "Why, I don't know," she said. "I haven't thought about it."

He strode past her to the side of the house, beckoning. "Come inside," he grumbled. "Something to show you. I bought my son a .22 for his birthday. I've got it on a gun rack in the den. I don't suppose you shoot, being a woman — my wife *hates* it — but what I say is if Harold doesn't go out and shoot something with it the very minute he turns sixteen I'm going to throw him out of the house." He shoved his hands deep into his jacket pockets, scowling back at Rebecca who was lingering. "It beats me," he said, "why women don't like hunting. And fishing. There is not anything more fun than that. Character-building, too. My old man had me out on the marsh with a rifle in my arms before I was two years old. Women! I'll tell you about women. Women have got themselves into this trouble out of their own choosing. They deserve everything they get. Bunch of fools, if you ask me. Silliest thing on two feet. Look at you, for instance. All sky-baby-blue in that silly raincoat and those silly shoes. Well, it's *feminine* all right, but that's all I can say for it."

Rebecca laughed, a low breasty chuckle that brightened her face. She loved insults. She wished he'd say something else — perhaps about her hair or her nice scarf or her blue pocketbook. She wished he'd put on his funny little cap.

"Come on," he ordered. "Want to show you that gun."

Rebecca was tempted. Few things pleased her more than seeing how other people lived. She could imagine herself inside browsing through his cupboards, checking out cereal boxes, opening the refrigerator door to read out the brand names on frozen foods. But she'd been looking at Estelle's house; she was certain she'd seen the front curtain move. "No thank you," she said. "Perhaps another time. I'm often in the neighbourhood."

"Buzz off then," he said. "Who asked you? I got better things to do."

* * *

The gnats had moved on from Estelle's door. They were now up around the telephone wire where it entered the house, a larger body now, black patch silently lifting and falling, swaying, against the clear blue sky.

"It's me again," Rebecca called, knocking.

The house was silent. Four or five rolled newspapers were on the ground beneath the hedge, soiled and wet, further indication to Rebecca that Estelle's love life had reached the cut-throat stage.

"I've brought you your reading matter!" she shouted, bent at the keyhole, thinking she detected shadowy movement inside.

"I'll huff and I'll puff!" she called. "Stand back!" Estelle didn't respond. A tomb.

* * *

The back of the house was deserted, too. Curtains were drawn over the windows, and a beautiful spider web had been spun over the upper portion of the door. Crumpled newspaper filled a hole down in the corner of one cracked window. Under the roof line stretched a series of old hornets' nests, or dirt-daubers' sturdy quarters. The garbage can was overturned, but empty. A rusty barbecue stand was down on its side in the tall grass. Numerous tin cans and milk cartons lay about; a huge cardboard box had been flattened by the rain.

Rebecca took her time contemplating the debris, seated in a white metal chair out near where a composting fixture once had stood. She smoked, and pitched her head back to catch the sunshine. She would have been happy if only she had a drink to sip on.

Gloves, she thought. Why haven't I bought myself a pair of nice blue gloves?

The silence of the place fascinated her. She realized she was genuinely enjoying this.

A large fluffy cat, golden in color, hopped up on the picnic table in the neighbouring yard. It took turns idly scrutinizing her and, just as idly, licking its fur.

"Gin," said Rebecca. "Gin and tonic, I think."

And she stayed on another ten minutes or so, enjoying the invisible drink.

Someone not far away was calling. A woman's fragile, unhurried voice repeating: "*Oro!... Oro!... Come home, Oro.*" Very musical, Rebecca thought.

A breeze played gently across her face, further subduing her mood, and she let herself drift along in a sweet, dreamy doze, seeing the world before her as though through a haze in which all things moved in tranquil, harmonic order, pleasant and kind.

The sun dropped down rays thick as a lattice fence, golden and alluring.

What splendour, she thought. I could be in someone's enchanted garden.

* * *

Afterwards, drawing the blue collar up against her neck, feeling somewhat chilled, she stepped again up to Estelle's rear window. She rapped on the glass, looking for a peephole through the curtains.

"Estelle? Estelle, darling, please open the door."

She heard a quick catch of breath within and could feel Estelle's presence on the other side of the wall.

"It's lovely out here, it truly is. You should come out and talk to me. He hasn't hurt you, has he?" She heard a whisper of footsteps, the creak of floorboards, and beat her knuckles sharply against the window. "Oh don't be unhappy!" she pleaded. "Please let me in. He isn't worth this pining, Estelle . . ."

The floor creaked again.

A cat squawked somewhere in the neighbourhood, much as if someone were repeatedly pulling its tail.

Rebecca stiffened; she shivered. She whipped her head around, certain that someone had stolen up and was about to hit her on the head.

No . . .

A very old man with an enormous stomach, wearing a checkered shirt and carrying his shoes in his hands, was out on the steps next door, watching her. He leaned against the door frame, putting on one shoe. Then he leaned the opposite way and put on the other.

"I think she's left that place," he said. "I think she moved out four, five days ago."

Rebecca smiled at him.

The man backed up, slowly withdrawing into the house.

Nearby, someone was singing, or perhaps it was a radio.

Rebecca stared a moment at the dusty, faded newspaper stuffed into the window crack. "I've got my troubles too, Estelle," she said. "My phone rings every night. It's that man I told you about. He refuses to let up. Every night I think, 'Well, tonight he's going to threaten me' . . . but he never quite does. He's extremely cunning. What do I do, Estelle?"

When Estelle didn't answer, Rebecca went up on tiptoe and tugged the stiff paper free. Then she went up again on tiptoe, straightening her arm, and poked her hand into the small opening. She worked her hand past the jagged glass and past the curtain edge and thrust her arm deeper into the room. It felt cold, very cold, in there.

Something brushed or cut or struck against her flesh and with a faint cry of pain, of fear, she snatched back her arm. Shards of glass tinkled down, her heel twisted in the uneven dirt, and she stumbled back, holding in her breath; she staggered, banged one knee against dirt, then lost her balance totally and landed gracelessly on one hip.

Dizzily, she got to her feet. Her coat sleeve was torn, scar in the blue fabric scarcely larger than a dime; a straight line of blood was popping up in droplets across the back of her hand. It stung.

"You've cut me, Estelle," she said, her voice calm, amazed.

She had a clear vision of Estelle inside the cold room, pressed against the wall, eyes slitted, knife poised, waiting for her again to poke her arm through.

But she wasn't sure. It could have been the glass.

She licked the line clean, hastily pulled free her scarf, and wrapped it around her hand.

"That was uncalled-for, Estelle. That was very mean."

She drew back, watching the window.

"But I forgive you."

At the corner of the house she turned, calling again.

"I know you're not yourself today. I really wish you'd let me help you."

* * *

She went once more to the front of the house and sat down on Estelle's stoop, brooding on this turn of events.

No, the fault wasn't Estelle's. The fault was Arnold's.

She unfolded one of the newspapers. The moisture had soaked through and the sheet had to be peeled apart. Displayed across the front page was a photograph of Nureyev leaping, his legs flung wide, bare buttocks to the camera, arrow pointing to where his tights had ripped. DANCER SHOWS TRUE FORM, the caption read. But Rebecca shivered at the black headlines. Shivered, and let her head swoop down against the page. 58 DIE IN BLOODBATH . . . OIL RIG GOES DOWN OFF NEWFOUNDLAND, NO SURVIVORS . . . WARSAW ERUPTS.

Yes, she thought, and my mother is dead, my husband has left me, I have no children, hardly any life, and no one knows anything at all — or cares! — about poor Rebecca.

But when her head came up she was ruefully smiling.

Yes, all true, she thought, but we shall continue the investigation.

She turned, peering through Estelle's keyhole.

"Peace Promised for One Zillion Years!" she shouted. "Happiness Lays Golden Egg! . . . Man Steps in Pothole, Breaks Leg!"

She removed the scarf from her hand and closely observed the wound. "Nineteen Stitches Required!" she called. "Noted Plastic Surgeon Called In! . . . Lady Recovers from Heartless Attack!"

The tear in the coat bothered her more. She wondered whether a good seamstress could save the day.

A boy was approaching, yet some distance down the street, slouching, his hands deep into his pockets, small black case tucked up under one arm, his face white as plaster in the sunlight.

Harold.

The man who had been washing the car was no longer in the yard, nor was the car. A woman now stood out in front of the house, arms crossed over her chest. She was looking past Rebecca at the dawdling boy. She wore a print dress, too bold for her thick figure; the hem hung unevenly and the grass cut off her legs. She called wanly to the boy:

"Harold! Harold! He hit me, Harold!"

Harold stopped. Now nearly abreast of Estelle's house, he looked not at his mother but at Rebecca coolly watching from the stoop.

"You don't live there," he said to her. "That place is deserted."

Rebecca loved this frontal approach. He was sullen, nasty even, but she wanted to reach out and hug him. He was abusive, yes, but it seemed to her that those who were most insulting were also those who most willingly offered enthusiastic praise.

"What's that under your arm?" she asked him. "Is that an oboe?"

The boy's face clouded. He kicked a shoe against the pavement, standing with his body bent like a quarter moon.

"I wish you'd play for me," Rebecca said. "I haven't heard an oboist play really well in years."

"Who are you?" he growled. "What are you doing in our neighbourhood?"

"*Harold! He hit me, Harold*," called his mother.

The boy put his case on the sidewalk and, crouching, took the instrument from it, polishing the bulbous end on his sleeve.

"I give the pitch to the whole orchestra," he said, standing, glaring at Rebecca.

He blew a strong, high note, which then seemed to falter — but the note came back stronger, more penetrating, thin, only a little plaintive, and it intensified and kept on coming.

"*Harold!*" called the mother. "*He really hit me hard.*"

His mother now stood at the edge of her yard, her hands twisting around the narrow trunk of a leafless tree.

The boy scowled at Rebecca. "Sure, I could play," he said. "But I won't. Harold only plays for money."

Rebecca nodded doubtfully, her thoughts drifting, watching the swarm of gnats at the side of the house, hovering a few feet above the scraggly grass.

"You're a very good-looking boy," Rebecca said. "I'll bet you must be every inch of six feet tall."

"*He hurt me, Harold!*"

The boy came up and sat down on the stoop beside Rebecca.

"I'm very advanced for my age," he told her. "I'm very unusual. In fact, I'm eccentric."

"Well, it is a strange neighbourhood," she said.

"Not that strange. The woman who lived here — what was her name?"

"Estelle."

"Estelle was strange. I saw her one night out back of this house, practically naked — in a flowing gown, I mean — down on her knees in front of that chair she's got back there, bowing and bowing, like an Arab. *That's* strange.*"*

Rebecca smiled. "Not if you know Estelle," she replied softly.

Across the way his mother advanced a few paces, her footsteps weighted, as if deep holes were opening in front of her. When she saw them looking at her she backed up, returning hastily to the tree.

The boy moistened the mouthpiece, allowed his head to settle deep between his shoulders, then played several quick, rather piercing, notes. "Listen to this," he said.

He closed his eyes.

He played.

When the last lingering note faded, Rebecca, only now opening her eyes, clapped enthusiastically. "Oh God," she sighed, genuinely moved. "You're going to be immortal."

The boy stretched out one hand, palm upwards.

"I'm bleeding, Harold!" his mother called.

Rebecca opened her purse. She looked thoughtfully at her bills, then unsnapped her change purse, and dropped two quarters into his hand.

The boy stared glumly at the coins. "What can this buy?" he asked.

"Happiness," Rebecca said. And she smiled in a bewitched way, as if indeed it had.

The boy walked away, pointing with his instrument to the swarm of gnats.

"Those gnats are mating," he said.

At his yard he turned and went on past his mother without a word and entered the house and a few seconds later she left the tree and scooted in after him.

Rebecca leaned back against Estelle's door. "The music was lovely, wasn't it?" she said. "I wonder where such genius comes from."

It seemed to her that from inside the house there came a whispery, half-strangled *yes!*

Rebecca stayed on, pursuing stray thoughts as they popped into her head. Harold's music, unquestionably very beautiful, had put the

Garden of Eden into her mind. A kind of dreamy, springtime garden. Yet now several hundred men, no larger than bees, were erecting a barbed-wire fence around the place.

She laughed. How silly.

"A blight has hit the garden," she said.

Men with rifles were up sniping from their towers. *Plunk plunk plunk!* Bullets stirred up soft puffs of dust in the arid soil.

Off in the corner, darkened, the Tree of Knowledge hunkered down, like a rat gone fat from too much wine and cheese. The bullets went on plunking.

Plunk plunk plunk!

Rebecca giggled. It's absurd, she thought, but what can be done about it?

"*Aim over their heads,*" a voice said. "*We don't want to harm anyone.*"

Rebecca's heart caught. She recognized that voice.

"*Well, one or two,*" God said, "*as an example.*"

Two or three hundred of the small bee people began to fall. They rolled down into the grass, kicked and lay still, or they screamed and went limp, snagged on the wire.

Plunk plunk plunk!

Rebecca leaped up, throwing her hands over her eyes. "Estelle," she said, "I've just had the most awful vision!" She knocked again on Estelle's door, and kicked at it, and put her eye against the keyhole, and for a moment believed she saw another eye looking back — but then decided this was nonsense, since Estelle lacked any such curiosity. No, Estelle, after such a busy day, would be spread out on her bed, damp cloth across her brow, claiming headaches, claiming troubles, agony too painful to mention.

I too was once like that, Rebecca thought. I believed I didn't have a friend in the world.

Like something shoved over the edge . . . and still falling.

But she had learned better long ago. People valued her. Friends were ever eager to see her. They let her know without any guile or trickery — without any reservations whatsoever — that their doors were always open.

"*Any time, Rebecca. For you we are always home.*"

She brushed off the seat of her raincoat, fluffed her hair, and started towards the street. "I'm going now!" she called. ". . . Take care of yourself! . . . Enjoyed visiting! . . . See you tomorrow!"

Maybe. Maybe she would see her tomorrow.

At any moment she expected to see Estelle yanking open the door, flinging herself down the path, embracing and pulling her back.

"Chin up, darling! . . . Accept no wooden nickels!"

But the red door remained firmly shut.

She wondered what Harold would be doing. Where Arnold would be in his orange Toyota.

What next? Who to see?

She'd go home first, laze around a bit. Have a quiet smoke, perhaps a nice gin and tonic. Watch the big, distant ships hulking ever so silently by on Fisherman's Bay. Watch the fog — watch darkness — descend slowly over the water.

Think this matter through.

Continue the investigation.

Wy Wn Ty Calld
Your Nam You
Did Not Answr

Marucha was six when she decided she would no longer employ the eighth letter of the alphabet either in writing or in speech.

"Wy?" asked her father, Huidobro, in his woodshed hard at work with hammer and chisel on his newest pig. "I don't compreend."

"Very good, Uidobro," said the girl. "You can see ow muc fun it will be."

"Wat if you fall in te river and must call for elp?"

"I will call '*Elp! Elp! Elp!*' and you will bring me to safety."

"Fine," said Huidobro. "But I am apreensive."

The child's mother Astrada, when it was her turn to be informed, was not instantly amused.

"Go aead, toug," she said, "if you must be a lunatic, because wat am I in tis ouse but a mop and pail?"

At her prayers that night Marucha said to God, "God, tis is Maruca Figueroa Jotamaria of eigty eigt Calle Noces de la Mil Lunas in te village of El Flores, Micoacan, Mexico, putting te bug in your ear once again. Save my sister Gongora Azurdia from furter umiliation on te sow-grounds and see tat Uidobro's soes are polised and please do someting about my moter's air."

That day Gongora Azurdia had fallen from the thoroughbred Egoro on the fifth jump and was now in the bed beside Marucha, covered in nasty bruises, one arm on a white board elevated from her hip by a metal rod.

"And pray God in te morning you will assure good fortune to us all."

"Stop tat talking to eaven," her father shouted from his own bed.

"I am sorry you do not like my air," shouted the girl's mother, who that very day had been a guinea pig at the Estrella de Oro Beautician's School. "Doesn't anyone like my air?"

"*Elp! Elp! Elp!*" shouted Marucha, and in an instant Huidobro was by her bedside conveying a glass of water.

In the night the girl dreamed that the "h" was a comet whirling the heavens, mad as could be for having been forsaken, and it was decided in her sleep that "E" was a letter of similar inconsequence.

Thus at breakfast the following morning, when Huidobro asked what Marucha would like to eat, the words that poured from her mouth made no immediate sense.

"I will at a ors," she said. "I will at a lim or a jalapna pppr or drink juic until I pop."

Mother and father stopped what they were doing.

Each patted a foot, waiting for Marucha to continue.

"I don't know wat I will at," she finally said. "Unlss you av somting trrific for m to at it may vry wll b tat I will at noting. Wat ar you ating?"

Mother and father suddenly beamed, clapping their hands together.

Her sister Gongora Azurdia sat stiff at the table with her arm elevated from her hip on the white board.

She was not happy to be in this family.

"I wish someone would tell me what is going on," she said.

The previous day she had pitched right over the stallion Egoro's head into a muddy pool of water.

"I wis somon would tll m wat is going on?" quoted Marucha Figueroa Jotamaria.

The parents had slept well; they felt uncommonly rejuvenated this morning. Huidobro had arisen early and in his woodshed with hammer and chisel had finished work on his newest pig. The pig now sat grandly on a fifth chair drawn up to the table like a regular member of the family.

The Huidobro pigs were famous throughout the region. Every village in the mountains where they lived had to have its Huidobro pig.

"I fl uncommonly good tis morning," said Huidobro.

"Tis as gon far noug," Marucha's mother said. "If no on is willing to improv rlationsips in tis ous tn as usual I must myslf pick up th gauntlt."

Huidobro kissed his wife on the lips.

"You ar t most fascinating woman I av vr known," he said. "I lov you madly"

"W all lov ac otr madly." Marucha said.

Her sister was in the act of writing something on the white board elevating her arm.

"Wat ar you doing?" the others asked.

She had been writing, 'Of all the animals in the animal kingdom I like horses best.' But she had written this in letters invisible to everyone but herself.

She would hereafter speak invisibly as well, since no one in this house ever paid the smallest attention to her.

"I am going out now," she said, rising from the table.

The other three looked at her with blank faces. "Did somon spak?" asked Huidobro.

"I tink it was t wind," said Astrada.

"I saw r lips mov," said Marucha.

At the doorway Gongora Azurdia turned, looking back at her parents and her impossible little sister.

They were chattering away at her empty chair.

"Wat did s say?" she heard Marucha ask?

"I don't know," said her mother. "Wr did s go? S is always disapparing witout a word to anyon. You would tink s wantd to liv wit tos stupid orss."

"On of ts days," she heard Huidobro say, tilting back in his chair, "I man to gt to t bottom of tis affair. I guarant to you all tat I will discovr ow s pulls ts disapparing acts."

"I op s dosn't try riding wit tat arm," said Astrada.

Marucha was no longer listening. She was eating as fast as she could. There was much to get done this day, in her view, and already it was getting old.

Huidobro had not yet eaten even a crumb, and wouldn't now, because Astrada was busy stashing away every little morsel of food.

Gongora Azurdia, fully invisible, was racing as fast as she could to
the stables.

Later, everyone in the village was struck dumb with amazement to
see that devil horse, Egoro, galloping one way and another, jumping
everything in sight, sometimes even their own crouched and trembling
figures.

As for Marucha, she had decided to abandon all letters of the alphabet. She filled the house with silence, which proved a great comfort to
everyone.

WHY AGNES LEFT

The woman with no hair has gone home. The body stocking woman has gone home. Agnes has gone. Everyone has gone home and so should I.

You should go home, my hostess Sulvie tells me. What are you waiting for? Everyone left hours ago, and Zephyr and I would like to get some sleep.

Zephyr adds her two cents.

The place is all cleaned up, no one would ever guess that a few short hours ago twenty-seven women were here talking, laughing, having a gay old time.

The place *looks* empty. Its emptiness has permeated my bones, brought me close to tears. It reminds me of a play on closing night when all the beautiful walls come down. Vanishing life. There and then gone.

Zephyr's two cents amount to this:

You should go home, Mr Banks. We don't know you all this well and in any event Sulvie and I don't allow men to stay overnight.

It isn't that so much, says Sulvie. We have no place to put you. The sofa isn't at all comfortable. You'd catch a cold sleeping on the floor.

Yes, says Zephyr. You'll have to go. Please leave.

It's true, I really must. I have no right to inflict my presence on these two no-nonsense, straightforward women.

Zephyr stands with my overcoat held high to receive my arms. Sulvie extends my hat. I slip my arms into the coat and button up. I put on the hat. A moment later, however — I can't explain it — I am again sitting down.

One more cigarette, I say. Let me finish this and I promise I'll get out of your hair.

Zephyr explodes. *God!* — and stalks off to slam a door.

Sulvie, too, is no longer content to reason with me. *Get out!* she all but screams. My patience is exhausted! Get out this minute!

I drag on the cigarette. They have removed all the ashtrays and I have to thump my ashes into the palm of my hand.

It was a lovely party, I tell her. One of the best I've been to in years.

She smoulders.

I'm amazed that you two could so quickly clean up the place. What a lot of mess!

She mushes a pillow into a chair. I'm not talking to you, Mr Banks. We have asked you nicely to leave. You refuse. You don't frighten us, if that's what you're thinking. Not at all. You have about five seconds, then Zephyr and I are going to physically throw you out.

No need for that, I say. Just let me have this last cigarette.

You said that an hour ago.

Was it really that long?

Her nostrils flare. Her face has changed colour, gone a deep red.

Zephyr re-enters, drawing the cord on a long blue velvet robe. She has very pretty feet, I notice.

I've called the police, she announces. If you want to avoid spending the night in jail you'd best pack yourself off this minute.

Sulvie has decided to cry. Zephyr tells her to stop snivelling, there is absolutely nothing to warrant tears. I am an oaf, she tells her, but I will be gone soon.

She's only tired, I say. She will feel better in a minute.

They glare at me. Both women have spent all day preparing for the party, no doubt, and they are obviously exhausted.

I am, too, for that matter. I must be. Otherwise, I would not find myself in this awkward situation.

My palm is quite full of ashes. I look about for a place to put them.

The two women watch. Zephyr taps her foot. They are quite certain my ashes shall at any second despoil their vacuumed sky blue carpet.

I slide the ashes into my side pocket. I pinch out the cigarette and drop it inside as well.

You're finished, Zephyr says. She opens the door and stands beside it.

Just let me wipe my hands, I say. I stand. Would it trouble you too much, I ask, if I had a glass of water?

Sulvie screams. Zephyr rushes over to comfort her.

I go in and draw a glass of water from the kitchen tap. Dishes are piled up on the drain-board. The counter and the twin sinks have been wiped clean. The entire kitchen sparkles.

Suddenly Zephyr is behind me, asking what I think I am doing.

Oh, I thought I'd help out, I say. Put away a few dishes, the two of you have worked so hard. It was a lovely dinner you served, by the way. Don't know if I mentioned it before.

Zephyr snatches a golden serving tray from my hand. *Out!* she yells. *Get out of here!* The dish clatters down.

Sorry, I say. Didn't mean to offend.

I thump out another cigarette, heading out into the living room in front of her.

Sulvie, on the sofa, has her head buried under several pillows. I flop down into the nearest chair.

Won't be a second, I say. Just let me finish this.

Sulvie looks up, is horrified, then again buries her head. Zephyr leans against the sofa back, snarling to herself.

Go on with whatever it is you have to do, I suggest. Don't mind me.

Neither replies.

I make a stab at explaining this business of the cigarette. When I was very young, I tell them, I made a vow to myself never to smoke on the streets. A lot of people do, I think. At home, driving, at a restaurant, at these places okay, but never on the street. It's one way of controlling the habit, you see.

Sulvie, without looking at me, got up and left the room. A few seconds later I heard water running in the bath.

Zephyr approached, stopping directly in front of me. If you don't leave, she said, her teeth clenched, I'm going to kill you. I swear I will, I am not joking.

I could see she wasn't.

She held the robe collar clenched under her neck. Her eyes were hard and blazing. Her skin was very white, all the make-up scrubbed off. Her hair needed brushing.

Who the hell do you think you are? she asked. We hardly know you. Know nothing about you. We didn't invite you. You practically ruined the party for everyone. You're a truly contemptible human being, do you know that?

I'm sorry you feel that way, I said. As far as the party-crashing goes, you know I came with a friend. My friend assured me you wouldn't mind, that the two of you were very open-minded about that sort of thing.

Yes, she said, her fists balled up at her side, but your friend had the good grace to leave at a proper hour. We didn't have to kick her out. As far as that goes, we hardly know her either.

This surprised me. It had been my impression that Agnes was on the closest of terms with these two women. That was all I had been hearing for months: what an amazing pair this Zephyr and Sulvie were.

She's almost a total stranger, Zephyr went on.

Don't talk to me about Agnes, I said. That woman can drop dead for all I care.

Zephyr was about to say something more when Sulvie appeared, going from the bedroom to the bath, a chocolate-coloured beach towel wrapped around her.

If that man isn't out of here by the time I finish my bath, she said, I am going to kill him.

Zephyr rushed over to her. I could hear them whispering. Zephyr was asking Sulvie not to leave her alone with me. She was frightened, she said. There was no telling what I might do.

It puzzled me that she should say this. I had not raised my voice to anyone all evening, had not got in anyone's way; since the party ended I had done little more than sit and smoke and say to them over and over not to worry on my behalf, that I'd be leaving soon.

The two women approached together and sat down on the sofa

facing me. They stared. For a long time the three of us maintained a strained silence. My ash dropped on the carpet, but I scooped it up so carefully it left no mark. Then Zephyr bounced up, shot at me, and began shaking my shoulders.

What is it you want? she demanded. Is it sex? Do you imagine we will let you sleep with us if you stay long enough?

Sulvie snorted. Fat chance! she said.

You're sick, Zephyr went on, now yelling, slapping at me. You're a cockroach.

He's a bore, Sulvie said.

I wish you wouldn't abuse me like that, I told them. I assure you I mean neither of you any harm. I find you both attractive, to speak frankly, but I certainly have no intention to make advances.

Then what do you want? both shouted at once. Why won't you leave?

I raised my cigarette, nodding at it, by way of impressing on them my firm intention to leave once this last one was smoked down.

Zephyr stopped shaking me. She sucked on a broken nail.

We were all startled when the phone rang. Zephyr snatched it up. She listened a moment, caught Sulvie's eye, then said:

Yes, he's still here. He absolutely refuses to leave.

I moved to take the phone, thinking it was Agnes checking up on me.

Zephyr jumped back. *Don't touch me!* she screamed. Sulvie leapt to her side, both looking panic-stricken. *You leave her alone!* Sulvie hissed.

I sank back down.

No! No! No! Zephyr yelled into the phone. We can handle it! We are quite up to handling this ourselves, thank you! She slammed the receiver down.

The two women returned to the sofa. They sat close together, Zephyr's hand gripping Sulvie's knee, Sulvie with an arm slung around Zephyr's neck.

I was steaming inside my overcoat. My hatband had tightened, giving me a bad headache. I had no more cigarettes.

I had stayed too long simply to get up now and casually walk out. I'd have to exert myself, do my best to win the friendship of these two. I couldn't have them thinking Agnes would waste her time on the contemptible creature they took me to be.

My mouth tasted sour. It seemed to me that if I didn't brush my teeth that very minute I would gag.

May I use your washroom? I asked. That final favour and then I promise you I shall be going.

The women said nothing. They were like lifeless dummies staring back at me.

In their washroom feminine scent abounded. Sulvie's unused bath water had been drawn extremely deep, its steam dampening the blue tiles and mirror. The water was coloured blue. On a white stool beside the tub were folded two thick yellow towels. Their tooth brushes were an identical white. The bristles of the one I chose were hard and cut my gums. I spat out blood, rinsed the toothbrush under a quiet trickle of water, and returned it to its holder.

I looked out. They had not moved from the sofa, although their heads had come together. Their backs were to me; I could not tell whether they were sleeping.

The bathroom was amazingly warm. My face was soaked with sweat. I felt almost too dizzy to stand.

A skylight occupied one entire half of the ceiling. A clever arrangement of shelves extended up to it and on these shelves rested scores of African violets all in bloom and thriving.

Agnes, too, had lately been collecting these dwarfish, uncommunicative plants.

I am a shower person. It has been years since my body has known the luxury of a long hot bath. I slid in, and kept on sliding. The water rose up my chest, my neck, stopping at last just short of my mouth. I sighed back with closed eyes, half-afloat now, very much at peace with myself, wishing only for a book, soft music, or a cigarette.

Sidebar to the Judiciary Proceedings, the Nuremberg War Trials, November, 1945

[The Speaker, in black judicial robes, reclines in an easy chair, occasionally sipping from a cognac glass. Behind him can be seen the flags of the victorious nations. Lights throw shadows from the cutout figures who comprise his audience.]

The craniologist who came to measure Heidegger's brain was made to stand in the rain by the front step while Elfride went to ask the famous philosopher would he be willing.

Heidegger was in his study, surrounded by a pile of open books. He told Elfride not to be absurd. He was not to be disturbed.

Elfride told her husband that the craniologist had said the task would only take a minute. At this Heidegger laughed a scornful laugh. "We shall see about that," he said. Elfride had to jump aside, so quickly did he exit the room.

The craniologist, no fool, had found partial protection from the rain under the roof's overhang. Heidegger, striding fast, was outside in the rain himself before he knew it — whipping his head about in search of the visitor.

He did not see the craniologist until the man spoke. "Over here."

Already they were both drenched.

What the craniologist saw was a short, thick-waisted man with a heavy face, a large, squarish brow, jet black hair, and an untended moustache patterned after the Fuhrer's.

The philosopher saw a stringbean mortician, astoundingly advanced in years, possessing an overlarge head.

Elfride had taken up a stance in the doorway, which Heidegger, as often was the case, had left open. The great man could not be bothered with closing doors. She looked at the two of them standing under the overhang, and at the rain splattering their shoes and the cuffs of their pants, and did not say to them what it occurred to her to say, that even dogs knew enough to come in out of the rain.

The craniologist was explaining his intentions.

Heidegger took the visitor to be a man of bureaucratic dullness, inflated with a sense of his own importance. This made the philosopher impatient and rude.

As for the craniologist, Goebbels' office had told him the Magus likely would be difficult — aloof, brusque, opinionated — and that he should persevere and endeavour not to offend, as Heidegger was under consideration for an exalted position within the Party. He had not expected a man of such small stature.

Elfride remained in the doorway, biting at a hangnail, but with an air that suggested she thought herself every bit as important as them.

"If you want anything," she said, "you will let me know. But I am not bringing my good china out here in the rain."

The craniologist stood up straighter. He told her that he had not come here to eat.

Heidegger told Elfride to stop bothering them with her trivialities.

After showing both of them — by a look that flooded her face — how horrified their comments made her feel, Elfride disappeared behind the slammed door.

"Women," the craniologist said, "have small brains." Heidegger did not leap to his wife's defense.

He was thinking that the craniologist had by far the privileged spot under the roof's overhang. Hardly any rain was falling on him. He was thinking that their shoes were wet and dirty and now Elfride was unlikely to allow either of them inside unless they entered in stocking feet. He could not abide the thought of having a stocking-footed craniologist walking over his polished floors and sitting in his chairs.

It began raining harder.

"Eva, I've heard," said Heidegger, "has intelligence."

Heidegger intended this statement as a test of the craniologist's own intelligence. He was not going to waste his time out here in the rain talking to an idiot. Eva *Who? Which* Eva? Those were his two questions, and the stuffy craniologist would either know the answer or not know the answer.

But the craniologist was not aswim in the dark.

"Eva has brains," the man said. "I stand corrected."

Heidegger scrutinized the craniologist's features more closely. *I stand corrected* were not words he could ever imagine himself uttering, any more than he could imagine the Fuhrer uttering them; it proved that the craniologist, however much he wore the mask of public esteem, perceived in his heart that he was very much an underling.

"Eva Braun and the Fuhrer are properly suited to each other," the craniologist said.

Heidegger had the impression the man was suggesting he had dinner with the Fuhrer and his darling every evening.

"Move a little," Heidegger said, elbowing the man. But the craniologist did not move.

Every now and then the wind was blowing the rain's spray into their faces.

The Heidegger house was set well away from the street. Under the thick hedgerow by the street a deformed cat, refused by the neighbourhood, was trying to find a dry spot. The soaked cat, to Heidegger's eyes, had a slimy look. The cat had been tormenting him for months by hopping up on the outside sill of his study and moaning at him.

"The effect this rain is having on our soldiers at the front is God's own misery," Heidegger said.

It had been raining in Freiburg and over all of Europe for a full three weeks. There were times when Heidegger felt he would never again see spring. He longed for his cabin in the Black Forest, at Todtnauberg. It was isolated there.

At Todtnauberg he could don Swabian peasant dress, brew tea on the stove, and think.

The craniologist had no comment to make on the war effort.

The craniologist had with him a leather satchel in which he obviously transported the tools of his trade. He seemed concerned that the satchel was getting wet. A moment ago the satchel was between his legs; now he tried stuffing it beneath his coat, though the satchel was much too large.

"How do you measure your brains?" Heidegger asked.

The craniologist looked surprised. He looked as though he thought this was information which should be under everyone's province.

"Various means," he said.

Heidegger snorted; he hated the vague.

"By eye, by feel, by —"

The cat abandoned the hedge in a run; midway across the grass, it stopped; then it scurried off in a new direction.

Good, Heidegger thought. The cat had developed a limp.

A week before, the cat had given birth to a single kitten.

"A cloth tape," the craniologist said, hardly opening his lips.

"Cloth or wood or German steel," said Heidegger, "you do not have measuring apparatus of sufficient girth to measure *Heidegger's* brain."

The craniologist smirked.

Heidegger told him: "The time that lapses between one Heidegger thought and another can not be measured any more than the content of the thoughts themselves can."

It seemed to Heidegger that the craniologist sneered. Someone, he thought, should report this man.

"I show you two spoons," the philosopher said. "One filled with lead, the other with gold. In the dark you would say both weighed the same."

"I beg your pardon," the craniologist said. "That is not true."

Heidegger's mouth dropped open. Not since old Husserl, whom he reviled with all his heart, had anyone spoken so to him.

Edmund Husserl, right here in Freiburg, had invented phenomenology; Heidegger, celebrated, had but scratched the bare bones of time and being.

The rain was splattering up as high as their knees now. His shoes were sodden.

The critique of words by yet more words, Heidegger thought. Before Heidegger that is all philosophy was.

"When I sleep my brain swells enormously," he said. "Elfride has noticed this. She has the visual proof not only of her own eyes but also in the wear and tear of my pillow."

The craniologist nodded. The statement did not seem to amaze him.

"When I am teaching, or talking to certain people — Lowith, for instance, in the old days — I can feel my brain swelling large as a melon. If I sat on a wall you would think me Humpty-Dumpty."

Elfride would have smiled at this joke; the craniologist didn't.

"The Heidegger brain is the potentate of the metaphysical," Heidegger said. "How can you hope to measure the metaphysical, when Heidegger has himself grappled with it each instant of his life? Even if your cloth tapes could span the metaphysical the hand meant to hold those tapes could not hold the volume of tapes required. Your cloth tape could not even span so much as the Greeks who relentlessly toil inside Heidegger's brain. How could you measure the one brain in the world which alone in the world charts the scope of time and being?"

"I can," the craniologist said.

Heidegger laughed. He was unaccustomed to doing so. His laugh sounded like a snarl.

The cat was meowing in the rain. Heidegger could not determine where it was meowing from. The cat was skin and bones. What kept it alive was a mystery.

"You could set around me a ring of buckets and I could pour my strange syntax into those buckets but you could never bring enough buckets to hold even my syntactical leavings."

A tick had developed at one corner of the craniologist's thin mouth.

"Am I losing you?" Heidegger asked.

A phrase hopped into Heidegger's brain: *from me and yet from beyond me*. Later he would endeavour to sort out what this meant.

The craniologist closed his eyes, as though in pain.

In his research on Heidegger he had learned that the philosopher had spent the summer of 1918, twenty-nine years old, as a soldier in the

Verdun district. He had hoisted and studied balloons. With data gleaned from these balloons weather forecasts had been made, necessary for the success of poison gas attacks.

The philosopher had not shown himself gifted. After two months influential friends had finagled his release.

"Look here at this shoe," Heidegger said, removing the same from his left foot.

"I don't want to look at your stupid shoe," the craniologist said.

Stupid? Heidegger's eyebrows lifted. The man was insufferable. Even so, Heidegger persevered.

"Notice how the heel of this shoe has worn inwards. Now look at this other shoe."

He removed his other shoe. His feet sank a few inches into the wet soil.

"The heels of both of these shoes, and the soles as well, are worn to the inside. How I walk is a thing you can measure but what this means, the relationship between the walking habit and the workings of the brain, is a thing your cloth tapes can not reveal."

Heidegger paused, tapping a stiff finger hard against his brow. He could feel his brain expanding, and wondered whether the craniologist would have the wit to notice.

The craniologist looked at him. Heidegger looked away. He had never with ease looked into another person's eyes. Something he saw in those eyes was disturbing to him. Elfride sometimes gripped his collar and shook him. "Look at me!" she would say. "Look at me!"

In his family they had never looked at each other; in that regard he was a victim of his humble origins.

"Also," Heidegger went on. "Also, look how worn both these soles are up in the toe area. You likely have never seen this before, not even in Eva Braun or the Fuhrer. When Heidegger has a thought, a brain wave — about nothingness, to mention but one example — his toes dig holes through the toughest leather. Before he knows it his toes are leaving bloody imprints on the streets. Every other month he requires new shoes. It is driving Elfride insane. But that, my friend, is called concentration. It is called *thinking*."

The craniologist looked to the ground where Heidegger was standing.

He looked at the wet black socks on Heidegger's feet, at his narrow white ankles.

At their feet lay a bed of empty shells, black walnuts left by squirrels. The door opened and they heard Elfride say, "Put your shoes back on, Martin. There's a war on. I am not going to spend the whole of my life tending to a sick man."

The cat appeared from nowhere, streaking between Elfride's legs into the house.

Elfride screamed.

The door slammed.

The craniologist flattened his satchel, then tried buttoning his raincoat over it.

"In the cat world which has the biggest brain?" asked Heidegger.

The craniologist did not answer. He was listening to raucous sounds emanating from the house.

A week ago, the pregnant cat had assumed its position on the sill outside Heidegger's study. It had stalked back and forth and scratched at the screen, meowing ferociously. Heidegger had just scribbled in his notebook, *No shelter within the truth of being.* Then the cat had again showed up, a slick, black, ugly kitten, newly born, dangling from its jaws. The kitten's entire head was in the cat's mouth. With its claws the cat ripped a hole in the screen. It stepped through and settled itself down in that space between the screen and the window. Heidegger had just written, *Elfride's stomach was last night made queasy by wine.*

The ridiculous cat, fortunately, had produced but one very small kitten. Horrified, Heidegger had watched it eat a second one, or the afterbirth.

"How do the Jews fare?" Heidegger asked the craniologist.

The craniologist remained silent.

"Who sent you?" Heidegger asked.

"I am not permitted to disclose that information," the craniologist said.

"What is your name?"

"That too is confidential," the craniologist said.

"Goebbels?" asked Heidegger. "Or someone higher?"

The craniologist's face remained indifferent to these questions.

"The Fuhrer sent you?"

The craniologist pressed himself flatter against the building.

"I have every right to know," said Heidegger. "The higher the office you represent the less reason I have to question your credentials. You will agree there are a lot of crackpots running about."

It seemed to Heidegger that the craniologist did agree to this.

For a moment they watched the rain. Heidegger put his shoes back on. The trees were heavy with rain. Rain was coursing down the street beyond the hedge and flowing in thick grey curtains down the facades of the facing buildings.

From his cabin windows at Todtnauberg Heidegger had a sweet view of the Swiss Alps.

The Swiss were a durable people but theirs was not a fated nation.

At Todtnauberg he could wear knickerbockers and his peasant caps. He could tread the slopes on snow shoes.

At Todtnauberg, until recently, he had enjoyed the company of Hannah Arendt.

Christmas time two years ago he and Hannah had unsuccessfully attempted cooking a goose dinner.

The craniologist was studying him; Heidegger caught himself licking his moustache. He had got into this habit lately, one infuriating to Elfride, whose own alienating habits were confined to those inflicted upon her by her father, the high-command Prussian officer. A dozen times each day he would hear her saying, "How did these crumbs get on the table!" She saw imaginary ants everywhere. She saluted the stove, the cupboards, the light fixtures. She could stand for hours on end mesmerized by the sound and sight of water running in the kitchen faucet.

Her taut body was accustomed to upholding her father's rigid standards on posture; when they made love her spine emitted cracking noises.

"I measured Einstein's brain," the craniologist suddenly said. "When he was in Berlin." The words seemed to spurt from his cramped lips. His eyes were blinking fast.

"I measured his brain twice. Once before his property was confiscated and again before he was born."

"In the womb?" said Heidegger. "You took his measure in the . . . ?"
The philosopher's tone suggested that not since his honeymoon had
he been so amazed.

Then he remembered that he and Elfride had succumbed to two
wedding ceremonies, Lutheran one week and Catholic the following.
That had amazed him. He would have to think a while now, to recall
why it had been so important.

He and she had prayed together in those days.

"Trotsky," the craniologist said. "Lenin. I've done them all."

Nietzsche, Heidegger thought. I'll bet the son of a bitch will next be
telling me he's done Nietzsche.

"Nietzsche, also. Now there was someone a man could talk to."

"You conversed with Nietzsche?" Heidegger could not believe this.
For years he had himself been conversing daily with Nietzsche.

"We were . . . intimate," the craniologist said.

Something in the sound of the rain must have led Heidegger's mind
to wonder. He became aware suddenly that the craniologist had mentioned a dozen more names of those immortalized.

"Wagner?"

"Wagner, of course."

They were both silent a moment.

"Napoleon, too," the craniologist said.

Silence fell again.

Heidegger stepped away from the wall. He didn't care how wet he
got. He was excited.

"Who didn't you do?"

"I don't do Jews. Einstein was the last."

"I hear Julius Streicher is insane. Is the insane mind larger?"

The craniologist rolled his eyes.

"Have you done him?"

"I have done the highest echelon of Reich officials."

"Whose is biggest?"

"I am not permitted to divulge that data."

"Holderlin? Our greatest poet? I would be curious to know whether
you have done him."

"Too much decay."

"Holderlin? Decayed? Our greatest poet!"

"Unlike Napoleon. Perfectly preserved."

"Jesus? What about him?"

The craniologist stared at Heidegger.

"Pardon me," the craniologist said. "But I would not walk in all that shit."

After a moment, Heidegger nodded. So here was another who had shed his faith.

"But I did Pontius Pilate. *Very* impressive."

Clearly this craniologist, built like a scarecrow, as emotionless as history, was another time-and-being man.

The door opened.

Elfride stood on the landing, hands on her hips. They waited for her to say something about the cat. But she did not speak of the cat. She had perhaps dealt with the cat as she had with its kitten.

She had dressed. She had done up her hair and put on lipstick. She had put on an alluring frock, with a silk scarf folding from a pocket, and had the niceties adorning her throat.

"Come inside," she said. "Both of you. Come inside *now.*"

The two deposited their shoes by the door.

"Take off those wet socks," she said.

They entered.

"Your office called," she told the craniologist. "I had no idea this project was all so scientific. I had a nice chat with Goebbels himself. He was most gracious. Quite an enchanting man."

Heidegger stared at her red lipstick.

She was wearing stockings. Stockings were precious. Something of significance must have transpired over the phone, for her to put on stockings.

"Did he say anything about me?" Heidegger asked. "Did he offer any hints?"

Elfride was studying the craniologist's head. The heels of her hands rested against her slim hips. A cigarette burned there between two fingers, the nails still damp with red paint.

She seemed mesmerized by what she saw behind the craniologist's thick brow.

But a moment later she emerged from this state.

"The poor man needs a towel," she said. "Martin, get our visitor a towel. A nice one, from the guest room."

In one thin hand the craniologist was holding up his dripping socks. Elfride, her face flushing, the flush spreading to her ears, suddenly lunged, snatching them from him.

"I'll give them a quick wash," she said.

Heidegger was still by the doorway, holding his. It stupefied him that Elfride would wash another man's socks.

"What about mine?" he said. "What about me?"

But Elfride was already scurrying away. They heard water running in the sink in the kitchen.

The craniologist entered the living room. He looked about for a second, then settled himself into the room's most comfortable chair.

From the hallway Heidegger watched him cross his legs; he watched the craniologist dangle his naked white foot. The skin was hairless. Raw scabs, spots of blood, showed on the nubs of his toes.

Beneath the chair crouched the deformed cat. Its lunatic eyes were staring fixedly at Heidegger.

Heidegger felt a shiver steal over him. A thought had just come to him, bewildering and frightening.

Hitler would lose the war. The Volk would not claim its rightful greatness.

[The Speaker falls silent. He drains the last of the cognac in his glass. He rearranges the judicial robes, buffs the toe of one black shoe. A door is heard opening. A new shadow is seen. A soft voice is heard. "Gentlemen. It is time to reconvene."]

GYPSY ART

Young Fazzini was apprenticed to an artist who made incredible boxes that were like airy castles, each with a thousand rooms and baffling appendages. One day the master said to Fazzini, "You don't understand art, or boxes, or castles. You need to run with gypsies and lose yourself in amazing adventures." At home Fazzini's parents were ever bickering at him. "Grow up," they said. "Avail yourself of every opportunity. Let not the smallest blade of grass go unnoticed." In other words, hit the road. So Fazzini struck off on the road, eager for any adventure. On the road Fazzini met a gypsy woman, big-boned and unruly. The woman took Fazzini to her encampment. He was the love of her life, she said, and requested the other gypsies refrain from spitting at him. Within the hour they were married. Fazzini could not believe his luck. He had been in love before, though never so deliriously. His wife tired herself out, proclaiming her love. They fell asleep entwined. All the gypsies were entwined one with another, Fazzini and his own gypsy somewhere in the middle. Then the gypsies hit the road. Fazzini had a headache. He wondered why it was he had awakened under the sour apple trees and where the gypsies had gone. Later on he realized his toe must be broken, since walking was such a difficulty. The sun was unbearable and the only shade in the vicinity was taken up with wild animals which hissed at him when he neared. Fazzini fashioned crude crutches from the branches of the apple tree.

The crutches hurt, his underarms were raw, but at least he could walk. Fazzini had been warned as a youth to avoid gypsies, but hadn't paid attention. He had felt contempt in those days for anyone so arrogant as to believe their calling in life was to issue advice. How many the times his mother had slapped his face? He did not want to go home again, but now he was going home because this adventure on the road had not worked out as planned. He had taken the wrong road. Next time he met a gypsy woman on the road he would know better. He wouldn't be so easy to fool. From time to time he rested by the road under the shade of more sour apple trees. Life would be all right, God, he thought, if you will deliver me a little food. A nice prosciutto would be divine. A bottle of vino, dear God, as well. Lately Fazzini had been talking to God as though God was a sweet woman. It paid to compliment Her, although in his personal opinion a good catholico should not advertise the fact. Deeply religious people should keep their feelings to themselves. The crutches felt fine now; such an ungrateful fellow he had been, complaining endlessly of every triviality. His toe had miraculously healed. It was a magic toe. People he passed on the road were of two sorts, civil or uncivil. They spat at him, or sought to set him off in opposing directions. More than one person offered the opinion that he appeared able-bodied. Why did he not secure meaningful employment? Fazzini trudged on; he had many a mile to traverse, and ambition was his guide. He was a mature fellow now — no longer the crass fool. If his family saw him they would be amazed. On a high meadow Fazzini discerned an encampment of gypsies. He hid behind bushes, throwing rocks into their camp. When they ran at him he also ran. Fazzini and gypsies just did not get along. "You gypsies," he said to them, "are the dregs of the earth." The maddened gypsies threw Fazzini in the river. This was round about the Spesso Fumo lowlands where the Spesso Fumo River finally allows itself to be seen. The gypsies jumped into the river themselves. They washed themselves, they sang. A gypsy with an ugly bruise on his forehead embraced Fazzini constantly. "Your stones have knocked sense into my head," this man said. "You shall henceforth be known as the King of the Gypsies." But once Fazzini was in their camp the gypsy women swore at him. They spat. They made him cook their gypsy food and wash their gypsy clothes. Even their gypsy feet. They made him tend the horses and dogs. They were at him every minute. The gypsies not badgering him were singing gypsy songs. Fazzini, in all his life, had never heard such ugly, uninspiring songs. One night when all the gypsies were asleep Fazzini crawled away from the gypsy camp on his hands and knees. He crawled until his knees bled. All along the escape route he was pursued by an insane crew of black flies. After a time he no longer bothered with the ticks pricking at his scalp. He was hungry and cold. He talked sweetly to his sweetheart God, complimenting Her at length on Her fine dress, but God wasn't fooled. She knew he was speaking only to hear his own voice. He changed his voice, which did not fool Her either. She wore fine jewels, though, and was quite radiant. She looked to him like She was on Her way to a party. His hands burned. All that lye soap that the gypsies had made him boil. So many boiling pots, so many pots that Fazzini was made to stir. Gooey stuff, hard on the limbs. His very elbows ached. The gypsies simply did not know how to live. They knew no other life. The refineries of life were unknown to them. Plus, babies everywhere, always crying, and only Fazzini to care for them. Crawling babies that went about on all fours until on their own accord they uprighted themselves and pranced about as mature gypsies yodeling senseless gypsy songs. It was sickening, if you wanted to know the truth. But what did Fazzini care? He was free of their lot now. He'd learned a thing or two. He had experience under his belt which he meant to put to good use. He wished his family could see him now. They would be amazed. Finally Fazzini decided he would stand up. Why all that crawling anyway? He guessed he'd crawled a million miles. Now it was raining; the heavens pouring down. What's that? Oh my God, yes, there's a road! Now, Fazzini thought, I know where I am. No more of this bush life for me. Immediately upon taking to the road, Fazzini found himself intercepted by an unruly gang of men who appeared out of nowhere. They wore slickers, carried umbrellas, did not heed the ferocious heavens, the pelting rain. This gang wanted right out to know whether Fazzini had seen anywhere in the vicinity a dirty band of roving gypsies. "Speak up," they said, "and we'll go easy on you." They slapped Fazzini around. They punched him one way and another. This gang, truly they were enraged. You trust a gypsy at your peril, they told him. They were on foot, they said, because the gypsies had stolen their wagons. Oh, and their horses too. And the womenfolk. The gypsies had set fire to their haystacks. They'd raided every hen coop and carried away good God-fearing children, to raise these children as mangy gypsies. The gang had been on the gypsies' trail for weeks. Now they were close. They could smell gypsies nearby. Come to that, Fazzini smelt like a gypsy himself. "If you want to know why we are swatting you, that is why." Fazzini objected. "I hate gypsies more than you," he said. "Those gypsies just have no respect for the common decencies. They are godless creatures. You would not believe the bizarre acts they had me perform. Chickens? Who was made to pluck those chickens? Your womenfolk? Forget your womenfolk. Already they are more the gypsy than the gypsies are themselves." Fazzini felt proud of himself. His tale of woe worked this gang of roughcuts into a frenzied state. They proclaimed their own virtues endlessly, firing off muskets right and left. Fazzini raised one finger in the air, and pointed the way the wind was blowing. Go that way, he said. You'll find those scurvy gypsies before the sun goes down. The gang was so enlivened by this news they decided then and there to have a party. To celebrate this turn in their fate, why not? Unloosen the jugs. Everybody have a good drink to make us mean, then it's onward to sweet revenge. One jug led to another and soon all were so wildly drunk not one of them, including Fazzini, could stand up. Fazzini did not know how it happened: one second he was by the river, his pee grandly arching, and the next second he was in the drink. He was in the Spesso Fumo River, which had finally showed itself. Fazzini had to swim like a rat. Agony, you want to know the truth. So many times he nearly perished. Glub-glub, Fazzini the drowned rodent. The river at flood stage, current sweeping him along. Debris flowing by him: rooftops, pigs, cows, fowl. The whole of the once dry earth flowing with him. He clutched at mud and wet grass, ferns, katydids, sprig of daffodil; not so easy was it getting ashore. He drifted miles and miles and no longer knew where he was. Finally the heavens relented, the rain softened, he was at eddy in a swirling pool. Fazzini cried out; the object he had been clinging to over the past hours, clinging to for dear life, was a swollen dead man.

Oh, dear God, Fazzini said. Oh, my Lord, I love Your shoes. What pretty feet! Bella! Bella! He tried pushing the dead man away — *go! go!* — but the eddy repeatedly floated the dead body back at him. The arms of the dead man flung themselves over his shoulders, the face time and time again tried kissing him. It tried crawling itself up over him. Rape! Fazzini thought. That dead man means raping me. What a come-down. May I never know tranquillity? All I wanted from this world was a dignified life. A little something to eat now and then. A warm bed. Flotsam, foam, and the dead man encircled him. Fazzini's legs dangled uselessly in the river's depths. "What's that?" Fazzini asked. "There, swimming by?" A giant turtle. Well, dear God. Fazzini threw himself at the turtle, catching its shell on either side. Astonished, the turtle whipped back its head. Its jaws clamped entirely through one of Fazzini's hands. The turtle dived and twisted in a frenzy of disbelief. Its feet clawed; it dived, it surfaced, it flipped over and over and over. It was a turtle thoroughly deranged. Fazzini's head reposed on the shell's muck. The turtle was now away from the eddy. Fazzini had courage; he was fighting for his life; he held on. He must have slept. When he opened his eyes the sun was bright, he felt warmth. He was akimbo upon the silent earth. Don't just lie there. Show your mettle, Fazzini told himself. You've endured the worst patch. Trudge, trudge. A thicket? A thicket, yes, so many vines and trees. So many squirrels jumping tree to tree. So many snakes. "And who," Fazzini asked of the black flies, "invited you?" Eventually Fazzini, trudging, saw a campfire at blaze within a clearing; he trudged towards it. He looked first for wagons but saw no wagons. The campers were not gypsies, then; his luck was looking up. In fact, the campfire was deserted, despite the flaring fire, cinders volleying to the heavens. I'll just warm myself, Fazzini thought. Yoo-hoo! I wonder if they have any grub. Fazzini warmed himself. He felt so much better now. Someone had been even nice enough to leave a nice green tent, neatly propped. My lucky day, Fazzini thought. He lifted the tent flap, and immediately felt faint. In a swoon, hot all over. Oh, God, he said, I love Your ears, Your nose, Your beautiful lips. Have I spoken of Your most incredible knees, Your ankles, Your fine, firm buttocks? "Grr and crunch," the beast in front of him said. Yikes! A giant black, grunting, creature stared back at him. Fazzini smelt it. It had a terrible smell reminiscent of smelly feet. The creature was busy eating something. It looked him over closely, but went on eating. A small fold-up desk had been set up inside the tent. On the desk was spread a large map. An explorer's jacket hung from a nail on the centre pole. Fazzini took the jacket; he took the map, which felt oily. Oh, my God, English biscuits! He quickly took these; he filled his mouth with biscuits. "Just go on," he told the beast, "with what you are doing." The creature nodded sagely. He and the beast were pals. The beast seemed not to mind what Fazzini took. It went on eating. It slurped and chomped, blood and gore dribbling from its chin and paws; the beast flung out one arm, offering Fazzini a long, dripping bone. Want some? Fazzini wasn't tempted. The biscuits had filled him. The beast watched him steadily, ever with a benign air. Afterwards, when the beast endeavoured to embrace him, Fazzini ran. That beast is worse than the gypsies, Fazzini thought. I'm not coupling with bears. Oh, Mother in heaven, how many pedestals must I set You upon? Never mind, my Darling. I will scour the land, mend each broken toe, or nose, or thumb. Each eyelid. He blundered through the thicket. He felt brave. Renewed. He wished his family could see him now; they'd take back more than one of their previous harsh words. Soon Fazzini realized he was hearing music. He turned one direction and another. He whipped his head about. He dropped down and lay first one ear and then another against the cold earth. Music wafted his way from every direction. It was all the same music, gypsy music. By my life, Fazzini thought, those gypsies are everywhere! Well, he'd avoid them. A person could only accept gypsy company for so long. Gypsies are entirely too demanding. One desires one's own kind, Fazzini thought. That is how God has made the earth. Let the gypsies stay to their domain and I will cling to mine. Fazzini went on talking to himself like that. After his ordeals, why not? Plus, black flies were after him again. Ticks burrowing. Big fat pussy ticks in his scalp, mean black flat buggers everywhere else. His hand numb from the turtle's snapping jaws. His hand ugly, throbbing, heated up big as a drum. I'll get that tended to, Fazzini thought. You need not worry on my account. "I like Your hat, God," Fazzini said. "That's a splendid hat. Let no one tell You different. Create Your own fashion, I say. Pay no attention to what the rabble say. Your hair looks wonderful too. And such lovely skin. I'll grant You the rouge is heavy, someone would say overdone, but I like it. Please Yourself, that's what Fazzini says." He fell silent. No need to get carried away; no need to layer on the compliments with a spoon. There was something to be said for straight talk. But why run the risk? When had straight-talking got him anywhere? It had landed him with gypsies, that's what straight talk had done. Onwards now. Trudge, trudge. In his new jacket. You'd think just once God would compliment him. *Say, now, Fazzini, lad! That's a spiffy jacket! Aren't you the cheeky one! Brava, Brava!* Indeed, Fazzini's view was that he cut a fine figure. Who wouldn't think so? Anyone with a fair gaze would be bound to be impressed. When he reached society, the quality people would see at a glance the kind of man he was. Style would carry the day. A soldier of fortune, yes! Tides betide. Before the moon set, without a doubt he would meet and marry a beautiful woman, marry and settle down. High time too, Fazzini thought. Time to shy away from this rover life, this existence without meat or merit. Yes, high time. It had taken him a long time to recognize the flaws in his character; now he was determined to set himself to mending these flaws. Youth, what did youth know? Sooner or later a person had to grow up. You had to work your way through it, didn't you? "Well, mother dear," Fazzini said, "that's my advice." Black flies coated his face; why flit here and there when already they'd found hospitable lodging for the night? First order of business, when he reached the city, was to do something about those flies. Then to the vineyard to slacken his thirst. To the Music Hall. All those high kicks, those heaving bosoms, all those naked legs! Yes, yes, if you would be so kind! *Cacciucco alla livornese,* why not? He'd want a good song to cheer him up. Not this crude gypsy zing-a-ling. Then to the studio of his artist friend, to re-apprentice himself. He too could build incredible boxes now, boxes each with a thousand rooms and anterooms, catacombs and towers, cat walks connecting one tower to another, and a thousand secret chambers holding incredible adventure behind every door. But, wait, here he was limping again. Those old war wounds, his broken toe, the bloated arm, each aching like the very devil. And beasts of the wild over there under sour apple trees consuming every inch of shade. Plus here came a caravan of unruly gypsies — gypsies astride mules, riding creaking wagons, herding along an endless sweep of ponies, lambs, swine, acrobatic goats, caged monkeys, plumed birds that hopped on one leg. Up there, putting bite to the lead reins, a fine, slinky-eyed woman, bare-breasted, under a wilderness of hair, one and then another luscious eye winking wickedly at him.

"Tell your fortune, good-looking. Read your future? Today only, special price!"

"Why, hello there," Fazzini said. "Gypsies, are you? Oh, I've known a gypsy or two in my life. Salt of the earth. My heavens, I even married one. Big-boned and unruly, brimming over with love. Are you by chance going my way?"

"Sure, sure," the gypsies said. "Going here, going there! Today only, we are on our way to our airy castle in the sky. Much gold there, pig roasts, love eternal, wine that flows as from a waterfall."

The gypsies saw he was a nervy deluded fellow, the innocent romantic. His face encrusted, possibly suffering a fracture of the larynx; just a plain pasty-faced boy too long adrift from home.

They placed him inside a cage filled with chickens, outfitting him with a long blade, a sack to catch the feathers.

Art, Fazzini thought. Art is my life.

I love Your smile, he said to God. I love the rustle of Your skirts, the sun in Your hair, Your gay laughter, the fragrance of Your lilac-scented skin.

He would pluck feathers from the confused hysterical birds; he would go at this task feather by feather. The simple life is not to be disavowed.

Save me, my Darling. I lick the very sweat of Thy hand.

THE BROAD BACK
OF THE ANGEL

What more can we do to ourselves? Is this the question that keeps lights burning in this house through till morning? One might think so; I do myself. We make a clean target. But is this appreciated?

Having tired of the blue umbrella, Gore now elects to have a silver ring inserted in his lower lip. Matila complains.

"Gore, Gore, I don't want metals on your face!"

Gore is himself uneasy: he goes out, he returns. He's up, he's down: a man in my condition notes the uneasy play of limbs. Here he comes again, his eyes bloodshot, his lips hanging low. The finish is silver, but anyone can see there's lead inside. For the expression, he says. Just the right lip for my day and age. I like it fine, he says.

Ta-dum, ta-dum. Who reaps the harvest of this merry-go-round? Is anything so cheap — and yet so expensive — as this way we live?

"Ah, friend," he says, "— you're not fooling me!"

What can the poor bastard mean?

Weeks go by. Months. No one in this house is sure. But this we know: the ring interferes, it affects whatever we do. Gore pines for soft foods, to mention one: for those that do not require the grip and churn of his lower lip. To appease our hunger we are obliged to take furtive walks in the cold night. In this neighbourhood? We remark to each other: how many others have you seen? Are those human — or inhuman — shapes?

And these uphill routes are hard on a man in a wheel chair. I prefer to remain inside, gnawing on the forbidden thumb.

And Gore? What a tease! Last night he stabbed the fork into his nose. For the expression, he said. Is not my countenance much improved? He can't eat — but puts on weight, even so. Look now how he drags the floor, how the boards creak and bend! You would think his feet were carved from this very wood. "I like it fine," he says. His motion arrested, how he drools! Saliva thickens on his chest, but is that a grin? My wife thinks it is.

"Get rid of it," Matila pleads. "Do!"

She commands, she entreats. Her desires have no effect and soon she is adding to the moment with her tears.

"Mrruff-mrruff," Gore remarks, his lower lip having stretched. "Mrruff-mrruff!" What is the man saying? Better he should say nothing, or go out and barter with neighbouring dogs. His voice is a throaty mutter that Matila hears in her sleep. My wife confesses: "Oh, Sam, I hear it too!"

Yet he continues to sing when he bathes, and I notice a glint of logic not evident in his eyes before.

We meet at the dining table and Matila holds aloft her fork — "What need have we for these?"

You would think our lives had no form but for this scheduled food.

But why am I telling you? My past life was more elegant, but was it more refined? I ask you now: how is yours?

Matila whines. Each new emergency ushers in the familiar notes *"Do-re-me . . . !"* My wife marvels: "Are your ears so condemned? She's in agony! Can't you at least project a friendly smile?"

The fact is I proffer what I can. I listen, but who am I to intrude? Indeed, Matila is whining — but is hers not the voice which brought me to this chair? The voice that keeps me here?

Whose screaming bullets are these that ignite my groin? Is it me — or Matila — on the receiving end?

But oh, how she howls. "I won't put up with this! Metals on his face! I'll sue for a divorce! Why should I suffer these mad extremes?"

And from some place in all this a practical — a reasonable? — voice is heard. "On what grounds?" It is my wife speaking, and her words reach me as if through a tube. Is it Matila, or myself, whom she addresses now?

Later, bedroomed, I can put this question to her face. "Oh," she says, "I am soft and patient with Matila's moods. I am with her, in her skin. I love her for her temper. For her moods. I find nothing objectionable in her incessant whines."

And I am asked whether I share these views. "It is Gore," she says, "whom I find too miserable to tolerate!"

Me? I take no sides. Though a love for Gore engulfs me even as she speaks. I too would have metals on my face. I too would have my expression improved. I poke out my lip and am disconcerted at finding nothing there. "Oh, *Gore!*" — that's the one sentiment my mind reveres. "Gore! Never mind that he's the fool! Never mind that he's the product of what he wears! That what he wears is what most wears at him!" This chair, I think, would fit him almost as well as me.

Delirium has its pause. I have not served in seven wars without learning something from them. A tolerance for the other side.

My wife is unmoved. "You cripples!" she says.

And thus I am wheeled again into the dark. "Think this issue through," she says to me. "I'm sure you will come to your senses soon."

And here in the darkness, what are the thoughts that occur to me? That women are unpredictable. That women pursue where nothing leads. That wives willingly betray whoever first betrayed them. That for a friend they would forsake either the gallant or hideous dead. That breasts and legs and man's imagined lust combine to create some holy orifice. That nothing eludes them like sweet sympathy. That no womb, empty or full, is worth the smallest sacrifice. That men are perhaps different after all. That the same darkness which greets me here drove her to drive me to its dingy embrace. Or that it is sleep which finally captures all.

Thus I nod.

How curious it is that in my black dream sweethearts continue to promenade in pairs. A hand inserts itself in mine — warm, fragile, a mysterious hand. We walk and walk and no one speaks. We never tire. Our pace never alters. But after a while our footsteps are heard passing on in front of us.

When I was a boy . . . but how distant I seem to myself. Was there ever a moment when I was not this clunking bull? When these two wheels did not frame my eyes? And my raw hands did not shove these knobs? Yet a boy's vision endures. There was magic in those innocent coils between heart and brain. Its presence makes me shudder in embarrassment, looking back.

This obnoxious spasm in my legs! I slap cruelly at my thighs, at my dancing knees. My wife sighs irritably in her sleep. My feet clatter loudly against the steel shoes which support my legs. I continue to box at these limbs, squirming high in my sweaty seat. This monstrous chair knows the disgust I feel.

My friend Arturo, dead now, had a story he liked to tell. "There was this poor man," he would say, "who owned nothing except one sorry mule. And the beast cost more to feed than he brought in. 'If I could teach this brute not to eat,' the poor man decided, 'my situation might gradually improve.'" Here Arturo always paused. "You must understand," he would say, "the significance this story has for me." And his lidded eyes would make their appeal. I would strut here and there, no doubt uncorking and pouring wine or slapping down yet another ale. I had no patience for Arturo's stories. He took life much too seriously, in my view. "So," I would finally insist, "— so, did this poor man teach his animal to go without food?"

Arturo's melancholy face would draw nearer. His hands would clutch my arm. "Yes, yes!" he'd say, greatly excited. "The mule learned to go without food! Took to it without complaint! But then the sonofbitch up and died!"

Morning. I have passed another night in this chair. It occurs to me, wheeling myself past an open window, that this was a story I told Arturo. Nothing cheered Arturo so much as a good story with a rousing punch-line. His fingers would lift and there would be his bloodprints on my arm: "Impossible! How people can be such fools!"

Poor Arturo.

My wife sleeps soundly now. She is bedded under a spangle of white daisies and yellow butterflies. My trembling limbs can make her toss, but Matila's rage bothers her not at all. Matila is fiery at daybreak, a person back from desperate frontiers.

"I want a divorce!" she screams. "I can't live with that idiot another day!"

Gore stumbles by, in one hand his razor, in the other scissors for close work about his hidden chin. His lip ring flashes brilliantly, but it is his silent tread that ignites my wife: "What is it?" she exclaims, on her elbows — "What's happening here?" She settles back, contented, secure, as Matila's screams erupt once more.

"I hate it! Hate it! Hate metals on your face!"

We are guests here, I remind my wife. Offer comfort, yes — but on no account should we interfere. I go on speaking while clothing from her closet is flung out. My wife at night is tented under seven layers of wool; in the day flimsy playthings decorate her flesh. "You kept me awake," she says, "with your groans. Arturo's dead mule story, I suppose." But then she's gone.

My wife is a committed woman. She is committed to these people. Her life, she would say, is wrapped up with theirs. Some measure of concern is due them, to be sure. They have provided us with a home. Elevator and washtubs have been installed. They do not deny us their food, such as it is. They would even give up their best bed did we not constantly refuse. Yet I am puzzled each time I labour to change my clothes: was I crippled when I arrived here?

Once again I wheel myself into their midst. Gore sees me and his eyelids fall. "On what grounds?" my wife is asking them. "You people have always been peculiar and extreme. You have always been somewhat ridiculous, as you know." Matila nods. Gore's head weaves from side to side. "Mrruff-mrruff," he appears to say, "— I like my expression fine." Matila groans. "There!" she says. "You can see how impossible he is!"

I have no opinion on this. One outrage is so much like another, and in any event no one thinks to inquire about my view.

My chair's shadow paints every wall.

"There are," my wife is saying, "your children to be considered."

And that completes it for this hour. Traffic is heavy for an instant and then I am alone.

Weeks pass. Months. How much time who can tell? Can more be done to ourselves? Through many of these days my chair is positioned dead into the corner walls. I marvel at this joining of walls. Cruel seam which divides my two eyes while wanting to overlap them in the making of the single eye I would have, the one eye that would have me. My neck aches. Muscles throb. So much wanton checking of activity at my rear — so much weary searching for intersecting lines that have no origin anywhere in this room. All lines begin — or end? — at the front door. I nod . . . and dream of passing through it into a sea of mud. Dreaming is the word we give to the life that frog eyes perceive. Body and head become one from there.

"Oh, Sam, Sam!" my wife laments. "Oh, Sam!" Her backside oils silently through the open door. These people are magicians: they appear and disappear and the air which made space for them is never satisfied. Shock waves flow tirelessly within a radius approximately four feet of this chair. I observe it, drab lump between two gleaming wheels. I try to move from this sterile centre and the void goes with me. Matila, drenched by her own tears, enters and places a peeled orange in my lap. Fat wedges so beautifully orbed. They repose on blue china like old lace, like a roadmap of the planet Earth. I lift the orange in my palm and hold it inches from my face. It stares back at me. It catches the light and for a moment I am able to probe its lovely depth.

Matila vanishes with a stricken cry: "He won't eat it! He's unmanageable! He's worse than a child, I can't do anything with him!"

The house shudders under the siege of feet running to her rescue.

Liquid dribbles through my fingers and down my arm. I hear my wife's raucous protest in a distant room: "God! Haven't we seen enough of his obstinacy! Must he drive us all crazy before he'll be content?"

The drapes are drawn. I sit in a dark pool, and what the eye perceives is a bed of decaying leaves in a stagnant pond. My flesh stinks, yet I would hold out for something finer: the drive of birds in silent flight.

What can I say for myself? I speak of Gore, of Matila, of my wife, I make passing reference to this chair — although nothing is further from my mind than these. I stare at my hands but it isn't these deformed knots I see. The eye is wretchedly endowed: images form prematurely along the optic nerve, introducing mystery patterns on the eye's darker side. It is this which accounts for the sensation often felt: that we are retreating even as our bodies move ahead. It explains too why a dog will chase his own tail.

We meet at the dining table and I find myself asking: Who are these people? What curious forces unite us here? My wife shoves me to the toaster. I am invalid but someone must perform these chores. With his new lip Gore cannot eat toast. He shoves soft bread into his mouth and groans.

"My new lip," he announces, "is catching on." Mrruff-mrruff.

He speaks the truth. Earlier today the postman rang the bell, wanting to display the polished ring he wears. Next week we may expect his wife to appear with her breasts exposed, drinking champagne through silver straws, wearing a hat cut for donkey ears. What lengths we won't go, to transmogrify these tiny lives.

When Arturo was a boy he had wanted a dog. The dog died, run over by a car while Arturo stood in the pastry shop buying a loaf of bread to support his mother's stingy meal. *My dog my dog!* he cried, and stood out on the pavement, ruined, holding the mangled dog in his arms: stopping traffic, stopping pedestrians who were properly horrified. *"Little boy, don't you know? . . . Little boy, you! . . . Little boy, don't you know you'll get blood all over your clothes? . . . Little boy! . . .*

In the meantime . . . well, it's always in the meantime, every moment that we breathe . . . in the meantime the dog's guts have spilled all over the boy Arturo's arms, the blood flows in a puddle around him, and Arturo — stricken! — what could he do except cry out in the most profound and absurd grief: *"No no no no you can't take him this dog is mine!"* And, weeping, squeeze the sopping beast more tightly to his chest.

Finally someone shows some sense — we are not total morons after all — someone says to someone else, "This boy is in a state, can't you see he is? This boy needs looking after!" And someone else has roughly the same idea and eventually the boy is approached: "Little boy, what's your name, where do you live, little boy? Your parents! . . ." And so on, though of course the boy is perplexed with grief, oh, you should have seen the tears wash over him. Even so, he intends to fulfil his purpose here, he's got the loaf of bread still in his arms, mixing with dog to the extent that no one can tell which is which. It requires three people to pry the dog from the boy's arms and three more to restrain him as he attempts to get the dead burden back. "Little boy, can't you see! . . . Little boy! . . ." And all the time the boy is screaming, yanking dog fur and guts back to his embrace: *"my dog my dog my dog my dog my dog my dog my dog! . . ."*

My wife wheels me out into the yard. "Stop muttering," she says. "What is it now? Your dead dog story, I suppose." She abandons me to the open sky. Had one the vision, I think, one could see through it and beyond. The weather contents me, although it was in this very spot that yesterday a rock struck my chair. Thrown by the small child who lives next door. The fence here is high, I could hear his laboured breathing as he climbed. And his father's quiet encouraging voice: "Did you *get* him? Did you hit him *hard?*"

We are intelligent, we have emotions, we have will. We have strength. Power innate and much of it at our fingertips. We have all this but we are helpless in every way.

Gore, for instance, makes a rare appearance beside my chair. "Our wives," he whispers, "are looking distinctly odd. I prophesy there soon will be trouble in this neighbourhood." Mrruff-mrruff. My wife arrives, elbowing him aside. "I am sorry," she tells me, "I have let you remain in the sun too long. Your poor face is on fire, do you hurt?"

She administers a white salve and I find myself struck anew by our pathetic efforts to cajole love out of where it hides. The salve worms under my skin, she delivers bromides, anodynes — tears wet my cheeks in gratitude and pardon me I nap.

When I was a boy . . . .

When Arturo . . . .

When . . . .

The boy's mother was telephoned. She came running over, found no one there, the street empty of traffic — no evidence of madness except for this puddle of blood in front of the pastry shop. She goes running back to her own house, and as she bursts through the front door she sees a half a dozen people she's never seen before, and hears one of them saying, "He's dead." He's dead, he's dead.

He's dead.

She rushes forward screaming, lamenting, wailing, pulling her hair, shoving everyone. Grief vanishes the moment she sees her boy standing in the room with the dead dog dripping from his arms. She hurls herself against the boy, shakes him, slaps him, twists and pulls him, all the time shouting I TOLD YOU TOLD YOU I TOLD YOU DIDN'T I TELL YOU I WELL MARK MY WORDS YOU WILL NEVER NEVER NEVER HAVE ANOTHER NEVER ANOTHER DOG! DIDN'T I DIDN'T I WARN YOU TELL YOU SO! She tears at the boy's ears, chops his head, pushes him, shakes the dog out of his arms onto the floor and stays there herself kicking at the dead thing, screaming at it, and now shoving the boy into the bathroom, ripping off his clothes, while the boy shouts back at her *my dog my dog my dog my dog my dog my dog my dog my dog!* . . . On and on.

I awake in my chair in the familiar corner, shivering, a grey blanket over my legs. I stare at my hands and for a long time cannot make my fingers move. Behind me Matila is weeping. She and my wife, like twins born only for such emergencies, are pacing the floor. Matila strides a short distance, my wife chases after her. Matila whirls, comes back again. My wife remains at her heels. Each time the distance shortens. Finally they are face to face. They exchange expressions of surprise, they cry out, and fall wounded into each other's arms.

"What can I do now?" moans Matila. "What now? It's no good telling me this is my own fault!"

"It's our fault," my wife replies, "for being here. You could have been sleeping in our bed."

"I couldn't stand it if you were not here," sobs Matila. "What was I thinking of? I must have lost my mind!" Her voice rises, levels off, follows an uncharted route filled with groans, demented appeal for compassion which she cannot grant herself. "At night it's so different! That ring! His lip! In the dark!" Tears burst forth anew with this declaration, her neck thickens. "I'm ashamed! I can't bear this humiliation I feel!" Her body folds, and my wife leads her to a chair. She sits and for an instant the grief recedes, Matila's body goes erect, she glares menacingly and shakes a fist at the vast wrongs done to her: "Another *baby!* The last thing this marriage needs! Now it will be months before I can divorce the prick!"

My wife pulls up another chair, sits so that their knees are touching now: "I don't know," she asserts. "Perhaps the responsibility will bring your husband to his senses. I've never felt that Gore was a hopeless case." She smiles, sends it crashing to where I sit. I respond with the simple movement of a single finger, which exercise suddenly arouses my stick legs. Lifeless, they thrash about in their hideous dance.

Days go by. Weeks. Lamps know all the wrong hours in this house. Matila's stomach swells, her belly is as immense as her new pride. Oh, Matila, the stiff-legged kangaroo. She smiles and the gleam is on us all.

"I have been neglecting you," my wife remarks. She brings hot water in an enamel bowl, plops herself on a cushion in front of me. Sponges my legs.

Gore moves from room to room, distracted, muttering to himself. "A child's perceptions are limited," he explains. "All the same a man would be a fool to take unnecessary chances." He has had the ring removed, wears a black cloth over his chin, is never seen now without the walking stick slung over his left arm. "The snow," he says. "Yesterday I fell, badly bruised this knee." Snow? Was it not yesterday I sat out under a high sun, sipping juice through a tube, recalling Arturo's dog? Arturo . . . afterwards, the next day perhaps, that very night . . . out in the backyard burying his dog, going at the earth with a splash of grunts, throwing soil the length of the yard, going down deep, throwing it up hard: *My dog! My dog! My dog!* . . .

Snow is indeed packing us in. To my mind we are stuffed here like souring Judases in a crate. Gore limps from window to window, tap-tap advances his cane. He halts beside Matilda, takes her fingers to his lips: "And how's my little girl?" Matila blushes, bows her head: she is capable only of whispered speech. Gore moves on to my wife whose hand likewise gracefully awaits. Her face, tinted, with its softened eyes, with its shadowy cheeks — do I recognize it from someplace? Yes, like features imperfectly chiselled at the centre of some clouded moon, viewed through my own foggy telescope. These quarters, from where I sit, are cast in aphotic gloom, much as if Mary Magdalene had come in out of two thousand lonely years of mud and snow to express herself through their wistful eyes. As if she had come in to say: "The life He gave me was not all He promised it would be." To be forgiven signifies a dubious advance; to forgive is to ripen into fulsome pain. Gore, too, by his affectations, by his doleful show of warmth, so perceives. Yet I envy him. Once I too must have limped, employed sticks, worn a pinned ascot; with some alacrity and conviction could lift and tease a woman's hand. Now these doorknobs I call hands crawl upward from my lap and scratch to recognize whatever growth exists above or beneath the skin: this circle of raised or indented dots, these fuming pools I call eyes nose and mouth.

Arturo before he died spoke of giving birth to a dozen perfect beasts . . . but before that buried his dog and pitched a tent for half a year in his back yard. His mother nightly stationed herself at the nearest door, shouting her restless warnings into the cruellest darkness she had ever seen: I TOLD YOU TOLD YOU DIDN'T I TELL YOU WHAT WOULD HAPPEN IF YOU GOT A DOG?

Come out here, Arturo replied, and I'll bury us all.

Seasons flush us from these careful holes in which we hibernate. Witness Matila flushed from hers. Arturo's photo removed from the mantelpiece. His mother forming wings or horns for whatever is to be her brief afterlife. Arturo and Matila, Matila and Gore: marriage is whatever our best locket holds. Our lives before we attain them come wrapped in dust. Arturo, brother and friend: in his family and in mine we arrived condemned. My bones are last to survive these wicked, privileged hours. Dust is all-knowing, all-powerful. It appropriates, even engenders where nothing else will. It has the weight of a thousand copper pennies over my eyes.

"But you must eat something!" insists my wife. "You're snake-thin, you're not getting enough nourishment to keep a frog alive!" She snaps her head away, startled by the note of triumph her voice can't conceal. The words, too, discomfort her: this frog shape is mine. This sack of snakes, dormant always, which forms my body from neck to thighs. My head twists up, I allow an arm its furtive crawl — my wife recoils, finds escape in the busy arrangement of silverware, while I acknowledge with found indifference that vanity thrives under the most obscene of conditions. Gore laughs. I look to find his face at the usual chair and for a moment can discern nothing in that space. Only a swirl of dust on the other side of some milky field. Gore goes on laughing.

"I've got his number," he says. "Old Sam is not fooling me!" My hand twitches back to hide again under the grey blanket which supposedly dignifies me. "Look," someone exclaims, "— he's crying!" "Oh, look!" another says, "what a rush of tears!"

My eyes are indeed aswim. But whose voices are these? How is it that strangers come to be seated here? Has someone invited them? Do I know these voices from somewhere? My wife is making the easy excuse for me: "Don't let him disturb you. He's probably thinking of Arturo's buried dog."

"Arturo?" One of these newcomers speaks Arturo's name.

"A previous occupant of this house." It is Matila bringing dishes, addressing the table with a festive air.

"Ah, Arturo," responds Gore, "— whatever happened to him?" He lifts his cane, pokes its tip to that space where I breathe.

"Everyone dig in," Matila says. Her apron falls casually over my knee.

"Eat, eat!" encourages my wife. "God knows how he lives." A murmur goes around.

I get enough. I get, in fact, more than my share. I get hers, I get Matila's, and Gore's. I get Arturo's too. I get whatever portion our dead mule most enjoyed.

These newcomers are ravenous. They can't remember when they've dined better or imagine how soon they're likely to have it so well again. Yet while juices drip from their lips they are already recalling the simplicity and beauty of life where they come from. What a glorious future, they assert, one may have there! My wife scoffs, but is too polite to ask why, if so, they have come here. Matila and Gore hold hands, speaking delicately of their tender hopes. "One child, a single child," Matila maintains, "may change the world!"

When I . . . .

I once . . . .

"Arturo's dog —" I begin to say . . . but my wife's laughter drowns me out. "Mrruff-mrruff!" she barks. "Mrruff-mrruff," Gore rejoins. Their laughter spreads around the table and orbits there. My knees quiver, my legs thrash under cover. This weeping does nothing to extricate me. Snakes snooze contentedly in the warmth of my groin. This frog tongue thickens when it greets air. This blanket is dead earth borrowed from a grave. I speak to you of my wife, of Arturo, of Matila and Gore, I make passing reference to mules, dogs, and this chair — yet nothing is further from my mind.

I remember a large house, panoramic grounds. The solemn expressions of ancestors in oval frames. The abiding sovereignty of one massive glass chandelier. My mother in her ghostly . . .

But someone's hand is resting lightly on my shoulder now. It occurs to me that it has been there for a long time. I look up into the face of one of our dinner guests. She has red hair, I notice, and a small pretty space between two front teeth. "I'm so tired," she says to me. Her voice is gay, her eyes amused, as if she means to tell me that she would not exchange this fatigue for anything in the world. "I'm plumb tuckered out!" Her words waltz merrily, she has the mood of a schoolgirl who has never known this condition before. Behind her other guests are expressing this mutual exhaustion — they stretch and yawn, yet it seems to me this dinner table has rarely seen such ebullience. Chairs are pushed back, the guests rise, and the air makes room for them. It shifts in a frenzy, eventually to settle where they stand. The woman's hand tightens on my shoulder. Her dress, cut low, is of darkest green, and I stare at her close, freckled cleavage. I would be content, I think, to let my head hang there. "We are new to the neighbourhood," I hear her say. "Will you consent to walking us home?"

The moment is awkward. My wife is stacking dishes, Matila and Gore sit as though dazed, staring at their wine glasses. So it is that I volunteer. I rise without difficulty from my chair. The woman smiles as if enchanted and wraps a hand over my arm. I glance back to see my wife's head cocked, her eyes large, her mouth rounded in mute surprise.

I lead our guests out the door, I advance with them along the sidewalk that led them here. I walk with the woman's arm light upon mine. The night has no scent, it has neither colour nor substance of any kind, yet there is nothing I do not recognize. We reach a certain corner and their footsteps pass on ahead.

I see them in the far distance and marvel at the broad backs they have.

Once Arturo, in passing, spoke of his mother: "She advances, with pail and mop and broom, to clean up battlefields. She —"

I return to find my wife crying, tears plopping into the white beauty of her half-consumed dessert. "How humiliating this is for me!" she is saying. "I'm worn out from all that man has put me through!" Gore lifts one drunken eye: "I told you," he says. "Old Sam wasn't fooling me!"

Matila rocks, arms joined over her breasts as if to force down the climbing child. "It was Arturo," she moans. "He would never forgive me for leaving him."

They return to their despondent watch of my empty chair.

The elevator chugs, it rattles, but it delivers me to this room. Matila's bed is perfectly satisfying. Far more comforting is it than the other in that adjacent room.

I like it better, to tell the truth.

I can stretch out in my full ease here.

It has the scent of talcum and fresh earth. It has Arturo's handprints on every wall. He and I: we were born and raised in rooms such as this. What has become of those oval portraits which were here? Whatever became of our glass chandelier? It cried — we all said it did — whenever anyone moved in rooms above or below. And someone, where I lived, was moving all the time.

"It is weeping," my mother would say, "for all the nice children you shall have."

Its beads caught the sun and flashed radiance everywhere.

This flesh is chilled. Eyes seek the darker side.

What is the hurry? The question is immaterial now, yet it is one which engages me.

In our family we were discreet: we mapped out our paths of solitude, and then we fled.

We followed wind gusts — always with an eye alert for the old family trails. "You go far," my mother would say, "but you do come home."

Matila is first to enter. Her shrouded face, in this light, seems rouged. She too has been crying and now her face further distorts. She whimpers, drawing up a chair. In a moment she will tell me that Arturo was no better than other men. That she could not live — could not survive — with him. That no woman could. She bends nearer, fixing her sight on mine. Her wet eyes glisten. She has not two eyes but pieces in a chain of jewels which could secure the world. The depths which open to me are incalculable; were I of a mind to I could follow this chain to places both beautiful and horrible.

The chain weakens; slowly it vanishes there. We see only what fronts us here. Matila bows her head and gnaws at the fist in her mouth. Her shoulders heave. Tears burst from her.

"It's your fault!" she cries. "You would not share yourself! Don't expect me to grieve! Everything was always such a secret with you! I feel nothing! Nothing! And Arturo would say the same!"

This vindictiveness is so shallow it barely touches me. I speak calmly of the futility of such assertions and denials. She pretends to hear nothing. She grinds both fists against her teeth, now sobbing all the more. To my mind it is fear and guilt convulsing her. It is Arturo trying to leap inside. "You deserved this!" she cries. "You deserve it all!"

My dog! my dog! my dog!

I am the mirror of her enraged eyes. We would both sweep me up like some long dead fly, poke me with sticks until I am driven to the most remote garbage pile. A person's eye is monstrous, it sees around and beyond the woman in this room. It sees the space that is missing here. It sees space tumbling in upon space, the rubble of waves where nothing upright moves. The ear expands. It asks the value of this daily sacrifice. Defending one's self is the last indignity. The ear is magic: it listens to nothing. Yet these bones continue to anoint themselves. The longest war is one of nerves. Love bends to its pleasure as it flees towards another transient ache.

The eye widens.

Flesh is all mouth and devours itself.

"Oh, Sam, Sam, you've done it at last!"

My wife's form shivers between these high bedposts at the foot of the bed. Her finger spins a meaningless insignia, while her nostrils flare with a poison old in her.

Incantations are aswirl throughout this house.

Her hands smack together, they clutch and wring. She would murder the last duty that has forced her here.

What have we done to our lives? What brings us to this mad rapture we call remorse? Snakes crawl out from my guts and I feel little more than a tingle in that cavity where they were. My own remorse is waiting to crawl inside. I lament these times. The dreadful vigour of seasons, the shove of year into year.

I can recall a large house, panoramic grounds. During his last years my father slowly cruising the fenced-off yard in his motorized chair. Myself at a high window watching him.

My wife claws at bedposts. "Why? Why? Why did it have to be like this?" Who am I to say which of us is haunted most?

The moon's pull is stronger than my own. These people by size are life-like. They walk, they speak, they will go on doing so. Others will take the place of those who stand here. I will reappear among the dust motes and give the kiss to every hand.

But now . . .

When I . . .

Mrruff-mrruff. . . .

My face takes the oval frame. Nothing is obscured. I see back all the way.

I rise, and return to my chair.

"This is madness!" the two women shout. "Why does he do this to us!"

What have we done to our women to so incline them now to these accusations? To this loyalty? To this melodrama? What have we done to ourselves that induces us to notice?

The single eye of the swivelfish, confronting phenomena, enlarges. The eye becomes all.

All that is outside will now come in.

Say no more, I tell myself.

Reveal nothing.

By morning no trace shall remain.

My dog! my dog! my dog!

Fazzini Must
Have You Ever
at Her Side

One evening in winter just after dark, Fazzini's son by a previous marriage, a mere child, hardly more than six, now living with his famous mother, was seen racing across Vicenza.

His friends, spotting him, called out, "Marco, Marco, where are you going so fast?" — but the boy flung himself along, taking no time to reply, inasmuch as his racing was indeed borne of emergency and panic and the direst need. He burst into his father's house just as the latter was sitting down to dinner. "Father, father," the boy said, "come quickly, for our mother is saying she will do away with herself."

The father at once leapt up from the table and now there were two Fazzinis racing across Vicenza, their foot-race borne of direst emergency, and no time in their running to reply to the curious bystanders on Vicenza's streets who called out, "Hey, you two stallions, why are you racing so, why don't you slow down and live, take time to enjoy yourselves?"

Between gulps of breath, oh, racing so fast, the father asked his son, "Your dear mother, the most precious of women, the happiest of women, why is she wanting to do away with herself?"

To which the hurrying boy replied, "Papa, papa, how you do astound me! Do you not remember that my darling mother is always unhappiest when she is completing a painting, and papa, papa, she may already have completed her painting and be yet this very second on the very brink of doing away with herself, so let's hurry, dear papa, and save this chatter for the more reposed moment."

So there they were yet again, racing — how many times in a single year to speed back and forth across the city to the woman who was about to do herself in, as she was ever about to do on those frequent and heart-numbing occasions when the one painting was nearing completion and the next not yet begun, and never perhaps to be begun, because with one painting done the artist so rarely could see herself setting down to begin another, and thus her life would be over, since what reason could she have to go on drawing human breath when she had not the smallest conception of what canvas she might next turn to — no, and never would again, for her brain was dead and her body dying also.

This she would say to the boy, her face and hands dripping paint, her brush hand furiously at work on the all-but-completed painting: "Oh my dearest boy, my most acutely enamored son, my sweetest heart, although I love you dearly and can not bear the thought of being parted from you, you who mean everything to me! But what am I without my painting, this poisonous art, this worm that drinks my blood? I am nothing, a no one, a meaningless cipher in life's treadmill, a nonentity and a groaner, a sniveller, a hack, bad-mooded and ill-tempered and totally unrecognizable even as a human being! Without my painting I will be no good to you as a mother and I will despair and my despair will ruin your life, my dearest son, as it has ruined so many others, not to exclude your loving father, oh goodbye my darling, though for the moment I live, I work, I paint in this fever, but come and kiss me, do, there, there's a sweet boy, do forgive me!"

So everyone in Vicenza who saw the first Marco and his son the second Marco running so fast looked up at the stars, and said to one another, "Well, my goodness, that Francesca, she must be about to finish her new painting."

So, then:

Quickly as one could speak the words, father and son burst into the painter's studio, those old and creaking paint-bespattered rooms high on the hill, with the warped doors, the creaking floor, the crooked walls, the ragged ceiling where a thousand spiders had spun their webs since time immemorial, but boasting high, clean windows which admitted good light even in cruelest winter, with a view from these windows of the Villa of the Famous Dwarfs who were known themselves to cavort about in a frenzy and hide their heads in agony whenever the painter Francesca was about to pronounce "Fini" to her new painting and splash on the wild signature which only another spider could decipher . . .

Why, yes, father Marco and son Marco, as alike in their jitters as the yolks from two eggs, sweat dripping from their eyes, their hearts pounding, their eyes bulging, entering —

Entering to see the dear artist at work so intensely with her paints and brushes in that smallest pocket down in the painting's infamous right corner that she scarcely could take time out to lift her eyes in acknowledgement of them, her hair a tangle of fiery vermilion and ochre and russet hues that might have been taken for ancient blood, that might have been sludge washed into her scalp from primordial rock, her brow furrowed in deepest concentration, her smock a sea of stains, and muttering to herself, "The light, the light, oh, for the presence of unremitting light!" — because daylight had indeed waned and here she was working now from the mere, intermittent, all but inconsequential illumination that a single cigarette could provide. Oh, *puff-puff,* the brief orange glow, paint paint, *puff-puff,* another quick stroke, brush work down in that tight, meanest little final corner, the painter squinting, *puff-puff,* her teeth gnawing first one and then the other lip, *puff-puff,* the curling ash, the brief glow of light, the quickest stab of paint, her rapt, tortured face but inches from the canvas . . .

Then, *Voila! Holy Moses! Jumping Jehoshaphat!* — a great shout from the artist (*"I'm done, done, fini, fini, fait accompli!" Skaal! Prosit! To my health!*) — and the paint brushes pitched across the room, a foot kicking aside the mountain of cigarette butts, wading through ash, a carpet of wrenched tubes, nubbed brushes, tin cans, discarded rags, as a hand clutches a wine bottle, as the artist swigs, the artist next clawing at her hair, burying her face momentarily within her frock's stiffened folds, muttering incantation to herself before flinging a massive new canvas onto her easel, that canvas sized, primed, ready. Then . . .

Only then lifting an astonished face to her wide-eyed visitors, that face lit with sudden, transforming radiance by the most heart-warming cheer, now exclaiming to this most-excellent duo of Marco Fazzinis, "Darlings, my treasures, in the nick of time! The very nick! My best painting ever, oh my lovelies, a work of genius with no known comparison — now, *now, shoo! shoo! Away from me, you gnats!* — those other immortals must step aside! Michelangelo, Masaccio, Masolino, Parmigianino, step aside! Oh, but not you, my darlings, come and hold me, let me embrace you, oh let me kiss your faces, and after the kisses, champagne, more champagne, champagne until we drop, my wonders, but one sip only for me, one only, and a quick brush of my teeth to extract from my jaws this vile taste that benumbs my mouth, perhaps afterwards a second sip, a third, and then it's onwards to my next work, my sweet stallions, because I am in the grip of delirious fever and must keep on, *on on on!* with no time out for dinner or the conventional human intercourse between closest friends, or even to properly greet you, my darlings, how nice of you to drop in and what on earth would become of me if I did not have you ever at my side?"

Hitting the Charts

Last night I was out doing the boogie.

Nothing at The Ruptured Duck, not much at Teen Town or The Gypsy Moth, but at The Hot Wire I read the vibes, contemplated my juices, and determined I was all set to get lucky.

My hour had been a long time coming.

It was a case of *Go Daddy Go*, of *macho macho* and *Disco Duck*, or give your heart to Old Mother Nature and *let the cool lady sink you on down*.

I got no money
and I got no friend,
Me by my lonely
and nearing the end.
I got no wife
and I got no love,
Me by my lonely
Living push and shove.

I located a lovely person, foxy # with drooping head, sitting alone at a table in a far corner the minute my eyelids cooled. This is the life, Dad, I told myself — and putting on my Ready For Anything face I hiked up my Truckstop Designer jeans and motored over.

"*Dance with me Henry,*" I cried, and gave her The Look.

Without giving me a glance or saying a word she hoisted herself up and like a stately breeze headed out to the floor. I followed fast behind, chasing the scent of Wind Song by Prince Matchabelli, as the music wheeled into high screech like a thousand jibjabs finally let out into the garden.

Ta-ta-tum ta-ta-tum, let the beat go on. I gave my hips their first twist and was off and running like a nag bolting the gate, throwing out my arms in a propeller spin so that no one could doubt which part of the floor was mine.

"I'm Jake," I told my partner on the up-breath, "how you making out?"

Nothing. Under her bangs her moon face looked like an opening cut out of deep hedge. Never mind. I went up on first one toe and then the other, bending like green timber. In my high school days Jake B. Carlyle had been known as the eagle of the dance floor and it was all coming back after 99 years.

Wang Wang Blues, I thought, *and Begin the Beguine, gonna take a sentimental journey.*

"You come here often?" I shouted.

No reply. Her sight was always on someone just behind me, never any movement up or down. Her noble head slid from shoulder to shoulder like a thing on rails.

"That's pretty groovy," I joked, "you pick that up in India?"

Not a flicker. Yet her very essence told me I was getting somewhere.

Butter in my hands, *yeah-yeah-yeah!*

I had come a long way in only a few hours. At the start of the evening the music had been like a rhino herd having a singalong with Mitch; I had left The Ruptured Duck and Teen Town a Hippo on skate boards, but now I was hitting my stride. Jake, I told myself, your azimuth is in its five moons, Jupiter is high, and the time is yours! I had come through four repeat years at the Transcendental Meditation Centre, gone fourteen months with the Technocracy crowd, for twenty-seven years had been a devout Rosicrucian, and for one season had been a scrub guard for the House of David. Had spent half a lifetime kicking pigeons or just generally floundering about, but now my head was in place.

Daddy don't step on my Dr. Scholl's shoes because my clock has turned and the hour is ripe! I have weathered Frankie Laine's Jezebel and Spike Jones' Beatlebomb and my ears no longer extended to my feet. I was Fritz the Cat and purring out loud over all of discoland *Oh Mama we are the most, we are hot-to-trot tonight, your feet are on fire and Bo Diddly I ain't.*

The platter ripped to its demise. Strobe lights blinked and for an instant they let the tape deck cool. "Buy you a drink?" I said, and fifty arms shot up — though my own sweet dancing partner was nowhere to be seen.

I was bathed in black mud, a sightless knave. *Frail*, I thought, *oh frail is thy hand in mine, my fair Caithleeene!*

"Open the door Richard," I cried, "oh Richard open that door!"

Never mind. I was at home with these hard-to-get types and felt confident that before the evening ended I'd have her licking from my hands. Already I loved her air of indifferent and placid mystery, her aura of divine and mystic depth; I loved the way her hair bounced above expressionless ears and how her chin never dropped and how the light wheel grazed like sheep on her face. She was mine all mine and just the kind of sweet perfection I was looking for. *Mama Mama Mama*, I cried to the rafters, *treat me good!*

The platter spun anew and I quivered in my tracks, going solo for a while. Two or three of those I bumped gave me dirty looks and one in a feather-duster skirt and a strontium 90 smile murmured in my ear, "You better slow down, Pops, your face is snow-white, you definitely got lily-pad gills."

"I'm cooking with gas," I told this smiler, "no need to worry," and gave her a toad-footed spin that had her eyes rattling in her head.

Oh Jelly Roll roll, cream me no cream and butter me no butter.

I was beginning to get the feel of my digs. Beginning to realize what I had been missing out on by not doing the boogie scene long before. Beginning to regret all my tortured years of Monday Nite Baseball and Friday Nite poker and Saturday Nite blues and the thousand bleak evenings sitting on my elbows.

Jake, I told myself, this is the high life, the real life, this is where it's at, old fossil-heart of mine, you're to turn over a new leaf dating from now.

No more four A.M. movies for me, with the final blip dropping like man's last breath across the snowballed screen. No more weeping in the solitude of all my betrayals and longing for dawn's tender mercy to tuck me up in my drunken bed.

Oh frail is thy hand in mine, oh frail is your touch, my darling Caithleeene.

I was clearly cut out for this fine night-life. It was *Groovy Greybeard Groovy* and proper time I took off my age-old bib.

I grabbed a spin with loose flotsam whose date was spewing up Labatt's 50 in a corner, and kept her there for a full ten minutes while the Gyroscopes wooed us with powerpack song and the smoke of cigarettes dropped from the black ceiling inch by inch and wrote death in the air with a thousand white signatures, and when finally she wiped off the sweat and said "Um tarred" I took my cues and hurried her back to her tongue-tied mate, murmuring *merci* and *toute la guerre* as a gentleman would, in the meantime keeping a wary eye out for my Dream Girl, the one fair lady in the whole of The Hot Wire whom I would woo and be wooed by and whom I would have.

But man is an island even at The Hot Wire and my Dream Girl was nowhere to be seen and it was all Lover's Lullaby for me.

I'll love her in the attic,
I'll love her in the cellar
I'll love her wherever
She's clearly ecstatic.

Oh frail your hand, Caithleeene. Oh your time was long time a-coming, Willie Mays.

I elbowed my way up to black marble bar and told the cherub behind it to splash down in front of me whatever poison was nearest to hand, hang the expense, my son.

Set'um up Joe.

A man in a trench coat wide as a flag gave me a hearty slap on the shoulder and asked if I was from out of town, footloose and fancy-free the same as him. "Portland myself," he shouted, "USofA, city county and nation built by God." But now and then, he confessed, he had to unwind. He fished out a card and waved it in front of me: CHARTERED

ACCOUNTANTS, it read, FITZ, DIBBS AND SLIDE — *We Have What Counts.* . . . "Dibbs," he said, throwing out a hand, "put 'er there." He laughed, the joker, and went into a quick crouch, all better to goose a young lady just then passing by. The lady shrieked and spun, though not before Dibbs was again upright and innocently staring off into the dim yonder. The lady stared at my outstretched hand which Dibbs had refused, then reared back and smacked her mighty fist against my face.

"Reprobate," she snarled, and scooted on.

Oh Daddy shoot me with novocaine! Oh Mama, tell me the news!

"Works every time," snickered Dibbs. "I pulled that trick on Fitz one time and he lost three teeth." He grabbed at my arm, pulled me along: "Let's go visit the Men's. In this sumphole I can't hear myself think."

I was grateful, once reaching the Men's, for my Life by Riley platform heels. They let me tower over Dibbs, shorter than a barber pole and about as cool, and moreover kept my flared cuffs dry.

"Portland's all right," ventured Dibbs, looking for a high spot to perch, "but there are things a man can't do in his own home town. Too many twinkies he has to look out for. In Portland, city of God, you wouldn't find me coming within a mile of a dump like this."

"Time waits for no man," I told this snake. "Shake, rattle, and roll." Scratches in the door behind which Dibbs hid himself told me to CALL GLORIA, first with the latest, last with the most. Stickers on the wall said NO NUKES and SAVE OUR SEALS and REMEMBER PEARL HARBOR and GOD ADORES A TURKEY.

"A man's got to break out of a rut," Dibbs was telling me. "Got to get his arms around something unfamiliar now and then. You got a paper I could read? Mind you," he said, "the wife don't understand, but I say what the hell, a quick poke never hurt anyone. These young people now, not worth a crap, but they have the right idea. I tell you it's places like this that's keeping old Dibbs feeling young."

I sloshed down my gin, hardly listening to Dibbs, floating back to the action on wings of song, thinking how I had found and lost my thrill on Blueberry Hill, on Mood Indigo and Rock Island Line. Sock it to me, baby, I told old Dibbs, these shoes were made for walking, now who's got the smack?

"My daughter, 17," Dibbs went on, "precious lamb, she's hot-to-trot for experience, can't wait to run off with the first dog-catcher sniffs up her skirt. Last week I caught her writing Ann Landers, complaining how her parents kept her penned up, 'they don't trust me,' she said. Oh I lit into her, I really told her where she stood. I smelt smoke the other day walking into her room, and my fist nearly took off her head. She'll think twice next time. She sees me taking a drink at home, asks 'why can't I have one?' I tell you I've got blisters from the times I've had to smack that child. My daddy smacked me around, what do you think, that I'd disapprove? How else you imagine I got where I am? Not long ago I came home, found some squirt kid trying to sneak away through the backyard. I pulled him back inside, punched his nose, kicked him in my den. My den is redwood panelled, most beautiful stuff you ever saw. I got 14 rifles mounted, collector's items, every one in working or-der. Blow the head off a moose, great weapons, I tell you a person don't even have to aim. I said, 'there they are, kid, take your pick.' 'Whut, huh?' he said — I tell you kids today don't even know human speech. 'You got it, kid,' I told this squirt, 'the next time you come nosing round my daughter you going to get my .12 ought right between your eyes.' Oh that kid scrammed, I tell you we're raising nothing but chick-ens these days. In my day I'm proud to say I was mauling cherries all over town, me and jailbait had a natural attraction for each other. You think I don't know what is going on? What kids have in mind? Now the Kooks you find in here, these laid-back dope fiends living off my tax — if I found my daughter sleeping around like these Kooks I'd choke her, no questions asked. She knows it too. Oh she hoes the line. A sweet girl, a precious angel. You should have seen that letter she was writing Ann, just as proper as you please. Me, I'd spend a week on it and still not have the commas right. That's education, that's what I'm paying for. I mean, a parent's got to contribute, right? Out here, out in the real world, well it's all going to hell in a handbasket quicker than the eye can blink, wouldn't you say? But I've got faith, I'm a bundle of love, none of that negative crap for me."

Groovy, I thought, *Oh Daddio, show me the way.*

"Oh boy!" Dibbs said, jacking up his pants, "that felt good, third time I been today, healthy sign, wouldn't you say?" — and without a sprinkle of water over his hands but with time to slick back his receding hair he was off and running, leaping back into the fray. "I can still git it up," he shouted back, "don't think I can't." He crowded a friendly neighbour off a bar stool and scrambled up huffing, his brow shining with sweat, while a multitude of white gulls dipped their wings in a slow circle overhead, part of the decor that gave The Hot Wire its classy name. The beat was whining out of a half-dozen ceiling vents with a kamikaze craze and the floor was pounding and at the tables a hundred good-time voices were screeching in gratitude. It was meal time at the Oasis and I was with it, baby, I was Johnny on the Spot, old Johnnie B. Kool.

"Long may your willy ream," shouted Dibbs, now off to the dance floor, grabbing at every feline shape, "I've got more notches than Billy the Kid and I mean to dip it while the dippin's good."

Oh Mama, I thought, *Oh hunter home from the hill, Oh man in the Grey Flannel Suit. Oh make me a pallet on the floor. Oh it ain't me, babe!* Gyrating couples shook past under waves of yellow, mauve and blue. I yearned to step forward and embrace each of them, to say *Oh you spinning swingers, what you see here is a man who takes his lessons from Father Time, from the Mole People who burrow every year in my yard. September Song and Autumn Leaves and Some Enchanted Evening, all that is smoke in my eyes. Shoot Tchaikovsky, give the mickey to Mahler, old B. is bleeding on the floor. I emerge each year new-born and ripe for action. I have shucked Paul Harvey's Decade of News, I'm Johnny Belinda On-the-Spot. Butter me no butter and Yule me no Yule, I want all your wooden nickels, old Dibbs and I will talk them into gold.*

Hubba-hubba, babe, wake up little Suzy, take me to the hop!

Oh frail is they hand in mine, how frail,
my fair Caithleeene.

A man with an undertaker's face, seated by the woman next on his list, leaned into my shoulder, said, "I'm from Saskatoon, that's my wife Munchie I'm with. Say hello to the nice man, Munchie." Munchie glowered, then showed her red tongue, pulling at my sleeve. "What a character," she said. "I was wed once and that was enough." I sank down beside this wind-swept pair, yearning for Saskatoon where I've never been, for the Mom and Pop I'd have there waiting for me to make something of my life. No doubt the woman I should have married was still waiting for me, waiting in Saskatoon. Her life had been ruined, mine too, because I hadn't had the good sense to stay where I was born and with what was good for me, this dream-time Saskatoon. She would have lived next door, would have initiated me gently into sex, would have urged me to put my life back together and not commit suicide after losing the race for high school presidency by 900 votes. *You can do it, Jake, I've always believed in you. Oh Jake, there's always next year. Oh Jake, you did this when they dropped you from the checkers team.* Happy kids, a sound business of my own, all waiting in Saskatoon. Big warm house, couple of cars, a good snowblower to keep our driveways clear.

I could have made it big in Saskatoon.

"Look at him," the undertaker man said. "Saskatoon's got him. Happens every time."

"Buy me some peanuts," his Munchie said, "how do you like my hair?"

Adios, Saskatoon.

When I hear you call . . . my love song . . . to me. . . .

I went in search of my dream girl. I tapped the wrong beauty on the shoulder and the boy-friend rose up from his chair to stand on my toes. The music was loud and I didn't take in the advice he was giving, though his beauty's voice left no room for any misunderstanding: *"Go suck eggs,"* she said. *"Cock your leg up to a fire hydrant, buzz off, me and him are here to have us fun."* Under these scrofulous urgings, I chug-lugged on.

Oh broken-hearted melody, oh melancholy baby, I'm coming round the mountain yes I am.

The floor was solid concrete but I could feel it vibrating. Before the place became The Hot Wire it had been Elmo's Body & Fender Shop. Under this very ceiling where gulls circled and lights flashed 3000 times to the single blink Elmo's drab crew had put on a new grill and bumper, new radiator, new hood and paint job after my erstwhile wife, unable to give up sweets and tormented by broken fingernails, had tried to drive her Volkswagen through our very own front door. Lovely woman, she'd sat on the red seat screeching out through broken glass that there *"was not power enough under the hood!"* Then to back up and come again, knowing I was in there somewhere.

I'm all for you, body and soul.

Where was old Elmo now, I wondered. And erstwhile wife, where was she? They too ought to be here doing the boogie, didn't know what they were missing.

Dibbs punched me on the arm, shoved me back against a wall.

"Got change?" he demanded. "Any change?"

"Oh yeah, yeah," I said, and commenced digging.

"A dollar? Two dollars? My old lady don't take collect calls any more not since our oldest went Yo-yo and cut out on us. Calls all the time, wants to speak to God. A fruit-cake, can you imagine, my son!"

He scratched at my palm, took what change I had.

"Got to report in, you know," he explained, going. "Conference, you know! Midnight oil, what Dibbs won't do to keep together house and home!" He smacked his brow, came back at me again. "How you fixed? Anything to spare? A loan? Woman over there with the navel cut, skinny as a playing card, I asked her how much, she gave me the wink. Let you have seconds, what do you say?"

I plonked down a dollar into his hand. Added another.

"Go for quality tonight," I told him, "it's all on me."

Ah, your hand in mine, Caithleeene.

Dibbs was insulted, then thought better of it and gave me another of his bosomy slaps on the shoulder. "Great guy," he said. "I knew you were a great guy. One of the gang." Grinning, he tucked my two bucks inside his fat wallet, and strode off to make his call.

Ah, frail, Caithleeene, but a champion of love as we set off across endless dunes.

Up a lazy river, Caithleeene. . . .
Rocky Mountain Fever, Caithleeene.
Rock of Ages, Caithleeene.

My erstwhile wife Rebecca June, driven into fits on account of my drivel and my habit of bending precious silverware and my eternal bad moods and my insistence on calling her *my frail Caithleeene.*

"Munchie's going!" someone shouted from across the room, and I looked up and there through air more shaded than the ocean floor was Saskatoon waving both arms, now pulling Munchie in front of me, shouting, "Munchie, say goodbye, Munchie, to the nice man!"

Munchie put her hands under her breasts and lifted them and blew me a kiss: "Goodbye, nice man!"

And I was moved, I was genuinely moved. I wept, and for the promise, even the promise, of a second kiss I would have followed her even *past* Saskatoon.

So much for your hand in mine, Caithleeene.

Dibbs came back. "No answer," he said.

"Ten o'clock, 12 o'clock rock," I told him. "Blue Moon, Standing on the Street Corner, Mercy-mercy, Mr Percy."

"Guess she's out visiting her mother."

"Swing low," I said. "Looking over Jordan."

He spilled the coins back into my pocket. Slumped his shoulders. Ah yes, old Dibbs was subdued.

"Takes all the joy out," he said. "You never know *what* those bitches will do! Oh well. I'm turning in."

I took the door with him.

On the street, breathing fresh air, he shrugged and I shrugged, and each turned and headed off our separate ways.

Ah, frail your hand in mine, Caithleeene. Yours and Dibbs'. Sisters and brothers on the lam.

Shh-boom, shhh-boom . . . old buttermilk sky . . . Boo-boo-ba-boo of the night. . . .

I got no money
and I got no friend,
Me by my lonely
and nearing the end.
I got no wife
and I got no love,
Me by my lonely
Living push and shove. . . .

Two old ladies, arm-in-arm and peck-pecking their canes, looking straight ahead, were approaching me on the sidewalk.

Black glasses.

Blind.

I steered over, hugged back against a street-front door. Held my breath.

"Good evening, young man," the two together said.

They passed on.

Ah, frail, Caithleeene. Frail. But still here. Still mine.

BIOGRAPHICAL NOTES

BRIEF BIOGRAPHICAL NOTES on some of the people called to give evidence for or against me:

MARCELINE ABLE (1964–   )   Material to come.

WANDA LEE CASSLAKE   My Dead Friend.
Wanda Casslake came into my life nine years ago when I was thirty-five and branching out and never left it although she quit her own for reasons that remain to be extricated by someone better equipped to deal with biographical history than I am. Natural actor and wonderful human being. A pleasure-loving woman with a generous heart who always made the most of her appearance, on-screen or off, and only wanted everyone to think the worst of her. Bust like a boy's. Married to:

ROBIN HARVEY (1935–   )   Actor.
On camera, he rarely knew what to do with his hands: one had to take enormous care with angles because his head tended to photograph excessively large. The Floating Wedge, as this is called in the trade. The best a critic could ever think to say of him (*Great Speckled Bird*) was that he knew "how to undress casually while indifferently smoking a joint." He could at times surprise us, but he was, for the most part, an

awful bore. Robin found little in life about which to be enthusiastic. He was fond of reminiscing over the recent past. If I went out with Robin and Wanda for a night of drinking and relaxation after a gruelling day on the set, Robin's sole delight was in reminiscing over what the three of us had done the previous evening. Actually, he was never sure what we'd done and would remain unsure even after we had told him. Powerfully built, but with a slow, uncomplicated mind.

Canadian. Most of the people in these Notes are. I cite this with some hesitancy, since in my view the information yields little that is vital. Circumstance is relevant, origin is not, and accident is the father of mankind. National origin has significance relative only to transitory phenomena. It was for this reason that the stork, flying through skies belonging to no one, was selected to carry our early burden (trademark, by the way, of our first eight films). Such oddities of persuasion received frequent airings by Wanda and me. Robin Harvey found these musings of no consequence and normally went off to talk and drink with other individuals, some of whom no doubt were only too happy to tell him what he had done the previous evening. Wanda — who made a point of never telling me where she was from or what her family situation had been, just as she would never reveal her age or why she had married Robin or admit that she had ever read a book — Wanda, being the argumentative type, naturally disputed all notions relative to the common brotherhood of living beings exclusive of any vital differences incurred through country of origin, religion etc., foo-fawing for that matter *any* lofty ideas I might propose.

"Why then," I might ask her, "do you continue to work? Work without a higher purpose is a pokey thing indeed."

I do it for the money, came her inevitable reply. *I do it because I enjoy titillating the hicks, and because being denigrated by a society made up of people who are not as honest about themselves as I am affords me considerable masochistic kicks.*

"If I thought that," I would tell her, "I would fire your can tomorrow. You are a great artist and through your art we are reshaping the planet."

Oh, Martin, she would say in her fiery yet sad little way, *you are only trying to find an excuse for this terrible thing we do.*

Wanda Casslake took the opposite view on every question I ever raised, from the simplest to the most abstruse, even arguing that her breasts were "of quite the normal size" — this despite ample proof to the contrary which for years flowed through 16mm projectors every Saturday night at a hundred private cinema clubs and societies around the world. All now confiscated, I should explain. Scheduled for destruction the minute my last appeal is refused. Nothing of her remains in my possession except ten stills shot one sour, forlorn evening a week before her death. But not shot by me. These photographs, incidentally, I have wanted unpublished for the good reason that Wanda's flat chest does not lift them above the obscene. They have no redeeming social value. They are as dirty as they come. Which is why I held on to them. The point I would make about their existence is that filth remains filth until someone with a humanist perspective comes along and transforms it, often through art, into a thing that takes the measure of the beauty and depth of human life.

Police continue to snoop about, paid informers lurking on every corner.

"I want those pictures, Martin," Robin tells me.

"Oh, shove it," I tell him. "Wanda was adamant in maintaining that she owed nothing to you, that her marriage to you was largely accidental, regrettable, barely worth the paper that made it official."

I'll sue you, he says.

Opportunist, 5′ 8″, balding, something of a card shark, proponent of the *laid-back life* and for that reason a happy choice for roles opposite Wanda as his every indifferently delivered line and gesture served to symbolize a) the dehumanization of oppressed working classes everywhere; b) twentieth-century man gone soft through luxury; and c) that intelligent women will always give themselves to brutes too dense to value what they are receiving.

Drinks too much. Recently converted to Catholicism.

Her co-star through the twenty-three films comprising the *Night* series.

Less said of him the better.

RITA ISLINGTON (age approximately 42) Education, occupation, marital status, etc. unknown.

A short time ago, fresh on the heels of my incarceration and release on bond, a woman showed up at my door, announced that her name was as listed above, and that she had an interest in buying her sister's photographs, no questions asked — though she hoped my price would not be unreasonable.

"Who was your sister?"

Wanda Lee Casslake.

"I never would have known." A shrug of her shoulders. "Who told you I have them?"

I can't say.

"Did Robin send you?"

I suppose you mean her husband. I have never met him.

"How did you find me?"

Through your lawyer.

"Are you acting on behalf of yourself or for others?"

I want only to salvage what remains of my sister's reputation.

"She was a great actress."

I do not agree.

"Where was Wanda born? What were her parents like? For a long time I've been very interested."

Such questions are not pertinent to this negotiation.

"Are we negotiating?"

I hope so. I do not like to have my time wasted.

"Have you ever worked in cinema?"

You are prying. Let us talk price.

"What in your view constitutes a reasonable sum?"

I think you will find my offer liberal.

She opened her purse. As it turned out, the sum offered was liberal indeed. My black onyx bowl was soon stacked high with her currency. "No," I said.

No?

For the first time she seemed to be about to lose her temper. I sensed, if I may say so, a whiff of danger.

You will not sell them to me?

I sensed, emanating from her, an uncompromising hatred. Her skin had gone white. A moment later she smiled and my suspicions seemed ludicrous. On an impulse I decided to let her have the negatives. *Without charge.* The last is important to the view I have of myself, which is why I have it italicized. I have never made money unfairly off any person and would certainly not do so off Wanda. I did what I could for Wanda. I tried to make her happy, without becoming too involved.

Don't get too close to me, Martin, she would say. *Don't get involved.*

I gave her a job, propped her up when her faith in herself was low. I lent her money and saw to it that her child was taken care of when Robin wouldn't and Wanda herself was in no shape to do so. The material we had to work with professionally was often of dubious quality though I did my best to imbue it with substance. (This is equivocation: the fact is I yearn to burn my bridges and start over.) But I did these things with no intention of acquiring credit for myself. I did them out of the simple belief that we owe loyalty to those we would call our friends, and with full knowledge that had our situations been reversed she would have done as much for me. Wanda was argumentative, she liked to make people believe that she had not a brain in her head; in fact she was an extraordinary woman who repudiated her own vast gifts out of a deep-seated psychosis I could never probe but which the camera often understood.

"Would you care to see the child?" I asked Rita Islington.

I believe not. I do not care for children.

Strange Rita Islington.

I surrendered the negatives to her for no other reason than that she intrigued me. In the years I had known Wanda she had never mentioned having a sister. Yet how frequently do I mention my six brothers?

I trusted her.

She reeked of scent — an exotic perfume almost as permeating as incense. She wore spiked heels made of a lovely soft leather the colour of the sky. Her co-ordinated purse boasted a musical signature. Her hair was fully a yard long, with a high sheen even in my dimly lit reception-room. She refused to take off her glasses, the lenses of which were so curved and dark I never saw her eyes, despite my frequently assumed stance to this or that side of her.

Pardon me. Am I making you nervous? You appear unable to stand still.

Her voice was throaty, mellifluous — as if it liked to recline on a velvet cushion when not in use. Her language was precise, which characteristic heightened an already regal bearing, reminiscent of that developed by Marlene Dietrich while under the baton of Josef von Sternberg. Moreover, having once offered payment of money (there was never any hint that she was prepared to go further), she seemed not at all surprised that I refused it:

Gallantry still lives, n'est ce pas? — and allowed her ungloved hand to rest in mine longer than form would concede necessary. Nor did she make any objection to my stated intention to retain as my personal property the single set of prints made from those very negatives and which occupied in plain view the walls enclosing us. *Mmmmm,* I recall she said, *I find this affection you have for the small bosom incomprehensible.*

"I was fond of Wanda."

I noted that she appeared herself to be normally endowed, though her dress was not of a style to call attention to this.

She had visibly lovely legs, and the most beautiful lips I have ever seen on a woman.

Since she gave no indication of hurry, I offered her coffee. She declined. She did not drink of the bean, she said. I then offered alcohol, and this also she refused. Though she did say a moment later that she would drink with me if I insisted. By this hour she had arranged herself comfortably on my sofa, and had already, without looking at them, dispatched the negatives to her purse.

"Why should I insist?" I asked rudely. "I would hardly be likely to compel a total stranger to drink with me." As a matter of fact, my composure was broken. Prior to her arrival I had been drinking steadily.

Is it true, she wanted to know, *that you were my sister's lover?*

"Never," I said. "I am married — or was — and treasure fidelity."

How odd, she laughed, *for a porn king.*

Such statements intimidated me.

She wore a fur hat, in addition to other finery. I vividly recall this because my estranged wife had only recently lost a similar hat. My impression, before making a proper study, had been that this woman was wearing my wife's property.

"How did you come by your nice hat?"

It was the gift of my first husband.

"You have been married then . . . more than once?"

You are notoriously inquisitive. This, I would guess, is of value to one of your calling.

"It wasn't a calling. It was simply something to do. Easy money. Corn for the butterballs."

That does not correspond with my sister's image of you.

"A rabid fanatic?"

She rose to go, once more offering her hand. I kissed it. I don't believe I have ever done that before. Even in jest. I opened the door. A drab light spilled in from the hall. I suddenly did not want her to go. I felt like a man about to go over a cliff on a bicycle (*Night Plus Morning*, 1973). I could hear loneliness rushing at me in full stampede.

"Don't go yet. Please."

Goodbye. You have been most kind.

That remark turned the trick. My spirits lifted. I no longer had any interest in keeping her.

Her ankles disappeared inside the Rolls Corniche Mark II parked at the curb.

ELAINE HIGHTOWER WOLFE (1942–) Female Caucasian, born in Manhattan, matriculated at Wyoming State Christian College for Women (BA) and Colorado University at Boulder (MA in Human Resources). A former waitress, car-hop, interior decorator, receptionist, currently part-time media/projects critic for erratically published journals. Emigrated to Canada in 1967, married five years later, no children.

My estranged wife.

Writes from time to time an uninspired, thematic, therapeutic verse which is then set to music and given the occasional performance at well-attended feminist meetings. Does a nice softshoe when drunk (rarely).

The most marvellous of women.

Identifying scars: on her lower abdomen, which I shall not tell you about.

For the period of time with which these Notes are concerned, she was living apart from me, though in the same neighbourhood, until such time as, in our counsellor's phrase, "we got our priorities sorted out." The above disclosure has hidden reference to a) the vanity of Elaine Wolfe which drives her to want and need an independent life, and b) the relative insecurity of Elaine Wolfe which drives her to want and need a husband, together with c) outside pressures which insist that she not throw away her life. We are both entrapped and our emotions made banal by the afterburn of love achieved through six years of wholesome matrimony.

Eyes: blue.

Chin: erect.

That she is a pretty woman, an intelligent and humorous woman, and a powerfully intense personality is affirmed often enough by

EDWARD HIGHTOWER (1919–   )   Father of the above

OLIVE HIGHTOWER (–   )   Mother of the above

GERTRUDE HIGHTOWER MEWS (1896–   ) grand-mother of the above

and sundry relatives and friends (see Notes below). A wealth of additional values peculiarly her own has been likewise aggressively advanced, to wit:

Elaine is a fine woman, a tower of strength.

Elaine has only your happiness in mind.

Elaine is selfless to the extreme. There is nothing she wouldn't do for you.

You had better get a hold of yourself or you are going to lose this veritable jewel who is unabashedly still in love with you but is no one's fool, who adores the ground you walk on and has never looked at another man but who cannot forever be treated as a doormat. Moreover, she has charm, a sweet disposition, money of her own, and a character that is positively radiant. You are going to wake up one morning an old man alone if you don't soon come to realize and appreciate that an angel is what you have.

Agreed, and then some.

No sooner had my mystery caller, Rita Islington, departed than did Elaine Wolfe arrive to remind me of these many paragon qualities (not that *she* would; her presence, I am saying, did so), while at the same time hoping to wring out of me the identity of the woman in question, together with that mission which had summoned her to my door.

Who was she? What did she want? Oh, Martin, you're not going to make those films again!

Because we can't stand to make another unhappy we often opt for the quickest cruelty. I immediately took to the telephone, not at that time disconnected, dialling one

PETER MAHONEY (1918–   )   Noted attorney, city council member, twice unsuccessful candidate for mayor on the NDP ticket, author of the monographs *Divorce in Las Vegas, The Scottish Decree, Totem and Taboo,* etc.

"She is harassing me," I told this man, and he immediately divined that my reference was to Elaine Wolfe. He asked that I summon her to the phone. I complied and judge that he reminded her of the delicacy of the situation, that he and her parents' lawyers were working diligently to iron out an agreement which he could promise her would in due time be resolved to everyone's satisfaction, including the court's.

But I don't want a divorce, she told him. *I don't even want this separation.*

I was then recalled. *Guard against depression,* he warned. *Don't do anything silly.*

"I'll get twenty years."

He laughed. *We shall see.*

"If we thought we had some chance of getting Angelia," I said, "we could hold on."

My wife wept. We both wept.

Does it have to be like this? she cried.

"I don't know."

I forgive you. If that's all that's standing between us. If there is anything to forgive.

We hugged, fondled and continued to weep. "It helps," I admitted, "but you know very well there is no way out. You have your future, not to mention your reputation, to think about."

I don't care about that! It's my place to stand beside you!

I reminded her that her parents' hearts would be broken, their health thrown in jeopardy, if she took up with me again.

"Already your father has had one mild attack. That comes directly to my door."

Yes, but Angelia! Unless we're together Angelia will surely be taken away. It's that bitch Marceline's fault! I could wring her neck!

"She's a friend of the court. We can't touch Marcy."

Oh, Martin, why did you ever have anything to do with her!

We wrung our hands, moaned until our throats hurt, ranted over the injustices done to us by society and friends, searched about helplessly for a ray of sunshine, and finally threw ourselves together on the floor and found brief happiness in that physical union which assuages the bleakest hour.

Oh, love, oh, beauty!

Christ, I love a passionate woman.

Weeping without hope, she then fled.

I was utterly distraught, a crawling wound, too worn out even to endure the long struggle toward bliss via alcohol. In my self-pity I reached for the one kind review my work has ever received, seeking pathetic recompense from

MICHEAL OBLE (–)   Semi-reputable freelance art and film critic, Assistant Librarian at the Spadina Street branch of the Toronto Public Library, author of the celebrated article (*en Route*, the in-flight magazine of Air Canada, June 1978, pp.29, 40, 51), *Pornography with a Message: The Underground Films of Martin D. Wolfe.*

The most recent of the 23 films of M.D. Wolfe opens with a massively detailed, nearly interminable sequence made up of the same repeated, gradually expanding scene. Fade in on a barren plain where

a clump of ant-like creatures congregates. Viewed by a single hand-held camera at considerable distance, a lone figure appears. Puffs of smoke drift up lazily into an overcast sky. The figure falls. As the smoke wafts away we have superimposed, the camera infinitesimally nearer, an all but exact re-enactment. This time one can faintly hear the pop of gunfire a few seconds after the figure has again collapsed. Superimpose and begin once more, the same scene imperceptibly nearer, the action extending a few frames longer.

Our audience begins to fidget and some to demand a return of their money.

It turns out before long that our victim is a woman; with each re-birth of the scene more and more flesh is exposed. Is Wolfe giving us, then, an elaborate striptease? Those hesitating in the aisles decide to reclaim their seats. This may after all be the show the posters promised.

More smoke and gunfire. We are well into Biographical Nights *before it comes to us that what we are perceiving is not what we have perceived; and by the time this 90-minute feature drives to its close the original seven-second opening takes all of one hour to recount and has become another narrative indeed. Along the way, the distant, rather pretty gunfire has given way to machine-gun bursts, rocket fire, and in the end to full-scale battlefield explosions which are inte-grated with the sustained shrieks and howls of ferocious dogs. Over-heard fragments of speech become diatribes, though here too there are surprises, for the language is no longer English. The once barren plain has become a mirage in which any environment is possible. Wolfe can even manage to find in it room to continue his obsessions with factory interiors. Figures seen initially in military uniforms, later in priestly robes or in the elegant attire of heads of state, are next seen as beggars, convicts, amputee veterans, and eventually as the working-class representatives without which no Wolfe film is com-plete. Nothing is secure, Wolfe appears to be telling us. Nothing is to be counted on. Place is totally unreliable. Who we are is the most spe-cious of inventions. Wolfe's few converts will know, however, that whatever else this director may be, he is not a mere illusionist. His scene employs mirage as metaphor but inside that mirage much is*

279

hardcore naturalism. Thus when the camera swings away from a tight shot of the face of our old friend Wanda, looking more enigmatic than ever, we are not altogether astonished that the wide lens reveals the familiar over-large, bobbing head of Robin Harvey as he does his sexual labour over her. Blue-collar Harvey this is — hungover, laid-back, no doubt thinking of his wages as he looks indifferently out at us. Clearly his mind is not on Wanda. He sees us, it would seem, and nods a non-committal greeting. The camera withdraws farther. We are inside Wolfe's infamous textile factory. As far as the eye can see, a thousand looms are projected, repeating this act of bestial rape, of intermittent harmony. The factory hums with vicious lust, though the greater horror resides in the machines which roar on in the production of more and more undistributed profit.

Wolfe has moved out from the most distantly objective portrayal of one victim's story into the dark and tangled heart of material in which perpetrator, victim and spectator blindly collaborate. He confronts his audience with the bitter notion that misconceptions which apply to his subject matter apply to our own lives as well. Guilt weighs heavily on us all, he would have us acknowledge, but the eye which finally perceives truth is the one that must make the largest sacrifice. His is the one to educate priests, reform heads of state, dismantle the military, deliver us into good and secure biographical night. A sense of shifting guilt permeates this film, as indeed it does much of the Night *series in its entirety. All parties absorb a share — the working classes, for instance, with which Wolfe is most allied, in their* need *for heroes, even in their* need *for God. Yet he repudiates the belief that they have a need for someone, human potentates, to tell them how to run their lives. Better God, he argues, than us. Their virtues are seen as constant and surpass the ill or goodwill of those who would so instruct. Identities shift in his films in order to dramatize a theory of universal brotherhood but once that is seen he wants us to recognize that the main weight of guilt never shifts. It is an incorrigible property of that elusive party so rarely physically present where atrocity prevails. The people who exploit and kill Wanda in this film are indicted but the burden of guilt flows elsewhere. This ultimate source is nameless but one can never doubt that it exists, or that it is plotting new crimes even as this one transpires, or that at all cost it must be tracked down. Wanda, unfortunately, does not suspect. She believes in her heart that this is happening to her because of something she has done. She does not aggressively resist her destruction partly because she views this end as rightful payment for her vanity, for her few moments of pleasure, for wanting something better. It is this twisted nobility of spirit, this forlorn innocence that moves us so and for which she earns our begrudging respect. We leave the theatre with sex-drive diminished, with the lust to revenge her permanently intact.*

But are Wolfe's films high-class porn, or are they art? One is beginning to hear murmurs of support. More than a few have passed up Swedish Hotbox *and* The Devil in Miss Jones *for* Biographical Nights. *Martin Wolfe, we can suppose, does not live in hell; his films, however, remind us that he would be vastly happier if the public his films are aimed at were less content to do so. Despite their intensely sexual nature, his films make deeply religious statements so arduous in their pursuit of change that, left to their own devices, they might in time confound the Pope, foment revolution and topple governments. That they are made in the first place is an expression of the director's optimism and faith.*

Biographical Nights *exposes with startling clarity the design which has persisted through the whole of this man's cinematic career. He radically marries pornography with earnest morality. Base lust is his symbol for greed in all its forms. Pornography is the vessel which transports his devious socio-political message, geared to lure an unsuspecting public into the theatre — and out of it a different person. It is for this unique premise that he might be justifiably attacked. Undoubtedly, his defence would be that while the New Wave gave us masterpieces, it politically affected little. One can almost hear Wolfe laying down the ground rules to his incredible and infinitely patient Wanda: "The most permanent revolution begins by gathering its harvest from the bottom. If we can reform drunks and degenerates, if we can turn a nation of confirmed voyeurs into activists, we can reform anyone. Your hot breath, your boy's chest, and Robin's glazed eyes, will render them susceptible." His aim, I believe, is to crack*

heads wide open. To this end he disposes of Freud, incorporates
Masters and Johnson, and goes Marx one better.

OBLE, OBLE, my eternal thanks to Oble. A review I was all but
tempted to send to my mother. A few thoughts are wrong but I cannot
quibble. When this item first came to our notice, my wife and I, with
Robin and Wanda, booked a table at Antoine's and held an extended
post-mortem. Elaine read it, read it again, cried, and went back to it
once more. "It's so right," she gushed. "Beautiful, it's beautiful." Her
eyes shone. She wriggled close, unable to touch me often enough. I
couldn't eat my escargots or dip my bread in their juices without poking her in the ribs. "You're wonderful, oh, Wanda isn't Martin wonderful?" The pleasure this man Oble gave her, how I wish he had been at
the table. She had never been more radiant, so much the Pike's Peak of
Love. It grieved me that I had no more reviews to show her, no trophies
to pull from my pockets. I felt wretched, thinking of all the years I had
made this fine woman endure public disgrace. And how I, too, needed
that praise . . . doubt piled upon doubt, scorn heaped upon scorn, all
receding now.

Robin's mouth silently shaped this or that imponderable word. "I
don't get it," he muttered at last. "What does this turkey mean? Was I
hung over? Why can't he just call it a good skin flick and let it go at that?"

When Wanda read it she howled. She laughed so hard and so long
we were obliged to apologize to Antoine and his other guests. "Oh-oh-
oh!" she gasped, "this is killing me! What a hoax! Oh, Martin, did you
have to pay him a lot of money?"

Elaine, wounded for my sake, turned on her in a fury: "That isn't
true, you're a beast to say that."

"It is true, our pictures are garbage, that's all they are, Martin's not a
saint and I'm not Garbo, if the public had any sense we'd all be in jail."

Elaine burst into tears. She wrenched at the table-cloth, spilt her water, shook violently all over, quite fed up with our companions.

Robin appealed to us all. "Look, we're here to have a good time, forget our troubles. Let's behave ourselves. I'm confused about that mention of rockets. I never saw any rockets."

"If they want to call *smut* political and a means for social change,"
stormed Wanda, "that's their business. All the *Nights* pictures are trash!

Dirt! Filth! Slop! Nothing more!" She was in a rage, bristling, her beautiful eyes steaming with venom.

"You're frightened," I told her. "Why? Why does it scare you that the films might be good? That they might be worthwhile?"

"I know who *I* am! I know *what* I am too. I don't need any jerk cinephile to justify my existence!"

Elaine too was primed for war, in no mood to let this coarse assessment slide. She banged the salt shaker on Wanda's salad plate, picked up a fork and raked it over the table like a dagger. "You were wonderful in that picture!" she shouted. "You are a fine human being! A wonderful mother! Martin's too modest, I don't suppose he's told you that he gets letters from strangers saying how you have changed their lives!"

"One," I corrected. "One letter."

"Yes! From a man reborn! From a man martyred in Ethiopia because of what the *Night* pictures did to him."

Wanda reddened. But she did not speak, her thoughts deflected by Ethiopia's unknown dead. I was devising a theory about Wanda. It would destroy her, I sensed, if she ever came to realize that she'd somehow come out of whatever foul, stench-infested, brutalizing place she'd started from and developed into the extraordinary person she now was. If it ever dawned on her that she *was* out of it now. No one is ever *safely* out of it. There is no green benign place, no happily anointed field, no sanctuary where one may cast off the memory of what one was. No amount of sophisticated cinema talk, none of the high-fashion clothes or expensive restaurants or the nice car and lavish apartment she could now afford could convince her that she had not been murdered once upon a time. These outer trappings were fine, they gave pleasure, but the heart and soul that is murdered once is one that stays murdered forever. It marches on . . .

Look, Martin, I heard one of them say, *he's plotting out our next picture.*

. . . it marches on in our false bones, enjoying good food, good music, physical love, the company of friends, it takes luxuries and comforts as they come, but it will not be deceived. It knows this delicious camouflage can't resurrect what has been permanently destroyed. Wanda would allow no one to tamper with this horrible, abiding

283

vision. That vision must not be altered because to alter it she would have to forgive. And nothing — whether person, place or God — deserved forgiveness of those crimes committed against her, the mundane stench of which she breathed daily. They deserved reminders. The steady vigil of accusation. This was the film I had always wanted to make of Wanda and never had. Eternal victim. Everpresent accuser. Perpetual riddle of human life. A straight narrative, no tricks, no gimmicks, an old-fashioned tale, one that parents could take their children to see.

The ardour of expression at our table had thinned. Elaine was squeezing Wanda's hands across the table, her shoulders routed between two candlesticks. "One letter," she was saying. "But such a letter! Lives made over — that's what art can accomplish!"

Wanda squeezed out a thin laugh.

"What I object to in all this review business," said Robin, "is how critics can only talk about directors these days. One mention he gives me, one stinking line! If I hear another word about Russ Meyer or Bertolucci or that crowd I'll throw up."

"Not here, I hope," teased Wanda. "Not tonight." She smiled at my wife. Eyes gone lazy. Her enigmatic face. "I apologize. Pay no attention to me. You know I never know what I'm saying." She lifted the champagne bottle out of its ice-bed and poured our glasses full. "I didn't know I was part of a revolution. Guerrilla action, is that what it is, Martin? Me, a poor girl off the farm in . . ." She paused, batted her eyelids at me, inserted a thumb briefly in her mouth: "Look at Martin, he's suddenly all ears. I almost gave away where I was from. You're such a pest, Martin, so boring — as if it matters where I was born or how poor or rich my parents were. For all the years I've known him he's been itching to hear me confess that I was born an orphan, raised in a church home where I was beaten and went unfed, or that if I had a father I was kept out of school and raped and made to sleep under the front porch with dogs."

"That's Martin to a T," piped in Elaine as if this remark struck her as a sudden revelation. "He's got theories about us all. Because I was overly protected in my youth he's convinced that even today I need a nanny in my room and the light on when I sleep. It's only through subterfuge that I ever got to see his films. I had to lie and claim I was shopping or seeing friends."

I raised my glass in a toast to these two teasers.

"What do *you* think?" Robin asked me, jabbing a finger at Oble's review. "Do you take this brainy stuff seriously?"

"Yes," the women chorused. "Tell us what you think!"

My wife's hand cruised along my thigh as she snuggled her head against me.

The truth is that, between one thing and another, I was close to tears. "I do think," I said, "that except for Elaine, this is the first truly nice thing anyone has said about me since I was twelve years old."

"Boo!" croaked Robin. "He's drunk."

The women regarded me with wonder, smiling tenderly, warmed to see so much sentimentality exposed. "Oh, God," mourned Wanda, "he's going to cry now. He always does on the set."

"When *I* was twelve," joked Robin, "I was looking to reform school as a step up in the world."

"You still are," observed Elaine, shushing him. She turned to me. "What was said to you at twelve? Can you remember?"

"Vividly. My mother came in from work one day and found me sweeping. Into the corner where I had the dust-pan waiting . . ."

The women's eyes never left me. They were enjoying this moment, yet at the same time feared the cavalry would charge over the next hill and whisk me to safety before I could reveal my secret.

"He was desperately poor," said Elaine by way of illumination. "His mother, alone, had to raise seven children. Martin had no shoes and when his teeth rotted they were extracted by slamming doors. He won't forgive anyone for this. He holds us all responsible."

"What did your mother say?" asked Wanda.

"She said I was beautiful. That I had a beautiful soul. She told me I had the spirit of an angel."

Wanda sighed, not masking her disappointment, murmuring, "Now that's true deprivation" — no doubt recalling her own forced labour as a child and finding my gallantry feeble by comparison. "To hell with this," remarked Robin. "I'm tired of hearing about disadvantaged people." He excused himself and left the table. My wife contentedly massaged my thigh. I survived the brutal confession. We stuffed ourselves with food and kept the champagne flowing.

It was a fine evening. Our last together with Wanda.

MARY NAPELS   (b.d. & description withheld by request)

Helpful neighbour, homemaker and good sport, nicknamed "Mosie" by her friends: "Hello, Mosie."

Hi, Martin, how is my favourite convict this evening?

Contributor of $500 toward my bail. Overweight, but doesn't like to be reminded. Confronts every issue with brutal fact.

You deserved it, Martin. I hate your films. I don't care that they are part of our sexual liberation. I'd rather be uptight with Queen Victoria. I don't care about your good intentions. Your condemnations smack of the celebratory. I recall with a shudder that scene from Peppermint Nights *when you have Gring meditating on his victims like Narcissus bent over his image at the pool. I bathe a long time after viewing your films.*

"Why did you put up money for my bail?"

One feels protective of fools. And you've toned down the vulgarity, you've become more tasteful of late.

Dropped by only yesterday evening, by appointment, and helped me cook a succulent dinner.

Don't worry. I won't jeopardize your chances for getting Wanda's kid returned. I'm perfectly willing to tell the judge you'd make a lovely parent.

For this repast we were joined by

SANDRA OLSON (1939–   )

A semi-official visit. Former enemy, now new-found supporter and co-conspirator, a Family Affairs investigator.

How's tricks, gang?

she asked, plopping down beside the crab dish a bottle of Spanish burgundy with a home-made label.

I come with greetings from Angelia Latishia Casslake who pines for her return to the pornographer's bosom. Now, don't weep, Martin, but this altercation with your wife worsened your case.

"There is no altercation. She left because her parents promised her they'd die of a broken heart if she stayed with me."

We can hardly tell that to the court. Nor can we tell it that her father has threatened your life. We are up the familiar creek, honey bunch.

We weep, all three. One good cry leads to another and soon Sandra is regaling us with vivid reports of her own fanatical and brutal father whose stated mission in life had been the terrorization of all females and the blowing up of all foreign embassies and banks on home soil. To succeed in the latter he was often obliged to be out of town, for which his family gave incessant thanks to their dimly perceived saviour. I held her hand while she told me of the nightly beatings and humiliations, and how reprieve came at last when one of his Montreal bombs prematurely exploded. Later on, with Mosie off to her bed, I told Sandra Olson something of my own story.

Martin Martin Martin I feel so sorry for you!

"Oh, I don't know. Other people have survived worse nightmares."

I should have curled up and died! It's awful, awful!

That my tale was more terrible than her own she conceded, and this, I judge, made her feel better — as it did me — about facing the dawn which by this hour was nearly upon us.

I'm going home now. Try not to worry.

"Oh, you're a joker, Olson, you are."

I could not sleep. Donning a disguise that would fool no one, least of all myself — slouch hat, upturned trenchcoat, a walking stick to complement an imagined limp — I aimlessly followed footpaths, lanes and alleys in the neighbourhood, gaining forlorn solace in thinking about

MIRANDA PROBST   (now in her eighties) My high school French teacher. Children's counsellor and church organist, retired. She befriended me when I was a youth and isolated from my peers.

You were such a nice, awkward, almost backward child. Much too sensitive for your own good. So shy, so honest. I told you I would pass you but you said you deserved to fail. You must come and see me again before I die. What have you done with your life, dear boy? You must tell me sometime, I know it would make me proud. My friends here will be green with envy over this new shawl.

"POOPS" THOMAS   (about my age) Obese boyhood chum, the only person I was ever able to torment without fear of reprisal. Nothing known of his adult life. Where are you, Poops? Have you found happiness?

LEO YSELOVICH (–)   My high school history teacher who pushed the cycle theory with such malice and vengeance that I have not abandoned it to this day. Born a Dukhobor, old religious sect exiled (7,000 of them) to Canada from Tsarist Russia in 1898 after years of famine and persecution (*Night of the Tsars,* 1974). He wore the same sweater year after year and seemed always to walk over the same path dogs had taken a moment before. Tall, bespectacled, a chain-smoker. Elderly now and possibly deceased. I like to think he influenced lives more complimentary to him than mine. Hounded out of the public school system at age fifty-six for alleged homosexuality, not heard of since.

RUDOLPH PUCARD (1926–)   A servant of the people.
RCMP vice detective. Pucard had but one goal, to "send smut merchants back where they came from." Grim, bedevilled little bachelor a shade up from Maigret. Attended perhaps fifty screenings of the *Night* films in search of a psychological edge to be used against their perpetrators. Became, as a result, confused. Grieved deeply over Wanda's suicide.
Wanda: *I like him fine. Have you ever noticed that his right eyelid droops? I like that.*
My arresting officer, January 1978. *We've got the Able girl's statement, sonny-boy. It's a crock of scum but the department wants you and they don't care how.* Refused to testify under oath at the pre-trial hearing that the accused had unlawful carnal knowledge of one Marceline Able, minor, and that he did thereafter with reprehensible greed force her to work for him on the street as a common prostitute.
My lawyer: *Your Honour, I object to the nasty manner in which the prosecuting attorney has dropped this ugly charge.*
Me: *It's all a filthy lie, Your Honour.*

The Judge: *I would advise the honourable defence attorney to restrain his client or I shall have him gagged.*

My lawyer: (whisper): *Shut up, you fool.*

The Judge: *Detective Pucard, to your knowledge was the accused this child's pimp?*

Pucard: *Your Honour, I uncovered no such evidence.*

The Judge: *Hang the evidence. In your line of inquiry did you assume he was so engaged?*

Pucard: *No, Your Honour.*

The Judge: *Well, we've got to stop this vile business somewhere. Objection denied.*

ALBERT ROSEN (1931–1978)   Fascist, rabid anti-Semite and lifelong cinema freak.

The only documented case of a man whose character was reformed through film. After seeing the *Night* series, this stranger wrote me, he was committing his life to a war against evil. Shot down outside a mosque in Addis Ababa, Ethiopia, Sunday, 21 March, 1978, by guards of the red terror, while attempting to distribute food and medicine to the poor. A nail driven into his chest, attached to it a note which named him the people's enemy. One of 148 verified dead, mostly children, shot or hacked to death that day. Another day after so many and so many. His body and theirs littering the streets, removal forbidden. Notes pinned to bodies read: *This mother's son put the people's well-being above ideology.* (Amnesty International Bulletin.)

—— WOLFE (1936–1936)   Born dead. My sister.

SISTER MARY OF ST. DAVID (–1978)

Raped and murdered on this street corner one month ago, criminal party not yet discovered. One Christmas eve three years ago she passed Elaine and me right about here, transporting on her shoulder an undecorated tree.

It is an evil thing that you do, Martin. My prayers go with you.

"Mine with you, Sister."

SO MANY OTHERS

Nameless and unknown, disfigured in the memory, strangers, friends and shadowy walk-ons. The truck driver for Maple Leaf Foods who on a road past Long Beach, BC, pulled Wanda Lee Casslake too late from her carbon monoxide end to everything.

The motor wasn't running any more. I reached in, turned off the ignition. She toppled over. I don't know how long she'd been dead.

On the front seat a note: *Let Elaine and Martin have Angelia, she'll be happy with them.*

So many more. Over the faces of all these, superimposed, enduring year after year, the innocent, amazed eyes of a boy from nowhere, looking forward through time at me. My own eyes. My own, the same eyes, looking back at him.

"How goes it, old friend?"

My eyes never close. There is nothing you do that I can't see.

"Will you never be satisfied?"

You may have fooled Oble but you shall never fool me. A thousand people have passed before me, Martin, but you are the biggest disappointment of all.

"I'm tired now, old friend. I'm going home."

You've disgraced me, Martin. People like you have no home.

Dawn. True dawn. A red wash above the city, the air fresh for a change. I tell you much is to be said for living one's life by the sea. The milkman making his rounds. A street cleaner high in the orange cab of his giant machine. Rows of parked cars, the occasional cat or dog. Another night survived.

When I get back to my building I find my wife curled up on the hallway floor. Asleep. The hall isn't heated, a thin coat stretches from her head to her feet. Mouth a little open, her eyes puffy, her hair a mess. Her hands are ice-cold.

"Elaine," I say. "Elaine, you have got to stop doing this."

She awakens in a fright, then sees it is only me. She stretches her arms, yawns noisily, and scrambles to her feet.

You keep moving the key.

"Yes, to keep you out. But you've got to stop camping in the hall."

I know. This time I think I caught a cold.

She walks in behind me, turns on the lights, and begins immediately to clean up the place.

Sloppy housekeeper. Whoever is looking after you now.

She tires, however. She fluffs up a pillow, sits on the sofa, plops the pillow on her lap.

I've decided. Martin. Hell or high water, I'm not leaving again.

"We've been through all this before."

I sit down beside her. Her head lolls, or mine does, and her arm falls softly around.

We're so tired, she says.

She sneezes, grabs a tissue and blows her nose. The tissue floats down. We stare in front of us. There is nothing to see but bare wall.

It's our chance of getting Angelia back. If my parents die of shame they'll just have to. I'm staying, Martin.

"I guess so. If you're sure."

I'm going to bed now.

"I'll join you if I may."

We do not bother to remove our clothes. We drag ourselves to the bed and tumble in. Our backs curve, our knees bend. We are twins, lengths of soft curving flesh harpooned to the mattress by a single throw. To diffuse the light Elaine sweeps hair across her face.

Be quiet, she moans. *Don't say a word.*

I have grit in my eyes; it's this that causes tears.

Five minutes later we irritably sigh, kick like gypsies in a dance. Sob and sink down again. A pillow smothers her.

You're thinking, she accuses. *You've got to stop it, Martin, I can't sleep.*

MARCELINE ABLE

Viper. Liar. Killer of this sleep. Amorphous runner, derelict from the lost lagoon, guide for the lunatic's museum. Freelance jibber-jabber who single-handedly brought my mogul's empire tumbling down. *He put his hands all over me sir and when I said I wouldn't I wasn't that kind of girl he hit me and threw me down and then he did it to me so help me God I wouldn't lie about a thing like that and it went on for days and days until I was so sore I couldn't move all my pleading with him done no good and finally he was tired of me I guess and he said if I worked for him on the street he'd look after me he said a girl like me pretty and young and kind of classy you know I could make a lot of money on the street and he'd see to it I got a good share I told him I didn't want to but he made me sir he said it was all I was good for. . . .*

Discovered by Wanda, loitering on a street corner one day *(Hey, Miss, could you spare a quarter?)* and hired by her for part-time child-minding work.

You can see that she needs help, Martin. She's loony, she's a bit confused, but she isn't dangerous, I'm only doing what you would have done for her in my place, and you know all the trouble I've had getting someone to look after Angelia.

"She's bad news, Wanda."

No, she isn't. You should have seen me when I was her age. The responsibility will be good for her. You're always preaching compassion, I should think you'd show a little now.

A runaway, as it turned out. Hitch-hiker, acid-dropper, vagrant, groupie, Moon disciple, racist, back-stabber, shop-lifter and compulsive whiner:

Everybody dumps on me!

Hating above all things the square and the phony.

I hate a phony, don't you just hate a square, Martin?

I went without appointment one day to Wanda's place and knew something was wrong the minute I knocked on the door. It was Marcie who finally came. "Where's Wanda?" I asked and she said *Wanda's shopping, how would I know where Wanda is?* Strange, something about her that wouldn't let me go away. "What's going on?" I asked, "where's the kid?" *Oh, the kid,* she said, *the kid, I guess she's around somewhere.* And then giggles leading into hysterical laughter as she backed against the wall and slumped down. Angelia in the kitchen, weeping hopelessly, barricaded inside the cramped cabinet where the garbage was stowed. *Well, she was freaking me, Mister, suppose you just motor on out of here.*

"Wanda, Wanda, you've got to get rid of that nut you hired."

What harm can she do, be patient, she's only trying to find herself.

Charlie Manson's great granddaughter.

He was always coming on to me grabbing at me wanting me to ball with him I wouldn't of minded so much except he was always coming on so righteous like you know and know-it-all just like my parents he was always dropping by the place when Wanda was out and I could tell what he was after but I gave him the cold shoulder I wouldn't have nothing to do with him I guess he's got a thing about young girls or something he's kinda up-tight about sex you know weird. But me I was just looking after the kid the way I was s'posed to and I did good too which wasn't easy the kid was always wanting something a real attention-grabber if you know the kind I mean well the kid was like that something awful but I was looking after her see and ignoring Martin. It wasn't till later I found out he was in the porno business that nearly blew my mind when I heard that because he'd always seemed so straight to me him and Wanda was real close and at first I thought they had a thing going but I don't know you never can tell with people and I was looking out for myself I mean I had my own life to lead right? But then him and Elaine they started ganging up on me they told all sorts of stories on me to Wanda and I could tell the way she was looking at me she had her doubts and then there was that time when she lost her money I know she thought I stole it though she never said nothing about it she was real tight you know wouldn't spend a dime on herself anyway they told Wanda I was really fucking up the kid which really freaked me they said I was mean to the kid I even beat her but that was an outright lie. What's true though is that I was after Wanda to get me a role in one of their pictures I could be a pretty good actress I think if anybody ever gave me the chance I'm very photogenic to tell the truth. I know what they'll tell you they'll say I told them I'd do anything to be in the movie business I'd even do it with a black or a Chink any kinky thing they wanted but that's just a rotten lie like I told you I didn't even know that was the kind of picture Martin makes. So when I told them they could chuck it I wasn't having anything to do with dirt like that well that's when Martin raped me nearly as I recall I'm a little confused now what with it being such a terrible ordeal I went through and when the policeman arrested me for soliciting that's when I told him how come I was in this bad spot which I'm telling you about on my own free will. . . .

Deranged, demented, vicious. An idiotic little jerk. Empty-headed for the most part. Even ordinary at times. Even at times, God help me, amusing:

I was with a Moog Synthesizer man before I come here.

"With who?"

We were really grooving on each other for a week or two, crashing out at this deserted house he knew about, about ten of us. Funny thing was, every morning we'd wake up and nobody could find their shoes. We'd all be walking around dopey-like on the freezing floor asking each other where's my shoes, who's got my shoes, what happened to my fucking shoes?

"What had happened to them?"

Well then one night I saw him. He had this toesack and he was scooting from bed to bed cramming all the shoes he could find in this bag. And then he went outside in the snow and threw them every which way far as he could, every one of them. Then he came back inside and went to sleep.

"Would he throw away his own?"

No, that's why he was doing it, that was his whole idea. So we'd have to wear his, taking turns, I mean wearing his while trying to find our own. Hiking boots, about size twelve.

"Didn't anyone suspect him?"

Well we were pretty stoned, most of us either coming off a trip or taking off on one. No, he'd sort of stay in his sleeping-bag all day grinning, he really got off on it, seeing us walk around in his shoes. He was trying to make friends is what he said, loaning out his shoes. He said it made him feel real good, like Jesus when he threw bread upon the water and the crumbs turned into swans, that's the funny way he talked.

"Why did you leave him?"

Oh, they practically killed him when they found out he was throwing their shoes out in the snow. And he was kind of a drip you know.

She could be nice, she could lay a faint finger on the heart-strings when she was in a sentimental or depressed mood:

You people, you and Elaine and Wanda and even Angelia sometimes, I know you want to love me, I know you try to. It makes me feel kind of creepy, you want to know the truth, I never felt that way before. I keep asking myself when's the hatchet going to fall.

Mindless. Totally without conscience. Yet we rarely felt her evil was intentional, that it was motivated, that she had any reasons for the way she behaved. One day Elaine and I, talking about her, worked ourselves into a nervous state, and went running over. *Hurry, Martin, she's doing something terrible, I can feel it, can't you?* Horrible scene.

Marcie in the bathroom trying to stuff Angelia's head down the commode.

Why did you do it, goddamn you, Marcie, what's wrong with you?

A shrug. *I don't know.*

I don't know either. It's God, I think.

GOD

God is the proven traitor. I sometimes think his body is the rot in this air. That the battle for our souls was lost, our fate sealed incalculable ages ago. At the very minute we looked and began to fabricate something better than ourselves. That's when we killed God, at the very instant we in our image created Him. Not, as is usually supposed, to explain our origins or sweeten our destiny — but simply to shift the blame elsewhere. We strung the bastard up. That's when we did it and that's why.

* * *

It is Elaine, rising petulantly out of sleep, who first hears the banging on our door. *Quick*, she says, *get it before I wake up.* She flops back down, groaning, hand over her ear. I get to the door somehow. My neighbour Mary Napels is there. She glares at me, striding inside.

Have you seen it? Have you seen this vile rag? It's hideous, you'll never be able to adopt Angelia now!

She thrusts a rolled newspaper in my hands. I look stupidly at her and ask her what time it is.

Open it! she shouts. *Let's see you explain your way out of this.* She grabs the tabloid back, yanks the sheets flat, and drums a finger violently on the page. *There! It's disgusting, how could you let them do this?*

DEATH STALKS THE BEACH

the headline reads

AS SMUT QUEEN HAS LAST PARTY

Wanda with her flat chest, in her birthday celebration with Robin, black boxes to obscure genitalia and to hide Robin's eyes, smart lawyer's device for staving off libel suits. My photographs, last gift from Wanda. At last victorious, giving the one performance she always claimed for herself and giving it in *The People's Inquirer.*

Elaine sways barefooted in the doorway: *What is it? What has gone wrong now?*

Mary rushes to her. *It's Martin, he's sold those photos to a scandal sheet. Nonsense.*

A bottom-of-the-page insert claims my attention: a grim, cloudy photograph captioned HER DEATH CAR. Not Wanda's car, not even a real beach, but a studio blow-up of what a real one is. Through the early morning mist I can just make out the grey curved stem of a woman's neck, the dead face lodged between window and seat, so elegiacally turned. "Professionally posed," the parenthesis informs. "Meanwhile, her long-time director and bosom-chum Martin Wolfe, awaiting trial for the alleged rape of a juvenile, continues his efforts to adopt the queen's small child. Get 'em while young, eh Martin?"

MARTIN DEWITT WOLFE (1934–)   Film-maker (now retired). *Night with Wanda*, etc.

"I give up, Elaine. I quit." I pass this new bouquet to my wife, to let her have a whiff. I give her such imaginative gifts, she might say. Human smut skilfully disguised as a gift to all mankind. Thank God for the press, which keeps us abreast of ourselves. Thank God. The last picture show. It's over.

How could you do it, Martin? Mary Napels is weeping at the tombside. Somebody has swiped the last crumb off God's plate.

"I didn't. Somebody else did."

That woman, Elaine cries. *Rita Islington! Wouldn't that be it, Martin? You gave her the negatives. But why? Why would she do such a thing to her own sister?*

"Why not?" I say. But then I look at the two women, both of them horrified. Weeping and yet ready and able to give solace. I know well that look in my wife's eyes; it is frequently there, frequently inquiring: *Have you lost faith, Martin? Oh, no, Martin, you couldn't!*

I'm sorry, Martin, my neighbour says. *It just seemed too much, the final straw. You know? I had no right to suggest . . .*

She comes over to give me a hug. Elaine comes too and the three of us stand holding on to each other. One more word and we would weep like a fountain.

My wife breaks suddenly away from our triumvirate, shaking her fist at the sky: *Angelia!* she shouts. *How are we going to save her?*

ANGELIA LATISHIA CASSLAKE (1974–   )   An innocent child. The star of my next film:

The most recent film of M.D. Wolfe opens with a massively detailed, nearly interminable sequence made up of the same repeated, gradually expanding scene. Fade in on a barren plain where a clump of ant-like creatures congregates. As the scene comes closer we notice that these figures are strangely reminiscent of demons on a canvas by Brueghel, gnomes leering from behind haystacks etc. Each time the scene is replayed our vision is improved. For instance, we observe that the item being wagged by each of a crowd of chanting, hydrocephalic idiots is in fact the grotesque and elongated human penis. Another group whom we had originally supposed to be gossipy old women becomes eventually a chorus line of judges, each one of them bewigged. We are ten minutes into the film before it is possible to see that the idiots surround a fire. Bound to a stake in the centre of this blazing pyre is a little girl, not more than four years old. Off to the left is another victim, who looks remarkably like Wanda Casslake. She is being stabbed repeatedly with pitchforks, wielded by two other women, one elegant and austere, the other a mad-eyed juvenile. The Wanda-woman rises again and again, bleeding and struggling over to the fire as if she would give succour to the child at the stake. At last Wanda expires, her death rattle being amplified stereophonically throughout the theatre. One of the idiots, however, is seen on closer inspection to be a film director — he wears dark glasses and an Italian open-necked shirt; he has a folding director's chair strapped to his shoulders. With him are two women, very impressive types. We soon discover that these three are in fact attempting to rescue the little girl. Pretending to add faggots, they in fact remove the most treacherous. The director loosens the cords which tie her while the two women create a diversion — they writhe provocatively around the bodies of the idiots, licking their own lips and cupping their naked breasts as if to offer a drink of milk — he takes the child from the fire and places her piggyback where the director's chair was previously strapped. He adjusts his dark glasses and gives a blast of the whistle round his neck to alert his friends that the mission has been accomplished. Unfortunately, this also alerts the enemy — so that the two women and the director have to run like hell, the idiots barking after them while the judges blow tin bugles and stomp their heels. But they make it. All the way across the expanding screen they run, miniature angels seemingly getting nowhere, so tiny the camera's eye barely perceives them. The idiots and the judges abandon the chase and attack each other. In this way is the foe at last vanquished, harmless dots bleeding into the barren plain.

FADE OUT.

FADE IN: EXTERIOR. FLYING STORK, SWADDLED BABY. PAN.

CUT TO: DISTANT "X" ON BARREN PLAIN.

CUT TO: SWOOPING BIRD.

Acknowledgements

The author thanks the magazine editors in whose pages many of these stories first appeared: *Descant, The Fiddlehead, The Antioch Review, Antaeus, American Voice, The Malahat Review, Crazy Horse, The Literary Review, Event, Canadian Fiction Magazine, Wascana Review, Mississippi Review, Prairie Fire, Exile,* and *Matrix.*

Thanks also to the editors of Canadian Classics (Metcalf), Best American Short Stories (Elkin), Best Canadian Stories (Metcalf and Blaise), Illusion Oe: Fables, Fantasies and Metafiction (Hancock), Canadian Short Fiction Anthology (Belserine), Canadian Short Stories: From Myth to Modern (New), An Anthology of Canadian Literature in English (Bennett and Brown), The Bedford Introduction to Literature (Meyer), Carnival: The Scream in High Park Anthology (McFee), Making It New (Metcalf), The New Canadian Anthology (Lecker and David), Writers in Aspic (Metcalf), Statements 2: Fiction Collective (Baumback and Spielberg), The Art of the Tale: An International Anthology of Short Stories (Halpern), The Art of Short Fiction: An International Anthology (Geddes), and Elements of Fiction (Scholes and Sullivan) for reprinting many of these stories.

Special thanks to John Metacalf — and to Dan Wells and the Biblioasis gang — for giving these stories a new life — and to Tim and Elke Inkster for sustaining so many of us for so long.

HITTING THE CHARTS
was typeset in Adobe Garamond by Dennis Priebe,
printed offset on Rolland Zephyr Laid and Smyth-sewn
at Coach House Printing. A limited edition
of 25 copies was hand cased
by Daniel Wells.

BIBLIOASIS
WINDSOR, ONTARIO